To Donald,
May justice always be served

Kevin Foley

WHERE
LAW
ENDS

Kevin Emmet Foley

www.pronghornpress.org

Where law ends, there tyranny begins.

—William Pitt

For Susan, Patrick and Katie

Foreword

If it is true that the victors write the history, then the story of what took place in Bannack, Idaho (soon to be Montana) Territory in the winter of 1863-1864 has been told mostly by the Montana Vigilantes and those who supported them. It was the self-appointed lawmen, after all, who fashioned their own sterling legend and then made sure there was nobody left to dispute it.

Henry Plummer is among the most enigmatic and intriguing characters in Western lore. Little is known about him other than that he was handsome, articulate, successful, and lethal with a handgun. So it is easy to believe that Plummer stood out in the ramshackle mining towns and camps around Grasshopper Creek and Alder Gulch. A former marshal, he was also the logical choice for the miners when they decided to elect a sheriff. What most didn't know was that Plummer had a sordid past from which he was running.

What followed will likely never be fully known, but it is clear that Plummer's mistakes finally caught up with him. Yet, questions about Plummer remain. Was he an honest sheriff framed by the vigilantes as many believe, or was he the devious ringleader of a criminal enterprise, as the vigilantes charged? Were the Montana Vigilantes heroes who had no choice but to take the law into their own hands, or were they really cold-blooded and calculating mass murderers?

The pursuit of justice is always difficult, and pretty much next to impossible when it comes 140 years after events took place, so we can only speculate about Henry Plummer's guilt or innocence. The vigilantes did their best to make sure he would be remembered as a villain, so I have chosen to depict him otherwise in this historical novel.

Part One

From the Journals
of
Noah Coffey

1

Virginia City
Idaho Territory
January 30, 1864

Kincaid just left me. He carried a message from the Citizens Vigilance Committee demanding an interview with me tonight. Kincaid also made it clear I should get my affairs in order.

The blowing snow batters the window as I look onto the main street of Virginia City. So much blood has been spilled into the frozen mud out there that I can scarcely remember the faces of those who died. There was Ives and Zachery. Then Colgan. Then Mayfield and his uncle. There was Yeager and Brown, Bunton and Dutch John. The horrible night when they hanged Helm, the sickly Frank Parish, and the rest from a beam in the unfinished building; then there was the drunk Joe Slade and poor Joe Pizanthia, whose only crime was being foreign. I heard they shot him a hundred times before they burned his body to ashes.

As I said, so many faces and so many names to go with the faces.

It is cold this late afternoon, perhaps a little below zero. Winter's icy grip won't begin to let go for many more months. Spring was when I planned to leave the territory and never come back. It would seem the committee has other plans for me, however. I have opened a bottle of whiskey. The liquor burns in my gullet on the way down but, thankfully, it calms me. I am not a drinking man as was Exeter Colgan, my predecessor here at the newspaper. Well, maybe I drink more than I should these days but only because the thought of facing the committee freezes me inside, as I'm sure it did for all those before me, guilty or innocent.

I look out my window through the watery light as the sun sinks behind the distant Beaverhead Mountains producing an arc of vivid golden red rays. The wind has picked up as it often does here in the late afternoon, blowing the snow into drifts against my door.

My thoughts turn to my Connecticut home, in a farm hamlet called Coventry. I think of my father, Ezekiel Coffey, the local schoolmaster, his harsh and lean Puritan countenance glaring out across a classroom full of terrified boys, his hickory switch never far from hand, dealing out his own form of justice to those he considered slow or backsliding. I wonder what Father might think of the justice about to be meted out to me by the committee. He would certainly appreciate its historical significance. His son would be the second man from Coventry hanged by the neck (the first being the patriot hero of the revolution, Nathan Hale). Curious I remember that. I probably have Father's switch to thank.

I glance at the current edition published just two days ago. Actually, calling the *Virginia City Tribune* a newspaper is an exaggeration. It is merely a two-sided sheet of cheap newsprint. Of course the war is on everyone's mind so I dutifully transcribe accounts from the newspapers Nathan Carter sends me in order to tell my readers about the great conflict that engulfs the nation. My eye falls on this item:

A Great Battle at Chattanooga

—

A Union Triumph

—

If True, Enemy is Swept From
Missionary Ridge by Federal Forces

—

WHERE LAW ENDS

More Than 5,000
Rebels Are Dead or Wounded

—

Gen. Grant Commanded

—

Many Prisoners Are Taken

—

Federal Casualties Light

I know there is a lie in that headline somewhere but without a reliable correspondent on or near the front, I have no idea where the falsehood might be. "Federal Casualties Light" sounds suspicious. No matter, as I have quite painfully learned in recent days, fact and fiction in Virginia City are matters of perspective.

Also reported are the more mundane community events in this edition. There's the death of old Clem Murray (frostbite—a common enough problem here—corrupted his feet and gangrene set in). A new fire company has formed in Bannack. There is an account of a Hungarian miner's "slooshing" a goodly amount of color at the western end of Alder Gulch despite the thick ice. And here's something from our esteemed head of public education, Professor Thomas J. Dimsdale, late of Oxford, on the opening of a singing school at the Masonic Hall.

I turn the broadsheet over and again regard the item that has earned me my interview. I knew this was ill advised when I set it in type. I sip my whiskey and the north wind howls out of the high passes.

No fiction in that headline. I know because I was there. Outside my window, a horseman dismounts. He is a small, rotund man draped in a heavy black coat, his hat pulled low. He wears shiny black boots and gauntlet gloves against the cold. I cannot see his face but I know it is X. Beidler.

He glances at me through the window, and I cannot make out his expression because his face is nearly covered with a black scarf. But I do see his eyes, and they are a remarkable liquid black, cold and penetrating. He ties his big bay gelding to a post, looks at me again, then huddles into his coat and strides off toward the Masonic Hall at the top of Wallace Street.

What an appropriate name, I think to myself. X. He will be one of my judges and, contrary to common law, one of my jurors. Quite possibly, he will also be my executioner, seeing as how he enjoys that role so very much.

I must return to my work. I have the next edition to prepare. I stand and walk across the room's dusty wooden floor, past the small rotary printing press and the piles of old newsprint to a small side table where I've collected copies of newspapers from Salt Lake, San Francisco and finally St. Louis.

The *St. Louis Informer* is many weeks old, having made its way west to me via Salt Lake City. It contains perhaps the most current glimpse of the outside world as we are likely to see this side of the Rocky Mountains. We are isolated here in this lost and lawless corner of Idaho Territory, as the reader may have deduced, in a land not greatly changed since Lewis and Clark's famed Corps of Discovery blazed through it some sixty years ago.

I see General Ulysses Grant is pressing the rebels in northern Georgia and Knoxville is under siege. Brownsville in Texas has been captured. The Federal Navy continues its blockade of Savannah and New Orleans. More talk of British intrigue in the war.

Technically, we're in the Union if you listen to the civic leaders here, but many of my readers support the Confederate States of America since they come from places like Arkansas, the Carolinas, and Alabama. Very few are without a strong opinion one way or the other, so tension forms fertile ground within which violence takes root, sprouting bitter fruit far too frequently in the form of knife fights, gunfights, and fist fights.

But there is something more than simmering political hatred here— something far more toxic. There is greed. The miners toiling in Alder Gulch are greedy. The merchants who supply the miners are greedy. The petty criminals who followed the miners and merchants into the valley are greedy. The assayers are greedy. The cardsharps are greedy. The painted whores that service the miners, merchants, and mendicants are greedy. And the committee is greedy. How else to explain Biedler's fine gelding outside my window, once owned by Captain Slade? Or the cabin in Nevada City that used to belong to Jack Gallagher, which Sanders now rents to a dry goods merchant?

Gold. Greed. Gore. Could there possibly be one without the others? Could there be a more fitting motto than those three words for Virginia City?

I put the whiskey to my lips and drain the glass. The image of the Mormon's panicky blue eyes comes to me again. They are wide with shock and disbelief that he was dying so young.

Back to work. I begin to set type for the next edition. I do not know when or if it will be published so I wait to set the date on the masthead. I busy myself setting the St. Louis account of a speech given by President Lincoln at Gettysburg. For a politician, it seems very brief.

My skill at typesetting was a bonus for Colgan. He was not adept at setting the lead type; all thumbs. But I had acquainted myself with the trade in the city of New York while employed as a correspondent at the *New York World*. I enjoyed setting type. It was exacting and methodical, much like the law I saw practiced in the city's courts, where I served as the newspaper's correspondent after my graduation from Yale.

My father was most unhappy with my decision to become a "scribbler," as he called newspapermen. He wished for me to follow him into teaching and had tried to gain for me a situation at Amherst College where one of his Yale classmates was the chancellor. But I enjoyed writing accounts of the news, especially the proceedings in the courts, where I could see the many faces of justice. There a man could be legally tried by a jury made up of his peers before a judge elected by the people under the constitutions and criminal codes of the state of New York and the United States of America. A condemned man might disagree with the verdict, but he would be hard pressed to argue he had been denied due process. I wish I could say the same for the manner in which justice is exercised these days in Alder Gulch.

I am absorbed in my typesetting when a fierce rap on the window startles me. It is Nellis Kincaid again, his dirty face squashed against the glass. What an ugly man. He jabs his finger in the direction of the Masonic Hall up the street. I draw my watch and see it is almost seven o'clock. It is dark and the wind has subsided a little. Long icicles hang like fangs from the eave over the boardwalk outside my door. A dog barks. I hear bellowing laughter explode from the saloon across the way. A carriage slowly rolls by outside, the driver and passengers looking like great cloth sacks. Time to meet the committee.

I wipe my hands on a rag and then slowly don my coat. I walk back to my desk and open a drawer where I find what I now need. It is a very old copy of the Constitution of the United States. I found it in Colgan's desk after he was murdered. It is printed on parchment and I wonder if it wasn't indeed an original copy of the laws on which the republic was founded. The brittle paper crumples a bit as I finger the document searching for a passage. I find what I seek and, after carefully folding the document, I slide it into my jacket pocket, turn the lamp down, place my hat on my head, and make my way out the door of the *Virginia City Tribune* office, perhaps for the last time.

2

New York City
December 15, 1856

I have been engaged here at the *New York World* for five years and have been recently made a city editor. But I am frequently bored reading the prosaic news copy of lesser newspapermen than myself. That is not to say I think I am a superior craftsman, but rather that I might be better engaged in serving the *World* as its criminal courts correspondent as I did before my "promotion." So it was in this frame of mind that several days ago I encountered an interesting news account of the California gold fields in an old edition of a Sacramento newspaper I discovered in the *World*'s offices.

The florid writing told of "great opportunities" and the "chance at adventure" for anyone brave enough to make the dangerous overland trek to California. I had placed the newspaper aside and continued my work, but occasionally, when I felt bored, I picked it up and read the account again. "Magnificent mountain scenery" beckoned. "Riches beyond your dreams" awaited. "Fecund acres for but a few dollars" were promised.

Thoughts began creeping into my mind as I stared at an endless stream of birth notices, marriage notices, death notices, business announcements, arrests, burglaries, betrayals, executions, and escapes. Surely there was a place for a newspaperman in California, I thought to myself, and especially one with the skills of a typesetter. In fact, I might well be able to start my own newspaper if I encountered the right circumstances for such a venture. While I received ample remuneration for my duties at the *World*, certainly there was nothing of a personal nature holding me in New York with my mother long dead, my father recently deceased, and no siblings. I lived in a small boarding house off Trinity Street where I paid for my room and board by the week.

The weather is foul today so perhaps it is the cold sleet that makes up my mind for me. I arrived this morning at my desk soaked to the skin and mud splattered. Shivering, I sipped black coffee and once again picked up the Sacramento newspaper. "Endless sun falls across golden fields." That sentence was all I needed to read. I have made up my mind to go to California. I have a goodly sum saved and will take the railroad and boat journey to St. Louis. From there, I will try to find a wagon train heading to California.

St. Louis

February 4, 1857

This is an awful place. The Mississippi River stinks to high heaven and drunken Indians of every stripe crowd the sidewalks. You are as apt to see a gentleman wearing a tailored suit of clothes from London, a bowler, and a monocle as you are to see wild-eyed river ruffians dressed in buckskins and braids speaking some sort of French-Indian patois.

I have rooms at the Empire Hotel, grandly named but far from regal, I can assure the reader. I have decided it would be a good idea to search out my journalistic colleagues at one of the several local newspapers here. From them I may be able to collect intelligence about wagon trains preparing to go westward and maybe even more information about what I can expect along the way.

I soon learned a celebration called *Mardi Gras* is underway. I have never heard of such a holiday but discover virtually every adult male I encounter is drunk (as well as some females of questionable character). I also learned this *Mardi Gras* holiday lasts several days. On my way back to the Empire, I passed a small building and, glancing through a window, saw a smallish man bent over a desk diligently writing. He wore an eyeshade and sleeve protectors. I realized

I was looking at a newspaper office. I stopped and took note of the publication's name stenciled on the glass door: The *St. Louis Informer.*

I stepped into the office but the man at the desk took no notice. He dipped his pen in the inkwell and scribbled away in a tight, almost illegible hand, occasionally shuffling through some notes written on scraps of paper. I thought of the poor typesetter who must decipher that copy.

"May I help you?" he asked without looking up.

"Yes, you may," I responded, introducing myself as Noah Coffey, late of the *New York World.*

"My, my," he replied as he looked up at me with a sardonic smile, "the *New York World,* is it? And what, Sir, brings you to St. Louis? We are seldom visited by esteemed members of the Fourth Estate from as far east as the metropolis."

He was a middle-aged fellow of pallid complexion with several teeth missing. On his nose were perched grimy *pince nez.*

I explained my business to the man, who introduced himself as Nathan Carter, owner, editor and chief correspondent for the *Informer,* a newspaper he publishes once per week.

"If I had the money, I could publish everyday," he observed. "We have enough skullduggery and mayhem in St. Louis to fill fifty pages."

I told him I didn't doubt it, based on what I had seen thus far during my short stay, and then enquired about what he knew of wagon trains.

"There are trains assembling all over Missouri and Arkansas," he declared. "They'll cross the continent starting in the late spring and be in California by early November. Barring the unforeseen, of course," he added.

I frowned and he continued.

"Wild fires are common as are flash floods, tornadoes, sand storms; buffalo stampedes are not unheard of. Then there are fevers, quicksand, hail, freezing blizzards in the mountain passes, blazing heat in the deserts, contaminated water. Or no water at all."

He sat back and gave me an appraising look. "Wagon trains are a risky business, Mr. Coffey. And I haven't yet enumerated the dangers posed by human beings along the way."

I absently tapped Carter's desk with my fingers. Of course I knew about the Indians. Comanche, Cheyenne, Sioux, all bloodthirsty and ready to fall on any insufficiently armed wagon train. I had heard the tales of the massacres; of white men left staked out in the sun naked; of women savagely violated and murdered; of children enslaved.

"Nevertheless…"

"Nevertheless, you're going to California. Yes, yes, I understand." He smiled kindly and peered over his dirty glasses. "I thought of doing the same myself once a long time back. Young man, would you care to join me for dinner at my home?"

We made our way along the sidewalk past loud, drunken backwoodsmen and brigands. A pair of toughs exchanged fists in the middle of the street while a bawdy woman screeched at them from a window, her ample white bosom spilling from the loose bodice she wore. Embarrassed, I turned away.

"Charming, no?" my companion sarcastically inquired. "The Soulard District has attracted the *crème de la crème* of society, as you can see. The French influence I should think." He explained that things had not changed much since Lewis and Clark launched their expedition from the city at the turn of the century.

"Captain Lewis was so utterly appalled by what he found in St. Louis, he made his headquarters on the other side of the river!" Carter declared.

We walked up the bluff and were soon on paved streets. We turned a corner and found Carter's row house several doors down. His home was rustically appointed but comfortable. Mrs. Carter appeared presently, an ample woman of perhaps forty years with a broad and pleasant Germanic face. She wore an apron dusted with flour. Surprised to see a guest, she offered a curtsy and kind smile. Carter introduced his wife and explained to her that I was joining the family for their afternoon repast.

We sat at the small dining table and Mrs. Carter soon appeared carrying a platter of roasted beef and potatoes and another plate of freshly baked bread. A young woman followed her through the kitchen door with a pitcher of cold buttermilk. Carter introduced his daughter, Rebecca. She looked nothing like her father or her mother, and I thought she was beautiful with a small graceful figure, warm brown eyes and flaxen hair drawn back in a genteel style. Her smile was charming, and as we dined, she revealed a quick wit and a great knowledge of current affairs. I guessed her at perhaps twenty years of age.

"We are in a treacherous place should hostilities break out between the states," she declared, her eyes flashing. "Some have slaves here and some do not. This is a land partly settled and partly quite primitive, as I'm sure you saw in the streets Mr. Coffey. I cannot imagine what might happen if there was war."

Her father smiled ruefully. "Well, yes daughter, primitive, but it is still civilization, although I know it doesn't always appear so to outsiders." He looked my way.

"I can assure you, Miss Carter, that New York City can be equally uncivilized based on my days reporting on criminal news in that city," I observed. "All that is different is the brand of reprobates there."

"Mr. Coffey is headed to California," Carter interjected.

"Really?" Rebecca asked, her eyes bright. "You're traveling west? How exciting!"

"Indeed I am," I replied proudly. "Your father and I were discussing wagon trains at his office and I hoped he might know where I could locate one preparing for the trek. When I get to California I'd like to perhaps found a newspaper…that is my business. I'm a newspaperman like your father."

"Yes, and like any good newspaperman, I hope you have a strong affinity for the truth, Mr. Coffey. I believe I was explaining to you some of the dangers you might encounter…"

"I expect danger," I interrupted Carter. I didn't want him digressing into tales of Indian savagery in front of the ladies.

"There's been trouble with Mormons," Carter replied flatly. "Some have emigrated and established what they call a 'kingdom' in the Utah Territory. A bunch of lunatics, if you ask me, with their latter-day saints and polygamy. But they've apparently done quite well in that wasteland."

I had not heard about this development. In fact, what I knew of Mormons was that a fellow New Englander, Joseph Smith of Vermont, had claimed to receive a revelation of some missing biblical testaments from an angel. It all sounded far-fetched to me, but the Mormons must be a religious people, Christians, and thus peaceful.

"Well," I suggested to Carter, "is it not a good thing that the Mormons have established themselves in Utah? That is more than halfway to California.

Wouldn't their presence there be a benefit to parties headed west?"

"I think not," he said shaking his head. "They want to secede from the United States and they view outsiders as their enemies. Some Mormons say they were persecuted, beaten, and some of their number were murdered in Illinois and Missouri. I don't know about that one way or the other. I do know they have not welcomed emigrants on the shores of the great salt lake where they have evidently set up their capital. If you ask me, the Mormons are looking for trouble."

But white men, and Godly men at that, not receiving and assisting their Christian brethren? It didn't seem likely. I cleared my throat.

After a long pause Carter continued. "Very well. I know of a train being assembled down in Arkansas by a Captain Alexander Fancher. You may have heard of him. He distinguished himself as an artillery officer during the late war with Mexico."

I had not heard of Fancher but he certainly sounded like the kind of man who could lead a wagon train.

"You'll have to travel to Carrollton in Arkansas by stage coach. I don't know when Fancher plans to leave exactly, but I would guess late April or early May at the latest. They must be through the high mountain passes before winter. There are several routes westward, but I expect Fancher will take the Oregon Trail."

Mrs. Carter had remained silent throughout the meal. I noticed her eyes flicking back and forth between her daughter and me. When I caught her glance she raised an eyebrow and smiled slightly.

The ladies began clearing the china and Mrs. Carter soon presented us with a huge apple pie and pot of fresh coffee. I complimented her on her table, noting that I had not enjoyed a home cooked meal since leaving New York. After stuffing myself with Mrs. Carter's delicious confection, I made to be on my way. Mrs. Carter stepped from the kitchen and, with some hesitation, invited me to attend a small dinner party she was giving in two days time. I noticed Mr. Carter blinking his eyes in a confused fashion. I, of course, accepted as I had no plans for at least another week. My eye caught Rebecca's as I bid the Carters goodbye and she smiled brightly at me again.

3

St. Louis
March 21, 1857

The reader may have divined that Mrs. Carter's dinner party was hastily arranged for my benefit. It may also be apparent that Rebecca and I were destined to fall in love. Indeed, my stay in St. Louis lasted for some weeks after that fateful dinner and subsequent dinner party. I worked at the *Informer* for Carter, who was able to pay me a small stipend and was glad for the help. When the young man who set type and ran the printing press took ill, Carter was surprised and pleased to see that I could easily fill in.

Last evening, Rebecca and I strolled along the riverfront north of the city away from the noise and crowds. It was unseasonably warm, the sun sinking, golden light spilling over the surface of the river. Chunks of ice that had begun their journey upcountry in Minnesota Territory flowed downriver along with tree trunks, shattered boats and canoes, and all manner of detritus.

I stopped and nervously told Rebecca the time for my departure had come. Her eyes were fiercely fixed on mine. I looked away and then, awkwardly, asked if she would marry me and accompany me west. Her face softened.

"Of course I will marry you, Noah." She smiled, then. took my hands in hers and suddenly kissed me.

I walked into the *Informer*'s office this morning and found Carter much as I had when I first set eyes on him, bent over his desk, writing away. I interrupted him and told him I was bound forArkansas in two day's time. He gazed at me a moment over his glasses.

"Mr. Coffey, I believe you might have some unfinished business with my daughter."

I nodded lamely and he smiled up at me. "You may have her hand if that is what you've come to ask me," he smiled. "You are a fine young fellow and I've no doubt as to your future."

I was shocked, pleased, and not a little confused at his approval. I had doubted Carter would allow his only child to make the trip west because, after all, it had been he who had spelled out the risks.

He must have read the emotions on my face because he quickly added, "I am not worried, Sir, for I know you will see to Rebecca's comfort and protection."

Carrollton, Arkansas
April 29, 1857

Alexander Fancher is quite formidable, a strapping man of fifty or so years with a booming voice and commanding presence. He has assembled just as formidable a wagon train for our journey west. Any misgivings I may have had upon my arrival in this remote outpost have been allayed at the sight of forty or fifty sturdy wagons, one thousand head of cattle, hundreds of horses and about one hundred and thirty emigrants. All the men and older boys are well armed and strong looking fellows.

I noticed that many of the men and women featured dark complexions and discovered that a good number of them are descended from the Cherokee peoples of Georgia and the Carolinas, brought here forcibly along the scandalous "Trail of Tears" some twenty years ago.

The train, I am told, will travel north through Kansas where we will pick up the Oregon Trail, then onwards through Nebraska Territory and Utah Territory, then south to the Old Spanish Trail in New Mexico Territory. This will lead us across the desert to a place called Pueblo de Los Angeles in California near the Pacific Ocean. From there, the emigrants will part company. Some are destined for the gold fields while others will seek the lands between the Pacific Ocean and the Sierra Madre Mountains. Evidently, some of their number have preceded them to this "central valley" and reported the land to be extremely rich and the growing season year-round. Farming has clearly been a successful endeavor for many in the party if one judges the quality and quantity of goods carried in the train's wagons, and many no doubt believe they can multiply their prosperity in California.

Fancher was striding about the encampment this morning making ready, and I followed him hoping he would give me some assignment. He wears a big Colt revolver on his hip, probably the one he carried in Mexico. Stopping for a moment at a barrel, he dipped a ladle into the water it contained and sipped. His eye fell on me and he nodded in my direction.

"Coffey is it?" he called out, wiping his lips with the back of his hand. "New York City. Am I correct, Sir?"

I told him I was indeed from New York but born and raised in Connecticut. "What do you know about fighting?" I must have looked shocked at the question because he grinned. "Fighting, man. What do you know about it?"

"Nothing, Captain," I stammered, "I'm a newspaperman."

He removed his sweat-stained hat and nodded his big gray head knowingly. "Well, Sir, you will need to know how to fight when we're on the trail, that's for certain. Every man here can fire a carbine, rifle or musket and you must be ready, too. We may encounter hostiles out on the road, and I don't mean just injuns, Sir. There are desperadoes, Mexican banditti, road agents, assassins, and other such scum. We ain't gonna stop when they tell us to, offer 'em coffee and crumpets and then hand over our goods and stock, Sir. We're going to fight 'em, kill 'em as necessary, and keep moving west. Am I clear?"

"As crystal, Captain Fancher," I replied.

"What sorts of arms are you carrying?" he demanded.

I was embarrassed to tell him. "I have a pocket pistol..."

He made a face, then ambled over to a nearby wagon and pulled from it an old flintlock musket. He handed it to me. "Can you load it?"

Years earlier I had hunted deer in the forests around my home with a smooth bore muzzle loaded weapon not unlike the one I held. My grandfather

Ebenezer had fought the British with it at Trenton, Brandywine Creek and finally Yorktown. I told him I thought I could load, so he watched me fumble with the pan, the horn, the ball, the wad, and the ramrod.

"Good God, Coffey!" he laughed, "that Sioux'd have you scalped and skinned before you had that load home. Let me show you, son."

He took the weapon from my hands and proceeded to load and prime it with efficient precision.

"You should be able to get off a coulpa shots a minute if it gets hot out there. Why don't you practice with this ever' chance you get. Shoot some targets or game. We'll need you at some point. Here, take this, too." He handed me a savage looking tomahawk with a blade sharp enough to shave with had I a notion to use it for that purpose. "You can return the musket and horn to me when we reach California."

I thanked Fancher and made my way to the wagon I'd purchased when we'd arrived in Arkansas. It was small but sturdy and well maintained with a white canvas tarpaulin stretched in an inverted U shape over its bed. I had bought two healthy oxen to pull it as well. My meager possessions were stacked inside along with the linens, and clothing Rebecca had brought from St. Louis.

We'd been married at Rebecca's home, a young minister presiding over the simple ceremony. Despite my protests, Nathan Carter had made her a dowry of one thousand dollars in gold, probably all the money he had in the world.

I shouldn't like to write in detail about the carnal for fear of offending the reader. I will say our wedding night at the Empire Hotel was a new and exciting experience for both of us. Rebecca was unembarrassed and even brazen in her passion and I made up for my inexperience with endurance. We lay in our bed most of the next day, a cool spring breeze flowing through the room.

Not long afterwards, Rebecca had bid her parents a tearful farewell at the stage depot before our journey and she had sat at the window weeping and waving as the coach began to roll.

Now on the western edge of Arkansas, I watched Rebecca bloom. She helped the other women with the communal cooking, cleaning and looking after the small children. Tonight was a fine evening so Ned Kent, a kindly farmer whom I'd gotten to know, brought a small harpsichord from his wagon, and Mrs. Kent began performing an open-air concert of charming minuets. To my astonishment and delight, Rebecca asked the woman if she might play, and proved to be far more talented than Mrs. Kent. Her slim fingers moved across the keyboard without hesitation and I recognized several airs and suites by *Herren* Bach and Handel that I had heard in the concert halls of New York.

The bonfire was burning down as the assembled emigrants applauded Rebecca's impromptu performance. Presently, Fancher appeared in flickering light. "It's time we turn in folks," he announced. "We move out at daybreak. I aim to put fifteen, twenty mile behind us before we camp again, so sleep tight all!"

Rebecca snuggled in next to me on a feather mattress in the bed of the wagon. Just outside, I heard my oxen contentedly chewing their cuds. A coyote barked and his mates answered. An owl screeched as it fell on some helpless rodent. My last thought as I drifted off was that certainly the Fancher party was ready for any hardship the trail westward might present.

Somewhere in Kansas
May 10, 1857

The days are long and intensely boring. I sit on the bench and watch the backsides of my oxen as they plod along behind the wagon ahead of us. Flies buzz around the beasts and occasionally one attacks me. Rebecca is comfortably seated behind me, out of the sun, busying herself with her knitting and other womanly pastimes while chatting with me about her childhood days in St. Louis and mine growing up in Connecticut.

I learned her father had taken over the *Informer* after its first owner died. It had once been the city's most important newspaper, but because Nathan Carter's editorial views concerning certain municipal business dealings with certain citizens clashed with the old St. Louis French-descended aristocracy that ran the city, advertising revenues fell off to the point where he could barely make ends meet.

I told Rebecca of my mother's death when I was just two and my father's prominent role in my life. He had been very stern, I said, but he had educated me well and I knew I would succeed in whatever I endeavored to do thanks to Father's discipline.

In the evenings we usually stop at a spring and pull the wagons into a loose circular formation. Water is fetched, sometimes we hunt for game—usually deer or antelope—and the women prepare a wonderful feast. With such a large contingent, the ladies have organized themselves in order to make the cooking chores easier. The cuisine, while rustic, is filling. A slab of broiled venison loin and a heaping pile of beans, preserved tomatoes and fresh biscuits is a wonderful way to conclude a long day on the trail.

After supper, some of the men repair behind the wagons for smoking, drinking and cards. Others bring forth fiddles and jaw harps and play jaunty tunes while we sing along. I am not familiar with the music, it being of an unusual backcountry flavor, but it is very enjoyable, nonetheless.

Fancher has formed guard units among the men. All of us are under orders to keep weapons loaded and at hand should we be attacked at night. My unit guarded last night so I tumbled into the back of our wagon after the meal and music and fall into a deep slumber almost immediately.

We rise before daybreak. There are latrines for ladies and girls to one side of the train and those for men and boys at the other. We wash and take breakfast, usually biscuits, grits, bacon, and hot coffee. Then it's another day on the bench watching the backsides of my oxen while growing calluses on my own.

Nebraska Territory (?)
June 1, 1857

We encountered today the most pathetic band of Indians, the dozen or so men and women frail and barely clothed and their children filthy, naked and starving. They had erected lean-tos of sticks and worn out blankets against a tree next to the trail and held out their hands to us beseeching food as the train passed.

The children looked at us with hollow eyes, their faces caked with dirt and mucus while their mothers made plaintive noises.

Rebecca bit her lip. Wiping her eyes with the back of her hand, she stooped into the rear of the wagon. I reined in the oxen and Rebecca reappeared with a canvas bag filled with beans, some cured ham, and two of our extra blankets.

She handed the bag and blankets down to one of the Indian men who had trotted forth from the sad assembly. He accepted the gift without expression or a word of thanks and stepped back.

"Move it, Coffey!" bellowed the driver of the wagon behind me. "Ferget them damned injuns!"

I felt my face flush with anger and made to step down from the wagon but Rebecca's hand stayed me. Angrily, I whipped the flank of one of the oxen and our wagon jolted forward. The pitiful Indians silently watched us roll away.

4

Nebraska Territory
June 17, 1857

A fever is sweeping through the train. Rebecca has caught it, apparently tending to the sick. Two infants have already died and I fear for my wife who now lies in the wagon bed in the throes of the sickness. Mrs. Gowdy is with her, applying cool compresses, but the heat here is breathtaking and certainly isn't helping to alleviate Rebecca's condition.

Fancher has called a halt until the sickness passes. The wagons are circled and we can only wait. Fortunately, there is a clear, cold spring nearby so water is not a problem today.

This evening, Fancher, along with some of the other men and me, sat around the fire, the group hanging on every word of Fancher's war story.

"Our artillery blasted away at Chapultepec castle for hours, but them greasers was dug in and fightin' like hell," he said. "Finally, orders come to attack, so the infantry moves up and before long the fightin's hand to hand. I move my artillery up and we fire canister and shot into their lines. They was courageous, them greasers, but they died wholesale."

He drew the Colt I'd seen him carrying. "One of 'em decides he's gonna charge our guns, this little fella all decked out in a beautiful red tunic, white britches, shiny boots an' a green shako with gold tassels on it. He comes at our line o' artillery with his sword flashing—officer, I guess. But his men, they don't follow him. He don't know that, so, while my boys are reloadin', I draw down on the Mexican and put one right through his head...or so's I thought. His shako goes a flyin', he looks surprised, but he keeps a comin'. So I cock my piece and aim agin, and this one catches him square in the head, just as he's about to slice one o' my gunners stem to stern."

Fancher puffed his cigar and shook his head thoughtfully. "That little Mex officer was one brave bastard...a dead bastard, but a brave one!"

The men all roared with laughter as they nodded their approval. "Not long after that, the greasers surrendered Mexico City to old Winnie Scott and we got ourselves some pretty fair territory in the bargain, includin' California."

I pictured the poor Mexican as the round blew his head apart and shudder, praying I'll never have to fire a weapon at one of my fellow human beings. I rose, said goodnight to the others and found my wagon.

Rebecca was asleep, her face slick with sweat. I dipped the towel in a bucket, wrang it out and pressed it against her forehead. She opened her eyes and offered me a weak smile. I kissed her cheek and then took a pair of blankets, making my bed under the wagon for the night so as not to disturb my wife.

Nebraska Territory
July 12, 1857

It has been cloudy and warm with occasional rain. But the most troublesome feature of this rolling prairie today is the awful stench that hangs in the humid air. We've come upon scores of bison carcasses stretching for the better part of a mile on either side of the trail. They appear to have been shot several days earlier and simply left to rot. There is no shortage of the great dusky animals hereabouts, but to see so many slaughtered to no apparent purpose is disturbing. We got upwind of the stench and the train stopped for the evening.

We were followed by a fierce looking band of Indians for most of the day so Fancher ordered us to circle the wagons in a tight formation next to a creek sheltered by cottonwood trees. Guards have been doubled during daylight hours as well as at night. Fancher seems particularly worried about the livestock, so the drovers have herded the cattle and horses close in to the circled wagons.

We have done well so far. With the sad exception of the two babies taken by the fever, there have been no deaths among the party. Rebecca is back to herself and tending to some injured men. One broke his hand repairing a wagon wheel. Another cut his foot with an axe as he chopped firewood. A rattlesnake bit a third man on the leg. All will recover.

Ned Kent joined me for a short walk along the stream and I asked him about the decaying bison.

"Not, sure Noah," he replied, "but I believe they was killed for sport."

I wondered what kind of sport it was to kill the bison. When I haven't seen them thundering across the prairie in their endless herds they generally appear to be quite placid, docile, and even curious, actually ambling toward our wagon train, I suppose for a better view. The hapless creatures deserved a better fate than to be shot and left to decompose.

This behavior among my fellow whites may well explain some of the Indian hostility I've heard about. I am told the Plains Indians rely almost entirely on the bison for food, clothing and shelter and no doubt resent the wanton killing of the beasts along with our encroachment on their ancient tribal lands.

It began to rain in earnest just as the ladies were serving supper. We ate our food hastily and all of us, except the night watch, turned in.

I lay snug in the wagon next to Rebecca, lulled to sleep by the steady patter of the rain on our canvas roof before I was jolted awake by a nearby shotgun blast followed by terrifying high pitched shrieks. I threw on my clothes and jumped from the wagon, musket and tomahawk in hand. The fire had died down but I could see several oilskin-clad guardsmen were standing in a circle. I joined them and saw that an Indian with a painted face lay on the wet ground at their feet, coughing up blood, a gaping hole in his chest. He appeared to be just seventeen or eighteen years of age.

"Sum'bitch tried to get inside my wagon," said one of the men, a fellow called Baker. "Had me a little buckshot surprise ready fer 'im."

The Indian groaned and tried to roll over. One of the men kicked him in the ribs and the poor boy vomited blood on his boot.

"Godammit!" the man yelled before he kicked the helpless Indian again. At that moment, Fancher strode up.

"What in the hell happened?" he asked. He then looked down at the Indian. Without a word he drew the Colt and shot the boy in the head.

"Drag that carcass over yonder and let the coyotes have their way with it. Don't want the ladies nor kids to see 'im in the daylight."

I must tell the reader I was completely shocked and sickened by the acts of brutality I had just witnessed. Even as I write this, my fingers shake. I have never seen a man killed and I never dreamed I would watch a man—no, a mere boy—dispatched in such a casual manner. I am shaken to my soul.

The next morning dawned clear and cool. My mind numbed by the previous night's killing, I walked to the fire where Rebecca and other women were preparing our breakfast. I picked up a coffee pot and abruptly stopped myself mid-pour. The man across the fire from me was wearing on his belt a bloody clump of hair and skin. I didn't know the fellow, but he was one of the train's Cherokee descendents. He was talking to his friends and pulled the gory trophy from his belt to display it. I threw the coffee on the fire in disgust, my stomach churning.

Fancher called out that it was time to move. The wagons were quickly loaded with cooking implements and children and the train started its slow, bumpy procession across the plains with armed outriders on both sides and two score of drovers calling and whistling to the livestock some distance to our left. My wagon was toward the rear this morning. I glanced back over my shoulder and saw three mounted Indians atop a hill above the gully where we'd left their associate.

"What happened last night, Noah?" Rebecca asked as she fearfully stared at the Indians. I held the reins and told her what I'd seen. Horror washed across her face. I decided to leave out the part about the man with the scalp

.

Nebraska (or Utah) Territory
July 29, 1857

We are several days out from Salt Lake City, according to an army patrol that joined us for the night. They are from Fort Bridger, a day's ride west. A Lieutenant Marcus Reno is leading the patrol. He's a young man, no more than twenty-two, recently arrived at his post after graduating from West Point. His troopers are a rough and ready looking lot, rangy men in blue uniforms, most speaking with Irish brogues, seated around the supper fire gratefully lapping up the delicious stew and biscuits the ladies have prepared.

"Miss, I haven't enjoyed a meal so since leaving me old mother in County Kildare," a trooper said to Rebecca with a rakish grin. I stepped forward and, placing my arm around her shoulder, silently let the soldier know Rebecca was spoken for.

Later, I saw Fancher and Reno sitting on some nearby rocks, quietly discussing the train's route, I supposed. Reno gestured west then shook his head doubtfully as Fancher spoke. They were quiet for a long moment, before the young lieutenant rose and shrugged. Fancher, his brown face wrinkled with concern, sat for a moment more and then returned to his wagon.

5

Nebraska (or Utah) Territory
July 30, 1857

The troopers were gone before sun-up, headed back to Fort Bridger. At daybreak I heard a commotion and stepped down from my wagon, rubbing the sleep from my eyes. A man holding a Kentucky long rifle was at the center of the circled wagons, excitedly speaking and gesticulating to Fancher and other men. I quickly learned that more than five hundred cattle and horses had been stolen during the night.

"Don't ask me how, Cap'n Fancher...I don't know...we was up all night but there weren't no moon. They musta' slipped in and took 'em off quiet like, a few dozen head at a time. Looks like the bastards headed south!"

"Shit!" barked Flancher in a rage. "Fuckin' injuns." (I apologize to my more gentle readers here as I know this rough frontier language may offend some. But it is necessary to relay the captain's language so the reader may better appreciate the urgency of the stolen livestock. For many emigrants in the Fancher train, the horses and cows taken by the Indians represented the sum total of their wealth.)

"Boys, we gotta get 'em back right now!" Fancher looked around at the gathered men. "Teddy, you take Jimmy and Wes, you're the best trackers here, so git goin' and find 'em!" The men bolted to their horses and were saddled and off in less than a minute.

"Folsom! You, Jake, Tom and Fanny get a coupla dozen armed men on horseback as quick as you can. Then follow the trackers! They'll need your guns when they find the injuns. Hurry up now!"

The four emigrants ran in different directions and it occurred to me that the captain had thought to prepare them for something like this before we left Arkansas.

Fancher was staring at me.

"Coffey, can you ride fast?" I hadn't been on horseback since leaving New York, and then only to take gentle Sunday rides aboard rented nags in the woods of northern Manhattan Island.

"Yes, Sir," I replied without thinking.

"Good! Go after Lieutenant Reno's patrol and bring 'em back here fast...we'll need their help. They got an hour's head start on you. Go, man!"

Rebecca watched Ned tack one of his black geldings for me, her knuckles at her lips. I mounted, glanced back at her once and then drove my boot heels into the horse's flanks.

It was easy to follow the troopers' trail through the tall grass. Within ten minutes, I had spied the dust their column was kicking up maybe a mile or two away. They were walking their horses and I was riding, however clumsily, as fast as I could. Small bushes jutted here and there and I dodged around rocks and clumps of scrubby trees, but the prairie seemed an endless sea of long, dry grass.

I presently rode down a hill faster than I thought prudent, then up another when, without warning, I came face to face with two painted Indian warriors on horseback at the crest of the hill. The Indians had been watching the soldiers ahead and had not seen or heard my approach. They were as alarmed to see me as I was to see them. I yelled and drove the gelding full tilt past the astonished Indians. I realized my only hope was to outrun them to Reno's patrol.

The Indians whooped and gave chase. My heart was suddenly in my throat as visions of butchered settlers left for the vultures flashed through my brain. I raced toward what I hoped *was* Reno's patrol and not some other band of Indians waiting for the two chasing me to catch up.

Behind me I heard the Indians laughing, no doubt amused by my riding exhibition. One was suddenly alongside me wearing a grin. His face was slashed with black and red chevrons and golden feathers flew from a leather thong tied to his hair. He wore only a breechcloth and had no saddle. He reached out and playfully slapped my horse's rump. I saw the dust cloud just ahead over the next rise and realized then I wouldn't make it.

The Indian, meantime, had pulled from his belt what looked like a war club. At that moment he was snatched backward from his mount just as I heard the sharp crack of a carbine. I looked ahead and, there, at the top of the rise twenty yards away was the same Irish trooper I had fancied was flirting with Rebecca. He'd just lowered his gun and was reloading as he waited for the other Indian to come into range.

"Sure now, me lad, you almost lost your hair!" the soldier declared as I slowed next to him. "'Twas lucky for you I took notice o' them two heathens."

I could scarcely breathe, much less speak. I saw in the distance Reno leading his men back toward the sound of the shot. I looked to my pursuers and saw that the surviving Indian had draped the body of his partner over the dead man's pony. He mounted his own horse and trotted off to the east, his comrade in tow. The Irishman had decided to hold his fire.

Reno arrived with his mounted soldiers. All were coated in fine white dust. I quickly explained the theft of the horses and cattle to Reno, who called his sergeants forward. They conferred and then, at a full gallop, we all rode east.

The train was as I had left it, wagons circled, armed men stationed around the inside of the ring awaiting an attack. They waved their hats when they saw us and one of the men pointed south. We cut around the train and followed the direction of the men who had earlier given chase.

Unaccustomed to the saddle and demands of the ride, my buttocks and thighs were beginning to burn. I ignored the discomfort, determined to ride as hard as the soldiers. It was an hour before we finally overtook Fancher, who had stopped at a rivulet to water his mounts. The trackers were nowhere in sight. Fancher had a force of twenty or so men with him, all heavily armed with shotguns, carbines and side arms.

Reno dismounted and his horse drank while he and Fancher briefly parleyed. The lieutenant beckoned one of his men forward and I realized this particular soldier, absent the long hair of his people, was an Indian. Reno pointed south and the man mounted and was gone at full speed.

"We lost the trail," Fancher said to the group at large, obviously angry. "They got five hunnert head and we can't find 'em! Damn it all!"

We let the horses rest for a few minutes more, and then mounted. Reno dispatched outriders on our flanks and now at least forty men strong, we followed the Indian soldier. We rode south at a trot, the sun blazing, the waves of heat shimmering off the endless plain ahead. I guessed the time at noon when we finally stopped next to a copse of scrubby trees. The horse soldiers were clearly immune to the rigors of the ride while I was exhausted and it had only been six hours or so since the discovery of the missing horses and cattle.

The soldiers drank from their canvas canteens and gnawed some dried meat. Our men looked fatigued as they sat in what little shade the trees provided, some with their eyes closed. I joined them, brushing flies away from my face as I tried to doze. I was presently awakened by a yelp. I rose to my feet and watched as the Indian soldier dashed full tilt into our midst, leaping from the saddle before his horse had halted.

He saluted Reno and made his report: "A mile ahead, Sir. They killed the trackers!" Reno looked into the Indian's face for a moment, the color draining from his face.

"Oh my God!" Fancher cried out in anguish.

The three men, Teddy, Jimmy and Wes, the best trackers in the Fancher party, had been butchered, their scalps, clothes and horses taken. I will spare the reader the awful details of the three unfortunate men's deaths other than to say they had been left for the buzzards and flies, their entrails pulled from their bodies and left in reeking gray piles.

Fancher was disconsolate. He kept muttering, "I gotta tell Jimmy's ma about this…"

I learned from one of the men that Jimmy was his nephew.

One of the emigrants brought forward blankets, but Reno waved him off.

"I'm sorry, friend, but we'll have to do that later. The hostiles are not far in front of us now. They wasted too much time doing…this. We have to go on."

The scout found the attackers' trail so we rode hard, my entire body aching, my head pounding, my face sunburned. As we approached a barren hilltop strewn with rocks, the Indian soldier, whom Reno had dispatched ahead of the main force, was dismounted and running toward us waving his arms. We came to an abrupt stop as he approached Reno's horse, again saluted the officer, and gave his report, which I overheard.

"Just the other side of the hill, Sir! They're watering the stock down there in the draw!"

Reno called his sergeants forward, took his spyglass out of a case, dismounted and went to the top of the hill with his men. Just before they reached the crest, they all got onto their bellies and crawled forward. The lieutenant glassed the draw. He spoke with the older of the two sergeants and the Indian. He nodded at something one of the soldiers said and then returned to where we stood with the horses.

"It's good. They must believe they are not being pursued," Reno declared. "Maybe twenty, twenty-five hostiles and it doesn't look like they've been there too long. They may even be thinking about camping where they can't be seen."

Reno then looked over his men and ours as he decided his plan.

"I'm going to have one squad move around to the opposite hill above the creek," he finally said. "I'll keep another squad here and then place two squads at either end of the draw, out of sight. Those are the only two ways out with that much livestock."

Reno looked at the old sergeant. "Sergeant Higgens, I'll take this hill with my men. Mount up and lead your squad east around to the opposite hill. Stay out of sight. Wait for us to open fire in…" he pulled out his pocket watch, "thirty minutes. Let's kill as many as we can in our first volley."

The sergeant and ten soldiers were on their horses and shortly out of sight.

Reno eyed Fancher, still stricken at the discovery of his murdered men. "Captain Fancher, listen to me. Those boys are gone and you need to get your stock back…we will help, but I must have your complete attention or those hostiles will surely get away."

Fancher nodded his head, then his eyes seemed to clear as they focused on Reno.

"Take ten of your best marksmen on foot down to the east end of the draw," Reno said. "Stay out of sight behind the trees and rocks there and, by God, be prepared! I am certain they'll try to make for that end of the ravine when the shooting starts because it's downhill. When they come your way, you can turn the stock back into the draw and kill some of the bastards."

Fancher nodded grimly then turned to his men and pointed at those he wanted to accompany him.

"All right then, I need ten more men on the west side. You people be ready, because that will be their escape route when they discover they're cut off. I want the rest of you to stay here to guard the horses of those of us who are dismounted."

Fancher made his choices and the lieutenant detailed a pair of corporals to accompany each of the emigrant platoons. I was assigned to stay with the horses together with several teenaged boys and some men who appeared to be older than fifty. One of the latter fellows didn't like his assignment and swore under his breath. I am not ashamed to report that I was relieved.

Our men departed to the east and west on foot, screened by the hill. Reno and his soldiers crept to their positions and I saw the lieutenant again consult his pocket watch. I was happy to finally be out of the saddle and sat on the ground after tying the reins of a dozen horses to the branches of a scrubby tree. I watched Reno and his squad fifty yards away at the top of the hill and sensed the mounting tension.

The lieutenant once again glanced at his watch, said something to his men, then, taking a kneeling position, Reno carefully aimed his carbine as the other soldiers followed his lead. A moment later, there was a report and suddenly the soldiers were on their feet shooting down the hill, their fusillade shattering the silence of the still afternoon. In the distance, I heard answering shots as Higgens's platoon on the opposite slope opened fire. Between shots, there were whooping and cries from the Indians trapped in the draw with the stolen animals. The soldiers rapidly fired and reloaded. I saw one man take aim, shoot and then flash a wide grin.

I could hear the dull thunder of two thousand hooves as the Indians tried to drive the horses and cows to the east, just as Reno had predicted. Suddenly, firing erupted on the left, followed by more whooping. The soldiers on the hilltop were reloading and waiting.

The gunfire in the east crescendoed then slowed. I heard the hoofbeats increase in volume along with the braying and whinnying of the panicked animals. The Indians were making a desperate try for the western end of the draw. The soldiers on both hills began firing again. Then, the shooting on the right commenced in earnest.

"Let's move down there! Spread out and fire at will!" Reno called as he drew his pistol. He turned back to us and yelled, "You men, stay put!"

The gunfire at the end of the draw was growing sporadic and then it stopped altogether. I heard several intermittent shots ring out. I looked at my fellow horse guards and all were excited with curiosity. Finally, the old man who didn't want to look after the horses angrily spit tobacco juice and walked defiantly up the hill.

"Fuck it boys, sounds like they's havin' all the fun...let's go kill us some injuns, too!" he yelled down to us over his shoulder.

All of the others ran up the hill except for the youngest boy and me. He might have been fifteen. We realized we were alone. I pulled a carbine from a saddle scabbard and opened the breech to make sure it was loaded. I also had a Colt I'd borrowed from Ned stuck in my waistband.

We heard some more shots, but otherwise, an eerie silence had descended over the draw.

I watched the crest of the hill and the boy looked off in the other direction. I had the carbine cocked and was just turning back to the boy when, out of the corner of my eye, I saw an Indian rushing at me from behind a horse. I turned to face him. He was small and wiry and held a deadly looking knife at the ready. Gaudy red and yellow paint slashed his face and he wore buckskin breeches and a chest protector of bone. He lunged at me with the blade, but I stepped aside and, without thinking, struck him in the face with the butt of the carbine. Stunned, the Indian spun around, blood pouring from his broken nose. His teeth gritted, his eyes desperate, he lunged again, the blade of his knife piercing the sleeve of my shirt and slicing into my arm.

My heart pounded as I again brought the butt around, this time catching the warrior in the back of his head and sending him sprawling. As he scrambled to his feet I leveled the carbine and pulled the trigger. The weapon misfired, the ball weakly hitting the Indian in his chest protector but doing no damage. The brave smiled evilly and snatched up his knife with a whoop. He lunged, and as he did there was a shotgun blast next to my ear. The top of the Indian's head disappeared in a spray of blood and brains. He dropped like a stone to the ground, gore pouring from the cavity in his skull. My ear ringing, I turned to see the boy standing behind me, enveloped in the smoke from his weapon, his face a mask of horror.

We managed to recover all of the cows and horses save a dozen head that had been inadvertently shot in the melee along with all the Indian raiders. Reno forbade scalp or trophy taking and we left the Indians where they had died. I walked across the battlefield in the draw and understood that Reno's plan had been flawless. The first shots from the opposite hillsides cut down most of the enemy. There were a half dozen dead at the eastern mouth of the draw killed by Fancher and his men. The remainder had been slaughtered running west.

With my slight wound, I was the only casualty. When Fancher learned that men charged with guarding the horses had abandoned their posts, his pent-up rage exploded.

"You sons o'bitches coulda killed us all if'n we'd a lost our mounts way the hell out here!" he roared. "We got a long goddamn way t'go and if any a you fools fails to follow my orders again I will leave you and your people behind, so help me God!" The guilty men hung their heads in shame in the face of Fancher's tirade.

When he'd regained his composure, Fancher looked at my wound before one of the soldiers bandaged it.

"Noah, thank you," he said, patting my shoulder. "You and that young'n there did good. That damn injun woulda run off with all the horses an' we'd a been in a helluva fix." He smiled weakly and then went to speak with the boy who had killed the Indian. The youngster stood off by himself, his back to the rest of the party. I saw Fancher put his arm around the boy's shoulders and say something to him. The boy turned toward Fancher and buried his face in the big man's chest.

On our return to the wagon train, we stopped to bury the dead trackers.

It had been easy to find them because a cloud of buzzards circled over their bloating remains. The soldiers kindly dug the graves with the short shovels they carried while we prepared the bodies for burial. Fancher said a few words over the dead men before we departed.

We arrived back at the train well after dark, all of the men and soldiers exhausted with the day's exertions. We discovered a band of Indians had attacked the circled wagons in the early afternoon but the defenders had easily driven them off. It fell to Captain Fancher to inform the trackers' families of their loved ones' sad fate. He gathered them together at the far end of the circle and we heard pitiable weeping and crying for some time afterwards.

Rebecca, alarmed to hear I'd been wounded, cut off the bandage and was relieved to see the injury was only slight. She washed the cut with strong soap and hot water then rebound it. The other women fed the men and soldiers beans and biscuits. After I had eaten a little food, I staggered to my wagon, my thighs and buttocks on fire, and fell fully clothed onto my bed. Rebecca kindly removed my boots and let me sleep the sleep of the dead.

6

Utah Territory
August 8, 1857

We have passed through several Mormon settlements and our reception has been decidedly hostile. We have tried to purchase flour, milk, corn and other staples but the Mormons angrily refuse to sell and demand we leave their "kingdom." Several farmers have issued dark warnings of what might happen to our train if we continue through their "State of Deseret." Fancher is dismissive of them, saying when we get to Salt Lake City, merchants there will welcome us.

Yesterday, we came upon three wagons by the side of the trail. One of them had its rear wheels listing outward, the axle snapped in half. Three men stood around staring at the broken wagon as though it might miraculously repair itself while a gaggle of women and children sat off to one side in the shade of a cottonwood tree.

Fancher stopped the train and joined the men. I and some others ambled up to see if we might lend a hand.

"You fellas have a spare axle, don't you?" Fancher asked them.

I looked more closely at the emigrants and realized they were all filthy, their clothing threadbare and patched in many places. The men had a rough backwoods look about them and based on the poor condition of their wagons and the few worn out cows and horses they had with them, they seemed desperately poor. Their women were likewise slovenly and their underfed children were barefoot with sores about their faces and bodies.

"Hell no!" barked the tallest man. He spat a long stream of tobacco juice into the dust. "Hopin' we could trade fer one o' your'uns."

Captain Fancher stared at the man in disbelief for a moment. Without spare axles and wheels, any emigrant was taking his fate in his hands crossing the continent. "Where you folks from?" Fancher finally asked.

"Ozarks." The man spit again. "We's mountain folk. Train left us behind t'other day when this here happened. Goddamn wagon master wouldn't he'p us. These my brothers and kin. Headin' to Cal'forn'a fer the gold."

Fancher shook his head. "I reckon we have a spare axle…fellas, let's get one and help these folks."

One of our men was a blacksmith and, assisted by the three brothers and a number of us, he quickly had the wagon mounted on rocks and the wheels off the shattered axle. An hour later, the repaired wagon was ready to roll.

One of the Ozark brothers produced a brown earthen jug from his wagon and offered it to Fancher and the others. Fancher hoisted it into the crook of his arm and took a pull. His eyes instantly bulged out of his head as he swallowed and then coughed.

"Good God damn! What in the name a jumpin' Jesus is that?" he coughed.

"Bash-head I makes," the man said with a leer that exposed rotten teeth.

"Say Cap'n," said the tall Ozark man, "Ya reckon we can join up with y'all seein' how's yer headin' west?"

Fancher eyed the three mountain men and then looked over their ramshackle wagons. "If'n you have more trouble we ain't gonna be able to wait up for you. We're on a schedule and I aim to make up for some time we lost on the trail back yonder."

"Yes, Sir, Cap'n Fancher," the man replied with a squint. "We ain't gonna have no more trouble. Thank ya kindly."

"All right, then, let's move out."

Salt Lake City
August 10, 1857

We had trouble from the moment our train entered Salt Lake City, which turned out to be an unremarkable collection of clapboard and brick buildings arranged around an impressive church the Mormons refer to as a "tabernacle." Tents and wagons surround Emigration Square. Tall mountains called the Wasatch loom to the east.

It wasn't long after we'd made camp before one of the Ozark men got drunk and brawled with several locals. Fancher pulled him from the fight and had him shackled to a wagon wheel where, despite the presence of our women and children, he stood screaming the most profane oaths I have ever heard.

Later, one of the other louts found a saloon and, after too much drink, started boasting that he had cut a Mormon farmer's throat back in Missouri and that he "was damn proud to send the bastard's soul to hell!" He was beaten senseless and left in the street where several men from our train found him sprawled incoherent.

As if this isn't enough, we have learned that none of the merchants here will sell their goods to "gentiles." Several men and women have made attempts to buy at various stores and have been impolitely told to leave. I am shocked as are many others at the vitriol these so-called Christians spew.

Fancher returned this afternoon with a detachment of emigrants, one of whom was a lay clergyman. The wagon master was white with rage.

"I went to see the church leaders," he told us bitterly. "Fat son of a bitch name o' Young was happy to explain he had instructed Mormons hereabouts they'd be thrown out of their church if'n they help us! We need to move on from here," he said through a clenched jaw. "We got enough supplies to get us to New Mexico Territory. To hell with these bastards."

The next morning we rolled south out of Salt Lake City with several armed Mormons riding close behind to make sure we didn't stop until we were well away from the city. At sundown, we made camp near the base of the mountains, already snowcapped at the higher elevations. It was quiet and subdued as we took our supper and went to bed. There was no music.

Utah Territory
September 12, 1857

The trail had led us through the desert and past other Mormon settlements, where word of our train's approach preceded us together with the dire warnings of the church elders should anyone offer aid. Even so, upon leaving the last town, Cedar City, Fancher's mood began to brighten but not before another one of the Ozark toughs beat a Mormon merchant with an axe handle, claiming the man had insulted him.

Our wagon train has been climbing into the barren mountains for some days. As we gain altitude, the days grow cooler and the nights are actually quite cold. Cedar trees, juniper, and other vegetation provide a welcome respite from the barren waste through which we'd trekked after leaving Salt Lake City.

Each night, we build cheerful fires and the pall is slowly lifting as we near our destination.

"We'll be out of Utah Territory and away from them Mormon sons of bitches in a few more days!" Fancher declared to a group of us gathered around the fire last night. "I guarantee you, boys, them New Mexicans will be damned glad to see our gold!"

As the sun fell this evening, I watched a beautiful meadow come into view as we crested a ridge. Purple and gold late summer flowers that blanketed the valley seemed to wave at us in the freshening breeze as if to welcome our arrival. Rebecca smiled and held my arm tightly. The train made its way down the bumpy trail to the valley floor.

The scouts dispatched earlier by Fancher to find a suitable campground led us to a spring. We organized the wagons into a loose circle some distance from the water and soon the ladies had a bullock on a spit over a roaring fire. The cool evening air was filled with the laughter of children and the wonderful aroma of roasted beef and fresh baked biscuits.

Ned and some other men were sipping from a bottle and I joined them for a tot. We were chuckling at some joke when Ned suddenly pointed back up the trail we had descended not an hour before. There, a half-mile away, a dozen Indians stood on the ridgeline silently watching us. With them there appeared to be several white men.

7

Utah Territory
September 14, 1857

I have only a few moments to pen some tragic lines. Indians attacked us yesterday. We had not circled the wagons tightly enough, believing ourselves to be safe and secure in this picturesque valley. More than a hundred savages caught us completely by surprise after stealthily murdering our guards in the predawn hours. A pitched battle ensued at daybreak. During the attack, a score of Indians penetrated our perimeter, scrambling around, through and under the wagons. I along with the other men of our party met them head on.

It sickens me to say I shot one of the attackers dead with Fancher's musket and was forced to kill another with my tomahawk after he had jumped on my back and we fell to the ground. I sharply elbowed the Indian in the ribs and he released his grip on my neck. Like his fellows, he was small and dark with wild hair, nearly naked and screeching incomprehensively. I drew the tomahawk from my belt and leapt at him as he struggled to get to his feet. The blade struck his thigh and he let out a scream as he fell backward. I lunged again, this time landing on top of the savage. I raised the hatchet over my head, and without thinking, drove the blade into his chest, blood spraying over me from his severed arteries.

Then on my feet, drenched in gore and heaving, I saw Ned shoot an

Indian in the belly with his Colt revolver. Fancher, wielding a shotgun, blew the brains out of another. A huge man I didn't know clutched a raider from behind and slit the Indian's neck open with an enormous Bowie knife. Women and children were huddled at the far end of the circled wagons wailing and crying while they watched the battle's horrors unfold before them.

Bodies of emigrants and Indians were sprawled everywhere on the ground, blood splashed across the trampled grass. I could see several wounded attackers moving, but one of our men busied himself dispatching them with his revolver. Realizing the battle within the perimeter of the wagons was over, a number of the women with stronger constitutions, including Rebecca, came forward to tend to our wounded. Some Indians continued to ride past on their ponies firing carbines or loosing arrows at us. Our men returned fire, occasionally bringing down a raider. After thirty more minutes the assault was over and the Indians had disappeared.

By nine o'clock, I could see the day promised to be clear and warm. We piled the dead Indians outside the perimeter and covered our own eight dead in the bed of one of the wagons. I changed my blood-splattered shirt and washed the gore from my arms and hands, then reported to Fancher. He put me to work with other men digging trenches within the perimeter where the women and children could shelter if we were attacked again.

As we dug, I noticed Fancher staring at the ridgeline above us. I followed his gaze and was shocked to see six white men in long coats and black hats watching us. How long had they been there? Had they witnessed the assault? Why hadn't they done anything to aid us?

Fancher declared he thought the men were Mormon allies of the Indians. "They tol' the savages to attack us," he concluded. I found that incomprehensible. The Mormons may wish us gone. But dead?

Utah Territory
September 15, 1857

Three men were sent to retrieve water before daybreak but they must have been surprised and killed by Indians (or Mormons?) because we heard gunfire and they never returned.

The Indians harass us with gunfire repeatedly from the ridge overlooking our improvised fort. The women and children in the trenches are terrified. Our cows and horses, which we'd been able to protect up to now, have been driven off and scattered around the valley floor. We are low on ammunition and food.

There was some excitement this afternoon when an emigrant shot an Indian who had ventured too close to our wagons. Upon closer inspection, we realized the dead "Indian" was in fact a white man of middle years who had cleverly applied paint to his body and face and cloaked himself in a blanket. This is a puzzling development, but Fancher said it proves his theory that the Mormons are behind the attack

Utah Territory
September 20, 1857

I honestly believed we were saved when a tall, well-dressed man with a sympathetic manner approached us under a white flag. He appeared genuinely concerned at our plight. Captain Fancher and several of our senior men met him to talk. While they parleyed, Charley Fancher, the captain's twenty year old son, and several other husky young men, took the opportunity while the guns were quiet to fetch water. It had been foolish not to base the circled wagons closer to the spring.

Presently, the man completed his talk with Fancher and left. The captain walked to the center of the circled wagons with a look of consternation. After the men and some of the women had assembled around him, Fancher addressed us.

"That fella says his name is Bishop John D. Lee of the Virginia Lee family," he began. "Says he's an elder in the Mormon church and he's sick to see what the injuns done to us. I asked him why all those white men we seen ain't he'ped us. He tol' me they been tryin' to convert injuns to Mormon and couldn't interfere because he ain't got enough men to stop 'em."

"That sounds like a load o' shit, Cap'n," said one man. (Again, I beg the reader's indulgence). "What about that white man what was wearin' the feathers and paint?"

"Them goddamn Mormons put the injuns up to this!" cried another.

"Men...men!" yelled Fancher over the loud grumbling that followed. "We're outgunned. We got almost no amm'nition left and food an' water's runnin' out. The women and kids is in bad shape an' it's sure to get worse if'n we don't agree to do like Lee says."

"What's that?" asked the big man I'd seen cut the throat of the Indian on the first day of the siege.

"He says we gotta give up our weapons..."

There was a general outcry of protest. Fancher held up his hands. "Wait, men!" Fancher yelled. "Just temporary. He says we put our weapons in a wagon, the injuns see that, they'll let us go. When we're clear, Lee says he'll return our guns."

"What about the wagons and stock...we're takin' those ain't we?"

"No," Fancher said flatly to the assembly, his eyes on the ground. "He says we gotta leave 'em. For the injuns."

The men were stunned. Some of the women who had gathered around began shrieking and weeping.

"Lee said when we get out of the valley," continued Fancher, "he and his men will try to he'p us get back on our feet and on our way."

Several men fell to their knees, moaning and covering their eyes with their hands at this shocking news. Others shouted out angrily in protest, but Fancher held up his hands again. "We got no choice men!" he said with finality. "Think of yer women and yer kids. You can replace goods and stock but you can't replace them and they's sure to die if we try to fight it out!"

Rebecca was at my side. A mist of tears had formed in her brown eyes but she refused to let them fall. I was bewildered at this development. I held my hand up and Fancher recognized me.

"Captain Fancher," I began, "I believe it prudent to hold out a day or two longer. I do not trust these Mormons. You said yourself they encouraged the Indians. If we conserve ammunition, we may be able to frustrate the enemy and they will leave us alone. We've fought hard for three days and lost too many men to just take this Lee fellow at his word. I think we can hold them off."

Fancher looked me in the eye and I could tell he was carefully considering my words. Some of the men nodded their heads and others called out in agreement.

"Noah's right, Cap'n!" declared Ned. "Let's make a stand!"

Fancher finally took off his hat and wiped his brow with his forearm. His eye fell on four or five women and their small children who stood apart, the little ones clutching their mothers' legs, the women with stricken faces, wiping tears away. Fancher bit his lower lip. After a long silence, he stepped between two of the wagons. He waved at several mounted figures at the top of a ridge, then stood before us again.

"I just can't ask the women nor kids to suffer no more," he said quietly. "I gotta trust a man of God and hope to God I'm right." And with that, Fancher walked away.

Three wagons appeared. In the first, Lee and a number of his armed associates directed the men to place all weapons. There was some hesitation, then, one by one we piled carbines, shot guns, derringers, rifles and revolvers into the bed. When it was my turn, I dropped the borrowed musket and my pocket pistol on the stack of weapons.

As we were surrendering our arms, I noticed more men had appeared and were going through the surviving settlers, taking the smallest children by the hands and leading them to the second wagon in line. Fancher confronted Lee when he saw this but the Mormon leader smiled reassuringly.

"We don't want the small children walking a great distance. Nor the women or wounded," he added kindly as he pointed at the third wagon.

Lee called for the women, older children and wounded who couldn't walk to get into the last wagon in line. His men assisted them. Rebecca looked me in the eyes, quickly kissed me and joined the other women stepping up into the wagon. As they seated themselves, a column of fifty or so men appeared at the top of the ridge and marched to where we were assembling. Most were dressed in neat black suits. Many wore ties, clean white shirts and broad brimmed hats with rounded crowns. They varied in age from young to old men, some with whiskers or mustaches and others clean-shaven. All were armed with shotguns and a few had carbines. I glanced up to the nearest ridge and saw three other Mormons dressed in black mounted on horses, observing the proceedings from the high ground. I thought it odd that there was not an Indian in sight.

In the clear, crisp morning air the three wagons began to roll southwest along the rutted trail toward the far end of the valley. We men were ordered to form up single file and follow behind them. We did as we were told and then an armed Morman took a position alongside each one of us. Most of the wagon train's men, including me, were numb with shock at the events of the past hour. We stared dejectedly at the ground as we walked.

What happened next will surely sicken the reader. As we trudged along the trail, fifty emigrant men flanked by fifty Mormon men, I glanced at my guard. He was a young man with Nordic features. Beneath his hat I could see his hair was a startling white-blond.

Like most of the others he was neatly attired. He carried his weapon across his chest. Presumably he would protect me were the Indians to attack again. But he kept glancing up at the three mounted men on the nearby ridge, licking his lips, blinking the sweat from his icy blue eyes and wiping his lean face with his free hand.

As we came parallel to the mounted men on the ridge, I could clearly see the men on the left and right were in their forties and wore long beards. The man between them was older— much older. Gray hair hung from beneath his black hat and he had long gray whiskers.

The old man suddenly called out "halt!" and our column came to an abrupt stop as did the wagon filled with our women and wounded ahead of us. The lead wagon with the weapons aboard and the second in line containing the small children continued on.

The sun was warm on my back and a gentle breeze blew across the valley. I expected the old man to address us when, inexplicably, he called out in a deep voice that echoed off the ridge, "Men! Do your duty!"

With that command, each Mormon guard took a step back from his charge, leveled his weapon at the emigrant man alongside and fired. The blond man guarding me hesitated, his blue eyes wide with fear. The barrel of his carbine wavered. He licked his lips one last time then pulled the trigger. I was knocked off my feet by the force of the ball's impact and driven into a deep gully that ran alongside the trail.

I was unconscious for a few moments and then awoke on my back, laying in murky water streaked with my own blood. I heard more gunfire, men grunting, the hysterical shrieking of children, the terrified screams of women, small feet running past me on the trail above and big feet in pursuit, then more gunfire. I drifted into unconsciousness thinking I was dying. My last thought was of Rebecca. Why in God's name had I brought her here?

I awoke in the ditch shivering. My head was pounding and I could barely breathe as I stared straight up into the sky. It looked as though it might be sunset. It was silent save the whisper of the wind. I moved one leg and then the other. With great effort I managed to push myself into a sitting position, muck dripping from my sopping shoulders and back. There was a great deal of blood in the water around me and, other than a dull throbbing pain in my ribs, I had no idea how badly I might be wounded. I sat in this position as darkness fell and it grew ever colder. I drifted in and out of consciousness, my teeth chattering. I tried to stand once but couldn't find the strength. I slid back down the gully's bank and passed out.

Men's voices woke me. It was daylight, perhaps close to midday. I could not hear what the men said, but it sounded like four or five voices on the trail above me. I heard their footsteps move off toward where we'd left our wagons a quarter mile away.

It then occurred to me if I stayed in the gully I would be found or I would die of exposure. With great effort, sharp pain shooting through my torso, I got to my knees and then stood, my head just above the level of the trail.

I found I was staring directly into the dead face of Ned Kent, a bullet hole through his forehead, his mouth agape and full of blowflies. My knees weakened and I slipped back into the gully but managed to regain my footing. I looked in the direction of the wagons and could see four men, some distance away, dressed in black and carrying rifles, walking back toward the circled wagons.

I ducked my head and trudged through the gully, my ribs burning. After about thirty feet, I again raised my head and saw dozens of bodies, fully clothed, spread out along the trail. Flies were everywhere and buzzards had appeared to fight over the corpses, making no distinction of men, women or children. A little girl and boy lay beneath the body of a woman who had been shot, no doubt their mother. She had been unable to protect her children. Their throats had been cut open from ear to ear. At the sight of the butchered children, I fell to my knees sobbing.

I waited for dark, then, violently shivering, I painfully climbed out of the ditch. The stench of decomposition hung heavy in the still air. I could see more bodies along the trail and others splayed about the meadow, the forms of coyotes tugging at them. Dead children were everywhere, but I saw none under the age of seven or eight. It occurred to me the Mormons had kidnapped the smallest children in the first wagon. Suppressing the urge to vomit, I stumbled back toward the wagons bent double in pain.

As I approached, the silhouettes of five or six men were gathered around a fire that blazed at the center of the circled wagons. Six horses were picketed just outside the perimeter and one gave a start as I neared. I made my way around the wagons in the dark until I found the one that looked like mine. I pulled back a flap of the canvas cover and managed to climb up on one of the wheels and into the wagon bed.

In the pitch dark I recognized the feel of the feather mattress and comforter still neatly stacked where Rebecca had left them yesterday. Was it yesterday? I couldn't remember, my brain clouded in a dull fog of pain, rage and grief. I located my canteen, still full, and drank deeply. I ran my hand inside a chest and found a clean sheet. I pulled off my soaking, bloody shirt and wrapped the sheet as tightly as I could around my midsection. I managed to pull off my boots and trousers. I lay back naked on the rough wood of the wagon bed, pulled the comforter over myself and fell instantly to sleep.

8

"This here one's yours, Harold," a man's voice was saying. "Bishop Lee's taking the big one over yonder and I've got the one behind this'n."

Despite the pain, I bolted upright instantly awake and listened.

"What of the cattle and horses?" another voice asked.

"Most are being driven up to Salt Lake for Young and the other elders, I understand," came the reply.

"Well that's no surprise. 'Twas Young that ordered this," a third voice angrily declared.

Somebody spit. "It was a blood atonement, Noble," came a new voice. "These gentiles had to pay with their lives. That was explained to you, was it not? Their goods and stock are forfeit and belong to us now. It's the price they had to pay for their trespass."

"Yes, but…"

"Good," the new voice interrupted. "Now, let's get these wagons and the last of the stock out of here. It stinks."

The wagon where I lay secreted shook as oxen were placed in their traces. I lay under the comforter and prayed that whoever was preparing the wagon wouldn't look into the bed. A few more moments passed and then I felt someone take a seat on the bench. A whip cracked —my whip—and the wagon jolted forward. I could hear the clip-clop of a horse's hooves behind the wagon. There was considerable rumbling as the wagon made its way up the trail from whence I had come just days earlier. We were apparently headed back to Cedar City and if I was discovered, I would be killed.

The sheet tied around my chest was damp with fresh blood. I pulled it aside and saw the hole. It appeared the ball had struck me in a rib, probably broken it, somehow deflected off the bone, and exited through my right side. The skin over my ribs was bruised black and blue. Blood had coagulated around and in the holes. I dressed the wounds with some clean bandages Rebecca had kept in a box with her medicines.

I rose from beneath the comforter and, steadying myself against the swaying of the wagon, found clean clothing in another chest. I dressed, the din of the wagon rolling over the rutted trail covering any sounds I made. The driver's back was to me and he was whistling a jaunty tune. I crawled to the back and looked through the flaps. A gray saddle horse tied to the rear of the wagon was plodding along behind us. A half-mile back, I could see there were only a few wagons remaining in the valley. To the right of the wagons, scores of the dead emigrants lay among the flowers beneath a clear blue sky choked with circling black buzzards.

I turned my attention to the Mormon driving my wagon. His carbine was resting against his leg and I could see he wore a revolver in a holster at his hip. On the bench beside him were several more guns, no doubt taken from among those we'd naively entrusted to the Mormons. I glanced behind us again and saw we had a substantial head start on the other wagons. Bending painfully, I pushed some tools to one side and found what I was looking for. I stepped forward in the wagon. Ahead, over the driver's shoulder, I saw the trail leveled and widened, cedars and brush closed in thick on either side. We went slowly around a bend and out of sight.

My father had displayed grandfather Ebenezer's sword over our fireplace back home in Connecticut. The story went that he had killed a score of Redcoats with it. I drew the sword from its scabbard. The blade was dull, but I tested the point and knew it was sharp enough to serve my lethal purpose.

I took a deep breath as I chose my target on the man. Then, with as much force as I could manage, I rammed the blade completely through his neck just above the right shoulder. The Mormon went rigid before he violently twisted around, his eyes wide with shock and pain. I held the grip fast as his mouth opened and closed, reminding me of a hooked fish. Blood spouted from the wounds on either side of his neck.

Gritting my teeth, I wrenched the blade. He coughed up more gouts of blood and his eyes opened wide again then slowly rolled back into his head. His hat flew into the wagon as he made one last desperate grab for the blade. But I twisted the sword once more then pulled him back into the bed of the wagon by the hilt as his struggles slowed, and then ceased altogether. I withdrew the bloody blade and wiped it on the man's coat. The wagon never stopped, the oxen oblivious to the killing.

Panting and in great pain, I stepped over the body. The dead man's glassy eyes stared at me in horror. I calmed myself then sat on the bench. I steered the oxen on for another mile before finding a thickly wooded trail branching off to the left. Seeing I was not being followed, I turned the animals onto the narrow track and drove for a half hour more before bringing them to a halt.

It was about noon, judging by the sun. I pulled the dead man from the wagon, removed his holster and pocketbook, and then dragged the body some distance into the woods where I left it for scavengers. Returning to the wagon, I stripped to the waist and carefully cleaned the wound and replaced the bloody bandage. Then I sluiced water over the blood in the wagon and cleaned up the gore as best I could with the bloody sheet I had earlier removed from my wound. Finally, I checked all the weapons and saw they were loaded and ready.

The reader might understandably now think me a cold-blooded murderer, but certainly anyone would understand my state of mind. The Mormons had deceived us, lied before their God, treacherously murdered my friends with no quarter even for women or children, and then stolen our train's goods and stock. I felt nothing toward them except raw hatred and hoped only that the whistling man I'd slaughtered was roasting in hell. I decided that if I should ever encounter a Mormon I recognized from the meadow, I would kill him on the spot.

Well after dark I guided the wagon back down the trail and into the valley. All the wagons were gone. The pain in my side was searing. I stopped at the spot where we had originally circled the wagons, crawled into the wagon bed, my weapons arranged next to me and waited for daylight.

Rebecca is dead, shot in the chest. When I finally found her some distance away from the massacre—she had obviously run—she lay on her back in the grass looking as though she were asleep. Her once luminous face was gray and lifeless as I picked her up and carried her to the wagon. Weeping, I wrapped her small body in a soft blanket then dug a lonely grave in the field of purple and gold flowers.

Afterward, I took in the totality of the butchery. I wore a scarf around my face against the stench. Well past feeling any rage, I only felt sorrow as I surveyed the remains of the dead. More than one hundred and twenty men, women and children lay bloating beneath the warm sun. I recognized the corpses of Fancher, his son Charley, Mrs. Gowdy, Ned's wife and little daughter and many others. Most had been gunned down but others, particularly the children, lay with their little throats cut. Scavengers had desecrated all the bodies. Flies were everywhere and black buzzards circled or squabbled on the ground over the dead that crawled with maggots.

We had all been so optimistic back in Arkansas, dreaming only of the fortunes to be found in California while blithely dismissing the dire warnings of those who knew better.

Worried the Mormons or Indians might return, I was forced to leave all the dead unburied.

Agua Mansa Settlement
California
November 29, 1857

A week has passed since I arrived at this lonely hamlet. I sold the wagon, the oxen, and Rebecca's clothing and linens to a Mexican merchant. I kept the saddle horse and tack and, returning to the settlement's only accommodation, a squalid dun colored adobe inn, I sat in my room and wrote the letter to the Carters that I had been dreading.

Dearest Nathan & Susanna,

It is with a grieving heart I must report to you that your dear daughter Rebecca was killed on the trail. Indians attacked us in Utah Territory on the morning of September 13th but it was very apparent that they were acting as surrogates for Mormons who stood by and watched the repeated assaults, which lasted until the 16th. These were the same Mormons that you warned me of, Nathan. I only wish now I had listened to you, Sir...

I went on explain the difficult circumstances of the trek through Utah Territory and the hostility we had encountered at every turn. Then I wrote a very vague account of the battle and bloodshed in the meadow.

Captain Fancher made the mistake of believing the Mormon leader, Bishop John D. Lee, a supposedly honorable and Godly man. We turned our weapons over to Lee's trust until we escaped the Indian threat and then, as we marched along the trail toward what we believed was our salvation, the Mormons treacherously turned their guns on us...

I began to weep as I wrote.

...killing all of the men outright and then the women and even the older children, who they slaughtered without mercy. Rebecca was among those murdered. I shall never forgive myself.

I brushed the tears aside, opened a bottle of whiskey and drank from it. I finished my account by telling the Carters I had buried their only child in the lonely meadow where she had died.

In closing, I can only beg your forgiveness for bringing Rebecca west. I loved her with all my heart and wish I had been the one to die and not she.

I have sold our goods and am returning the proceeds along with $756 dollars that remains of the dowry you so generously provided on our wedding day. Captain Gifford, whom I met here, is traveling overland to St. Louis with a detachment of cavalry and has kindly agreed to carry this letter with him and deliver it safely to you, for which I am most grateful. He is also aware of the killings and has promised to bring them to the attention of the proper territorial authorities when he is in Washington next year. Perhaps the government will act and bring those guilty to justice.

If one day I should pass through St. Louis in my travels, I hope you will receive me. In the meantime, if you wish to write, please send your letter general delivery to the post office at Auroria in California. I am told Auroria is a burgeoning mining town where I may find employment.

I closed the letter, placed it with the funds in the envelope, sealed it and extinguished the lantern's light.

Part Two

Henry Plummer

Kevin Emmet Foley

9

Auroria, California
February, 1861

He lay on the filthy cot, blood oozing from the knife wound in his scalp, his head pounding in the aftermath of last night's binge at Irish Maggie's. What had happened? There was the question of the day. What *had* happened? How had he gone from being the toast of Auroria's Democratic Party, a newly minted marshal, and a successful businessman to an outlaw locked up in a seedy cell, all by the age of twenty-five?

Henry Plummer tried to rise, but the ache in his head and the piercing pain on it forced him back down onto the cot. He had gone to Maggie's for company, cards and a drink. Riley had been there, a loudmouth from Missouri who'd been trouble since he'd first shown up in Auroria the week before.

Plummer had mostly ignored Riley as he stood at the bar downing whiskey and bellowing challenges to anyone who would listen. But nobody heard him. A couple of the girls had tried to quiet him down at Maggie's urging, and he'd seemed to simmer for awhile until Plummer looked up from his cards at a disturbance in the parlor.

Riley had one of the girls by the wrist and was trying to drag her outside. Maggie intervened. She was an enormously fat, middle-aged woman with a headful of curls dyed a lurid red. Riley drunkenly shoved Maggie aside and made to exit with the girl in tow, telling her she was going back to his room at the Hotel de Paris.

Plummer rose and placed his cards face down on the table.

"Right back boys," he said to the three men.

"Let it go, Hank," one of the players who'd been losing said impatiently.

Plummer ignored him and stepped toward the parlor. Riley had one hand on the doorknob and was clutching the girl's arm with the other. She had dug her heels into the rug. The girl was young, with long brown hair and a painted face. She was gritting her teeth and cursing Riley.

"Let her go!" Plummer commanded. It was the lawman's voice he'd used a hundred times except now he didn't have the badge. But he did carry the LeMat .40 caliber revolver, a menacing engine that fired nine rounds from a magazine that revolved around a second barrel containing a charge of buckshot that could be discharged with a second trigger.

Riley turned from the door, eyed Plummer and sneered. "T'ain't none a your fuckin' business, fella!" Riley swayed, his eyes blurry. "Go sitcha se'f down an' stay outta it for'n you get hurt!"

Plummer had faced threatening drunks many times before and he could see Riley was close to collapsing. For a moment, he considered just returning to his card game. But the girl took advantage of Riley's divided attention, and suddenly bit him savagely on the hand that gripped her arm.

Riley swore as he yanked his hand back. He shook it, then viciously slapped the girl. She tumbled backward onto the floor. screeching. Her thin white legs flew in the air exposing her naked backside.

Plummer stepped forward between the prostrate whore and Riley, who snatched a hunting knife from his belt. He pointed the blade at the ex-lawman and grinned. Plummer calmly stood his ground.

"You don't want any of this," Plummer said, his voice and manner steady despite the whiskey. "It's late and you've had a lot to drink. Go sleep it off and come back tomorrow. I'm sure this young lady would welcome your company when you're feeling more yourself."

"Well listen you...you some kinda' a Yankee, ain't ya?!" Riley's grin turned cruel.

"Maine. Now why don't you go home?"

"First, le' me tell ya how we skinned Yankee nigger lovin' sons a bitches like you alive back in Mizura...better still, I believe I'll just show ya..."

With that the kid drunkenly lunged, faster than Plummer had expected. He deflected the blow, the blade flashing up through the crown of his black hat and slicing deeply into the skin of Plummer's hairline.

An explosion shook the room and a cloud of white acrid smoke enveloped the scene. Riley was lifted off his feet by the buckshot from Plummer's LeMat and driven back into the parlor's wall. He slumped to the floor, knife still in his hand, a wide streak of blood smearing the yellow paint. He groaned once, his startled blue eyes lolling back as blood burbled from his lips. Deathly silence hung in the air like the dissipating smoke until one of the card player's finally broke it.

"Damn it, Plummer!" he blurted. "You didn't have to kill 'im!"

Hot blood began dripping into Plummer's eyes. He holstered his weapon and pulled a handkerchief from his suit jacket pocket, staunching the flow as best he could. The cut was deep enough that Plummer could feel his skull bone.

"Yeah, he was drunk Plummer!" snarled another man. "Why'd you shoot 'im, fer Chrissake?"

The girl on the floor rose to her feet, her mouth bloody, and fled to the back of the house. The card players folded their hands, carefully recovered their money and made for the door, staring down at Riley's body as they silently slid past.

A group of miners at the bar soon followed. Plummer looked back at Riley. He was breathing shallowly but the blood continued to pulse from the deep wound in his chest, pooling around and between his legs. He could see then that Riley was no more than twenty and somewhat taller than Plummer's own five feet eight inches. The kid had a handsome face, chin whiskers and dark blond hair. He wore buckskin trousers and a fancy shirt under his long coat. His hat was cocked back on his head. As Plummer watched, Riley's eyes glazed over and his breathing stopped.

He felt faint and nauseous from the loss of blood and the effects of too much drink. He sat back in a chair and Maggie came over to him holding a towel.

He must have passed out because he woke to find himself lying on the bug-ridden cot in the jail he'd helped raise the money to build a couple of years earlier.

A deputy, whom Plummer recognized as Kennar, was seated at his desk reading a newspaper. He could hear the morning street bustle outside. Plummer felt his head and realized a bandage had been wrapped around it. The movement caught Kennar's eye. The deputy stood and walked to the cell.

"Mornin', Marshal," Kennar said in a friendly tone. Plummer was grateful that the lawmen in Auroria still called him by his former title and continued to show him respect whether they thought he deserved it or not. "Had the doc here earlier to take care o' that head a yourn."

Reed Kennar was an old man with a pinched face who'd failed as a placer miner. Plummer had hired him on as one of his deputies when he was marshal.

"Thanks, Reed."

"That Riley kid weren't no big loss. I had him in here fer fightin' an' shootin' inside the city limits." Kennar sat on a low stool next to the bars. "You feelin' alright, Hank?"

Plummer regarded Kennar's kindly concern and nodded.

"Anyways, Sheriff Crosby is out talkin' to witnesses an' so forth. Sounds like a case a self defense you ask me."

Plummer cleared his throat. "For anybody else, Reed. But not for me, I'm afraid."

"Aw Marshal, now come on. Them past troubles ain't got nothin' ta do with what happened over Maggie's last night. Kid stabbed you and you had t' shoot 'im...what was you gonna do?"

Good question, Plummer thought. He supposed the same could easily be asked about the death of John Vedder. There was presently a knock at the jail door. Kennar rose and walked to one of the barred windows that looked out on the street. He waved at the visitor and then opened the door. Plummer turned his head on the pillow and saw Noah Coffey enter. The newspaperman exchanged a few quiet words with the deputy. Kennar took his seat at the desk and resumed his reading. Coffey walked toward Plummer's cell.

"Henry," he began with a frown. "What the devil happened last night?"

A few years older than the marshal, Coffey had a quiet, reserved manner that reminded Plummer of the people back home in Maine. Like Henry, Coffey was well-educated and articulate, attributes that stood out for better or worse in a tough mining town like Auroria. He was a little taller than Plummer, thin but sturdy looking, with a lean, clean-shaven face framed by long side whiskers and brown hair worn a little longer than was fashionable.

"Some kid named Riley at Maggie's last night," replied Plummer in his truncated speaking manner. "Came at me with a knife, so I shot him."

Coffey looked down at the floor and shook his head. He removed his bowler hat and ran his hand through his hair. Soon after Coffey had arrived to work at the *Democrat*, he and Plummer had become acquainted, although the marshal had been out on bond at the time. They instantly liked each other and it wasn't long before they sought out each other's company for an occasional game of billiards or a glass of whiskey.

"This isn't good, Henry," Coffey finally said under his breath. "The Republicans running things don't want gunplay or violence of any kind. They want Auroria to be 'respectable.'"

"Then they should shut down all of Front Street's bawdy houses," Plummer said with a wry smile. "Oh, I forgot. Most of those esteemed Republicans you mention have interests in whores, gambling, and liquor."

"It's not a laughing matter, Henry," Coffey declared, anger edging his voice. "After the Vedder business and before that the mess with Wright and Johnson—they're going to want to hang you this time. You should not have come back here after you were released."

Plummer stared at his friend for a long moment.

"You're right, of course, Noah," he finally acknowledged. "A Democrat in a Republican jail cannot bode well for yours truly."

Despite himself, Coffey laughed. *No doubt about it*, he thought to himself. *Henry Plummer is the coolest, most unflappable man I know*. He recalled the story of how Plummer had arrived in Auroria in 1853 at the age of only seventeen. Like many before him, he had sought his fortune in the gold fields, journeying the three thousand miles from his family's New England home, across the Panama isthmus by mule train, then on to San Francisco by ship before he finally reached the foothills of the Sierras.

But unlike many others who scratched out meager livings panning for gold, Plummer had proven himself to be a clever businessman. He recognized there was more money to be made supplying miners than there was in actually mining a claim. Along with a partner, Plummer had started the town's first bakery before selling his interest in the successful enterprise back to his partner. Then he'd bought and consolidated a string of placer claims. The original claimholders had panned or plucked what gold they could find from their individual one hundred-foot-long sections of stream before moving on. They ignored the quartz deposits, but Plummer found a cheap and effective means of extracting gold from quartz using stamp mills and made even more money.

As his wealth and prominence grew, local Democrats took notice of the young New Englander who was wise beyond his years and placed his name on their 1856 ticket as a candidate for marshal. He narrowly won but soon became known as an honest and effective lawman, tracking and arresting criminals, collecting city taxes, and enforcing the city's fire prevention ordinances.

Coffey gazed at his friend with an expression of both admiration and pity. The ex-marshal lay quietly, bandaged head back on the dirty pillow, eyes closed, his hands folded serenely across his chest.

Reputations may be quickly won and quickly lost, Coffey reminded himself. *And a man's reputation is all he has here.*

10

The first blow to Plummer's reputation came with the tragic and unnecessary deaths of Sheriff Wright and his deputy, Davey Johnson. A young desperado named Webster had been terrorizing the county, robbing and killing miners and ranchers at will. Marshal Plummer, on his own initiative, had gone after Webster, tracked him for more than a week, and, remarkably, had brought him in single-handedly.

In Sheriff Wright's custody, Webster broke out of the town's temporary jail and fled. The embarrassed sheriff asked Plummer to help him recapture Webster, and the marshal agreed, but only if the pursuit was limited to three men. A half dozen local citizens led by Plummer's political opponent, Wallace Williams, demanded they be allowed to join the trackers. Wright and Plummer refused. Then Plummer, the sheriff and Wright's best deputy, Ted Garvey, rode out after Webster on a cloudy and moonless November night.

After several hours of hunting through the rolling hills, they discovered two saddled horses tied up in a wooded ravine. Plummer and Wright agreed an accomplice had left them there for Webster. The lawmen secured their horses some distance away and then crept back to wait in ambush among the tall pines and brush for Webster to retrieve his horses.

Despite the warnings about the dangers of a night chase, Wallace Williams had enlisted a posse and an off-duty deputy, Davey Johnson, and followed Plummer. They also stumbled onto the two horses. Hearing their arrival and believing Webster and his accomplices had arrived, Plummer, Wright and Garvey opened fire in the dark.

Shotgun blasts shattered the night as Wallace's men fired back. Plummer, by far the best with a gun, could see nothing so he fired his LeMat at muzzle flashes. Buckshot struck the tree trunk behind which he hid, spraying bark and branches over the prone marshal. He heard a familiar voice as the firing subsided for a moment. It was Wallace Williams commanding one of his men to take cover.

"Stop firing!" Plummer had cried out. "You're shooting at friends!"

"Who's there?!" came the reply.

"Wright, Plummer and Garvey!" yelled the marshal. "Who goes there?"

"Williams and Davey Johnson."

"God *damn* you stupid people!" Plummer raged. "We told you not to follow and this is why!" He stalked out from behind the tree and walked toward the voices. Somebody lit a torch. In the flickering light, Williams stood with the others. Deputy Garvey soon emerged.

"Where's Jim?" Plummer asked Garvey as he looked around at the other men. "And where the hell is Johnson?"

Williams glanced about, eyes wide with confusion. "We thought…"

"You *didn't* think!" Plummer responded, his voice oozing contempt. He felt like striking the fool.

"Over here, Marshal," another voice called from the darkness. "It's Sheriff Wright."

In the torchlight he could see a large caliber round, probably from Plummer's weapon, had hit Wright in head, blood and brain matter splattered across the ground. The sheriff's remaining eye stared into space, seemingly wide in astonishment at being killed.

"Shit!" Plummer bitterly exclaimed. He heard a groan in the darkness. They soon found Davey Johnson, sprawled face down on the ground. Plummer could see where the buckshot pellets had cut into the man's right shoulder and back. They turned the deputy over and saw bloody foam on Johnson's lips.

"He's hit in the lungs," Plummer said. "He's alive, but barely. We need to get him back to town right now."

Johnson had died the next morning and Webster was never recaptured, Coffey now recalled. During his testimony at the coroner's inquest that followed, Williams blamed Plummer for the gunfight and intimated that it was the marshal's weapon that killed Wright. He even accused Plummer of cowardice.

"*I suppose Plummer took to his heels after he fired*," Plummer had angrily read in the transcript published in the *Journal*, Auroria's Republican newspaper. In the unwritten rules of the mining towns, this was an insult that could not go unanswered. Thankfully, instead of a duel, Plummer chose to settle the matter with an open letter published in Coffey's newspaper, the *Democrat*:

> *Unlike Mr. Williams, my reputation for courage is dependent neither upon my own testimony nor upon the trumpetings of the press. I shall leave this subject, hoping that Mr. Williams may enjoy the reputation for which he longs, and I, such as I may deserve.*

> *H. Plummer, Marshal.*

Coffey had heard that Williams withdrew his accusation and Plummer was later cleared of any responsibility in the deaths of Wright and Johnson, but his sterling reputation as a lawman had been tarnished, nonetheless. Now, Plummer lay here, for the second time in danger of hanging.

The ex-marshal stirred and Coffey realized his friend had fallen asleep. Good. He needed his rest. He is a good looking man, Coffey thought to himself as he regarded Henry's peaceful face. He was of average height and wiry but he could certainly hold his own, be it pistols or fists. He also had a romantic streak, Coffey thought sadly, which had led him to the Vedders.

It had happened some months before Coffey had arrived in Auroria, but the tragedy was well known throughout northern California. John Vedder and his wife Lucy had arrived in town with their baby daughter one fine summer's day.

Plummer had made their acquaintance and rented them a cabin he owned.

A big man with a foul temper, John Vedder worked as a monte dealer at Carson's gambling house and it wasn't long before Plummer heard he was beating Lucy. In his role as a lawman, the marshal became immersed in the Vedders' domestic problems and, along the way, the story went, he'd fallen hard for Lucy, a beautiful blond woman with a fishwife's tongue.

Coffey was never able to get Plummer to discuss what had happened, but from the newspaper accounts he read and from everything his editor had told him, it was understood that Plummer had bedded John Vedder's wife.

One night, neighbors summoned Plummer to the Vedder cabin, where Lucy lay bleeding from her ears. Plummer took the woman and her child to the Hotel de Paris where he called for the doctor. Word of the marshal's intervention reached John Vedder at a saloon and he made his way to the hotel. When Vedder confronted Plummer, Coffey thought as he read the accounts of the incident, he must have been aware of the marshal's considerable skills with a handgun, but his rage and anguish probably overwhelmed his fear.

"You bastard!" Vedder screamed drunkenly, pacing about in the mud of Commerce Street in a misting rain, "Hidin' behind that badge. You ain't gettin' Lucy, Plummer, nor my baby!"

Plummer stood on the boardwalk beneath an awning that sheltered him from the rain. They were alone and Plummer could see the butt of a pocket pistol sticking out of the waistband of Vedder's trousers. Plummer silently eyed the tall man in the street and saw that he was swaying slightly, blinking drops of mist from his eyes.

"I've been looking for you, John," replied Plummer calmly. "I'm charging you with the assault and battery of Lucy Vedder. Now let's go."

Vedder's eyes grew wide at Plummer's audacity. "I been lookin' for you, too, Hank Plummer, you son of a bitch!" Vedder cried out in an anguished voice. "I'm gonna settle this score right now!"

"Don't, John." Plummer could see that it wasn't the mist but tears that Vedder was wiping away.

"Lucy's my woman!" he howled forlornly. With that he made a clumsy move for the pistol but the hammer caught on his belt loop.

For just an instant Plummer hesitated. Then he drew the LeMat and fired, the ball striking Vedder in the heart and sending him staggering backward. He dropped to his knees in the cold mud and manure, still tugging at the small gun in his waistband before he fell forward into the thick brown slurry, blood pouring from the exit wound in his back.

Plummer stood with the smoking revolver in his hand for what seemed a long time.

"John!" Lucy screamed as she bolted from the hotel door. She dashed past the marshal to her dead husband. Crying incoherently, she fell on him, trying to turn his big body over, blood staining her white dress, her hair hanging limply in the drizzle.

Miners, attracted by the shot, stood around, gawking and pointing at the scene. Deputy Garvey appeared next to Plummer. He glanced first at John Vedder's bloody body then at the marshal.

"Oh, no," Garvey muttered, realizing what had happened.

"Damn," Plummer muttered to himself as he slid the LeMat into his holster.

The marshal and the deputy walked silently to the jail. When he arrived Plummer removed his gunbelt and handed it to Garvey. "My place is here for now, Ted," he said to the astonished deputy. "Please try to ask Belden if he'll defend me."

Witnesses told the court that Vedder had been drunk and unable to defend himself when Plummer had shot him down. The prosecution, without expressly saying it, strongly suggested that his affair with Lucy had been the marshal's motivation for killing John Vedder.

Noah Coffey had begun work as a correspondent at the *Democrat* about the time the trial started and was in the court the day of the jury's verdict.

"Marshal Henry Plummer, you are accused of murder in the second degree," intoned Judge Harris. "The duly appointed jury of your peers has heard the evidence against you. What is your verdict, Mr. Foreman?"

The jury foreman stood. "Guilty as charged your honor," he replied and then took his seat, glancing Plummer's way as he did.

11

On the grounds that he had not received a fair trial in Auroria due to the heated political climate, the California Supreme Court in Sacramento granted Plummer a new trial. It was between the hearings that Coffey first met Plummer to interview him while he was out on bond and continuing to serve as marshal.

The second trial was moved to Marysville, but the change of venue didn't matter, Coffey recalled. His friend was convicted a second time and sentenced to ten years at the state prison at San Quentin. Plummer resigned as marshal. He never saw Lucy again.

Coffey rose and left the jail, Plummer still fast asleep. The day was sunny but cold. The jagged Sierras shimmered in the near distance as he made his way to the offices of the *Democrat*. The streets bustled with miners, mule trains, wagons, and horsemen. The Greek Revival false fronts of the buildings gave the town a façade of permanence, but Coffey knew such places were quickly abandoned once the gold ran out and the miners stampeded to the next strike.

"What news?" called out Page, the *Democrat*'s editor, when he saw Coffey enter the office. He was a rotund man with bushy muttonchops and tiny eyeglasses. He wore a green eyeshade and he had copy scattered on his desk before him.

"Henry Plummer killed a fellow named Riley last night at Maggie's," Coffey replied. "I understand Riley attacked him with a knife and Plummer had no alternative."

"Yes, Plummer never seems to have any alternative other than to kill a man," Page declared scornfully. "He settles matters with his deadly *pistola* then seems surprised he's charged with a crime!"

"He is most certainly not surprised this time, Mr. Page," Coffey replied. "He's laid up in the jail with a bloody bandage on his head. I think he understands there will be consequences."

"I'll warrant you're right on that score, my young friend! Plummer may well find himself on the wrong end of a rope. Go on then and write up your account for the afternoon edition. There's a good lad."

Coffey produced his account, laid it on Page's desk, left the office and walked back to the jail.

Sheriff Lee Crosby sat at his desk. An affable man in his mid-fifties, Crosby had replaced the deceased Jim Wright. He wore a sweat stained white hat and a leather vest. His mouth was completely covered by thick black mustaches streaked gray. Crosby didn't usually carry a weapon, his role more that of an administrator than a law enforcer, which he left to the deputies and night watchmen on his staff.

The usually cheerful sheriff was today quiet and somber. He looked up as Coffey entered, nodded, then glanced into the cell behind him, where Plummer still lay with his eyes closed. Crosby was a close friend of Plummer's, Coffey knew, and like many others, he owed his job to Henry.

"It's not looking good for our friend there, Mr. Coffey," Crosby said quietly. "Everyone who was at Maggie's last night says the shooting was unjustified." He paused, looking up at Coffey, his eyes sad. "I...I don't know what to do now."

"Do your duty, Sheriff!" Plummer suddenly called out from the cell.

Startled, Crosby almost jumped from his seat. "Hank, you're awake...I'm sorry..."

"For what?" Plummer asked, grimacing as he sat up. "For doing the job you're paid to do? Listen, Lee, you're a good man and a good sheriff. I'm here because I have to be. Now go gather the evidence and follow the procedures I taught you."

Dumbfounded, Crosby's mouth hung open.

"You need to talk to the judge," Plummer continued. "He'll want to convene a grand jury. Then, please see if lawyer Belden can meet with me later today or tomorrow so he can prepare my defense."

Crosby stared for a time at Plummer. Finally he nodded and silently left the office.

Coffey, who'd been taking in the exchange, slowly shook his head after Crosby shut the door, a wry look on his face. "Always the honest lawman," he said finally. "You're a rare commodity out here in California, Henry."

"It's the way I was raised, I suppose," Plummer replied with a sad smile. "My people were Puritans, you see. We have a strong sense of righteousness."

"Or self-righteousness, in your case," Coffey responded wryly. "That could get you killed."

"Maybe." Plummer rubbed his head. "Is this thing bloody?" he asked, tugging at the bandage.

"Yes, I'll get the doctor over here to change it."

"I can't stand filth," Plummer observed as he stood up. "Look at that cot. Look at my clothes. Would you kindly arrange a hot bath here for me and a clean change of clothing along with that fresh dressing, Noah?"

"Of course," the newspaperman replied with an exaggerated bow. "Will there be anything else, Your Highness?"

Despite the circumstances, Plummer burst out laughing, his fine white teeth and slate blue eyes flashing. He nodded at Coffey good-naturedly.

"Thank you Noah," Plummer finally said with a smile. "You are a good friend. If I get out of this fix, perhaps you'd join me on a trip back to the States. I want to go home. I've had enough of California and if war does break out, I want to be there for the fight. Even if it doesn't, I've made enough money here that I fancy I can make a fresh start back home in New England."

"I wish you'd done that after your release," Coffey observed.

"Maybe so," Plummer replied. "But think about joining me. I'd welcome your company."

As it happened, Coffey had also had his fill of California. It was far from the romantic place he'd read about back in New York and the work at the *Democrat* was unfulfilling. He had lately thought he might wish to pursue a career as an author, his initial effort being a first person account of the Mormon massacre of the Fancher party.

Even though that event was several years behind him, he often had nightmares about it. In them, Rebecca ran screaming from black vultures that tore at her flesh as a blond man looked on laughing. Sometimes in his dreams, he saw the dead and desiccated bodies of little children sprawled out in a field of purple and gold flowers, black coyotes gnawing their little arms and legs.

After he arranged with the barber for Henry's bath and a change of clothes and sent for the doctor to re-dress Plummer's wound, Coffey spoke to Judge Harris at his law office. There was no doubt that Plummer would be charged with murder, according to Harris, who had already scheduled a grand jury to meet with the witnesses in a week's time. He had also appointed a prosecutor with an eye toward a speedy trial.

"This is too much like the Vedder killing," Harris declared when Coffey had appealed to him not to press charges. "I never agreed with Plummer's politics, but I always liked the fellow personally. Unfortunately, he must answer for this killing. I'm sorry."

As Coffey ate his supper at his boarding house that evening, he read the story he'd written earlier in the day.

Henry Plummer Jailed in Death of Missouri Man

A difficulty occurred at a house of ill fame on Commercial Street between Henry Plummer and William Riley, aged 21 and lately of Huntsville, Missouri, resulting in the death of the latter. It appears that both were drinking pretty freely and got quarreling in the parlor when Riley struck Plummer on the head with a knife inflicting a deep wound in his scalp. Plummer at the same time drew his revolver and fired at Riley. The charge took effect in his chest and he must have died instantly.

Coffey knew if it got to a jury, there would be no mercy for Henry

Plummer. After the Vedder conviction, Plummer had been sent to prison at a gloomy, wind-swept fortress called San Quentin across the bay from San Francisco. Coffey had ridden along with the federal marshal's wagon in which Plummer and other convicted criminals rode shackled to the floorboards.

When they arrived at San Quentin, Coffey was not allowed inside the prison but could see it was little more than a dank, filthy dungeon jammed with convicts seemingly of every nation and color. They stood glaring out of the barred windows at Coffey, some yelling obscenities.

When he had next seen Plummer several months later in the prison's day room, his friend's face was ashen and drawn. He wore a uniform of rough gray wool. Plummer had a welt across his forehead where he said a guard had struck him with a club. On his feet were his own boots because the prison did not issue shoes.

"I'm told I could be paroled after several years here," Plummer glumly told Coffey in between racking coughs. "I hope that's the case because I don't believe I will last the full term, Noah."

The ex-marshal's words proved prophetic for it wasn't long after he had returned to Auroria that Coffey received a letter from his friend saying he had been moved to the hospital ward. The prison's doctor had diagnosed consumption.

The next evening, Coffey went to the Democratic Club's regular weekly meeting.

The room was uncomfortably warm and filled with twenty or so well attired men, clearly successful at whatever enterprises they pursued, quietly talking and smoking cigars around a large circular table.

"Ah, a member of the press joins us this evening," smiled Jared Stanfield, owner of a saloon at the other end of town. "Welcome Mr. Coffey. We appreciate your newspaper's support of our Mr. Douglas."

"Well, he appears to be the only man who can defeat Lincoln," Coffey replied.

"Agreed, Sir. If the baboon gains the White House, there will be war, that is for certain." Stansfield paused, eyeing Coffey. "But presidential politics is not why you've come here tonight, is it?"

"No it is not," Coffey said flatly. "I'm here about Henry Plummer."

The name caused a number in the room to glance nervously at one another, for Plummer had been president of the club just two years earlier. They had even run him as their candidate for the state legislature in 1858. Now he was in prison, convicted of killing John Vedder over a rumored affair with the victim's wife.

"What about Plummer?" Stansfield asked, concern in his tone.

"He's deathly ill. Consumption. The prison doctor doesn't believe he will survive the year."

Stansfield rubbed his chin and turned to the man seated next to him and mumbled something under his breath. The man nodded and Stansfield looked back at Coffey as though assessing him.

"Mr. Coffey, some here feel Marshal Plummer got what he deserved," he began. Several heads around the room nodded. "But others of us, me included, are not so sure. There were mitigating circumstances. Vedder was a lout and a coward who frequently abused his wife and threw her into the street. Plummer stepped in to protect Mrs. Vedder and her child as he was sworn to do. If he became...um...smitten with her, who can say? Mrs. Vedder herself testified in open court there was nothing between her and Plummer."

"Not to mention Vedder was armed and tryin' to draw down on the marshal," a voice said from the other side of the room.

"Aw, shut up, Bob!" replied someone else. "Vedder never had a chance against Plummer. He didn't even cock his piece!"

"Gentlemen!" Stansfield interrupted as he rose to his feet. "Marshal Plummer was a good and honest lawman. We can all agree on that point, can we not? He made a mistake killing Vedder, to be sure. But I personally don't believe he should rot in prison either, especially since we have a Democrat now serving as our governor."

Stansfield proposed a vote and Coffey was relieved when a majority of men raised their hands in favor of a petition to release Henry Plummer. Coffey drafted one there and then and those who had agreed signed it, including Stansfield and several other of the town's leading Democrats. He had the Sacramento stagecoach driver deliver it to Governor Weller's office. Three weeks later, Plummer was paroled after serving just six months.

12

Coffey finished his supper and left the boarding house. He walked along the main street of Auroria in the cold evening air and wondered again why Henry had bothered to return after his release from San Quentin. He arrived at the jail and walked in to find Plummer, Crosby and Kennar playing poker at the deputy's desk using matchsticks for chips, a fire crackling cheerfully in the potbellied stove.

"You've got a dangerous felon there, Sheriff," Coffey declared with a grin as he entered. "Why isn't he in his cell?"

Plummer looked up from his hand and smiled. He wore a clean black suit, was freshly shaved, and had a clean bandage wrapped around his head.

"Marshal ain't gonna break jail," Kennar said, not looking up from his cards. "I owes 'im too much money!"

"Who doesn't owe him money?" replied Coffey. He looked back at Plummer, whose smile began to melt away as he saw the expression on Coffey's face.

"What did he say?" asked Crosby, looking for the first time at the newspaperman.

"Judge Harris is pressing murder charges," Coffey replied.

Crosby and Kennar looked at each other and then at Plummer, who was nodding thoughtfully.

"I expected as much," Plummer finally said. "He has no choice, you know, with the Republicans running the show."

"It was self defense, Marshal!" Crosby exclaimed. "What in the hell is Harris thinkin'?"

"He's thinking I need to hang," Plummer said quietly. "I was lucky once, but not a second time, Gentlemen. No, I'm an example, now, of what happens to the disorderly element in Auroria." He flipped a card over. "Damn."

Coffey watched the torrential rain fall through his window as he finished his breakfast. On his way to the *Democrat* wrapped in his oilskin slicker, he saw a commotion in front of the jail. A group of armed men stood around Sheriff Crosby. He recognized one of them as the newly elected Republican mayor and two others as town councilmen, also Republicans.

"You go find that bastard!" Mayor Wiley was bellowing at Crosby as Coffey approached. "You get him back here or I'll take matters into my own hands!"

"Mayor, we tracked Plummer as far as we could this mornin', but the rain's covered up everything. He's away and I got no way of findin' him until this storm clears," Crosby said wiping his hand across his wet face.

"You son of a bitch, Crosby!" screamed one of the councilmen through the windblown rain. "You let him go, didn't you?"

Crosby glared at the man, his face red. "Why don't you go to hell, Bates!" And with that the sheriff turned and walked into the jail, slamming the door behind him. The mayor and councilmen stood for a moment, the rain sluicing off their shoulders and hats, before angrily stomping off toward city hall.

Coffey followed Crosby into the jail. The old sheriff was pouring coffee into a chipped mug. He could see the sheriff was smiling beneath his bushy mustache.

"Sheriff Crosby?"

"Well, what the hell'd ya' expect, Noah?" the sheriff replied as he spun around to face the newspaperman, his tone defensive. "I was gonna let Hank swing for killin' that trash Riley? No, Sir. We weren't gonna let that happen, no how."

Coffey stared at the man. "How did he get away?"

"Why, he escaped, Mr. Coffey!" the sheriff replied in a tone that affected shock at the question. "Not the first jail break we've had here, y' know!"

The rain ended two days later and Crosby launched a manhunt that, of course, yielded no trace of Henry Plummer. A letter arrived for Coffey at the *Democrat* several weeks after the ex-marshal disappeared:

My friend,

I am quite sure your readers were treated to a thrilling account of the former marshal's desperate escape from the Auroria jail. You have a way with words, Noah, so I know you made the "jail break" sound far more exciting than it actually was.

In fact, my former associates convinced me Judge Harris and his prosecutor were going to "stack the deck" against me. To my surprise, my cell door was "accidentally" left unlocked. Even more mysterious was my saddled horse tied in front of the jail together with my weapons, my money, and some supplies.

I am riding north to Walla Walla. I will contact you from time to time because it is my sincere hope you will accompany me back east once I have made my plans. I've had enough.

Your friend & servant,
H.P.

13

Fort Benton
Dakota Territory
May, 1862

After more than a month on the river aboard the side-wheeler steamship *Emilie,* James Vail had hoped to see something more formidable than the cluster of grimy hovels surrounded by smoky Indian encampments. As he disembarked, he saw a group of soldiers lolling around crates and bundles of freight as they were unloaded, laughing at a small clerk who consulted his consignment sheet one moment and chased Indian and white children away the next.

Passengers, mostly miners and merchants, followed the schoolteacher and his family down the gangway onto a rickety dock. Behind him walked his wife, Martha, their two small children followed by his sister-in-law, Electa Bryan. The soldiers eyed the beautiful young Electa as she lifted her skirts, making her way gingerly down the greasy plank to the dock.

James Vail stood in the center of the dusty fort and considered his options. Presently he was joined by Francis Thompson, a pleasant young man whom Vail had befriended on the seemingly endless voyage from St. Louis. Thompson had left his comfortable home in Boston and his studies at Harvard to work with a team of geologists conducting an exploration for a mining company.

"What are you thinking, Jim?" Thompson asked.

Vail shook his head. "Well, Francis, there is the hotel, but it doesn't look like a fit place for the ladies or children."

Thompson followed Vail's gaze and saw a ramshackle wooden building with the absurd name of Hotel New Orleans painted on its façade. A clutch of Indians sat cross-legged in front of the hotel waiting for handouts as loud, off-key piano music issued from the open door. An old man in dirty buckskins staggered through the entrance and kicked an Indian.

"You're right." Thompson agreed. "Perhaps we should camp nearby?"

Vail nodded but began to doubt the wisdom of his enterprise as he looked about him. He and Martha were devout Methodists who had made the journey west after accepting a position as managers of the Sun River Farm, an experimental ranch some forty miles from Fort Benton beyond the Great Falls of the Missouri. His mission was to help civilize the Blackfeet Indians and teach them farming. These idealistic goals overlooked the Indians' natural predilection to roam the plains following the buffalo herds as well as their aversion to being cast as lowly "diggers," labor Indian men felt was only fit for their women.

Vail was unaware of any of this. Driven by his desire to bring Christianity and education to the savages, he'd embarked on the adventure and had luckily made the association of Thompson en route. Now, the plan was to travel south toward the distant mountain ranges with the gold explorers, who would accompany Vail and his family as far as the Sun River Farm.

"Yes, that's a good idea," Vail finally replied. "My word, this place stinks!" As if to second this observation, a sow squealed from a nearby mud hole. Wolf-dogs roamed freely, some snarling and snapping at one another over the guts that hung from the carcasses of several butchered antelope. Flies covered the dead animals.

A government wagon and mule were waiting for Vail at the fort. He paid a Negro crewman from the *Emilie* to help him load it with the supplies and few furnishings they had brought from Ohio. He and Thompson helped the women and children on board and he noticed a look pass between the young man and Electa as Francis assisted her onto the bench seat. The five other members of his exploration team soon joined Thompson and, with their mining equipment loaded on several horses, they began the trip southwest toward the Sun River.

That evening they made camp alongside a creek. Wolves and coyotes howled throughout the night. Vail, as he lay awake on the ground gazing at the multitude of glittering stars, was suddenly struck by a sensation of being cast adrift in the vast emptiness of the western plains. A cool breeze made him shiver as he slipped off into a dreamless sleep.

The trail paralleled the Missouri River. At the Great Falls, the travelers paused to marvel at the cataracts that had caused the Corps of Discovery so much difficulty years earlier. A trapper they encountered led them to the point where the Sun River entered the Missouri and two hours later the government farm came into view.

In the clear afternoon air, the snowcapped mountain peaks glimmered in the distance. The mining explorers talked excitedly among themselves about the riches that lay ahead as the party crossed the swiftly flowing river at a shallow ford and rode through the farm's main gate. A palisade of logs arranged around the main house protected it from attack. A barn and some sheds of rough-hewn logs stood outside the improvised fortress. Vail was pleased to see corn had been planted in a nearby field.

As they rolled to a stop, a young Indian appeared from the barn and approached the wagon. Vail made his age at about eighteen and he wore trousers but was naked from the waist up, his skin the color of a chestnut. His raven hair was pulled back into two braids and he was festooned with bone jewelry and beads.

"I am Iron," he announced to the Vails with a stern expression. "I hunt for you. I talk for you."

Vail smiled and nodded at the Indian but was inwardly embarrassed by the young Indian's immodesty in front of the ladies. He would see to it the boy wore a shirt from now on.

"Hello!" a voice called from behind. Vail turned and saw a lad walking toward the wagon from an outbuilding, wiping his hands on a rag. He appeared to be about sixteen or seventeen.

"Hello," Vail answered with a grin, pleased that there was a white person, albeit a young one, associated with the farm. "We're the Vails. These gentlemen were kind enough to accompany us here."

"I'm Joe Swift," the boy replied. He was of average height with brown hair, ruddy cheeks and a bright smile. "I was starting to worry that you maybe ran into trouble."

"No trouble," replied Vail. "Just the usual delays on the river with sandbars."

"Where do you hail from, Joe?" asked Martha.

"Philadelphia, Ma'am," the boy said. "I left home some years back and hired on here as a hand. Welcome to Sun River Farm."

The Vails thanked Swift, bade farewell to the miners and began unloading their supplies. As he carried a chair into the house, Vail noticed Electa and Francis Thompson speaking near the farm's gate. Thompson nodded, took Electa's hand and, to Vail's surprise, bowed to her. He then joined his companions who were already hurrying toward the looming mountains.

Within a month, James Vail realized he was on a fool's errand. The only Indians he was able to coax into the farm were elderly men and women, whose families were only too glad to be rid of their sickly old people. The ancient men sat under a cottonwood tree, silently refusing any advances by Vail to learn cultivation or the Bible while the old women shuffled around campfires roasting meat that Iron brought in from the prairie.

"The Blackfeet don't understand farming, Mr. Vail," Swift explained one hot afternoon after the missionary had walked away from the circle of old men with a look of frustration. "They're hunters, like Iron."

The young Indian, who had said no more than ten words to Vail since he'd arrived, nodded his head in solemn agreement. "They follow the buffalo herds in the summer and hole up in their tipis in the winter," Swift continued. "It's how they have lived for years and years, Sir."

Vail was nevertheless furious with himself for having agreed to bring his family the two thousand miles from their quiet, civilized Ohio home to this wilderness. His wife and sister-in-law were stoic, but he knew they both saw the folly as clearly as he did.

One morning, toward the end of the hot, dry summer, as he tried to resuscitate the shriveled corn crop—any fool could see corn wouldn't grow in this dry climate—Iron galloped bareback on a black gelding into the farmyard. He saw Vail in the cornfield and rode to him, oblivious to the stalks he trampled.

Annoyed, Vail began to berate the Indian. "Dammit, Iron!"

"War party," the Indian declared.

Vail's breath caught in his throat. "Where?" he asked as Swift ran over to join them.

"Half day ride. West." Iron gestured in the direction from which he'd ridden. "Many warriors."

Vail was stunned. The Blackfeet he'd seen since he'd arrived were mostly peaceful but he had heard back in Ohio that, from time to time, they were liable to go on the warpath.

Joe stepped forward. "Don't mean they're comin' here, Mr. Vail," Joe stammered. "They... they could be after other injuns."

Vail wasn't going to wait to find out what the Indians had in mind. He glanced about nervously. The palisade guarding the home never looked more flimsy. "I'm going to ride to Benton to get help," Vail finally said. "I need you and Iron to stay here, Joe, and protect the women and children."

The boy started to protest but Vail cut him off. "Listen. We need help. We can't defend ourselves against an attack if one comes and I can't take the risk of riding with Martha, Electa or the children to Fort Benton. What if they fell on us while we were on the trail?"

"Yes, Sir, I agree..." Joe hesitated, "but..."

"I can get to Fort Benton in a day if I ride hard. There are soldiers there who are bound to come."

He left as the sun set and rode at a trot across the moonlit plain all night, stopping periodically to water his mount and get his bearings. The sun rose and the day became hot. He dozed in the saddle and was suddenly awakened by a nearby shriek.

He looked to his left and felt his insides knot as a dozen Indians, just a hundred yards away, rode in a single file parallel to his route. He fought the urge to spur the horse into a gallop and, instead, let the horse continue to walk. He held up his right hand, palm forward.

The Indians glared back at him, ignoring the sign. Vail gestured with his hand and pointed in the direction of Benton. Again, the war party disregarded the sign language Joe Swift had taught him. All the braves wore buckskin leggings and were bare-chested. Black, yellow and red paint decorated their faces and chests, making them all the more menacing. Several had carbines in buckskin scabbards and all were armed with lances and bows. A sudden image of his body pierced by dozens of arrows flashed through Vail's mind and he stopped himself again from charging away.

Vail and the Indian band rode side by side for more than a mile, the Indians staring at Vail, and Vail glancing nervously their way. The warrior in the lead suddenly gave a whoop and wheeled his pony away from the lone white man at a gallop and the party raced off, a cloud of dust billowing in their wake. Vail then realized he had been holding his breath and suddenly found himself lightheaded and gulping for air. He watched as the Indians disappeared over a distant ridge and then spurred his horse forward at a full gallop.

14

Vail arrived at Fort Benton just after noon, where he stabled his exhausted gelding and looked for an Army officer. He inquired after the post's commander and a soldier directed him to a cavalry captain at the dock.

"I'm terribly sorry, Mr. Vail," the captain patiently explained after listening to Vail's request for help. His eyes were brown and sincere. "I only have a small garrison here and I unfortunately cannot spare any of my men to assist you."

The tall captain spoke with a courtly southern accent and Vail wondered what the man was doing here with the war raging back east. The captain's face featured elaborate Van Dyke style whiskers, and when he removed his hat to wipe his brow, Vail saw his long, lush brown hair was heavily pomaded. As he put it back on his head, Vail noticed the captain's hat was not like those worn by the other soldiers at the fort. It had a wide, floppy brim with one side pinned against the crown and an enormous eagle feather sticking flamboyantly out the band.

"I might, however, suggest you recruit some men for the mission you have in mind," he added, with a note of genuine concern in his voice. "There are a number of people stranded in Benton at present. They were hoping to take the steamship back to St. Louis on its return voyage but we recently learned the boat turned back about halfway here. It seems the river is too shallow this summer, so there will be no transport downriver until spring at the earliest, I'm afraid.

Indeed, I was hoping to return to St. Louis myself."

Vail regarded the man. "I understand, Captain. Thank you. Your name?"

"Captain Nolan Harris Tofton the Fourth at your service, Mr. Vail," he bowed slightly as he shook Vail's hand. "Late of Ablemarle County, Virginia and the Virginia Military Institute."

"Thank you again, Captain Tofton," Vail replied, "and good luck to you."

He walked to Hotel New Orleans. Judging by the level of noise pouring through the open door, there appeared to be few other places to look for men who might be willing to help him. Vail entered and took in the saloon's dingy hot interior and the men crowded at the bar or sitting around tables playing cards. If it was possible, the saloon smelled worse than the street and a dense cloud of tobacco smoke hung in the air like a thick curtain.

A pair of drunken men supporting each other stumbled past him out the door. Vail made his way to the bar and ordered a small beer from the one-eyed bartender. The man poured the warm brew from a pitcher into a dirty glass and slid it over to Vail.

His eyes now adjusted, he scanned the room, trying to identify the kind of man who would be willing to help him defend his family and the farm. His eye fell on a well-dressed fellow wearing a black hat seated at a table playing poker ten paces away.

The man's face was handsomely chiseled and he wore neat blond mustaches. Next to him sat another man, also attired in a suit and playing cards. He was tall and lean and wore a bowler hat. At that moment, Vail was shoved violently from behind. He turned and found himself eye to eye with a broad, muscular man he thought he recognized. The fellow's hat was pushed back on his sweating bald head. He was eyeing Vail through a drunken squint.

"I know's you!" the drunk declared. "You're that fuckin' Bible thumper who's tryin' to teach injuns how grow corn!" He roared out a laugh and looked about. "How about that, fellas?! Grow corn!"

Several men looked Vail's way. One suddenly stepped forward, poking his finger into Vail's chest. "Yeah, he works fer the gov'ment! He's out at that injun farm on Sun River."

The first man grabbed Vail's collar. "Lemme tell you sumpin, Friend," the man sneered, his nose touching Vail's. "The only thing you should be teachin' the goddam injuns is how to disappear. An' then you oughta disappear, too!"

He shook Vail violently, then pushed him into the other man, who shoved the teacher to the floor.

"That's enough boys!" called a voice from one of the tables. "Let him go."

The bald man peered in the direction of the voice, ready to challenge whoever had spoken up but then turned his back without a word. Vail got to his feet and saw it was the handsome young man playing poker who had stopped the shoving. He politely waited for him to fold his hand then introduced himself.

"Good afternoon, Sir," Vail said, holding out his hand. "Thank you for intervening. My name is Vail. James Vail of Ohio."

The man looked at Vail's extended hand then shook it. "Henry Plummer," he smiled. "Of Maine and California. And this is my associate, Mr. Noah Coffey, from Connecticut and New York."

"Mr. Coffey," Vail nodded, shaking the other man's hand. "I am pleased to make your acquaintance, Sir."

"Yes, likewise," Coffey smiled up at the man. "What brings you to a place like this, Mr. Vail?"

"Well, I'm afraid I am in some trouble," Vail began, his brow knitted with worry. He explained his predicament to Plummer and Coffey, who quietly listened. "So, the captain has no soldiers to spare and I am greatly concerned for my family's safety."

"As well you should be, Sir," Plummer observed.

"I am hoping I might hire some men to accompany me back to the farm and help me defend it in the event of an attack," Vail's voice became hopeful. "I don't suppose you gentlemen would be interested? I'm willing to pay for your time."

Plummer eyed the man. He was short and thin, no more than five foot six or so. His brown hair had grown long and he wore a thick, unkempt beard. He was dressed in a dusty suit coat and trousers and wore an open necked shirt stained with sweat and grime.

"Can I buy you a drink, Mr. Vail?" Plummer asked as he rose from the table.

"I really don't drink, but I am awfully hungry. Would you and Mr. Coffey join me for dinner? I understand there is a cafe here."

Plummer and Coffey laughed together.

"Oh, that's what that place is!" declared Coffey. "We thought it was a latrine. Yes, we'll join you for dinner, Mr. Vail."

In the dilapidated shed that served as Fort Benton's lone eating establishment they were served a stew made of jackrabbit along with cups of black coffee that tasted several days old. They ate the meal silently. Finally, throwing the spoon into his empty bowl, Plummer looked intently at Vail.

"Why in God's name did you bring your wife and children here?" he asked.

"I have asked myself that same question every day almost since we arrived," replied Vail with a look somewhere between shame and remorse. "Some fool in Washington thought the farm would be an excellent way to pacify the Indians. Of course that same fool probably never met a Blackfeet Indian."

Plummer and Coffey chuckled at this and Vail continued.

"Our pastor heard about the farm manager's position and thought we— that is my wife, Martha, and my sister-in-law, Electa—he thought we would be ideal candidates. I operated my father's farm from the time he died when I was fourteen and the three of us are devout in our Methodist faith. I am also a schoolteacher as is Electa." Vail looked sheepishly at his audience. "It seems the Blackfeet have about as much use for husbandry as they do for learning the Word of God. Had I known that, I would not have come here."

After a pause, Plummer glanced over at Coffey who nodded. He looked back at Vail. "I think we can help you, Jim, but we'll have to be on our way before the snow flies. By then the danger of an attack will no doubt have passed anyway. Now that the steamer has been cancelled, we're making our way overland to Salt Lake City and then east to the states. I hope to fight in the war and Mr. Coffey here hopes to write about it."

Vail looked at both men gratefully. "Thank you gentlemen!" he beamed. "Do you think we should find more men?"

"I'd like to talk to that cavalry captain of yours," Plummer replied. "He may have an opinion about that."

They found Tofton at his office, situated in a decaying log cabin near the river.

"Good afternoon, Gentlemen," the captain greeted them as he looked up from some paperwork. "How may I be of service?"

They made introductions. "We've agreed to help Mr. Vail with his problem at the government farm," said Plummer. "I wondered if you thought a couple of extra guns would be adequate defense against a Blackfeet raid."

The captain twisted his chin whiskers between his fingers. "Yes, I believe so, barring an all out assault. If we were talking about a Sioux war party I might advise otherwise, but the Blackfeet tend to shy away from well-defended settlers. They prefer stealing horses to fighting, anyway."

Plummer nodded before eyeing the captain thoughtfully. "That seems to be an odd uniform for you to be wearing, Captain Tofton."

"Yes, it is," the officer replied dryly. "I was hoping to take the steamship to St. Louis, resign my commission there, and then travel through Tennessee back to my home regiment in Ablemarle County, Virginia, to take up arms in defense of the Old Dominion. Colonel Thomas Jackson, a professor of mine at Virginia Military Institute, requested my service in a letter some weeks ago. But alas..." his voice trailed off.

"Captain, why not join us?" asked Coffey. "Mr. Plummer and I intend to assist Mr. Vail and then travel overland to Missouri. I once made the journey so I know the trail."

"Excellent idea, Noah!" Plummer exclaimed.

Tofton nodded thoughtfully. "May I consider your proposal...sleep on it as it were?"

Plummer and Coffey looked at Vail. "I must return to the farm as soon as possible..."

"Of course, of course!" interrupted Tofton. "I'll have my mind made up by tomorrow morning. You need to rest in any event, Mr. Vail. I'll have my quartermaster arrange a cot and supper for you later."

15

Vail, Plummer and Coffey met at the livery stable just before dawn. They saddled their horses, then waited a few more minutes.

"Doesn't look like he is going to join us," observed Coffey.

Plummer shrugged and looked at Vail.

"I fear for my family if we delay any longer," said Vail.

The three men mounted and were riding southwest just as the sun peeked over a distant ridge. They presently heard hoofbeats and turned to see Captain Tofton riding toward them from the Army barracks. He pulled his horse up alongside and saluted sharply.

"Good morning, Gentlemen!" he called with a smile. "May a wayward Virginia cavalier join you?!"

Plummer saluted back with a grin as Coffey eyed the captain's unusual uniform. He wore a flowing blue cape against the morning chill and his hat was cocked on his head at a rakish angle. On his hip hung a huge cavalry saber that could not have been standard Army issue. Tofton indeed resembled one of the fabled sixteenth century cavaliers.

"What about your command?" Plummer asked, surprised the captain had decided to join them.

"I relinquished it to my executive officer, a young lieutenant from Indiana," Tofton replied. "Duty to my Virginia homeland trumps any obligation I have to the Yankee invaders."

They arrived at the farm close to midnight, exhausted and hungry. Vail was relieved to hear from Joe Swift that no Indians had been sighted during his absence. Martha let her sister sleep as she offered plates of venison and cornmeal mush to her guests, which they wolfed down. Vail bid his new friends goodnight and Swift showed them to a roomy hut that was supposed to house Indians receiving agricultural education. The three men spread their bedrolls on cots and were shortly asleep.

Autumn was in the air the next morning as Plummer, Coffey and Tofton walked the farm. The palisade of logs protected the front and sides of the main farmhouse while the river offered a natural barrier to its rear approach. It would be difficult to defend against a determined attack, Tofton observed, but he was confident that small war parties would avoid the place once they knew there were well armed defenders ready to keep them away.

The hot, nearly rainless summer had dried the grass around the farm to a brittle brown. Even so, several scrawny cows grazed on it while a collection of pigs, ducks, some geese and a few chickens milled about the barnyard. Vail presently stepped from the main house and gestured the men over.

"Martha will have breakfast up very soon, Gentlemen," he said cheerfully. "I see you are perusing the farm. Not very prosperous, I'm afraid."

"Those cows don't look well," Plummer observed.

"No, they've stopped giving milk because their forage has dried up," replied Vail with a sad shrug. "And our supplies are dwindling although there is ample game here abouts. So we're not starving."

"Who's the Indian fellow?" inquired Tofton, gesturing toward Iron, who was dressing a mule deer carcass that hung from a tree branch.

"That's Iron. Doesn't say much, but he keeps us fed. He's a Flathead, I believe. He calls himself a name I can't pronounce. Iron can shoot, though, so along with young Joe Swift, we have another able marksman if need be."

Plummer had stopped listening to Vail. He was gazing at a beautiful young woman who had materialized at the kitchen door. She was staring back at Plummer, her lips parted, her eyes wide.

"Electa," Vail called to the woman, "come here, please, and meet our gallant allies!"

"Electa," Plummer said under his breath as he watched her approach. Her thick brown hair was tied back loosely and her sparkling green eyes were cast demurely downward as she was introduced.

"May I present my sister-in-law, Electa Bryan," Vail said cordially.

"*Enchanté*, Miss Bryan," Tofton said with a smile. He removed his hat and swept it with a flourish. "Captain Nolan Harris Tofton the Fourth, of Albemarle County, Virginia, and late of the United States Army."

"This is Mr. Coffey," Vail said, somewhat embarrassed by Tofton's ostentatious display of southern manners. "I understand he is a newspaperman."

Coffey smiled at Electa.

"And this gentleman is Henry Plummer, a former lawman," Vail noted. "Mr. Plummer is on his way home to New England to enlist in the Union Army."

Plummer's eyes met Electa's. He touched the brim of his hat. "Miss Bryan," he said, looking into her eyes, "I am very pleased to make your acquaintance."

There was a long pause. "And I, yours," Electa replied with a blush. "Thank you for coming to our aid, Mr. Plummer. And you gentlemen as well," she added, smiling at Coffey and Tofton in turn.

Both men could not help but notice Electa and Henry's immediate and unmistakable attraction. She curtsied and left the men.

Vail cleared his throat. "Yes, well, men, you've reconnoitered. Any thoughts as to our situation here?"

Plummer looked at Vail. "Captain Tofton has the most experience among us fighting Indians. He believes we'll be safe unless the Indians decide to come at us in force…"

"An unlikely eventuality," interrupted Tofton. "You see, the Plains Indians usually spend the autumn months readying for the difficult winter. In addition, the Indian tribes here about are mostly Blackfeet and mostly pacified. I really don't think there will be much danger here after the first of October."

Vail looked relieved at Tofton's assessment.

"But we should be ready, nonetheless," Tofton added quickly. "There have been some attacks on emigrants and settlers in recent months."

"Breakfast is ready, Gentlemen," Martha called out from the kitchen door. "Won't you join us?"

Food had been laid out on the table in the cramped kitchen. "There is no coffee, I am afraid," Martha announced with an awkward smile. Like her sister, she was an attractive young woman, but the strain of raising two children in a desolate and dangerous place was showing. "We do have meat and cornmeal aplenty. James told me the steamship did not arrive with supplies from St. Louis, so we're going to have to make do with what we have until spring, I suppose."

Vail said a blessing over the food and the women passed the plates.

"The fact of the matter is I want to return home in the spring," Vail said. "The Indians don't appear interested in learning anything about cultivating crops nor raising stock. They just leave their old people here and move on."

"Not surprised, Mr. Vail," Tofton replied as he cut a slice of antelope loin. "But it's better than leaving the old people out in a blizzard, which is what they usually do."

Electa shot a look at Tofton and frowned. "I'm afraid it's true, Miss," the soldier said. "Their old people are a burden to them, especially when the weather turns savage."

"Yes, well, in any event, we will return to Ohio in the spring," said Vail.

Coffey had been watching Plummer as his friend snuck looks at Electa. Once or twice, Coffey noticed, she caught Henry's eye and the two exchanged smiles.

"Miss Bryan, may I ask what you do here at the farm?" Coffey inquired.

"I am a schoolteacher," she replied self-consciously. "Although I have no pupils to teach at present, as I am sure you have seen. But I have been trying to introduce Jesus Christ into the hearts of the elderly Indians who are here. I read the Bible to them with Iron's assistance. And, of course, I help Martha with the chores and the children."

Coffey watched her as she spoke. She had a light voice and a sincere manner. Her complexion was clear and her cheeks rosy from the climate. He thought she might be about twenty-three or four. She suddenly turned her earnest gaze on Plummer.

"And, Mr. Plummer, perhaps you will tell us about your life as a lawman?" she demanded with a mischievous smile.

Caught unprepared by her sudden question, Plummer was momentarily speechless. Coffey laughed at his friend's embarrassment.

"Yes, Marshal Plummer, tell the story about how you recovered Mr. Thomaston's stray hogs!"

Plummer turned red as Tofton chuckled.

"Well, I was able to track those hogs down and get them back to their owner," Plummer finally said, "But as marshal, I was also responsible for keeping order in Auroria—that's in California—so that meant frequently jailing Mr. Coffey here."

It was Coffey's turn to be embarrassed and Plummer grinned at the startled looks from the Vail family.

"No, I jest. Mr. Coffey and I are the best of friends," Plummer explained. "In all honesty, my job was not as exciting as the title makes it sound. I collected taxes and also had to enforce the fire codes. The town burned to the ground in '56, you see, and the citizens didn't want a repeat of that particular tragedy."

"He's being modest," Coffey said. "Henry was a fine marshal who brought dozens of desperados to justice."

"Did you ever hang anyone?" Vail asked abruptly. An uncomfortable silence descended and everyone looked intently at Plummer.

"Well, yes, I did," Plummer finally answered. "It was part of my job and I did not like it. May we change the subject?"

Vail realized he had been rude. "I'm very sorry, Mr. Plummer...a stupid question."

"I propose a reconnaissance of the area," Tofton declared to ease the awkwardness. "Let us enlist Iron and that young fellow Joe Swift we met last night to lead us on a tour. We can determine the lay of the land to better anticipate the movements of the savages."

There was a general agreement, but Vail suggested he stay with the women in case Indians showed up.

16

The bright morning sun gave way to rain squalls that rolled over the prairie from the north. The day grew colder as they rode across a broken landscape of sagebrush and tall brown grass blanketing the low hills and ravines. They crossed small streams on occasion or passed stands of cottonwoods with their leaves beginning to turn a vibrant yellow.

Iron led them in a wide circle around the farm. They saw herds of deer and antelope lying in the grass, oblivious to the cold drizzle that was falling. Plummer and Coffey chatted as they rode, while Tofton, mounted on his gray mare, played the role of cavalry officer, pointing here and there and asking Iron or Swift clipped questions about the terrain.

As mid-afternoon approached, the patrol began making its way back to the farm. They rode down a hill, came upon the Sun River and turned west, riding along its north bank. They broke through a stand of willows when Iron sharply reined in his horse and pointed to his right. There, a hundred yards distant, was a wagon lying on its side, clothing and boxes littered around it.

"Oh God!" Coffey choked, staring at the wagon. His blood ran cold as he remembered the scene in the meadow, his wife's small corpse at the mercy of the coyotes and wolves.

"Hold here!" Tofton commanded as he spurred his horse forward. The others waited by the trees until the captain signaled them. Plummer, Iron and Swift rode at a trot toward the overturned wagon, but Coffey hung back. As the riders approached, Tofton strode out from behind the other side of the upturned wagon, his face ashen.

"Bastards!" he exclaimed as he jerked his thumb to whatever lay hidden behind the wagon.

Clothing had been strewn over the grass on the bank of the river. Chests and crates lay about the ground broken open and splintered. Plummer saw a shattered fiddle and a child's doll. The mules or oxen that had drawn the wagon were gone.

They dismounted and walked to the other side of the wagon. There, a man lay with arrows jutting from his chest and neck. A young woman was sprawled nearby, obviously violated before she'd died the same way her husband had. Two small children, a boy of ten and a small girl of perhaps five had been stabbed with lances. All were scalped.

Iron walked to the man's body and, with some effort, pulled one of the arrows from the corpse's chest. He examined it for a moment. "Blackfeet," he announced.

"These people came through Benton four days ago," Tofton said quietly as he pointed at the dead man. "I spoke to him about the best way to get to St. Peter's Mission. He was an Irishman. Said his brother was one of the priests there and he was going to homestead on the Dearborne River near the mission."

Coffey rode up to the scene, took in the slaughtered family and quickly wheeled his horse away. Tofton glanced Plummer's way.

"Noah's wife was killed when his wagon train was attacked in '57," Plummer explained. "In fact, everyone was killed…more than a hundred people were butchered."

"My God!" exclaimed Tofton. "I hope the army tracked the Indians who are responsible!"

"Wasn't Indians," Plummer said as he looked Tofton in the eye. "It was white men that did the killing. Mormons."

"Mormons?! That can't be!" exclaimed Tofton in shock.

"It was Mormons," Coffey declared as he reappeared on foot carrying a shovel he'd found in the grass. "They shot the men and women. They cut the throats of the older children. They spared the smallest children, I suppose because they thought they wouldn't remember what happened. Then the Mormons stole our wagons and stock. I was there. I was the only survivor, Captain Tofton. Would you care to see the scars on my body?"

Tofton stared at the newspaperman. "No, Sir. I believe you," he finally replied.

Coffey's gaze turned to the dead family, rain dripping off the brim of his hat. "We should bury them," he said with a shiver.

Plummer put his hand on Coffey's shoulder. "You're right, Noah. It's the least we can do," he agreed and they began to dig graves. Swift found a Bible the Indians had overlooked and opened it.

"Says here their name was Brennan," Swift told the others as they finished burying the family. He read one of the flyleaves. "The man was named Dennis, his wife was Molly and the kids were named Sean and Maureen." Swift paused for a long time and Plummer could see tears in the boy's eyes.

"Why don't you read some words out of the book for the Brennans, Joe," Plummer quietly suggested. Swift nodded, found a passage and read the verses in a halting voice. Afterwards, they silently remounted and rode back to the farm. Swift kept the Bible, intending to give it to Father Brennan at St. Peters the first chance he had.

Vail's face was etched with worry as he listened to Plummer describe the massacred family that evening after supper had been served and the men sat alone in the tiny parlor smoking. Tofton had shut the door to the kitchen so the women wouldn't hear.

"We need to be ready," Plummer concluded. "Every weapon must be loaded and a guard posted each night until the danger has passed."

Vail nodded absently. This was far more than he'd bargained for back in Ohio when he'd agreed to manage the government station.

"I shall take the first watch tonight," Tofton volunteered. "I can sleep tomorrow after you are all awake."

"Thank you, Captain," Vail said as the officer donned his cape and hat. He picked up his carbine and bade everyone a good night as he stepped through the front door.

"Interesting man," Plummer observed after a moment. "Something of an anachronism, eh, Noah?"

"He is duty bound to the state where he was born and bred," Coffey agreed. "I daresay you'll find his attitude shared by many of the officer class of the so-called Confederate States of America. I believe this will be a long war."

"God, I hope so," Plummer responded as he exhaled a plume of cigar smoke. "I don't want to get all the way back to Boston and discover I missed the fighting."

"You may well encounter our Captain Tofton on the battlefield," Vail interjected. "What an irony that would be...allies here; enemies there."

The men turned in, passing Tofton on guard duty as they made their way to the bunkhouse carrying their weapons. The cold north wind blew with force and the clouds had given way to bright starlight and a half moon.

"All is quiet," Tofton announced as they passed by. "Good night again, Gentlemen."

The men rotated guard duty each night for the next week but no Indians appeared. During the days, Plummer, Coffey and Tofton helped Vail reinforce the palisade. As they were engaged in cutting down lodgepole pines one warm afternoon, Electa appeared with a pitcher of water. Plummer removed his hat and wiped his brow with his forearm, watching her as she poured water into tin mugs.

"Thank you, Miss," he smiled as she handed him one of the cups. "It's beastly hot work."

"Is the wall really so weak?" she asked in a nervous voice.

Plummer looked over at the thin wall of upright logs, many rotting, that was supposed to protect the farmhouse. He had decided it only served the purpose of reassuring Vail and his family. Plummer knew any war party could breach it in minutes.

"I'm afraid so," he said. Then he pointed at the pile of logs at his feet. "But we're taking the necessary precautions. There's no need to concern yourself, Miss Bryan."

"Please," she said, looking up at his face, "call me Electa."

Their eyes met and he returned her smile, Coffey noticed as he sipped his own water. He had observed them over the last several days and knew a romance was blossoming. The evening before, as the flaming sun disappeared over the distant western mountains and ignited a vivid sunset, he had seen Henry and Electa walking along the path next to the river. Plummer was pointing east and talking earnestly and Electa was intently listening. Then his friend reached out and took the young woman's hand in his, raised it to his lips and kissed it gently. The two had stood there for some time in the lengthening shadows. The spell was broken when Joe Swift appeared on horseback from behind some trees across the river from the couple and hailed them.

Plummer was an easy man to like, Coffey thought to himself. Joe was also under Henry's spell and, if Coffey was honest with himself, he was, too. But there was something more, Coffey reflected. After a moment he knew what it was. *Henry wore a halo of danger.*

"Blackfeet war party!" Plummer hissed. Startled, Coffey and Tofton bolted from their cots in the dark shed. "Hurry!" Plummer whispered. "They're just the other side of the river!"

As he threw on his clothes, an image of the slaughtered Brennan family flashed through Coffey's mind. He stepped outside into the dark and found the other men gathered around Henry. Vail, Joe and Iron quickly joined them. "There are ten, fifteen of them on the north bank," Plummer said quietly. "They didn't see me."

"If we ambush them, we'll have the advantage," whispered Tofton. "They're probably after the stock or they would have simply tried to kill us in our beds."

Plummer gave a sharp nod of his head in agreement and the men, staying to the shadows, silently made their way across the farmyard to the barn. As they approached, they heard a cow bellow and a horse whinny as if to confirm Tofton's guess at what the Indians were there to do.

Through a stand of willows next to the barn they could see several shadows moving around the corral.

"This way," Tofton gestured toward the river. "We'll cut them off."

They ducked around the far side of the barn next to the main house.

Coffey felt sweat dripping down his back despite the chill wind. Plummer had his revolver out, cocked and ready. Vail had a shotgun, while Joe and Iron were each armed with carbines. Tofton, Coffey could see, was carrying his savage looking saber in one hand and a menacing Army Colt revolver in the other.

Plummer peeked around the corner of the barn and there, twenty paces away, stood a half dozen warriors on horseback ready to drive the stock back across the river. One of them held ropes attached to six or seven other ponies belonging to the Indians in the corral.

Tofton came alongside Plummer, took in the scene, then ducked back behind the corner. After a quick deliberation, Tofton whispered instructions into each man's ear. When he'd finished with the orders, he stepped back to the corner, holding up three fingers, then two, then one. With that, the six gunmen silently stepped out from behind the corner of the barn. Before the mounted Indians saw them, each took his mark on the target Tofton had assigned him.

The fusillade shattered the stillness as five Indians were plucked from their mounts. The shocking roar of the gunfire spooked the loose horses and they scattered. The sixth Indian broke for the river, but the shooters ignored him while they reloaded or cocked their weapons. As they approached the corral, seven warriors leapt the fence trying to make for the river. Coffey could see they all wore buckskin shirts and breeches.

They never saw the white men as another volley of gunfire split the night. Through the muzzle flashes Coffey saw three Indians drop in their tracks. Tofton took aim with his Colt and cut down two more on the riverbank. The remaining two Indians dove headlong into the water and disappeared.

After the wind had carried off the last of the acrid smoke, the men found themselves standing amidst the Indians who'd been shot from their horses in the first volley. Two rolled on the ground holding their bellies and groaning. Tofton stepped over to them and dispatched each with his saber, blood spouting as he cut their throats.

Iron drew his knife and began scalping the dead raiders. Coffey watched in horror as the Indian pulled back the braids of one warrior and sliced through the scalp at the man's hairline. He ripped the hair back, flesh tearing away from the skull with a hideous ripping noise that nauseated the white men.

"Christ on His bloody cross, Vail!" swore Tofton. "Stop him!"

Iron ignored Vail's entreaties and the schoolteacher, unable to halt the Indian's savagery, finally gave Tofton a helpless shrug. The officer swore again and stalked away in disgust.

Plummer saw cows and horses crowded together at the far end of the corral, terrified by the shooting. He ran to the house, where several lights burned. Some of the old Indian men stood outside, having come from their cabins to see what the gunfire was about. Plummer shooed them away and then knocked at the kitchen door and let himself in. The women and the two children were huddled on the floor in the far corner behind the huge iron stove. Martha had a shotgun trained on Plummer's chest.

"Martha!" exclaimed Plummer. "It's all right! It's Henry Plummer! There were Indians…we killed most of them!"

Martha lowered the weapon and she and Electa stood, shaking with fear in their nightdresses. Despite the moment, Plummer could see Electa's shapely form beneath her gown and suddenly felt himself become aroused. His eyes met Electa's. Embarrassed, he stepped back through the kitchen door.

"Keep this locked. We'll be back shortly," he called over his shoulder.

Outside, the men had piled the Indian bodies among some trees, gore dripping from bullet holes and knife wounds.

"We'll bury them in the morning," Vail said in a voice that shook with emotion. Henry placed his hand on the man's shoulder.

"We had no choice, Jim," he said.

Tears in his eyes, Vail earnestly looked at Plummer. "This is not why I came here," he mumbled. "I wished only to save souls, not take lives."

Plummer took Vail by his quivering shoulders and stared into his face. "You had to protect your family, Jim!" he said sternly. "Remember the Brennans? That's what would have happened to Martha, Electa and your children, man!"

"That's enough, Henry!" Coffey said angrily, grabbing Plummer's arm away from one of Vail's shoulders. Plummer glared at his friend for a moment, then stalked off into the night.

Tofton, who had been watching the scene, suddenly declared. "Gentlemen, we had all better stay alert for the rest of the night. There could be a bigger war party nearby."

No Blackfeet returned. As the sun crept up over the farm, Joe Swift and Iron, the latter carrying his bloody trophies, went to their bunkhouse. Fatigued by the night's bloodshed and watch, the four men gathered at the house and silently ate their breakfast.

When they had finished, Plummer looked over at Vail. "I am very sorry about my behavior last night, Jim."

"Think nothing of it," Vail replied quietly. "You were right in what you said. They would most assuredly have done us murder."

Now Plummer gave Coffey a wry smile. "The heat of battle, I suppose."

"Understandable," Coffey nodded with an affable smile. "You are forgiven, Henry."

"As penance, I will stand guard," Plummer replied with a chuckle. "You gentlemen may retire and I'll awaken you around noon. Then I can sleep."

Vail, Tofton and Coffey gratefully did as Henry suggested. The women and children, also exhausted, had gone back to their beds after breakfast. Plummer stepped outside into the sunny morning and noticed the cottonwoods were shedding their golden leaves.

He lit a cigar and puffed on it as he thought of Electa, asleep in her nearby bed. He sat on the stoop, leaned his back against the house and closed his eyes, the babbling sound of the nearby river and the sun's warm rays lulling him. He must have dozed off because suddenly, there, standing before him was Electa. She wore a dressing gown, her light brown hair spilling seductively over her shoulders as she gazed down at him.

Silently he stood, removed his hat and kissed her gently on the lips. She embraced him and returned his kiss, which grew more passionate as they held each other. Plummer felt Electa's naked body beneath the gown and again felt himself harden. She must have felt it, too, because she pressed herself against him. Panting, Plummer stepped back, looking in her eyes.

"Electa," he whispered. "Marry me."

She looked stunned at the sudden proposal, then her expression softened and she smiled up at him. "Yes," she replied. "Of course I will marry you. I love you, Henry."

"And I love you," he said, feeling his heart pounding. She leaned into him again and held him close. She smelled of sleep and lavender soap. He wanted her now but she slowly pushed him back.

"When?" she asked breathlessly.

"As soon as we can get a parson here," Plummer smiled.

That afternoon, Plummer explained his intentions to Electa's sister and brother-in-law as they stood in the sun dappled yard. Martha appeared alarmed at the news of the sudden engagement, but her husband wore a broad smile.

"But...but what of the war and your wish to fight?" asked Martha, twisting her hands in her light blue apron, her eyes moist.

Plummer smiled at her. "I don't think I'm going to return to the States now, Martha. I wish to make our home here in the territory."

Martha looked relieved and dabbed the tears that were freely falling.

"That's capital, Henry!" exclaimed Vail. "It will be wonderful to have you in the family!"

They sat on a rock after supper looking down at the rippling waters that reflected another luminous golden sunset, a fat trout rising to tiny insects that had settled on the surface of a calm pool. Henry held Electa's hand in his and sensed the first contentment he could remember feeling for some time. He pointed at a doe and fawn that had emerged from a thicket just downstream. The deer lowered their long necks and drank from the river, taking no notice of their audience.

Electa was leaning against him. "Did you really hang men?"

Plummer was silent for a long moment. He considered the question and what it meant. Finally, he looked down at her. "Not men. A man," he answered. "A very bad man who needed hanging."

She turned her face from him and regarded the deer, which stood unmoving, like statues.

"There's more," Plummer continued. "I spent time in prison." He felt her tense as she sat up and looked at him intently.

"I killed a man in California who had been beating his wife," Plummer said quickly. "He confronted me with a weapon. I shot him in self defense."

"Why did he confront you?" she asked.

"Because he thought I was...having an affair with his wife," he replied, looking away from her gaze, embarrassed.

"And were you?"

He thought carefully about his answer. "Yes," he said finally. Electa sat frozen, blankly staring into the water. He went on.

"I helped her and her daughter find a place to stay...away from him. He'd brutalized her and she was desperate. She had no family of her own in Auroria...no one to aid her..." his voice trailed off.

"So you decided to help her," she tonelessly interjected.

"Yes... I... I helped her."

The river quietly gurgled at their feet. The deer wandered off into the thicket. Henry sat gazing down into the clear water, wondering if telling her the truth had ended their engagement.

"And they sent you to prison," she continued in the same expressionless voice. "How long were you there, Henry?"

"Six months," he replied. "Noah Coffey enlisted my friends to win a pardon for me from the governor of California. I would not have survived much longer behind bars. I am forever grateful to Noah."

She was looking at him earnestly again. "Have you killed other men?" she demanded. "Is there more about Henry Plummer I should know?"

"Yes. I have killed several men. All in self defense," he replied after a minute's hesitation. Electa looked away, then she silently rose up off the rock and walked quietly back to the house, leaving him alone.

Night fell. The evening was warm and Plummer recalled Indian summers back home in Maine as he walked to his quarters. Coffey stood outside smoking a cigar.

"Well, congratulations again Henry!" Coffey said cheerfully. "I would not have guessed you as one to tie the knot of matrimony, especially at such a young age."

Plummer didn't respond. He reached inside his jacket and withdrew a cigar. Coffey lit it for him and the two friends smoked in companionable silence for a time. Coffey sensed Henry's pensive mood and knew his friend well enough to let him speak about what was troubling him in his own time.

Finally, Plummer let out a sigh and leaned against the shed. "I told her about the Vedders and San Quentin," he quietly declared. "Stupid, I suppose."

Coffey regarded him. "I don't think so, Henry. Honesty is best. I know you agree."

Plummer nodded. "Perhaps," he said sadly. "But I could just have easily lied. Why was it necessary she know all about...that?"

Coffey patted his friend's arm. "When she considers your honesty with her, Henry, she'll recognize your faithfulness. She will know she's made the right choice."

Plummer looked over at Coffey. "Thanks, Noah."

Coffey smiled. "Well, I have drawn guard duty tonight," he declared. "So I'll be off on my patrol of the fortress. I believe Captain Tofton and Mr. Vail are engaged in a hand of whist at the house. With your permission, Sir." Coffey offered Plummer an exaggerated salute.

"Dismissed, Private Coffey," laughed Plummer.

17

Unable to sleep, Plummer lay on his cot listening to the soft breeze whistle through the eaves of the darkened shed. His hand rested behind his head as he considered the wisdom of revealing his troubled history to Electa. The door presently opened, leather hinges squeaking, and he saw a form slip through. His holster hung on a nail next to the cot. Silently he drew his revolver from it and placed his thumb on the hammer.

"Nolan? Is that you?"

"It's me, Henry," Electa answered in a raspy whisper. "I wish to speak with you."

Astonished, Plummer rose from his cot and stepped out into the yard, where Electa waited.

"I'm sorry," she whispered as she placed her finger against his lips. "What happened in the past is in the past. We have a future to look forward to."

He embraced her, kissing her gently. His hands moved over her body and she moaned at his touch before pushing reluctantly away.

"Wait," she whispered breathlessly. "Wait and I shall make you happy."

James and Martha insisted the wedding ceremony be officiated by a Methodist minister. Tofton told them the only Methodist church he knew of was in Lewiston, more than one hundred miles away. After some negotiating,

Plummer convinced them that a priest from St. Peter's Mission would be acceptable, and the Vails finally relented. Joe Swift volunteered to ride to the Mission forty miles away with the request for a priest. He took with him the Bible belonging to the massacred family.

A day after Swift departed, Francis Thompson, the young mining explorer, returned to Sun River Farm. Vail introduced the tall, boyish-looking felllow to Coffey and Plummer. Later, Thompson's quick smile vanished when he learned from Coffey that Electa was betrothed to Henry Plummer.

He leaned over a fence, dejected. "I wished to marry her myself," he said quietly to Coffey, who felt sorry for the heartsick young man. "That's why I came back here."

Coffey patted him on the back. "Well, I'm afraid Henry and Electa were thunderstruck when they met, Francis. They would have fallen in love no matter what."

After a few minutes Thompson slowly nodded his head.

Plummer, seeing the pair by the fence but unaware of Thompson's affections for Electa, strode over to them and clapped Coffey and Thompson on their backs.

"So Mr. Mining Explorer!" he said brightly to Thompson. "What can you tell me about gold in yonder mountains? Is it true? Are they plucking nuggets as big as walnuts out of the creeks?"

Thompson smiled thinly at Plummer and once again, Coffey realized it was difficult to dislike Henry.

"Yes and no," Thompson replied. "There are surface deposits all around the streams and in them, too. But you've got to do quite a lot of scratching to get at them. There's also considerable gold ore-bearing quartz around Alder Creek. But I think the most promising strike I heard about was made on Grasshopper Creek at a place called Bannack. I suppose it's named after the Bannock tribe."

Plummer had been listening thoughtfully. "Bannack, eh?" he said finally with a wide grin. "Mr. Coffey? Care to go into the gold mining business with me after the wedding? We'll form the Plummer-Coffey Mining Company and make our fortunes before we are thirty! What do you say, Sir?"

Coffey had been giving a lot of thought to his own future as he'd stood guard duty during the lonely nights. He had considered riding out to Salt Lake

City and then finding an eastbound wagon train or army column headed for St. Louis. From there he had a vague notion of becoming a war correspondent.

"Where is this Bannack?" Coffey asked Thompson.

"South. About two hundred miles or thereabouts."

Salt Lake City was south so he was at least headed in the right direction if he chose to make his way back to the States. "I'll tell you what, Henry," Coffey said, smiling at his friend. "I'll travel with you to Bannack and we'll have a look at the place. I will make my decision there. How does that suit you?"

"Right down to the ground, Noah!" Plummer laughed.

Joe Swift and a young Irish priest named Father Murphy arrived the following morning, just after breakfast.

"Father Brennan was prostrate with grief when he learned the fate of his brother Dennis and his family," the priest explained after he'd been welcomed. "But the Bible you recovered meant much to him and he asked that I convey his profound thanks to you."

The wedding was held that afternoon on the yard in front of the farmhouse, the sun casting long shadows as a cool breeze drifted through the tall cottonwoods and the golden leaves floated down on the celebration. Father Murphy, of course, had never officiated a Methodist wedding, so he decided to skip the wedding mass rituals and offered instead a brief homily before uniting Henry and Electa in marriage.

Martha served a wedding feast on a long table that had been set up in the yard. There was buffalo hump, a roast goose, corn bread and some kind of tasty roots Iron had found. After the meal, the men smoked and passed around a bottle of whiskey.

"Sure, I'll join you for a wee dram," said the priest as he took the bottle. "Then I must be on my way back to the mission to comfort Father Brennan."

Night fell, the north wind blew harder and it grew quite cold. James and Martha had vacated their small bedroom in the house so Henry and Electa could use it as their wedding suite. As the newly married couple climbed into bed together and Henry extinguished the candle, Coffey, Tofton and Thompson gathered beneath their window and began drunkenly serenading the couple. Only Iron and Joe Swift were sober and on guard duty.

> *"The sun shines bright on my old Kentucky home*
> *'Tis summer, the people are gay;*
> *The corn top's ripe and the meadow's in the bloom,*
> *While the birds make music all the day..."*

"My God, what awful singing...they're off key," Henry laughed as he held Electa in his arms. She smiled and kissed him again. As Henry and Electa made love, the singers gave up somewhere between the second and third verse.

They rode in the open wagon, a pair of mules pulling them through the valley, the mountains rising majestically around them, their snow capped peaks glittering in the golden morning sunlight. Coffey rode his horse on the right flank of the wagon while Tofton, in his dashing uniform, together with Francis Thompson, rode alongside on the left. It was cold and they could see the steamy breath of the mules as they labored along.

With the onset of cold weather, Tofton had judged the threat of Indian attack past, so two days earlier, Electa had bid a tearful good-bye to her sister, James and the children and promised to come back to the farm in the springtime. The Vails had given her some spare furnishings, housewares and fifty dollars in gold coins.

They'd made camp the first night and, as she lay with Plummer, Electa had sobbed miserably for most of the night, explaining through her tears that she and Martha had never spent more than a day or two apart in all their lives.

The next morning, Electa's grief eased a little and she began to smile. Electa seemed herself again, her body leaning against Plummer's. She was wrapped in a green wool cloak, a scarf tied tightly around her head against the chill as she took in the glorious scenery.

"You're in a good mood, this morning, Henry!" called Coffey. "You haven't stopped smiling since we took to the road."

"Yes," agreed Tofton from the other side of the wagon, "matrimony has done wonders for you, Sir!"

Grinning, Plummer looked at Electa, who blushed crimson as she smiled up at him. He patted her gloved hand and looked out ahead at the mountains. At noon, they stopped to rest by a brook that cascaded off a steep, rocky slope. They ate cornbread and jerked antelope meat as they discussed their progress toward Bannack. Coffey, who had been sitting on a rock, rose and suddenly felt dizzy and light headed.

"It's the altitude," Captain Tofton explained as he reached a hand out to steady Coffey. "You'll get used to it."

Plummer finished eating and ambled over to the brook, dipped his cupped hand into the water and took a drink. As Coffey and Tofton watched him, Plummer froze, then plunged his hand into the stream where he plucked a stone from the water. He eyed it, put it between his teeth and bit it, then looked back at his friends holding up his discovery.

"Eureka!" he called to them with a wide smile. "Gold!"

"He is the luckiest man I know," Coffey said to Tofton, grinning and shaking his head. Then he looked at Plummer again and his smile disappeared. "At least when it comes to making money."

They made camp and explored the stream. Thompson was excited at first but after two days and a half-dozen more nuggets and a few ounces of gold dust, it appeared they'd found all the gold the little stream had to offer.

"Well, I'm very encouraged, anyway," Plummer declared as they finished packing the wagon. "We've about two hundred dollars in gold and we haven't even staked a claim yet!"

18

They passed Beaverhead Rock the next day, so named by the Indians because the towering outcropping resembled the head of the animal commonly found in rivers and streams. The trail paralleled the Beaverhead River for ten more miles until they came upon a creek spilling into the river. Thompson stopped his horse and pointed upstream.

"Bannack's just up there," he said excitedly. "This here is the Grasshopper Creek!"

They followed the creek through a gulch and soon saw their first miners, busily panning and sluicing in the stream on their one-hundred-foot-long claims. The miners, hard looking men with thick beards and worn clothing, silently watched them pass by before resuming their work. Then the town of Bannack finally came into view. Coffey and Plummer exchanged disappointed looks.

Two rows of shacks and log buildings ran for a hundred yards on either side of a muddy main street. Tents were pitched everywhere and wickiups, a kind of conical lean-to made of tree branches, were erected haphazardly wherever there was any space. The dirty faces of women and children peered out at them from the crude structures as they rode by. Smoke billowed from dozens of stovepipes filling the air with a pleasing smell of burning wood. But as they entered the bustling main street, their nostrils were assaulted by the stench of human and animal waste.

Grasshopper Creek flowed alongside the town and it was jammed with more miners working their claims. To the east toward the mountains, the stream rose above Bannack into the barren, sage studded hills and Plummer could see there were still more miners working claims up there. The once clear water had been churned to a chocolate brown by all the mining activity.

Midway up the main street, Coffey saw that some of the buildings were large and well built, many with false fronts. He counted three saloons, a café, an assayer's office, a general store called Chrisman's which displayed shovels, pans and other mining equipment on the boardwalk out front, and a couple of places with signs saying they were hotels.

More tents and lean-tos were set up at the east end of the street and the ground around them had been churned into a sticky black muck. Coffey noticed that a band of Indians had wisely placed their tipis near a copse of trees a couple of hundred yards from the town, no doubt appalled by the filth the white men chose to live in.

The men said nothing as they reined their horses to a halt in front of a building that advertised itself as the Goodrich Hotel. The riders dismounted while Plummer helped Electa down from the wagon and the friends made their way into the hotel. It was a long, one story structure. The lobby was small and cluttered with furnishings that were far too big for the space. There seemed to be a dining room off the lobby. An aged clerk looked up as they entered.

"Good afternoon, folks," the old fellow greeted them. "Welcome to the Goodrich."

"Good afternoon," replied Plummer. "We require rooms."

"Ah yes," the man spun his register around and held out a pen. "I have three available at ten dollars each per night."

Coffey was stunned at the price. "Ten dollars?!"

Wearing an unctuous smile, the clerk eyed Coffey over the top of his gold rimmed eyeglasses.

"Sir, the Goodrich is the finest accommodation in Bannack," he said in a patronizing tone. "I believe you will quickly learn that the vast sums of money earned here have driven up the price of most everything."

Inflation wasn't a new concept to Coffey. The price of even the most common items had been unusually high in Auroria, but ten dollars for a hotel room worth no more than fifty cents per night was a shocking amount of money.

Now Tofton stepped forward. He stood over the clerk, his military bearing on full display. "Listen here, my good man," he commanded. "I am Captain Nolan Harris Tofton the Fourth of the United States Army's cavalry garrison in Fort Benton, Dakota Territory. My companions and I are on official Army business and we require rooms at the official army rate. Now, Sir, I expect you to accommodate my party or there will be severe consequences for taking advantage of the United States government. Do I make myself clear, Sir?"

The old man seemed to shrink under Tofton's unwavering gaze. "Quite clear, Captain. Um, I think we can provide you rooms at the government rate of, shall we say, two dollars per night?"

"That's an outrage!" roared Tofton, startling even Plummer who was trying to hide a smile. "One dollar per night per room and not a penny more!"

The man was visibly shaking. "Yes, yes, agreed Captain Tofton... I apologize for the confusion. Of course we want to cooperate with the army...indeed we do!"

"Very well," Tofton replied. "Now, Sir, we are quite hungry. Where might we board our horses and obtain supper?"

Still shaking, the man directed them to the nearest livery stable and recommended they come back to the hotel, pointing at the small dining room.

"Uh, Mrs. Quinn—that's my wife—will be ready to serve you at about six o'clock, if that is acceptable, Captain? I believe beefsteaks are on the bill of fare this evening..."

"As long as supper is included in the price of the room!" Tofton interrupted.

The old man started to protest and then thought better of it. "Of course, of course it is," he said with an uneasy smile. "Nothing is too good for our men in uniform...." His voice trailed off as Tofton fixed him with a steely glare.

The rooms at the Goodrich proved to be as dingy as the lobby. Toften had a room to himself while Coffey and Thompson shared one and Plummer and Electa the other. After they boarded their mounts and they'd eaten a meal made notable only by the small portions Mrs. Quinn had served them, Thompson suggested a drink and smoke at one of the saloons. Plummer looked at Electa with an inquiring eyebrow raised and she smiled and nodded.

The men entered an establishment called Skinner's Saloon. While it was freezing outside, the interior was stuffy and loud. It seemed as though every miner in Bannack was packed into the place. They made their way to the bar and, as Plummer ordered whiskey for all of them, Coffey noticed a barber had set up shop near the window, where he was shaving a customer. He also saw a row of cots lining the back wall.

While the liquor was poured, several miners eyed the newcomers' clean clothes and neat appearances. Several were rudely pointing at Tofton's blue uniform. Plummer, no stranger to being assessed in such a manner, coolly looked back at one of the gawkers, a heavy-set miner wearing filthy rags, and nodded.

"How do?" Plummer asked pleasantly as he lit a cigar.

Taken aback at the friendliness, the man nodded at Plummer. "You gents new in town?" the man asked, displaying a set of yellow teeth.

"Yes, Sir, we are indeed," Plummer smiled affably. "Looks like you've been working awfully hard, friend. Any color for the effort?"

The man's look turned suspicious. Then, realizing Plummer was simply making conversation, he shrugged.

"Some," the man replied, "but I think my claims is pretty well tapped out."

Plummer nodded as he sipped his whiskey. "Well, I'm interested in buying claims if you're interested in selling."

The man's eyes grew wide. "I...I might be..."

"How many claims do you have?" Coffey interjected.

"Five, all upstream to'ard the top of the gulch," the miner said. "How much might you be willin' to pay me fer 'em?"

"My friend here, Mr. Thompson, would like to have a look first, but if they have the potential I'm seeking we might go as high as a hundred per claim. In fact, you might pass the word to your associates, Mister...?"

"Benson," the man blurted. "Charlie Benson. A hundred a claim you say?"

"After we inspect them, of course," Coffey smiled.

Benson led them up a steep, winding path that ran alongside Grasshopper Creek. They climbed well above the town, passing miners shoveling sand and gravel off the bottom of the stream into sluices, long wooden boxes through which water ran carrying the the slurry along. Men eagerly picked through the tailings at the bottom of the boxes and occasionally found fragments of gold or small nuggets. Other miners, oblivious to the freezing air and cold drizzle, waded in the shallows, panning for gold.

They stopped and Benson pointed upstream. "I own this'n here an' the next four claims up. Say, what are you looking for, anyway?" the miner asked Plummer.

"Ah, that's my secret, Charlie," Plummer slyly replied. "But if I see it, I will know it and I shall make you an offer!"

Benson shrugged his shoulders then turned his attention to Francis Thompson, who was walking upstream along the far bank, occasionally sticking a shovel blade into the soft earth at the water's edge.

"What's he doing?" Tofton whispered in Plummer's ear.

By way of reply, Plummer held up his forefinger. "Watch."

At just that moment, Thompson was stabbing the shovel repeatedly into the same spot. He paused, then moved the shovel around, pushing aside loose soil. He got down on a knee and dug a hole with his bare hands. He eyed something in the hole, then looked up at Plummer and smiled.

This process was repeated several more times as they walked the five hundred foot length of Benson's claims. Finally, Thompson came up from the stream and had a short conference with Plummer and Coffey.

"Would you accept seventy-five dollars per claim, Mr. Benson?" Plummer asked.

The miner, having no idea what the value of the claims was, but certain there was no more gold to be had from them, immediately accepted. Plummer found himself wishing he'd offered fifty as they walked to the assayer's office, where Benson signed his claims over to Plummer and Plummer handed the money to the astonished miner.

"Charlie, would you like employment?" Plummer asked.

The miner looked sorely confused as he pocketed the cash. "Well...yes, sure Mr. Plummer. What'd you have in mind?"

"Please be up at your former claims tomorrow morning at seven o'clock and I will be happy to show you."

Later that morning, Plummer visited a blacksmith and gave the man some instructions and a drawing he'd made at the hotel.

"What in hell you want sumpin like that fer?" the blacksmith asked frowning.

"Mining," Plummer replied.

The blacksmith spat and said he had the materials required and he would try to complete the contraption by suppertime.

19

Set up on the edge of the stream now, the waterwheel spun in the creek's swift current, turning two gears which in turn drove a cam that lifted a fifty pound hammer up and let it crash down on a thick circular iron plate with a flange running around its circumference. Thompson had uncovered a chunk of quartz and set it on the steel plate as the hammer was going up. The hammer dropped, smashing the quartz into a dozen pieces. It dropped again, and the pieces were crushed still smaller. Another drop of the hammer turned the pebbles into dust. Plummer disengaged the gear and showed the crushed quartz to his friends and to Benson. By now, the stamp mill's racket had attracted the attention of the nearby miners.

"I'll be goddamed!" cried Benson as he gazed into the plate. The others grinned.

"Mr. Plummer!" declared Tofton with an amazed grin. "You are a clever bastard, Sir!"

Gold dust and several tiny nuggets were scattered throughout the rubble on the steel plate. Thompson carefully picked the gold out, placing it in a soft doeskin bag. He looked up at Benson while he worked.

"You see, Charlie, quartz deposits usually contain gold. But quartz isn't always present. On your claim, it is, from here all the way up. That's what I was doing with the shovel yesterday. But don't feel bad. You have to know how to get at the quartz and you have to know how to extract the gold. Mr. Plummer did this quite successfully in California."

Plummer stood up. "I'll pay you ten dollars a week to dig up and crush the quartz, Charlie. But only if you can keep your mouth shut about what you've seen me do here until I've bought more claims."

In the last month, Benson hadn't seen ten dollars worth of gold dust. "Yes, Sir, Mr. Plummer," he said. "I ain't gonna say nothin'…can I start right now?"

"Mr. Thompson is going to be my foreman," he said. "He will show you how to find the quartz. But remember, Charlie," Plummer's face was now inches from Benson's and he was tapping the side of his nose with his forefinger, "not a word."

Pooling his money with Coffey's, over the next five days, Plummer bought a dozen more claims and set up the Plummer-Coffey Mining Company. He had four more stamp mills built and hired most of the miners he'd bought out to work for the new company.

"Gentlemen and Mrs. Plummer," announced Tofton one night after supper, "I have enjoyed our association immensely but the time has come for me to return home to Virginia."

Surprised, Plummer looked at the tall cavalry captain. "I had hoped our business venture here might have dissuaded you from going to war, Nolan. Why fight when you can get rich?"

Tofton was shaking his head before Plummer had finished. "No, Sir, I am afraid nothing could alter my determination to help drive the Yankee horde from my home." He leaned back in his chair. "They want us to live life their way and, in the south, Sir, we have our customs and traditions that will never be changed."

"Like slavery?" asked Thompson dryly. The officer glared at the younger man and a brittle silence hung in the air among the companions.

"Yes, like slavery, Mr. Thompson," said Tofton stiffly. "We consider slaves an institution peculiar to our way of life. You may not know that my fellow Virginians, General Washington and his colleagues, Mr. Jefferson and Mr. Madison all owned slaves."

Thompson looked down at the table. "That hardly justifies one man keeping another in bondage, Captain Tofton," he replied quietly.

Tofton suddenly slammed his hand down on the table, his face red. "A damned abolitionist, is it?!" he cried, "Why, Sir, if you and I had not been so close these last two weeks I would..."

Electa wore a look of shock at Tofton's outburst. Plummer slowly rose and placed his hand on the captain's shoulder.

"Nolan, please, calm yourself. We are on the frontier. There are diverse opinions on these matters here. Of course you have to return to your home and we all understand why." He looked around at his friends. "You have helped us immeasurably and for that, Sir, I am—we all are—forever grateful to you." He held out his hand.

Tofton, glancing back at Thompson with a frown, rose and shook Plummer's hand. His fierce look began to soften.

"We might meet some day on the field of battle, Henry," Tofton said as he held Plummer's hand, "but you have impressed me as a wise and bold man in our time together. It is my hope we both survive the war to meet again one day as friends," Tofton turned to the others. "All of us together, again. As friends." He then shook the hands of each, Thompson's last.

At first light, Tofton rode out of Bannack, south toward Salt Lake City. Coffey, Plummer and Electa watched him ride over the far ridge into a sleeting rain, his great blue cape billowing in the wind.

"I hope he gets to Virginia," Coffey said. "I can't imagine it will be an easy journey."

"No," Plummer agreed, "but I do believe Captain Tofton will find a way for himself. I'll warrant you this: Nolan is not going to be left out of the war."

The winter slammed into Bannack one late November night. After several unseasonably warm days, the temperatures plummeted and the snow fell continuously for three days and nights. Mining along with every other outdoor activity came to a halt. The wind screamed through the timbers of the buildings at night and some of the miners who lived in tents were forced into barns or any other structure that couldn't be blown down. The saloons and brothels were jammed with men whiling away their time on gambling, women and liquor.

Plummer and Electa were forced to remain in the cramped cabin on Yankee Flats that he'd rented for them from a baker a week earlier. The crude structure sat on a trail alongside several other cabins across Grasshopper Creek from Bannack's main street. Coffey and Thompson were occasional visitors, but the newly wed couple spent much of their time alone, talking about details of their respective lives before they had met.

Plummer learned Electa had been the daughter of a successful Ohio farmer whose wife had died of a fever and left him with six small children. Later he remarried, and Electa's stepmother had proven to be a shrewish and greedy woman. When she was thirteen, her father had died suddenly and her older brothers had expected to take over the farm, but their stepmother sued them, claiming she was entitled to half of everything. The subsequent sale of the farm and stock had splintered the family.

"That was when Martha and James married and asked me to live with them," she explained as the fire in the small potbellied stove crackled away. "James heard of the Sun River Farm and decided it was a wonderful opportunity to help the Indians and bring them the good news of our Savior, Jesus Christ. Martha became excited, too. I suppose I had my doubts, but they were both so determined I decided to join them."

There was a pause and Plummer smiled at her. "I am glad you did, my love."

She blushed and looked back at him earnestly. "I am, too, Henry," she said quietly. Then her brow knitted and she glanced down at her hands. "Can you tell me now about the man you hanged?"

Henry shifted in his seat, then stood and walked to the cabin's lone window. It was frosted over. He rubbed the frozen condensation off of a pane with his fingers and peered out. The sun peeked through thick gray clouds and the blowing snow glittered like tiny diamonds in the morning sky.

"This man....this animal, really...killed a rancher and his family outside of Auroria where I was the marshal," he began, his voice a monotone as he remembered seeing the disemboweled corpses of the man, his wife and their three children. "His name was Comstock. He had worked for the rancher as a hand. My deputy and I picked up his trail at Yuba City and decided he was headed to Sacramento. We rode hard and got there, but discovered we had missed him by a day. We knew he'd been there because we found an old man and his wife dead in their cabin. They'd...um...died the same way the rancher and his family had been killed."

He turned from the window and slowly walked back to his chair and sat down. He ran a finger over his dark blond mustaches then looked up at her.

"There was no call to kill the old people or the rancher and his family. He murdered them all because he enjoyed killing," he remembered. "My deputy was a good tracker so we found Comstock one morning asleep on the ground. I arrested him and brought him back to Auroria. He was tried, convicted and sentenced to hang. I kept guard on him the night before his execution and he cried like a baby."

"Did he confess his crimes?" Electa asked, her eyes wide.

"No. He was a coward," Plummer replied flatly. "He was guilty, no question. We had found the rancher's pocketbook on him along with jewelry belonging to the murdered couple."

Electa nodded and waited for him to continue. "In the morning, we had to drag Comstock to the gallows. The rancher had many friends and they were all there to see him hang. He was a big man, so it took three of us to get him onto the scaffold and he wailed and cried his innocence the whole way..."

He broke off the story and looked at her. "Hanging a man is a brutal business. Do you really want to hear about this?" After a moment's hesitation, she nodded.

Plummer let out a sigh and continued. "He fell to his knees on the trap door, so I lowered the rope and placed the noose around his neck. The trap opened and he fell through it."

She involuntarily jerked back, her eyes wide with horror.

"He swung there for five minutes or so, his feet twitching," he said quietly. "He'd fouled himself..." he looked down remembering the grotesque sight; Comstock's tongue protruding ten inches from his gaping mouth, eyes bulging out of his head, and the stench of shit and piss in the cool morning air.

They listened to the howling wind for a long while. Electa went to him, placed her hand on his shoulder and leaned down to kiss his cheek.

"I understand," she whispered.

There was a knock at the door and she opened it. Coffey stepped in, shaking the snow from his shoulders and smiling. Plummer's mood immediately brightened at the sight of his friend.

"Good morning Mr. and Mrs. Plummer!"

"Good morning, Noah," Plummer replied as Electa took their visitor's coat and hat. "How does it look out there?"

"Weather's lifting, I'm happy to say," Coffey replied. Electa poured him coffee and handed the mug to her guest. "But I'm here on a political mission, Henry, not as a weather prognosticator!"

"Oh?" Plummer replied.

"Seems the miners want you to be their sheriff!" Coffey declared.

Plummer aimed his eyes suspiciously at Coffey. "Now, where'd they get that idea from, I wonder?"

"Not I, Sir!" Coffey replied in mock indignation. "One of them—man named Stevenson, I believe—remembered you from your days as marshal in Auroria. He's been telling anyone who will listen that you should take the post of sheriff here."

Plummer regarded Coffey for a long minute, his look skeptical. "I don't remember any Stevenson," he said finally.

"Oh, come now, Henry," Coffey said. "Miners stampede to the next strike, you know that! There are scores of men here that used to mine in California. I don't know him either, but my God, there were hundreds of the fellows in Auroria. Clearly you made an impression on this Stevenson."

"I prefer my *anonymity* here, if you don't mind, Noah," Plummer responded with a meaningful glance at Electa, whose back was to the men as she tended to the biscuits she was baking.

Coffey smiled. "Of course, of course. Well, think on it anyway, Henry. A position of power like that of the sheriff wouldn't hurt our mining interests, you know."

Plummer frowned. "I'm not clear on your meaning."

Coffey's smile became uneasy. "Well, you know, policing illegal claims, perhaps identifying...um...opportunities for us..."

"That's an impertinent suggestion!" Plummer suddenly shouted. "I have never abused my position as a lawman. Nor would I ever!"

Coffey cowered in his chair. "I'm sorry, Henry...I wasn't suggesting..."

"Yes, you most certainly were!" Plummer glared at Coffey who was staring at the floor. There was a long silence. Electa opened the stove and placed some split logs on the fire.

Coffey nodded finally. "Yes, I was making that suggestion," he acknowledged. "I apologize to you, Henry, and to you as well, Electa." He rose. "I suppose I had better be on my way..."

"No you won't, Sir!" Plummer interjected in mock anger. "You'll breakfast with us first. We can't let our business partner go starving now, can we Mrs. Plummer?"

"No, indeed, Mr. Plummer," Electa said with a smile.

Plummer reached over and patted his friend's hand as he looked Coffey in the eyes. "I accept your apology, Noah. Let's speak no more of this," Plummer said earnestly. Coffey, relieved he had not damaged the friendship, smiled gratefully.

Electa served them slices of bacon, corn mush and the warm biscuits with preserved fruit and coffee. They ate, made small talk and, when they finished, Plummer rose and looked again through the frosty glass.

"What happened to the last sheriff?" he asked.

Coffey, puzzled, chewed the last bite of biscuit. "They have never had one in Bannack. The town didn't exist eighteen months ago. They need someone to mediate claim disputes and keep the peace."

"Well, that's certainly what I did in Auroria," Plummer stated. He turned to Electa, who was watching him pensively. "And there was no law there either when I was elected marshal."

"But you said you wished to remain anonymous..." Electa said.

"I do. But perhaps I could help turn Bannack into a real town instead of the glorified mining camp that it is." Plummer gestured with a disgusted look around the crude cabin's interior. "Look at this place. It was all that was available to rent, but I aim to build a real house come spring. Maybe I could become Bannack's mayor or even the territorial governor if Congress ever gets around to establishing Idaho Territory, like I have heard it will."

"Would you have to be away very much?" she asked.

"No, I don't think so," he replied with an indulgent smile. "It's not a very big town. Yet."

20

One hundred miners were gathered in the Regal Billiard Hall because it was the largest indoor space in Bannack. The men were dressed in dirty, threadbare clothes, battered hats and boots crusted with mud. Their hands were red and raw, their faces wind burned. Some wore elaborate chin whiskers or full beards while stubble covered the faces of others. The stench of wet wool and body odor was overpowering.

Plummer and Coffey entered and the miners turned to the new arrivals. Several nodded and pointed in Plummer's direction as the lawman removed his thick fur-lined gauntlet gloves and heavy black overcoat. He was neatly attired in a blue suit foxed with buckskin and a wide brimmed black hat, which he left on. He eyed the crowd with an amicable expression just as Stevenson stepped from among the miners and clapped him on the shoulder.

"Hey boys!" he called. "This here's Hank Plummer if'n you ain't had the chance to make his acquaintance as yet!"

Stevenson was a tall, gaunt fellow with dark, deep set eyes and a mane of greasy black hair that hung over his shoulders. "Now, Sir, I was in California some years back and Mr. Plummer here was the marshal of Auroria and a helluva lawman he was! He was so good, the goddamn merchants who put 'im up for election got to hate 'im on account o' he made sure they paid taxes and minded the damn fire regalations!"

There was some laughter and a general buzz of approval.

"But Hank did a lot more. He collected the taxes and give it all to the town treasury liken he's supposed to..." There was more laughter.

"An' he brought in his fair share o' road agents and other thievin' bastards. He even hanged a son of a bitch what murdered a rancher an' his family. He's honest and he'll be fair when it comes to decidin' claims. So I nominate Henry Plummer here for Bannack's first sheriff!"

There was some applause and others looked at one another and commented as they nodded their approval. Coffey looked around and then called out, "I second that nomination!"

"So, now, any a you fellas got any questions fer Hank?" Stevenson asked the crowd.

"Yeah I do," called a miner at the front of the crowd. "You been a buyin' up claims right, left and center, Plummer. How you ever gonna be fair judgin' claim disputes?"

Plummer eyed the man. He was short and stocky with grime on his face. "I have considered that issue," Plummer said, "To be completely fair, we must appoint an arbitration board of ten or twelve of you to hear and settle disputed claims. I cannot and will not do that by fiat in any event..."

Several miners looked puzzled.

"I cannot by myself tell those involved in a claim dispute how to resolve it. I don't want that sort of responsibility. What I can do is try to work out the dispute with the parties and, failing that, call a hearing of the arbitration board. In the event a dispute arises involving the claims of the Plummer and Coffey Mining Company, I will recuse myself—uh...disqualify myself—from a role in the hearing. Mr. Coffey here will be our company's sole representative."

The stocky miner rubbed his chin. "Sounds fair enough, I guess," he said finally.

A few more questions came Plummer's way and he supplied the appropriate answers. "All right, Gents," Stevenson called. "All a you wantin' Hank Plummer to be sheriff raise your hands."

The vote was nearly unanimous. "Fellas," declared Stevenson. "We gotta pay Sheriff Plummer fer his services..." Now there was grumbling. Plummer raised his hand.

"Boys, I assure you I will not get rich as sheriff," he said. "I, like you, wish to see Bannack grow and prosper. I would assume the position of sheriff only with that goal in mind. I make my money with my mining interests anyway. I propose you pay me by the service: Twenty-five cents for summoning witnesses and jurors. A dollar for serving warrants, two dollars and fifty cents for attending court trials. And twenty-five cents per mile for my travel expenses."

"That's pretty damn fair, I say," declared Stevenson, who then called for a vote. Again, most every hand was raised. Taylor McKee, the assayer, volunteered to handle the assessments of the miners as Plummer's need for pay arose.

The Plummers passed a quiet Christmas with Coffey and Thompson. The new year of 1863 began as the bitter winter gripped Bannack and all mining ceased. News of the war came infrequently in newspapers arriving from Salt Lake City. The Union was losing, that much was clear, Coffey decided, as he thumbed through a five-month old edition of a Chicago newspaper. He sat in Skinner's, nursing a whiskey, waiting out yet another snowstorm that was blasting the town.

An old heavyset man came through the door, bundled in a coat and scarf, and made his way to the bar. He drank a whiskey and ordered a second as he unwrapped himself and tossed the outerwear onto a table. He turned and looked around the poorly lit room, which was occupied at that moment by some card players, a couple of miners asleep on cots at the back of the room, and a neatly attired young fellow seated at a table by the big stove. The man had a newspaper in front of him, which he was carefully reading.

"Greetings, Sir," the old man declared, stepping over to Coffey. "May I join you here by the fire? My very bones are frozen."

Coffey looked up, smiled and nodded at the chair across from his seat. "Certainly," he said. "Did you travel through this weather today?"

"I arrived last evening from Deer Lodge before the storm began blowing in earnest," the old man replied. "I stayed at the Goodrich Hotel...my word, ten dollars per night that innkeeper gets for a room there!"

Coffey took in the threadbare suit and wide face made red by wind-blast and whiskey. He had bushy mustaches and eyebrows, and long gray side-whiskers.

"My name is Noah Coffey, Mr. ...?"

"Colgan. Exeter Colgan!" Coffey and Colgan shook hands. "I own the newspaper in Virginia City."

Coffey had heard there was a paper in the mining town some forty miles east of Bannack but he had never seen a copy of it.

"I am pleased to meet you, Mr. Colgan," Coffey replied with an easy smile. "Like you, I am a newspaperman by training. I was a correspondent for the *New York World* some years ago and the *Auroria Democrat* in California more recently."

"Really?" Colgan asked, his voice full of surprise and his eyes wide. "Then what a propitious encounter indeed!"

"Oh?" asked Coffey, "how so?"

"I am in need of an editor, Sir! That's what necessitated my journey in this terrific storm. I had to travel to meet a gentleman from Lewiston in Deer Lodge whom, after an exchange of letters, had agreed to take up the post. But he never appeared there to meet me. So much for hiring a newspaperman sight unseen, I should say!"

Coffey chuckled. The man had an engaging personality he instantly liked.

"Will you join me in a drink?" Colgan asked and, without waiting for a reply called out, "Barman! Bring my friend Mr. Coffey here a..." Coffey held up his empty whiskey glass.

Colgan, Coffey quickly learned, had been a newspaperman since his boyhood ("Ink in my veins!"). He'd begun his career in Albany, New York, and had moved from Boston to Washington before gravitating westward to Columbus, Louisville and finally, St. Louis.

"St. Louis?" Coffey interrupted. "Do you by chance know a Nathan Carter, there?"

"Carter...Carter," Colgan looked at the ceiling, "*St. Louis Informer*, I believe?"

"Yes, that is he!" Coffey said, his voice rising with emotion. Colgan eyed the younger man curiously. "I am—I was—his son-in-law. I married his daughter Rebecca in '57. She... died some months after our wedding."

"I am so sorry, my dear fellow," Colgan quietly replied. "Yes, I knew of Carter but I never met him. If I may say, he had a reputation of being a little too outspoken for his own good."

"Yes, that was Nathan to the letter," Coffey replied, recalling his first meeting with the small, sickly looking man.

"Well, Sir, might you be interested in my situation?" Colgan asked.

"Situation?" Coffey replied, confused. "Oh, you mean as editor? No, I'm afraid not. I am a partner in a mining enterprise here in Bannack."

Colgan looked disappointed but nodded his understanding. "Yes, I can see where the prospects of making your fortune in gold would eclipse any interest in scribbling..."

The door suddenly blew open and Plummer stepped into the saloon. He glanced around and spied Coffey.

"Sheriff Plummer!" Coffey cheerfully called as Plummer approached. "Meet Exeter Colgan of Virginia City..."

Coffey interrupted himself because he could see that Plummer was preoccupied. The sheriff absently nodded at the stranger then looked at Coffey.

"I have to leave for at least several days," Plummer began. "John Camden's lost his herd in this storm. I am going to try to help him recover his cattle. Thompson is coming with me. Can you look in on Electa while I am gone?"

"Of course," Coffey replied. The Camden ranch was thirty miles west of Bannack in a remote corner of the rolling high desert. "Camden rode all the way here to ask your help?"

"No, his son Paul did," Plummer replied grimly. "The kid almost froze to death."

"Good Lord!" Coffey exclaimed. Paul Camden was about twelve years old. "Where is he now?"

"With Electa. She's fed him and bedded him down." Plummer glanced at Colgan and then looked back at Coffey. "Thank you Noah. I will see you soon."

With that Henry Plummer was gone into the blizzard.

The boy was asleep under a quilt. Electa had his clothes drying before the stove. She handed Coffey a mug of tea she had poured from an iron kettle and sat in a chair across from him and resumed her knitting. The wind shook the flimsy roof of the cabin and a draft of cold air from a chink in the floorboards blew across Coffey's ankles.

Over the steam, Coffey watched her. Her brown hair was loose and her eyes shone brightly as she concentrated on her needles. She looked up at him suddenly, caught his gaze and blushed. Embarrassed, Coffey blinked, cleared his throat and glanced out the frosted window.

"It's going to be a long ride in that weather," he declared suddenly. "But I've seen Henry do this before. He knows his business."

Electa looked out the window and nodded. "I still worry. I can never, ever remember cold like this in Ohio."

"No," he replied as he sipped his tea, "Nor in Connecticut, either. It's as though we have arrived in the Arctic regions. I half expect to see white bears next!"

Her lilting laughter filled the small room and Coffey thought it sounded musical. He regarded her again and then caught a faint whiff of her scent, the pleasant fragrance of lilac soap. She was intent on her knitting and then she looked over at the sleeping boy.

"More than thirty miles. Can you believe it?" she asked Coffey, "He's just a little boy."

"Camden had no choice but to send him," Coffey replied. He recalled talking to the rancher weeks earlier and remembered the boy was the eldest of Camden's six children. "It's truly amazing he made it to Bannack at all. It speaks volumes about the fortitude of the people who settle here."

She put her knitting aside, slowly rose and walked to where the boy slept, reaching down to stroke his hair.

"This is a hard place," she whispered.

Plummer returned a week later to the day. Coffey was sitting in the lobby at Goodrich Hotel reading a book when the sheriff walked in.

"Henry!" Coffey called as he leapt up from his chair. "We were worried!"

"No need to be," Plummer replied as he pulled off his coat and removed his snow-covered hat. His face was stubbled and raw from windblast and sun. "It took us awhile to find the strays. Two were frozen solid, so old Camden gave us one of the beefs. I dragged it back here. Sold it to the butcher for two hundred dollars and split the money with Francis!"

Coffey shook his head. "Always finding a way to profit," he laughed. "Well, I am damned glad to see you alive and well, Sir! Have you been home yet?"

"No," Plummer replied curtly. "I need a drink to warm up first."

Quinn poured whiskey into a glass and Plummer washed it down gratefully in one gulp. His eyes watered at the sting of the liquor on the back of his throat. He placed the glass on the bar and the innkeeper poured another. Coffey watched his friend.

"How'er Electa and the boy?" Plummer asked as he took a seat.

"They're both fine. Paul eats like a mule."

"I am glad to hear that. He was near dead when he rode in," Plummer declared. He sipped the liquor and held the glass up at Coffey. "Join me?"

Coffey looked at the bartender who poured him a whiskey. The two friends sat chatting for an hour and then Plummer rose and pulled his coat on.

"I'll be off, then," he declared as he threw some silver coins on the bar.

Coffey resumed reading the book he'd purchased two weeks earlier from a drummer who had passed through Bannack. It was a history of the Napoleonic Wars written by a British officer who had fought the Little Emperor's forces at Waterloo.

It grew dark and the wind picked up as yet another storm began to blow through Bannack. Quinn stoked the fire in the big potbellied stove in the corner and brought another whiskey over to Coffey. Some merchants entered and quietly began a game of poker.

Coffey finished his drink and then made his way back to the room he rented in Yankee Flats from Chrisman, who owned the general store. Huddled in his overcoat, he carefully crossed the icy footbridge over the Grasshopper, the creek frozen solid. As he passed in front of the Plummers' cabin he heard loud, angry voices inside. He hurried by without stopping.

21

As Chinook winds warmed the valley floor, Bannack began thawing out. Snow and ice melted furiously and was quickly replaced everywhere by thick mud. Dead animals, buried in the snow, were exposed and began to decay in the warm sun. The miners once again worked their claims for, while winter was by no means over, the thaw made it easier to break the ice away and begin panning and sluicing. Before long, the stamp mills were pounding away at quartz and little by little, the gold found its way out of Grasshopper Creek.

A freighter hauled by fourteen mules made its way into Bannack from Salt Lake City laden with food, lumber, clothing and other goods. It was the first one seen in Bannack since late autumn. Sour moods lifted and talk turned from the oppressive cold to the hope of quick fortunes. A miner showed up at Skinner's and boasted of striking gold in nearby Rattlesnake Creek. Soon, many miners had abandoned their Grasshopper claims and moved out to camps on the banks of the Rattlesnake several miles away. Henry Plummer was on hand to buy the claims for ten cents on the dollar as they rode out of town.

"Thanks Sam," Plummer said brightly as he handed twenty dollars in greenbacks to a miner for his claim. "And good luck out there. You should do well."

The miner grumbled something and left the sheriff's office. It was a one-room affair in the back of Chrisman's store that Plummer rented for five dollars a week. From his window overlooking the Grasshopper, Plummer could keep an eye on the new jail that was under construction behind the store as well as his claims along the creek. As he watched the workmen he'd hired place the rough-hewn logs, he recalled how he'd had to pry the two-dollar assessment out of most of the merchants in Bannack to build the jail.

"Wouldn't it just be easier to hang 'em, Hank?" one had asked him as he reluctantly handed over his coins.

He watched through the window as Francis Thompson was setting up a new stamp mill with the help of Coffey and Charlie Benson.

"God damn you Charlie! Be careful!" screamed Thompson as the miner dropped the heavy hammer assembly into the mud. Coffey helped the miner lift it out and set it on the mill's frame.

Plummer smiled to himself as he walked out onto the boardwalk in front of the store intent on dinner at the Goodrich. He eyed the mud and animal droppings in the street then carefully crossed, trying to place his newly polished boots in whatever dry spots he could find.

"Afternoon, Sheriff," Quinn called as Plummer entered the hotel. "There's a big fella in back been askin' about you."

Plummer paused, frowned, then slowly walked into the saloon. He kept his hand on the LeMat as he entered. The room appeared vacant except for a figure seated in the far corner backlit by the window behind him. Plummer ordered a whiskey, which he slowly sipped. He casually turned and looked the stranger's way.

"You remember me, don't ya, Plummer?" the figure asked.

"Cleveland."

The man responded with a roar of laughter as he stood and approached the bar. Tom Cleveland wore a full beard that was flecked with food and dirt. His clothes were shabby and his boots were covered with mud. He wore a Mexican style hat back on his head, and despite his laughter, his tiny black eyes beneath a heavy brow darted warily around the room.

"Been a long time, Plummer," Cleveland laughed. "Ain't seen you since..."

"That's *Sheriff* Plummer!"

Cleveland instantly stopped laughing. He stood over Plummer, the top of his hat brushing the saloon's ceiling.

Despite his bulk, Plummer stepped over and grabbed Cleveland by the arm. "Why don't we step over to my office for a private talk, Tom?"

Plummer led the way back across the street. He closed his office door, sat in his seat and studied Cleveland, who remained standing on the other side of the desk. The sheriff said nothing and as the silence grew increasingly uncomfortable, Cleveland began to fidget, his black, rat-like eyes bouncing around in his head.

"Sure am glad to see you's healthy, Hank," Cleveland finally blurted.

"I'll tell you for the last time," Plummer said in a monotone. "It's Sheriff Plummer."

The eyes stopped darting for a second and stared at Plummer.

"Sorry, *Sheriff*," he said, his tone mocking. "Leastways, like I said, I am glad you is healthy."

"How did you find me, Cleveland?" Plummer demanded. He was growing impatient with the big man's pretensions of goodwill and his feral odor. "And what is it you want?"

"Well, Sir," Cleveland replied. "Army fella in Benton mentioned your name an' said you was at that gov'ment farm. The one at Sun River. I went there and Jim Vail tol' me you was in Bannack. I thought I might find me some work with you minin' gold, seein's how close we was at Quentin…"

"You talked to Vail?!" Plummer exclaimed.

"Sure. I tol' him we was ol' friends…"

"You're wrong Cleveland," Plummer snarled, "We were *never* friends."

Plummer shot to his feet. Even though he was six inches taller and one hundred pounds heavier than Plummer, Cleveland appeared to shrink under the sheriff's withering glare. "And do not mention San Quentin around me or in this town again. If you do, I will shoot you down like a dog."

For emphasis, Plummer snapped the LeMat out of the holster. He leveled the weapon at Cleveland's chest and cocked it, producing tiny beads of sweat on the big man's expansive forehead.

"Now, you want a job?" Plummer asked. He pointed out the window. "You go down there and tell my foreman I want you to clear ice. He'll give you the tools. But if I hear you mention that place or anything about me from back in those days, you are a dead man. Do we understand each other?"

Plummer holstered the piece and glared up at Cleveland, who

offered him a smirk.

"Yes, Sir, Han…Sheriff Plummer. And thank ya' kindly."

As the big man left the office Coffey entered, squeezing past Cleveland's bulk. He stood for a moment observing his friend. Plummer's face was gray, his lips white.

"Henry?" Coffey asked gently. "Are you all right?"

Plummer nodded. "Shut the door," he said as he took his seat and shifted his gaze out the window overlooking the creek. "That was Tom Cleveland. Remember him?"

Coffey thought a moment. "The prisoner in the cell across from yours at San Quentin?"

"Yes," Plummer grimly replied. "And now he's here. In fact, I just hired him."

Plummer watched through the window as Cleveland made his way through wet, knee-deep snow to the creek where he stood before Thompson. As he spoke to the foreman, he pointed back at the office and Thompson nodded and handed him a pick ax and shovel and pointed upstream. Cleveland started ambling in the direction indicated by Thompson.

"Why?" asked Coffey.

"Because if I order him to leave town, he will start talking. And I can't just kill him. So I will need to keep Cleveland close," Plummer explained. "At least until I decide what to do about him. If he starts running his mouth here I will be forced to leave. Nobody will care about the circumstances behind my…conviction…only the fact that I was sent to prison will matter to them. I'll be ruined in Bannack."

He's right, Coffey thought to himself, *a reputation often took years to attain and could be lost with just a careless word or two.*

Plummer finally stood and looked at Coffey. "I have to leave for a few days again. Business in Nevada City," he explained. "I have to hire and deputize a couple of men there. Will you look after things for me?"

Coffey nodded his head as a wave of anguish swept over him.

That evening, as the sun set, the warm air brought out the first flood of tiny insects. They didn't seem to know another cold front would soon arrive and eradicate them entirely. They were just happy to be flitting around in shadows, oblivious to their impending doom.

Yankee Flats was asleep as Coffey slipped from his room at the Chrisman house and crept through the dark passages between the shacks and cabins. He let himself into Plummer's cabin and, undressing, found Electa ready for him beneath the quilt. She wrapped herself around him and thrust her hips into his. She bit him to stop herself from crying out as Coffey plunged into her. She rolled him over and rode him, her head back as she was racked by the pulsing sensations. He cupped her breasts in his hands and closed his eyes as he shuddered. She reached down and put her hand over his mouth, stifling his moan.

The room was too warm. Coffey and Electa lay naked on the bed, slick with sweat. She kissed his neck and caressed him beneath the sheets. He felt himself stir even though it had been mere minutes since he had climaxed. He looked down at her and wondered why Plummer ever left Bannack. Electa was insatiable and while Coffey's experiences with women were limited, she was clearly capable of pleasing a man. What was wrong with Henry?

It had started a month ago. Both were shocked when, as they stood at the window watching the snow fall, Plummer away again, they had fallen into each other's arms. It had been spontaneous and electric, born of loneliness and mutual desire. Afterwards, Coffey had been miserable and ashamed. But he'd stayed silent when the sheriff returned and so had Electa.

"This is dangerous," he whispered to her. "People talk here and I'm worried rumors will start."

"We're too careful," she replied. She gripped him firmly. "And you are far too stealthy, Mr. Coffey." She began stroking him as he closed his eyes. After they had made love again, he kissed her, rose, dressed, slid back through the door and disappeared. He prayed he was indeed stealthy as he crept through shadows on his way home. Henry Plummer would surely kill him if he knew.

Tom Cleveland stood swaying in the center of Skinner's Saloon. He held a whiskey bottle in one massive hand and a revolver in the other. He could barely stand as he glared at the crowd of miners. Some warily watched the pistol. Others ignored him.

"Lemme tell you bastards sumpin!" he declared. "There ain't a single man hereabouts who I cannot beat to a bloody pulp!" He took a pull off the bottle but most of the liquor found its way into his filthy beard. His beady eyes flickered as he grinned, exposing sharp little teeth. "Who wants a go a round with me? Who wants a dance wi' Tom Cleveland? Not even the great Henry Plummer wants t' deal with me...I could tell you stories about that son of a bitch..."

"Come on Tom," a miner finally yelled over to him. "Put that pistol up and take it easy!"

Cleveland glanced over in the direction of the man then raised the revolver and fired it through the roof. The ear-shattering blast momentarily stopped all conversation.

"You shithead, Cleveland!" cried Cyrus Skinner. "Get that gun away from him, somebody!"

Buzz Caven rose from his chair. He was a small man with a bantam rooster's temper and predisposition to fight. He had a wiry frame and thick wrists. He strode up behind Cleveland, reached around and snatched the revolver from the drunken man's hand. Cleveland lurched to face Caven with a growl, but the small man brought his boot up between Cleveland's legs and kicked the big man's testicles. Cleveland dropped to the floor clutching his balls as the spectators roared with laughter. Caven handed the weapon to Skinner.

"Thanks, dep'ty," Skinner grinned. "Let me buy you a drink."

Plummer walked in at that moment. He glanced at Cleveland lying on the floor then over at Caven. "What was the gunshot I heard, Buzz?"

Caven, a man of very few words, tilted his head in the direction of the groaning Cleveland lying on the filthy wooden floor.

"Runnin' his mouth again, Sheriff," Caven said flatly.

Plummer walked over to Cleveland and helped him to his feet, walked him to the saloon's door, then pushed him into the street.

"He say anything?" Plummer asked matter of factly as he took a seat across from the deputy. Caven shrugged absently, completely absorbed by the cards in his hand. "Buzz? He say anything?"

"Oh, some bullshit about stories he could tell...I weren't listnin' to him,

Hank," Caven replied as he stared at his cards. The man was Plummer's least favorite of the three deputies he'd hired in Bannack. But Caven was a man of action, the kind Plummer would always want covering his back.

Plummer stood up and walked out into the street. It was fiercely cold again. A front had moved in from the northwest that morning. Cold rain had turned to sleet by afternoon. Now it was snowing and the mud was beginning to freeze in the street even though it was almost April.

He found Cleveland leaning against the wall of the blacksmith's shop, doubled over and retching. As he got close, Plummer caught the stench of the man's dirty body and his vomit. With each gasping breath, Cleveland emitted a steamy cloud of vapor that stunk of rancid alcohol. When he heard the sheriff's approach, he stood up and stared, horrified, as he watched Plummer draw the LeMat from his holster.

"You have some stories to tell, I understand?" Plummer asked, his voice tight with rage.

The rat eyes darted about. "Naw, Sheriff...I was talkin' about..."

Plummer slowly cocked the hammer. "I thought we had an agreement."

"We do! We do, Sheriff Plummer!" the big man cried desperately. "Oh God, please don't kill me!" Plummer stepped back in disgust as he realized Cleveland had urinated in his trousers.

"You see this middle barrel here?" he held the pistol up between Cleveland's eyes so he couldn't miss it. "There's a big charge of buckshot in there. I will put it through your head if I hear you have mentioned my name again, drunk or not. Last warning, Tom."

With that, Plummer uncocked the weapon, slipped it into the holster and strode off, disappearing into the black night. Cleveland began weeping as he slumped down the wall before he fell onto his backside into the cold mud.

22

Thompson sat on the wagon's bench, ready to leave for Salt Lake City. The weather had warmed as the Chinooks blew down through the canyons. Rivulets of water coursed through the thick sludge in the street, so pedestrians were splashed with slop whenever a wagon or horse passed by.

"I should be back in a month's time, Henry," Thompson said as he prepared to depart. "Anything else you can think of?"

"No, the tools and the stamp mill parts are pretty much it," Plummer replied. It was cheaper to buy parts like the gears he needed than have the blacksmith fabricate them. "If you can find me one of those Spencer repeating rifles, I'd sure appreciate it. But I hear the army's buying all that are manufactured these days."

Thompson's list included food, dry goods, blankets, new clothes for Henry and Electa, and the lumber needed for the house Henry was planning to build. Plummer touched his hat, smiled at Thompson and stepped back as the wagon rolled away. He walked back over the footbridge to Yankee Flats, so named because those with Northern sympathies had made their homes there while the miners favoring the South lived in the town proper. He found Electa in the cabin. She, like most all of the town's respectable women, stayed off the streets of Bannack.

He saw she was in a melancholy mood again. Plummer said nothing as he poured coffee into a cup. He sat at the small table and began perusing a newspaper that had arrived earlier in the day on the stagecoach from Virginia City. He heard a sniff and turned to regard Electa. She had tears in her eyes. She was staring off through the window at the willow trees just outside. Tiny green buds had begun appearing on their wispy branches.

He rose and walked to her, knelt in front of her and took her hands in his. "I am truly sorry for bringing you here, my love," he said quietly. "I know this is a rough place."

She didn't look at him. He watched as a tear dropped from her eye.

"God I miss, Noah," he declared as he stood up. "He always made you laugh. I wonder how he is faring in Virginia City."

More tears fell and she dabbed her eyes with a handkerchief, but said nothing in response.

"It's nice of him to forward the newspapers to us. He knows how much I miss the doings of the outside world," Plummer remarked, trying to sound cheerful. "My, what a fine day. Would you care to walk with me out to the meadow?"

She shook her head.

Plummer felt himself growing impatient with her. "Very well," he said, his voice growing stern. "Then I have business to attend to. There has been a robbery on the road to Alder Gulch. Road agents."

She didn't reply. He glared at her for a moment, finished his coffee, and left the cabin.

Dillingham was ready to ride. The tall deputy was of a better class than Caven and the others Plummer had found for the job. Miners were too busy trying to get rich and ranchers had better things to do then serve as lawmen. So he'd had to settle for reformed troublemakers and, in Ned Ray's case, an ex-criminal. That he himself had once been a convict was not lost on the sheriff as he mounted his new horse, a black gelding he'd named Lincoln.

"Nice mornin'," Dillingham observed as the two lawmen followed the trail out of Bannack and across the desert of rock and sage that was still sprinkled with clumps of snow.

J. W. Dillingham was about six feet tall, with a long, handsome face. He wore neat mustaches and kept his face shaved. His clothing was always clean and his boots were free of dirt. Plummer thought he might be about thirty years old. Dillingham said he was from Texas, but had no particular sympathies for the Confederacy. He had been a Ranger down around his home in San Antonio before the war, where he had fought Comanches along the Rio Grande.

The two men had met one night at the Wisdom Ranch, a way station for the stage that ran between Deer Lodge and Bannack. Both men were sheltering from a bitterly cold night. Over supper, Dillingham had agreed to become a deputy, although Plummer knew it was only a matter of time until the Texan moved on. Still, he was Plummer's favorite deputy and by far his best trained and most capable.

"Indeed it is, Jack," replied Plummer, still preoccupied by Electa's mood. "Did Wells give you any more information this morning about the killing?"

"He thinks it might have been Horan and a couple of others," Dillingham said as they rode side by side through the crisp morning air. Just ahead, the snowcapped mountain peaks of the Beaverhead and Ruby ranges jutted into the blue sky. "Wells was a fool to try to make that trip loaded down with dust like he was and only his boy to ride shotgun."

Virgil Wells and his sixteen year old son, Jamie, had attempted to take their gold out of Nevada City to Bannack, where Wells had heard he could get a better price for it. Their wagon had been stopped in the Ruby Valley by three masked road agents during the late afternoon two days ago. One of the robbers, Wells recalled, had long blond hair. The boy had tried to make a play with his carbine and was shot down as his father looked on.

The distraught Virgil Wells had appeared at Plummer's office the night before. Plummer had looked at the boy's mangled body in the bed of the wagon. Bullets and shot had nearly cut him in half. Dillingham had gently calmed the father and coaxed from him the story of what had happened. Along with his boy, he'd lost at least five thousand dollars in gold dust and nuggets.

"John Horan," Plummer declared. "Well that figures. I almost shot him in Bannack a couple of months ago."

The sheriff remembered Horan as a young man with a high regard for his own prowess with a pistol. He had arrived in Bannack in February and had immediately raised hell. He'd gotten into a brawl at Skinner's with some miners then pulled his Colt when it looked as though they would beat him to death. Plummer had walked in toward the end of the melee, just as Horan backed his four attackers into a corner and looked as though he was going to shoot them all.

"Enough!" Plummer had commanded. Horan cut his eyes to the sheriff and grinned.

"These sons o' bitches need t' be taught a lesson, Mr. Plummer," Horan had cried out, his voice on the edge of hysteria. "They're goddamn nigger lovers and think that cocksucker Abe Lincoln's gonna whip the South!"

"Well, that happens to be what I believe, too," Plummer replied without missing a beat, his own pistol leveled at Horan. "Now put the gun in your holster and be on your way out of town, Johnny. And don't come back."

Horan slowly turned his head, his maniacal grin twitching. He'd lost his hat in the fight and his hair was a blond tangle that hung to his shoulders. Blood trickled from his mouth and nose and he had an ugly bruise under his eye. He regarded Plummer with wild blue eyes, then slowly holstered his Colt.

"Sure, Sheriff," he snarled. He picked up his hat, shot one last menacing glance at the miners and pushed past Plummer as he left.

Plummer wasn't surprised that Wells thought Horan was the desperado. He had heard rumors that Horan had been a road agent in California and that he had even ridden with the notorious Rattlesnake Dick in Nevada. He remembered the crazy look in the kid's eye and shuddered.

The day of searching was fruitless and by nightfall, Plummer and Dillingham were camped along the Ruby River, twenty miles west of Virginia City. They'd built a small cook fire and the deputy had fried some bacon. As they finished eating, they heard rustling in the nearby sage. Dillingham froze and Plummer drew the LeMat as he rose to one knee.

"Hello the camp!" a voice called from the darkness.

"Who goes there?" Plummer challenged.

"A friend! I means no harm," the voice replied cheerfully.

"Come!" called Plummer. They watched as a figure appeared from the sagebrush. It was John Horan. Plummer glanced at Dillingham and shook his head as he holstered his weapon. The young man walked into the campsite leading a handsome spackled mare.

Horan's eyes widened in surprise as he recognized Plummer, but he made no hostile move. "Well, Sir, if it ain't Sheriff Plummer!" he exclaimed good-naturedly. He looked in Dillingham's direction. "And you, Sir?"

"He's my deputy, Jack Dillingham," Plummer interjected. "Welcome, Johnny. You hungry?"

Still reeling from his chance encounter with the two lawmen in the vast rangeland, Horan blinked a couple of times and then grinned. "Sure am, Sheriff. Smelled that there bacon a mile off!"

Dillingham handed a tin plate heaped with bacon and cold biscuits to Horan, who grabbed it without thanks and began cramming food into his mouth. The fire crackled as a gust of cold wind lifted tiny sparks skyward. Horan finished his meal, licked his fingers and pulled a flask from his vest. He held it out to Plummer. "Drink?" he asked with a smile, his eyebrows raised.

Plummer took a sip and passed the flask to Dillingham who followed suit.

"Why are you way out here, John?" Plummer asked quietly as his deputy handed the flask back to Horan.

"On my way to Nevada City," Horan responded, his eyes blinking rapidly. Plummer guessed he might be about his own age. He was clean-shaven except for a clump of chin whiskers. His thick blond hair hung from his hat in a loosely tied ponytail. "I got me some business up that a way."

"What kind of business?" Plummer asked.

"Well, no offense intended, Sheriff, but that ain't none of your business," Horan replied with a lopsided grin.

Plummer shrugged. "Just wondering, John, that's all. Since I ran you out of Bannack, what have you been doing to keep yourself busy?"

The grin disappeared. "This an' that. Mostly a little minin'."

"Oh?" Plummer coolly replied. "Anything else I might be interested in?"

Horan stared across the fire at Plummer. "No, Sir, I don't think so."

Plummer pursed his lips and nodded. "The reason I ask, John, is because there was a killing out this way three days ago. A kid got himself shot by three masked road agents. His daddy was robbed. You know anything about that?"

As he was speaking, Plummer noticed Horan's eyes were growing wider. Seeing Horan distracted, Dillingham had reached behind his back, found his pistol and held it ready, out of sight.

Horan abruptly rose to his feet and began walking briskly to his horse. "Can't help you at all with that one, Sheriff," he said over his shoulder. "But I'm obliged for the vittles..."

"Stop!" Dillingham ordered. "Turn around, drop your piece, walk back over here and set down." The Texan was standing, his revolver on Horan. Plummer watched from where he was seated as the kid did as he was told. The sheriff held his LeMat on the prisoner as Dillingham walked over to Horan's horse and began going through the saddlebags.

"You really can't help us?" Plummer asked. "It would go a damn sight easier for you if you could."

Gritting his teeth, Horan stared into the fire and said nothing.

"Looks like you're doin' real good minin', young fella," Dillingham remarked as he walked back to the fire. He dropped a brown leather bag next to Plummer's feet. The sheriff opened the drawstrings and peered into it as Dillingham trained his Colt on Horan.

"Well, I should say so!" Plummer exclaimed.

"Two more pokes like that in the saddlebag, Hank. His share. And then there's this," said the deputy as he handed a carbine to Plummer. The initials *J.W.* were clearly etched into the wooden stock.

"Well, I know for a fact this piece doesn't belong to you, Jack," Plummer said to Dillingham as he studied the weapon. "So it must be Jamie Wells's. I'm sure his pap will identify it as such just like he'll identify his gold here." He looked up at Horan and frowned. "That was the boy's name, Johnny; Jamie Wells, the kid you killed the other day."

Horan bit his lip and nervously glanced over at Plummer. Despite the chill, there was perspiration running down his face. "It weren't me what shot that boy, Sheriff!" he suddenly yelled, his eyes crazy.

"Well then who the hell killed him, Horan?!" Plummer demanded as he stood and pulled the man to his feet. Dillingham was shocked at the sudden change in the sheriff's tone and mood. "You best tell me, you bastard, because

I'm going to hang you either way!"

Horan's blue eyes darted around as he considered the consequences of blowing. He made his decision to say nothing. Plummer shrugged again, pulled some twine out of his saddlebag and tied Horan's hands behind his back.

"Have it your way, John," he said quietly as he cinched off a knot. We'll take you into Bannack in the morning. The miners court can deal with you."

There was just one lawyer in Bannack, so Plummer appointed Morris Reynolds to serve as the trial judge. He was a nervous middle-aged man with a long, crane-like neck and pronounced jaw.

"But, Sheriff," Reynolds had protested, "I'm only familiar with civil law."

"You studied criminal law, didn't you?" Plummer asked.

"Well, yes, of course, in law school many years ago, but as I say…"

"Then you know more about it than anyone else in Bannack."

Plummer appointed himself prosecutor and the town's only doctor was Horan's counsel. All miners who attended would serve as jurors. The trial proved to be a chaotic affair held in Cyrus Skinner's saloon. Men spilled out of the cramped barroom onto the street and miners made loud comments throughout the trial while others ambled in and out for drinks. Skinner was only too happy to supply the liquor, the trial proving a boon to his business.

Squeezed into the back of the room were some of Horan's friends, one of whom was Tom Cleveland. Arms crossed or hands fingering their side arms, the group glared out at the miners seated or standing around them throughout the testimony. Some of the miners watched them warily and began to realize the danger they'd be in if they didn't vote to acquit Horan.

Plummer was the first to testify. Then he had Dillingham tell the court of finding the carbine and gold. He held up the weapon and bag as evidence. Then Virgil Wells was called to the stand. He was about forty, stooped and haggard looking, with several days of growth on his face. His eyes were rimmed with red as he took his seat, where Plummer led him through the events of the robbery.

"…and Mr. Wells, is one of the men who shot your son Jamie present in this courtroom?"

Voices called out from the crowd of miners and Horan's gang hissed.

"Silence!" cried Reynolds, who was warming to the task of serving as judge. "You *will* be silent!"

"Yes, Sir," the bereaved father said quietly. He pointed at Horan who sat ten feet away. "John Horan was one of 'em."

"That's a fuckin' lie!" yelled Cleveland in a drunken voice.

"You! Leave this courtroom immediately!" Reynolds commanded, his face red with embarrassment at the foul language.

Caven pushed through the crowd and grabbed Cleveland's arm. The little deputy began pulling the unsteady giant toward the door and some big miners assisted him, getting up from their chairs and shoving Cleveland roughly from behind.

"This ain't right!" Cleveland screamed as he resisted. "You can't convict Johnny on the word of that lyin' sheriff. Hell, he's a convict hisself! I know all about Sheriff Henry goddamn Plummer!"

In the turmoil that followed Cleveland's ejection from the courtroom, Plummer stood staring at the floor as he felt his stomach turn somersaults and the burning on his face. Several miners glanced Plummer's way and Reynolds was now staring at him. Plummer slowly regained his composure, ignored the looks and began his questioning again.

"Mr. Wells, how do you know it was John Horan?" he asked. "You testified the men were all masked."

"I could see that blond hair a his hangin' to his shoulders," replied Wells. "Ain't nobody I ever seen 'round these parts wears their hair like that 'ceptin Horan."

Plummer asked several more questions and then rested his case.

The judge called Plummer forward. "What in the hell was Tom Cleveland yelling about, Henry?" he asked.

"Cleveland? He was drunk again, Morris," the sheriff replied. "He was going to say anything that came to his head to disrupt the trial. It's late. How do you want to handle the poll?"

Reynolds considered the question then looked at the toughs at the back of the room. "All right, Gentlemen," he called out to the assembly. "You've heard the evidence against John Horan. He's accused of the murder of young Jamie Wells, late of Bannack. He is charged in a second count of armed robbery of Virgil Wells."

Horan's friends began loudly protesting but Plummer looked their way with a scowl. "You men!" he shouted, pointing at the group. "Shut up or I will jail you right now and charge you all with obstruction of justice!"

Plummer recognized Frosty Stump, who pointed back at him.

"Hey, Sheriff...what was Tom talkin' about when they dragged him outta here?"

Enraged, Plummer pulled the LeMat and strode toward the knot of Horan's friends, pushing his way through the crowd. He knew Cleveland had been talking after all and cursed himself for not shooting him when he had the chance.

"What was that?" he asked as he stood before Stump, who was about Plummer's height. He wore a soiled dandy's suit and plug hat. His face was narrow and one of his eyes was cocked in the wrong direction. "You had a question about the legal proceedings here?"

Stump tried to back up but he was already against the wall. "Just that Tom there made a point about your viability as a lawman..."

"*Viability?*" Plummer mocked. He placed the LeMat's barrel against Stump's nose. "That's a big word for you, isn't it Frosty? Well, here's my viability." He pushed the pistol's muzzle into Stump's nostril. The man's eyes opened wide in terror. "You and the rest of this trash get out. We're about to poll the jury to see if your friend Mr. Horan goes free or hangs."

Plummer stepped back. Stump and the rest of Horan's friends filed out without another word.

"I want two of you men here," Reynolds declared as he pointed at a spot to his left. "And I want two men there." He pointed to his right.

Four miners came forward and did as directed. The judge continued: "You men stand side by side facing toward me with room enough between you for a man to pass. Then I want those who believe Horan is innocent to pass between Jim and Dan there and those who think he's guilty to walk between this gentleman—I am sorry Sir, I do not know your name—and Sonny there. When you have voted, I want you to leave the courtroom. Deputy Caven, will you count the innocent votes? Sheriff Plummer, will you please count the guilty votes?"

Nearly all of the miners passed between the human gate that represented guilt. Horan's friends were allowed back into the saloon and theirs constituted the majority of innocent votes. When they returned to the street in front of Skinner's, fistfights broke out between Horan's supporters and the miners who had voted guilty. Dillingham and Caven managed to wedge themselves into the brawl and restore order.

After the poll was completed, the judge let all the miners return. "John Horan, you have been found guilty of murder and armed robbery. This court sentences you to hang by the neck until dead. Sheriff?"

A cheer went up at the prospect of a hanging as Plummer stepped forward, tied Horan's arms loosely behind his back and led him outside. Caven and Dillingham pushed through the crowd and led Plummer and the condemned man to the gallows a carpenter had constructed earlier in the day in a lonely gulch a hundred yards from the main street. A stout beam had been anchored between two upright posts that stood about ten feet high. The crowd of miners followed the doomed man's procession, with several of the bigger men holding off Horan's friends with barrel staves. Reynolds and Plummer had decided earlier that the execution would be carried out immediately to prevent any rescue of Horan.

The early spring sun was falling behind the hills as they reached the gallows. Horan wore a defeated look and seemed to Plummer as though he'd accepted his fate. The noisy crowd gathered around, shoving and calling out at the condemned Horan. Caven and Dillingham held the excited spectators at bay with their shotguns while Plummer helped Horan onto a scaffold that stood four feet off the ground. He removed Horan's hat, pushed the blond locks back and set the noose around his neck, letting the hangman's knot rest on his right shoulder.

Horan's blue eyes met Plummer's. "Sheriff, I did steal Wells's gold and the gun, but I swear I didn't shoot that boy," Horan said quietly, his voice earnest.

"John, who did kill the kid? I can't save you now, but I can make damn sure whoever it was that pulled the trigger swings, too."

Horan swallowed, started to speak, then shook his head and looked at the ground beneath the scaffold. "Can I pray at least?"

Plummer nodded and stepped back.

"Oh God," Horan called out as he looked skyward, "please accept my sinner's soul. I ain't been a good man but I ain't never killed nobody neither. All I ask for is Your forgiveness when I get to the gates of Glory!"

Without another word, Horan stepped off the scaffold. Plummer watched as the man kicked and lurched at the end of the rope. Horan's blue eyes bulged and the front of his trousers were wet. The crowd cheered and some shots were fired in celebration. But not all of the men were joyous. In the waning light, Plummer could see others staring in shock at the dead man's final spasms.

"That's it. Go home now," Plummer at last commanded.

On a nearby hill overlooking the scene, Electa looked on, her face a mask of horror.

23

The cabin was silent and dark. The wind had come up, rattling the eaves as Plummer lit a candle and looked around. Electa had been sitting in the dark staring into space. Plummer silently took off his coat and hat. He went to the basin and splashed water on his face, then dried off with a small hand towel.

"Now I know what you do," Electa said in a toneless voice.

Plummer looked at her face in the guttering candlelight. It was completely expressionless. He poured water into a glass from a pitcher at the sideboard and drank. He could hear in the distance the celebration continuing at Skinner's. An occasional gunshot rang out and drunken men whooped and hollered.

"I'm a lawman, Electa," he replied, but his own voice sounded unconvincing, even to him.

"Yes, you're a lawman," she said, her voice rising in anger. "And from what I saw tonight you appear to enjoy the work you do."

He felt bile rise in his throat. "You saw?"

"Yes, I saw everything you did!" she replied through hot tears, "I heard that man's pitiful prayer. I saw you put the rope around his neck!"

"Goddamn it, Electa!" he snapped. "Horan was a murderer! You *didn't* see the body of the Wells boy he killed but I did! He *had* to hang!"

"Yes, and the great Sheriff Henry Plummer is just the man for the job!" she cried out. "You're no better than that man you hanged. You killed him! And you *liked* it!"

He stepped forward and slapped her hard across the face with the back of his hand. She screamed in pain and surprise at the sudden violence. Then she stared at him silently, tears streaming down her face, a red welt growing on her cheek from the blow. He was breathing heavily as he abruptly turned and left the cabin.

On the walk up the street, Plummer seethed with anger and remorse. He had never before struck a woman, let alone one he loved as much as he loved Electa. Coatless and hatless, he stepped into Skinner's. The saloon was still jammed, even though it was well past midnight. A miner sat in the corner, eyes closed, scraping out off-key tunes on a fiddle. Thick smoke from dozens of pipes and cigars hung in a dim haze. Plummer gulped back a whiskey, then heard a familiar voice on the other side of the room.

"Horan didn't have no fuckin' chance!" Cleveland declared in a loud, drunken voice to a crowd of men seated around a large table by the stove. "You call *that* a trial? You can't believe a goddamn thing Plummer nor any of his deputies say...they're the law in Bannack? Shit! They're nothin' but criminals theyselves..."

As he finished speaking, Cleveland saw Plummer's murderous eyes. Several miners who'd been listening to Cleveland followed his eyes to the sheriff at the bar. Men standing or sitting between Plummer and Cleveland quickly backed away.

"Sheriff, Tom don't know what he's saying," one of Cleveland's companions appealed. It was Frosty Stump. "He's drunk...and ain't nobody listenin' anyways."

"I've had enough!" Plummer declared, his voice firm. "Stand up Tom."

"He ain't armed, Sheriff!" called a miner seated next to Cleveland.

"Then give him a weapon!"

Skinner walked around from behind the bar holding a holstered Colt. He handed it to Cleveland, then looked at Plummer. "Take it out in the street, Sheriff. Please?" pleaded Skinner.

Plummer ignored him. "Put it on!" Plummer ordered Cleveland.

The big man stood dumbly holding the gun belt, seeming not to understand what it was for. "Hank...Sheriff Plummer... I... I can't fight you," Cleveland said, his voice almost a whisper. "You'll kill me."

"That's right, Tom. I *will* kill you." Plummer's voice was as cold as his gray eyes. "In fact, you'll be the second man I've killed tonight."

Cleveland began to weep. He looked down at the belt and slowly, reluctantly strapped it around his thick waist. "Sheriff Plummer...I ain't no match for you..."

"Shut up you coward!" Plummer cried out. "Fight me like a man."

Several miners tried again to intervene.

"All of you, shut up!" Plummer said between gritted teeth. "Cleveland knows what this is about and it has nothing to do with anybody else here. If you don't want to watch, leave."

"I ain't no gunfighter, boys," Cleveland pleaded, his wet beady eyes darting around the saloon. "This ain't a fair fight!"

"I'll let you pull your piece first *and* cock it," Plummer replied. "But you *will* fight me."

"Come on, Sheriff, let it go!" cried a man behind Plummer.

"Yeah, Plummer, this ain't right!" called another. "Tom's been drinkin' in here all night! He's just got a big mouth is all..."

Plummer ignored them all. "Make your play, Tom."

The bearded giant hesitated. His hands shook. He swallowed hard before focusing his rodent's eyes on Plummer. For once they stopped dancing in his head and, despite their dampness, his eyes turned dark and resigned. His huge hands stopped shaking.

"Pull and cock? Right, Plummer?" he asked.

Plummer nodded once.

Cleveland swallowed again, then quickly drew the Colt and pulled the hammer back, aiming it at Plummer's chest as he did. He pulled the trigger. Nothing happened. He had only cocked the weapon to its safety position. He hadn't pulled the hammer back to full cock. He realized his mistake too late. Plummer drew the LeMat, and just as he'd promised Cleveland, he fired the center barrel containing the buckshot into the big man's forehead. Cleveland's Mexican hat was snatched off his head as brains and blood splattered the wall behind him. A bloody flap of skull and hair now hung loosely down to the dead man's shoulder.

Cleveland stood staring with sightless eyes for many seconds as men dumbly stepped back to the farthest walls of the room. He swayed slightly. His lips moved as though he was trying to speak, but he collapsed forward across the table in front of him, splintering its legs and crashing to the floor.

"Jesus, Mary and Joseph!" cried an Irishman nearest Cleveland. His face was pale as he stared at the gaping wound on top of Tom Cleveland's head just inches away.

"All of you, get out!" said Plummer as he holstered his weapon. "Saloon's closed."

"You murdered Tom!" Stump said defiantly as he stood before Plummer jabbing his forefinger in Plummer's chest. "We all seen it. You might be the law, Plummer, but you can't shoot men down like dogs fer nothin'!"

Plummer looked down at the prodding finger. "Take your hands off me or I'll kill you, too."

"I'm takin' this up with the miners court!" Stump declared as he dropped his hand. "You ain't heard the last a *this* killin' you son of a bitch!" With that he stalked off with several other men who were muttering condemnations of Plummer as they left the saloon.

162 Kevin Emmet Foley

Part Three

From the Journals
of
Noah Coffey

24

Virginia City
Idaho Territory
April 12, 1863

Since arriving here a month ago I have been discouraged by Colgan and his drinking. He shows up each morning and looks over some of my work but by eleven o'clock he is usually gone, claiming an "appointment" which always seems to take him to the Bale of Hay saloon. Along with writing dispatches, I am responsible for selling advertising and running the old cylindrical printing press. Colgan was well pleased when he discovered the latter skill because he was able to dismiss the old man he had setting type, thus saving himself a salary.

We publish the *Virginia City Tribune* when we have enough copy and enough advertising, which is to say about every three to five days. This leaves ample time for me to consider the wisdom of taking Colgan's situation. Letters from Electa arrive for me on the stage from Bannack every few days. She is lonely and bitterly unhappy in her marriage. I have not answered any of them, and the last several have sounded increasingly desperate.

I could not betray Henry any longer. I told her that the last night we were together. I love Electa but she is, and always will be, Henry's wife. He was surprised when I told him I had decided to take the position of editor here. He begged me to stay on as his partner in the mining enterprise, but when I insisted on leaving, he paid me handsomely for my stake in the company, shook my hand and wished me well, saying we would see quite a lot of each other as his jurisdiction extends to Alder Gulch, which includes Virginia and Nevada Cities.

Still, I was surprised to see Henry walk into the office this morning. It was the first time I had laid eyes on him since leaving Bannack. We had a pleasant exchange, speaking mostly about the newly organized Idaho Territory, but he seemed distracted and unhappy. We shared a drink and then went to the café for something to eat. He ate little and said less. I finally asked him what was troubling him and he suggested we return to the *Tribune* office.

"The miners court is going to try me for killing Tom Cleveland," Henry told me, his voice subdued.

"You killed him?!" I was now frightened for Henry's life.

He nodded somberly. "He was talking," he explained simply and succinctly. "I had to shut him up."

I regarded my friend for several long minutes. He was gazing out the window of the office at the street, which was once again busy now that the long winter was finally in retreat. I thought about our days together in California and about his time in prison. It seemed Henry's past was closing in on him. If he was convicted, or, even if he wasn't, this killing might have well destroyed any hope he had of a political career in the new territory.

"What can I do to help?" I asked quietly.

"Can you testify on my behalf in Bannack?" he asked.

"Testify?"

"Yes," he replied. "As a character witness. You also knew Cleveland back in California and you can discredit him and the things he was saying about me in Bannack." He shot me a meaningful look. "Should that come up."

I considered what he was asking me to do and it sounded suspiciously close to committing perjury. I only knew Tom Cleveland slightly from my friend's days at San Quentin and Henry most certainly didn't want to bring his own prison term up in court, so I wondered what he really wanted me to say.

"If I return to Bannack to face charges, I want to know you'll help me defend myself," he continued. "Otherwise, I will ride on to Fort Benton, send for Electa and then try to get back to the States on a steam ship. *Will* you help me?"

It was clear to me at that moment that Cleveland had raised enough doubt about Henry's reputation to cause my friend concern as to whether he would be acquitted. He could run or he could face the consequences.

"Of course I will help you, Henry," I said finally, although it was Electa I was thinking of. "The first thing we should do is get something in print. Let me interview you and then write an account of what exactly happened. We go to press tonight, so I can go back to Bannack with you and copies of the *Tribune* to spread around town. That could help change some minds."

Henry blinked and smiled for the first time since he had arrived. "The power of the press!" he declared.

Colgan walked into the office at that moment. "Ah, the esteemed Sheriff Plummer! Good morning, Sir!"

Henry glanced at me as he caught the scent of alcohol on Colgan and his unsteady gait as he walked to his desk. I rolled my eyes at Henry and began writing the account of what had happened at Skinner's, occasionally asking questions of Henry about the gunfight and aftermath. Several minutes later, we heard Colgan snoring at his desk.

I handed the finished copy to Henry, which he read carefully, his head slowly nodding. He handed it back to me with a smile of relief.

"This could really help me, Noah. Thank you." He then rose from his chair. "I need to see Ned Ray while I'm here. He has agreed to serve as my deputy in Virginia and Nevada. Says he's got some other men I might deputize."

"Ned Ray?!" I asked in disbelief. "He's a troublemaker, Henry. He's no lawman, that's for damn sure."

"Yes, I know. I know," he replied, his hand up, his tone exasperated, "but he's the only sort of man that will take the job. No miner wants to do it, so that leaves the dregs, I'm sorry to say. I'm going to have Jack Dillingham supervise the deputies here, including Ray. Jack's the Texas Ranger I told you about. He's a good man."

I finally asked the question I had been holding back because I already knew the answer. "And how is Electa?"

He shook his head and looked down at the floor. I had never before seen Henry Plummer look so sad. He was near tears.

"She's very unhappy," he replied, his voice barely audible. "I am gone quite a lot and she doesn't like what I do. She said she wants to return to the States…to Iowa, to be precise. She has an uncle there who owns a farm."

I felt a wave of guilt wash over me. Henry must have taken my expression for pity.

"It's probably for the best, Noah," he sighed. "She's young and has always lived a sheltered life with Martha and Jim. There is no Methodist church in Bannack. She can't even venture into town on her own so I cannot blame her for feeling lonely and hurt." He studied my face for a moment, and then continued. "But there's something else wrong; something she won't discuss with me. Anyway, it's all my fault."

Another pang of guilt shot through me as Henry rose and shook my hand. I watched him through the window. Neatly attired as always in a spotless blue suit and expensive black hat, he ambled slowly down the boardwalk in search of Ned Ray. Nothing good could come by Henry deputizing the lowest common denominator in Virginia City.

Bannack
Idaho Territory
April 20, 1863

I arrived in Bannack three days ago with David Pemberton, a Virginia City lawyer. We took the stagecoach from Virginia and Henry greeted us in front of the Goodrich Hotel as we arrived. He had rooms arranged for us and, it being late in the afternoon, to my consternation, he invited us to dine with him.

Electa's green eyes were sad but she tried to maintain a cheery demeanor as she served us the roast chicken and dumplings she had prepared. We men made small talk but I stole sidelong glances at my former lover and felt desire well up from deep inside, a sensation that was quickly followed by self-loathing. All the while, Electa picked at the food on her plate, avoided eye contact with me and said very little.

We finished our meal and Henry suggested a walk and a smoke. Electa shook my hand without looking at my face and bid us all goodbye.

We went back to the Goodrich Hotel and sat at Henry's favorite table near the back of the saloon off the hotel's lobby. J.W. Dillingham joined us. He was an impressive man, tall and well spoken. Whiskey was poured and Henry passed around cigars. A few hotel guests and some merchants sat around the saloon. Most of the miners preferred Skinner's, I recalled, because whiskey was cheaper and the surroundings were less refined.

"A stroke of genius, this," Pemberton said as he handed me a copy of the *Virginia City Tribune* with a knowing smile:

Bannack Sheriff Henry Plummer Kills Desperado In Gunfight

—

*Tom Cleveland Was a Convict at Infamous
San Quentin Prison*

—

Threatened Sheriff & Mrs. Plummer With Violence

—

May Have Been Accomplice of Horan's

I wasn't proud of my handiwork, but the thrust of the account was basically true. After I arrived and spoke with several acquaintances who had witnessed the "gunfight," it was obvious to me Cleveland had been helpless. There was nobody better with a gun than Henry, a fact well known to most everyone in Bannack. Nevertheless, Henry was facing a murder trial tomorrow and he was not at all confident of the outcome.

"I will have you take the stand, Sheriff," Pemberton said. "It is very important the jury hear your account of what transpired."

"Most of 'em were there," Dillingham noted in his deep baritone drawl. "And most of 'em have made up their minds 'bout Hank's guilt one way or t'other."

"Yes, but they need to hear about the threatened violence," Pemberton replied. "They need to know that Cleveland meant to harm you and most probably Mrs. Plummer." The lawyer looked intently to Henry for confirmation. "Yes?"

Plummer regarded Pemberton for a long moment. "Yes," he finally agreed. "And I have reason to believe, as does Deputy Dillingham, that Cleveland was part of the gang of road agents that killed Jamie Wells."

Dillingham was nodding, his long face thoughtful. "That's right, Mr. Pemberton," the Texan remarked. "I had me a long talk with Virgil Wells and he recalls one of the masked men what did the shootin' as big and with a beard stickin' out 'round the mask he was wearin'. That sure as hell sounds like Cleveland to me."

"That's actually irrelevant to the case at hand and hearsay to boot. But you might bring that up when I examine you tomorrow, Deputy," Pemberton said. "The judge may not allow that into the record, but, then, justice here is a rather informal affair so it might sway some of the miners. I understand many are sympathetic toward Mr. Wells's tragic loss."

Henry gave Pemberton a wry look. "It might also be helpful that the judge knows next to nothing about criminal law."

Bannack
Idaho Territory
April 21, 1863

"Informal," it turned out, was an understatement. The miners court was the first I had seen and it was a farce, start to finish. Held in Skinner's Saloon, the scene of the "crime," Henry's trial began at ten o'clock in the morning and it took both the prosecution and the defense until one o'clock to finish their opening statements. Men were packed into the room and hundreds more were outside its doors, trying to hear what was being said. Pemberton spent an hour describing Henry's selfless service to the community, his dedication as a lawman, and his reputation for kindness and equanimity.

"...Sheriff Henry Plummer, on his own initiative and with a seldom seen diligence, rode out into that freezing blizzard and for five days," Pemberton dramatically held aloft five fingers for emphasis, "for five days, Gentlemen, and assisted Mr. Camden in rounding up his scattered herd! Now I submit to you that such a man...nay, such a *law*man...is not the kind of person who would wantonly take the life of another unless he was *forced* to do so in the prosecution of his duties as sheriff!"

Miners interrupted him with catcalls and loud demands for punishment. Judge Morris Reynolds did little to keep the courtroom under control except to call for silence from time to time. What a contrast to the halls of justice I remembered in New York, where judges ruled their courts like kings.

There was a recess for dinner and, when court finally resumed, Dillingham was called to the stand. As rehearsed, he recited the facts. Yes, he said, Cleveland had been threatening Mr. and Mrs. Plummer, even though the sheriff had shown Cleveland kindness by giving him a job. There had been a confrontation in Skinner's Saloon, and Plummer had killed Cleveland when he'd drawn his weapon on the sheriff.

"That ain't what happened!" Frosty Stump called out. "Tom was murdered by Plummer is what happened!"

"Quiet, Stump!" barked Reynolds. "You'll get your chance."

I was called to the stand next and sworn to give truthful testimony.

"Now, Mr. Coffey," Pemberton began, "You knew Sheriff Plummer in California, did you not?"

"I did."

"And was he not a true and noble lawman there?"

"He was indeed," I said.

"And did he ever comport himself in anything less than a law-like way in the performance of his duties?" Pemberton asked.

I hesitated, but just for a moment. "No. I believed him to be in the right on most every issue," I carefully replied.

"Now, were you at all acquainted with the deceased, Mr. Thomas C. Cleveland?"

"Yes, I knew him," I said.

"And how did you come to know Mr. Cleveland?"

"I met him when he was a convict at the San Quentin Penitentiary in California and I was a newspaper correspondent," I said. "He was serving a term there for armed robbery, I believe."

There was a general outcry among Cleveland's sympathizers. Pemberton did not follow up with a question as to why I happened to be at San Quentin and I volunteered no additional testimony. The prosecutor, on cross-examination, also failed to ask me why I was at San Quentin in the first place and I was left to wonder how I would have responded.

The prosecutor next called Frosty Stump to the stand and I saw the man who had cried out earlier eagerly push his way to the chair. He wore a look of belligerence as he took his seat. He didn't wait for questions from the prosecutor, instead blurting out his testimony in a confusing and even self-contradictory series of declarations. Pemberton calmly rose when it was time to cross-examine Stump and stood next to him.

"Mr. Stump, you say that Tom Cleveland was armed?"

"Yeah, he was armed, but..."

"Just answer my questions, Mr. Stump, with a simple 'yes' or 'no'," the lawyer, said patting Stump's shoulder. "So you say, yes, Cleveland was armed. Now, did he draw a pistol in this confrontation with the sheriff?"

"Well, yeah, but..."

Pemberton closed his eyes and wagged his forefinger. "Just 'yes' or 'no', please. Did Cleveland make an attempt, any attempt at all, to shoot Sheriff Plummer?

Stump was staring at Pemberton. "Yes," he snapped, hostility dripping from the word.

Henry Plummer was called last. His testimony mirrored Dillingham's with one exception. "He didn't have a weapon when I first saw him," Henry explained. "One was provided by the saloon's owner. I offered him the chance to draw and cock before I drew my pistol. He drew and cocked his gun, but I was faster. I shot him through the head and he died before he fell to the floor."

"And this was in self defense, Sheriff? You had no choice? No choice whatever but to shoot Mr. Cleveland?"

"I had no choice," Henry declared with a level voice. "He had repeatedly threatened my wife and me and was making disparaging comments about my reputation and the reputation of my wife. I sought satisfaction as a matter of honor and challenged Tom Cleveland to a duel. He was killed in a fair fight. And that should have been the end of the matter!" Henry angrily looked out over the crowd of miners who had grown silent. "Instead I am *here*! Defending my honor against a specious murder charge!"

There were more cries from Cleveland's friends, but I thought I saw men nodding in agreement with Henry. Then the most peculiar jury deliberation I had ever witnessed followed. Judge Reynolds arranged two men on one side of the courtroom and two on the other. He asked those who believed Henry guilty to pass between the two men on his left and those who thought the sheriff innocent to pass between the men to his right. I shot Pemberton a bewildered look and he shrugged.

There were more catcalls and oaths sworn. Several miners began shoving each other and someone fired a gun in the street outside, where it was now getting dark. Dillingham rose from his chair and walked to the back of the room, towering over many of the jostling men.

"Y'all best simmer down back here or I'm gonna start arresting the troublemakers!" he drawled.

They quieted themselves and miners slowly began filing through the human gates. Many hesitated, talking among themselves before stepping forward. Others stood off, animatedly discussing the testimony then striding either toward the men on the right or the left, glancing Henry's way as they did. One man walked to the "guilty" side then stopped before changing his mind and walking between the two men representing "innocent."

All the while, several of Cleveland's confederates watched, making a show of pointing at some of the miners who'd voted for Henry's innocence.

This bizarre manner of polling went on for an hour and I lost count of the innocent and guilty votes. I was even sure I saw several men vote twice. The room was stifling and I loosened my tie and mopped sweat from my brow as Reynolds stood holding a sheet of paper.

"All right, all right!" he shouted as he held his hands high. The room grew quiet. "I have a verdict here. Sheriff Henry Plummer, you stand accused of the murder to Thomas C. Cleveland. This court has found you innocent of the charge, one hundred and fifty seven votes to one hundred and eighteen votes. You are free to go, Sir.

A brawl immediately broke out between Henry's supporters and those who'd voted guilty. There was an explosion of shattering glass as bodies were pushed through the saloon's window into the street. Dillingham and Caven were helpless to stop the mayhem. I watched as one man bit another's arm. A miner had a foe pinned to the floor and was trying to pry the eye out of the fellow's head with his thumbs.

Frosty Stump was waving a shotgun while he loudly threatened Henry. "I'll kill the son of a bitch myself!"

I looked frantically around and saw Henry placidly sitting at the front of the room, one leg crossed over the other, taking in the violent spectacle. He wore a strange look on his face, one I had never before seen. It was a kind of bemused smile that at the same time looked rather sad to me. He ran a finger over his blond mustaches, then slowly stood up, drew his pistol from its holster and fired a shot through the saloon's ceiling. It was a deafening report that caused my ears to ring and brought the melee to an immediate halt.

From the cloud of white pistol smoke I heard Henry's angry voice. "Justice has been served here! Now, if any one of you wants to settle a personal score with me, I will give you the same opportunity I offered Cleveland. You can face me and fight me like a man or you can shut your mouth."

Henry stepped out of the smoke, his eyes roaming over the room until they settled on Frosty Stump.

"Stump!" he called out in challenge. "You said something about killing me just now. Did I hear you correctly? Here's your chance."

Stump looked stricken and alone as men on both sides stepped away, leaving no one between him and Henry. I watched in stunned silence because I could see the same look of murder in Henry's eyes that Cleveland and the other men he'd killed must have seen before they died.

Henry calmly holstered his pistol, his eyes resting on Stump. The man glanced desperately to his left and right looking for help but there was none forthcoming.

"I am waiting," declared Henry.

Stump dropped the shotgun as though it were a red-hot poker and began backing out of the saloon, his hands high in the air. When he reached the door he slowly opened it and stepped out into the night. The room was silent.

"Anybody else take a notion to die tonight?" Henry asked.

For the first time, I saw the confidence and power my friend possessed and it was both fascinating and frightening. He had brought instant order to chaos and he had done it with a display of sheer nerve.

"Very well, then," he ordered, "this saloon's closed for the night. Go home. All of you sons of bitches!"

With that he pushed his way through the miners and walked out the door, seemingly oblivious to any danger posed by vengeful gunmen who might be lurking in the shadows outside. I half expected to hear shooting, but there was silence in the street. I looked at Pemberton who, like me, had been shocked by the scene he had just witnessed. We stood and joined the men filing out of the saloon.

I returned to my hotel room and found an envelope on the floor that had been pushed under the door. I recognized Electa's handwriting on the envelope.

Dearest Noah,

It greatly pained me to see you last evening knowing we carry the guilt of a secret affection that may never again be realized. I made a great mistake marrying a man such as Henry. He is kindly but he is seldom here. He also has a streak of violence I never saw at Sun River Farm. He frightens me. I watched him hang a man and I have heard he killed another in a gunfight for which he is being tried. His sense of justice notwithstanding, I feel Henry is far too accomplished at executing his fellow human beings. Meanwhile, I am desperately sad and lonely here without you. I must leave Bannack. I have decided to return east as soon as possible. I have discussed this with Henry and he has given me leave to do whatever will make me happy. Perhaps some day we will meet again. I long for your embrace my love.

Yours always,
E

25

Virginia City
Idaho Territory
May 10, 1863

I made the acquaintance of an unusual man today. His name is Professor Thomas J. Dimsdale. He stopped by the *Tribune* office to ask Colgan if he would print an item about a private academy he was planning to open at the Masonic Hall at the top of Wallace Street. Colgan agreed to run the item and introduced me to Dimsdale as he was leaving for one of his morning "appointments."

Dimsdale was a small man dressed in a neat black suit. His short brown hair was combed down on his head and parted in the middle. He had bright, animated eyes that danced as he spoke. He was engaging but he coughed frequently, explaining as he did that he suffered from an unknown lung disease. He was clearly an Englishman and a well educated one.

"Oxford. Jesus College," he explained, "I arrived in Nova Scotia two years ago to assume a teaching post. But with the damp and cold climate there, I became quite ill. A friend suggested I travel west so I might take advantage of a dry climate. I arrived in Red River Colony on the plains, but I could find no suitable employment there. I learned from a wagonmaster that Virginia City was booming and it occurred to me a school might be a necessity, so, *voila*, here I am!"

I asked him what he thought of the town.

"Well, frankly, Sir, it reminds me of London's east end what with the ruffians and doxies up one side of the street and down the other," he replied. "Is there no law here?"

"As a matter of fact, no there isn't," I replied. He blinked at me. "The United States Congress forgot to write any criminal or civil codes when it established Idaho Territory in March. I daresay the Civil War being waged just outside the capital city's limits probably distracted the House and Senate. I understand the territorial legislature means to correct the oversight but they won't meet for some months. So, in answer to your question, there is no law here whatever; at least there are no written laws. But there is something called the 'Mountain Code.'"

"Do tell," he said, stifling a cough.

"The miners are peaceable for the most part. They almost always try to resolve their disputes without bloodshed." I explained. "In fact, they may look like a filthy rabble to outsiders, but many have at least a rudimentary education and there is a strict code of honor as you might find anywhere—among the aristocracy in your country for example. To question a man's honor or his courage is to invite a challenge for satisfaction. Sometimes that can turn deadly although more often than not, it gets resolved with fists."

He nodded thoughtfully at this, so I continued. "But with gold and quick riches come another class of people entirely," I continued, "They look for ways to prey on the miners..."

"Banditos and desperadoes, I should think," Dimsdale interrupted.

I laughed and he frowned at me in confusion.

"No, professor. Not banditos or desperadoes or road agents, although there is the occasional robbery. No," I said, "I refer to the local merchants."

He nodded as he comprehended my meaning. "The grossly inflated prices for goods and services are what you speak of."

"Yes, indeed," I replied with a smile. "These people have no shame. They charge the miners five dollars for a tin pan because they can get away with it. There's collusion among the storeowners, saloonkeepers, hardware drummers and even the whores. It's contemptible in my opinion."

"You will be happy to hear then that it will cost only one dollar a week to enroll a student in my academy," he smiled. "And that will include daily singing lessons."

"That seems quite fair, Professor," I replied with a smile. "Here's to an Oxonian acamedician and the bright light of education in a rough and tumble frontier mining town!"

"Precisely," he said through a cough. "Thank you for your kind assistance, Mr. Coffey."

With that, Dimsdale left the office. He'd brightened my day considerably because just before he arrived, I had received a letter from Henry that explained Electa was bound to leave for Iowa in a few days' time. He asked if I could come to Bannack to see her off.

I found Colgan at the Bale of Hay and explained I would be in Bannack for several days. His eyes were misted over by the affects of liquor and he waved me off with his hand.

Bannack
Idaho Territory
May 11, 1863

I arrived in Bannack a little after noon and located Henry at the Goodrich Hotel. He was sitting by himself, although I saw there were a number of respectable looking men in the saloon.

He smiled and greeted me with an earnest handshake. "Thank you for coming, Noah," he said. "It means a lot."

We ate dinner at the hotel and then Henry suggested we take a walk up the slope of the barren ridge that overlooked the main street of Bannack. We stood next to each other in silence at the crest of the rise regarding the muddy main street below and the busy miners standing in the creek that wound like a snake alongside the town. The spring runoff was heavy and the usually placid Grasshopper Creek was a torrent of murky water that made mining work difficult.

"Look at those fools 'slooshing' down there," Henry grinned as he pointed out a pair of miners, obviously new to placer mining, struggling with shovels and splashing water and mud over themselves as they attempted to dump gravel and sand into their long wooden sluice box. One miner inadvertently poured his shovel load of slurry down the front of his partner who in turn pushed the man with the shovel into the creek. Henry and I roared with laughter.

"Wasn't that us just last year?" I asked, wiping tears from my eyes.

"No, that was never us!" Henry laughed. "We at least had enough sense to let somebody else work the shovels!"

We continued our surveillance and I pointed out to the other side of town at what looked to be a tall corral gate. "What's that over there?" I asked.

"Gallows," he replied. "That's where I hanged Horan."

I said nothing in reply.

"You know, Noah, Electa accuses me of being too good at my job. At enjoying it, even."

Of course I knew all this already so I stayed silent.

"Every man I have ever killed richly deserved his fate," he continued, his voice rising with emotion. "It fell to me by happenstance or my own initiative that I was the one who pulled the trigger or slung the rope. But I am not a murderer. I am a lawman. I hate disorder...I refuse to let anyone criminally inclined have his way with honest men."

Henry's words struck me as not a little hollow as I thought back to his narrow acquittal in the Cleveland killing. He'd had more in mind than justice. So who was he trying to convince? He had been thinking of his name and reputation when he shot Tom Cleveland.

"I understand, Henry," I replied. "But your sense of justice...it's, well, difficult for a woman like Electa to understand. This is a hard country and you're a hard man. She's not the kind of woman who can easily adapt to..."

Henry was eyeing me now and I stopped speaking. "You seem to know quite a lot about Electa," he remarked. I detected a hint of suspicion in his voice.

For a long moment I stared without flinching into his blue-gray eyes. "Are you interrogating me, Sheriff Plummer?" I asked, my heart racing. Henry blinked and then turned his head away from me slowly.

"No. Of course not," he said finally, his tone quiet and embarrassed. "You've known Electa as long as I have. I know she's shared her feelings with you."

We walked back down the steep rocky hill and crossed a footbridge over the creek. A path led us to Chrisman's store and Henry's office.

"Electa leaves on the morning stage for Salt Lake and then she's on to Iowa," he said as he sat at his desk. "I'm going to ride with her as far as the Eagle Rock ferry on the Snake River. Will you join me? I'd be honored by your company."

"Certainly, Henry," I replied. "But I'm quite tired from the journey. I believe I'll rest awhile after I've bought or stolen whatever newspapers might be available here. After your trial, we're short on news in Virginia City."

He shot me a rueful smile. "I'll have a horse saddled and ready for you. Thank you again, Noah. You're a true friend."

Eagle Rock
Idaho Territory
May 18, 1863

We had left Bannack in a dreary rain but now the weather was warm and clear. The wide river was shimmering this morning as we approached the ferry landing. The high desert rose up around us and to the east the ragged peaks of the Tetons gleamed against the azure sky.

Henry had ridden much of the way alongside the stage so he could converse with Electa through its open window. My horse loped alongside Henry's and occasionally I would ride out ahead of the stage. The low rolling hills hereabouts are covered with sage and juniper. Big jackrabbits would spring out from behind them from time to time spooking my mare. It's desolate, but as I rode, I perceived a kind of sublime beauty in the purple sage, the rock formations and the clouds that rolled across the sky like the great ships I remembered sailing out of New York harbor. This contemplation of my surroundings helped me keep my mind off what now lay ahead.

At the way stations, Electa and I had exchanged glances but we'd said little to one another. Henry tried to make the best of the sad journey by telling stories and laughing, but his affectations of jocularity seemed strained to me. Electa was leaving and I thought Henry felt very much as I did.

At the ferry landing, the flat boat was just arriving from the Snake

River's southern embankment. It shortly discharged a wagon that appeared to be carrying a well-heeled family of emigrants who were headed north in the direction from which we'd just come. A distinguished looking gentleman sat alongside a younger fellow on the bench. Both wore formal looking black frock coats and black hats. As they rolled off the ferry, the younger man wheeled the wagon over to the side of the road and he and his companion dismounted. Women I took for their wives rode on seats in the wagon bed. The men helped the ladies down while several children spilled out from the rear.

There was a small store, a saloon and a couple of privies at the landing along with a number of Indians who stood around or sat in the dust impassively watching the activities of the white men.

Henry dismounted and assisted Electa and another lady out of the stage. He turned back to me and smiled.

"You're awfully quiet today, Noah," he observed. "Let's go wash the dust out...that might cheer you up."

I could have responded that I believed Henry's cheerfulness seemed odd for a man about to lose his wife, perhaps forever, but I said nothing, shrugged and followed him toward the misshapen cabin that served as the landing's saloon and cafe.

The two men I had seen arrive on the ferry were standing at the bar, their hats off, sipping tall glasses of cold tea. The older of the two was of medium height with hair graying at the temples. His thick full beard was streaked with white and his eyes were dark and severe. They seemed to me to be fathomless. The younger man was of average height and clean-shaven. He regarded Henry and me over his glass with soft brown eyes as we entered. He had a high forehead, receding hairline and a weak chin. With his hat off, he appeared considerably less distinguished. I nodded at them and Henry ordered whiskey for us. The young man made a face as the bartender poured the liquor.

Henry turned to the pair and touched the brim of his hat. "Gentlemen," he said with a smile. "A fine day for traveling."

"Indeed it is," the older man responded with a thin smile.

"I'm Henry Plummer, sheriff of Bannack," he declared as he held out his hand. The older man shook it, his eyes brightening.

"Sheriff, is it?" he said. "Well, it appears we're in the same line of business, Sir."

"Oh?" replied Henry.

"Yes, I'm a lawman, too," he declared. "In a manner of speaking. My name is Sidney Edgerton. I am the new chief justice for Idaho Territory. President Lincoln appointed me in January, but as you can see, we're only just now arriving from Ohio. In fact, we are bound for Bannack, ourselves."

"Well, Judge Edgerton," Henry smiled, "let me be among the first to welcome you and Mr. ..."

"Oh, I'm sorry," Edgerton said, "this is my nephew, Wilbur Sanders. Wilbur, meet Sheriff Plummer and his associate..."

"Noah Coffey," I interjected, holding out my hand. "I'm the editor of the newspaper in Virginia City. That's some miles east of Bannack."

"I see you are a drinking man, Sheriff Plummer," Sanders sniffed after he shook my hand. "Is that a good idea for a man entrusted to enforce the law?"

Henry coolly ignored the impertinent question as Edgerton chuckled apologetically.

"That's very rude, Wilbur," he admonished the younger man before looking at us. "I'm quite sure the sheriff is always fit to perform his duty. Wilbur, like me, is an attorney by training and takes the law quite seriously."

Sanders eyed me for a moment, finished his tea and, without excusing himself, walked to the door. "I will prepare the animals, Uncle," he remarked. "We must push on soon."

"Please excuse him," Edgerton apologized. "He's tired from the journey and has lately become irritable. He's a staunch teetotaler and doesn't approve of those who imbibe."

"Then he has come to the wrong place," I smiled. "Raging rivers of whiskey flow in the mountains where you are headed, Judge Edgerton, so I expect your nephew will have some difficultly making acquaintances."

"Just so, just so," he agreed and then looked at Henry again. "Sheriff, are you due back in Bannack soon? I would like to meet with you when you return to discuss what you know about the territory. I should also wish to learn what I can about its legal apparatus."

Henry and I couldn't help but laugh. The judge shot us a look of confusion and annoyance.

"I'm sorry, Judge, we aren't laughing at you" Henry smiled. "I am afraid you are *looking* at the legal apparatus!"

"I don't understand," replied Edgerton.

I explained to Edgerton that the territory had no criminal or civil codes.

He listened intently and then scratched his head when I finished. "So, then, Sheriff, pardon my ignorance, but what is your legal sanction? I mean, by what authority do you act in the name of the law?"

"My fellow miners in Bannack," Henry replied. "They elected me by popular vote to keep order and resolve disputes."

"I see," said the judge, although he continued to look confused. "Well, President Lincoln didn't inform me that I would preside over a territorial legal system without any laws! How curious."

"Doubtless he has other things on his mind what with the rebellion," I observed. I then told the judge of the plans to form a territorial legislature that would remedy the problem after elections were held and it met in the spring of 1864. This appeared to alleviate some of his concern. He consulted his pocket watch.

"We must move on, gentlemen," he said. "Is the trail well marked and safe from here to Bannack?"

Henry said it was but also advised him to take more water than he thought he needed and to stand guard at night. He also promised to meet the judge after he was settled.

With that Edgerton thanked us, shook our hands, and took his leave. We finished our drinks and joined the passengers as they began to board the stage. Henry and Electa walked to the river's edge and I turned away. As I did, my eyes fell on one of the stagecoach passengers, a man I had not spoken to during the journey but one I recognized as a regular at the Goodrich Hotel's saloon. He was well dressed and groomed and he was speaking to Edgerton and Sanders in an animated manner. Occasionally he would look in Henry's direction as he spoke and once pointed at the sheriff while Henry's back was turned to the conversation. The stage driver presently joined the men. His name was Curtis, a fellow I had also seen in Bannack throughout the winter.

Edgerton was listening intently to the traveler and then he looked at Curtis and asked him something before shaking his head, an angry expression on his face at whatever response the stage driver made. I noticed Sanders had folded his arms across his chest and was glaring in Henry's direction. I didn't know what to make of the scene I was watching so I walked away, slipping my hand into my pocket and fingering the envelope I carried.

Henry and Electa approached. I smiled at her and she dropped her eyes.

"Back in a moment," said Henry. Electa looked up at me and smiled. Even though we stood in the crowded ferry landing, I suddenly felt we were alone again as we had been on those passionate nights we had spent together.

"Electa..."

She reached up and placed her forefinger on my lips. "Find me when you can," she replied. "I love *you*, Noah, not Henry. My uncle has a large farm near Davenport in Iowa. His name is Samuel Meaker. People will know him if...when you ask in Davenport."

I slipped her the small envelope, which she placed in her dress. "I love you," I whispered. I strode away, blinking back tears. I found my horse and climbed into the saddle, pulling my hat brim down low over my eyes. Henry appeared, embraced Electa and helped her back aboard. The stage rolled out onto the ferry and other passengers paraded onto the boat's deck. A bell rang out and the ferry floated out into the river, the current's force pulling it across as a boatman manipulated a drive wheel on the overhead cable.

An hour later we were again riding north after passing the slower moving Edgerton party. "Henry," I asked, "do you know the man on the stage... the well dressed one?"

He thought for a moment. "Oh, yes, Butler," he said. "He's a card sharp."

"Card sharp?"

"Yes. A poker player...high stakes."

"I never saw him dealing cards," I replied.

"You never went to Miss Levereaux's house, either," he replied with a grin. "Not as I recall, anyway."

There were several houses of ill repute along "Bachelor's Row" off Bannack's main street and Miss Levereaux's was by far the most notorious. But what I found shocking was that Henry, married since arriving in

Bannack, had been there at all. Gambling and drink might be an understandable attraction to him, but the women there were the saddest looking collection of prostitutes I had seen this side of the Bowery. Could Henry have been carnally involved with one or more of them? The very idea deeply disturbed me.

I said nothing for some miles. Maybe I was disappointed in him, a new and strange feeling to have for a man I admired as much as Henry Plummer. As we rode, he occasionally commented on a coyote that followed us for a few miles or a distant herd of antelope that charged across the plain. I looked over at him.

"What about Curtis, the stage driver?" I asked. "Do you know him?"

"Not really," Henry said. "I understand he drives the Bannack-Salt Lake City route whenever the weather is fair. But you remember him, don't you? He was one of Cleveland's friends...at the trial."

26

Bannack
Idaho Territory
May 23, 1863

Francis Thompson rode in from Salt Lake City this morning, just a day after we had returned to Bannack from seeing Electa off. Henry and I happened to be standing in front of Chrisman's store as he arrived, his wagon loaded with mining equipment and supplies. He saw us and waved as he brought the wagon to a stop in front of us.

"I see you are safely returned, scalp intact," Henry called up to him with a smile.

"And it's good to see you, too, Sheriff Plummer," Thompson grinned. "No Spencer repeaters for sale in Salt Lake but here's a gift for you nevertheless!" He unwrapped a chamois cover and handed Henry a handsome double barrel shotgun with a gleaming walnut stock. "It's English made!"

"I can see that in the workmanship!" Henry beamed as he accepted the shotgun and a box of cartridges. "This is wonderful, Francis, thank you!"

The young man grinned at Henry. "And I have some good news, too," he declared. "I encountered Tofton alive and well in Salt Lake..."

"Tofton!" I interrupted. "My God, I would have thought he'd be on General Lee's staff by now!"

"Well, you know Tofton," Thompson said. "He's always planning. He told me when he got to Salt Lake the Mormons shunned him when they saw his uniform. But he explained to some of their city elders he had resigned from the army and was joining the Confederacy as soon as he could."

Henry listened and then smiled wryly. "That makes sense," he replied. "The Utah Mormons hate the U.S. government."

"Exactly!" Thompson said excitedly. "Some of the Mormon ladies made him a handsome Confederate colonel's uniform..."

"Colonel! He gave himself a promotion already?!" Henry cried. "I guess I shouldn't be surprised!"

"Yes, and the Mormons are helping him assemble a battalion of Confederate troops as well!" Thompson said.

"How?" asked Henry. "Mormons won't fight for anybody."

Thompson shook his head. "Army deserters from garrisons all over the western territories have found their way to Salt Lake City for the same reasons Captain—or "Colonel"—Tofton went there. They're southern boys who want to fight for the C.S.A."

"So he's putting together a command," Henry added. "That's brilliant!"

"He's riding for Texas when he has enough men assembled," Thompson said. "Meantime, the Mormons in Salt Lake are housing and feeding his command."

As Thompson had been speaking, I felt rage welling up inside me. "Those treacherous bastards," I spit angrily.

Henry and Francis looked at me with stunned expressions. I then saw Thompson's fair face burn red. "Sorry Noah. I forgot how you felt about those... people," he said quietly after a moment.

Embarrassed silence hung until Thompson finally broke it. "Oh, and one thing more. I encountered a party on the trail and guided them here."

"Oh?" replied Henry.

"Yes, a big freighter owned by a man named Lloyd Magruder. He's headed to Virginia City to open a store. Claims he can to get the best price there for his merchandise."

Henry glanced at me and shook his head. "Another thief. Yes, I'm sure he'll do quite well. You said something about men with him?"

"Magruder met them on the trail. He hired them as guards."

"They have names?" Henry inquired.

"Well, let's see," Thompson looked skyward, recalling the men he'd met. "There was a fellow who did a lot of talking...name of Howard. Doc Howard. Another called himself Red Yeager. There was a gentlemen who said he was a graduate of Yale medical school...um...Steve his name was...Steve Marshland. Then there was a Mayfield, Carter...a Bunton...Page, Lowrey..."

Henry's lips were pursed and turning white. "And you guided them *here*?!"

Thompson looked confused. "Well, not here...I showed them the cut-off to Virginia. Henry, I..."

"Francis, those men are renowned cutthroats and robbers!" Henry interrupted. "They were terrorizing Lewiston when I was up there a couple of years ago. Doc Howard *is* their leader! And if Steve Marshland's a doctor of medicine then I'm the archbishop of Bannack!"

"Henry, maybe you're confused," Thompson replied defensively. "These fellows were quite pleasant and of good manners. And helpful, too!"

"Oh, I'm sure they were," Henry said sarcastically. "You led them right into a thieve's paradise!" He looked up at the young man whose head was hanging in shame.

"Francis, you didn't know who they were," I declared with a harsh look at Henry.

"I'm sorry, Francis," Henry apologized. "You had no idea. Why don't you go unload and then come back up here and give me their descriptions? You say you showed them the cut-off?"

Thompson nodded. "Yes. That was just after daybreak. Magruder was driving the freighter. Howard and his men were the outriders."

"There isn't much traffic on the cut-off," I said to Henry.

"I know," he replied as Francis cracked his whip and the wagon began to roll down the muddy street. "Francis," Henry called out. The young man looked back over his shoulder. "Thank you for this lovely piece!" he said holding up the shotgun. "It is beautiful!"

WHERE LAW ENDS

Virginia City
Idaho Territory
May 25, 1863

There is no trace of Magruder. Along with Deputy Dillingham, Henry and I rode the cut-off trail that led around Bannack all the way to Alder Gulch and we never saw the freighter, the merchant, or his "guards." Upon arrival in Virginia City, Dillingham made inquiries at the general stores but, as Henry had feared, there was no word of Magruder's arrival, it being major news whenever freighters delivered their goods from Salt Lake.

"Damn it," swore Henry as we stood on the boardwalk in front of the *Tribune* office. Dillingham cut off a plug of tobacco, put it in his mouth and began chewing thoughtfully. After some moments, he spit brown juice into the dusty street.

"Hank, you reckon they diverted to Nevada City?" he drawled. "I know Francis said Virginia was Magruder's destination, but maybe…"

Henry was already striding down the boardwalk to where his horse was tied. Dillingham glanced at me with a bemused look and followed the sheriff. In moments they were riding down Wallace Street at a gallop toward Nevada City. I returned to the newspaper office and began catching up on my work.

Virginia City
Idaho Territory
May 30, 1863

Professor Dimsdale paid me a visit this morning but his demeanor was markedly less friendly than the last time I had seen him. After some small talk about the warm weather and his new school, he looked at me coolly.

"What do you know of your associate, Sheriff Plummer?" he asked me with his clipped accent.

"I beg your pardon?"

"The sheriff. What do you know of his…background?" he asked again with a hint of impatience in his voice as though he were addressing a particularly slow pupil.

"Why do you ask?" I finally replied.

"I had occasion to meet the new territorial chief justice last week," Dimsdale said. "Mr. Sidney Edgerton of Ohio, a most impressive man."

"Yes, I've also met the judge. He and his family are residing in Bannack," I said.

"Just so," he replied. "Well, it seems Judge Edgerton has been making some quiet inquiries into Sheriff Plummer's history. What he has learned is rather alarming and, how shall I put this? Not a little unsavory."

"Oh?" I replied stiffly. I felt my temper flare for a moment, but I got control of myself.

"Yes. Rumor has it Plummer was himself a criminal in California," Dimsdale continued. "Evidently he has killed many men and even spent time in prison. The judge is quite concerned that Plummer will resume his nefarious activities now that he is ensconced in the territory's richest gold mining region."

I was indeed alarmed but not for the reasons Dimsdale assumed. I thought back to the day at the ferry landing and the conversation I had observed.

"The judge is mistaken," I declared after a moment's hesitation. "As with law officers everywhere, Sheriff Plummer has made enemies among the criminal classes in his jurisdiction because of his vigorous enforcement of the law. You probably heard about his capture of John Horan, who killed a boy in the commission of an armed robbery? Doubtless it is these scum who are attempting to smear Henry's reputation. I wonder if Judge Edgerton knows just how popular Sheriff Plummer is among the miners he serves?"

The professor held out his hand defensively. "Yes, yes, he's popular. No doubt of that," he said with a weak smile. "He's a good politician and evidently effective in the dispatch of his duties. But there are other, um, prominent citizens in Bannack and elsewhere who share the judge's concerns about Plummer."

Clearly, Edgerton had sent Dimsdale here to question me as a sort of investigator. "I must return to my work, Professor," I said as calmly as I could manage. "Please tell Judge Edgerton and those prominent citizens you mentioned that they are wrong about Henry. I've known him for a number of years and can vouch for his reputation and his ability as a lawman. Good day." I opened the door for him and he reluctantly took his leave, a perturbed look on his face.

I sat at my desk for some time, gripped by an ominous feeling. As I contemplated the meaning of Dimsdale's visit, Dillingham walked through the office door. He nodded at me as he entered and took a seat across from me, propping his booted foot on a chair.

"Afternoon, Noah," he greeted me. "Why the gloomy face?"

"Oh, I just got a little bad news...nothing important. Personal," I replied. "Any sign of Magruder?"

"Yep," replied the Texan. "They went to Nevada all right. Couple of the merchants there said they bought goods from a group o' fellas that owned a freighter. They don't remember no Magruder bein' among 'em."

"Did you track them?"

"Yep," he said. "Had 'em a day's head start. Followed the road as far as the Ruby River but lost 'em at the ford. Sheriff and me is pretty well sure old Magruder is coyote bait somewhere's out there on the cut off trail." He pulled a cuspidor over to his seat with his foot and released a long stream of tobacco juice into it.

I said nothing. Henry's instincts were not only correct about the gang, but they had taken just a few days to come to fruition.

I finally looked up at Dillingham. "So, why are you in Virginia City?" I asked him.

"Hank wants me to wait an' see if any of 'em show up here," he replied. "He 'spects they will sooner or later."

27

Virginia City
Idaho Territory
June 5, 1863

The day began auspiciously but ended tragically. At about ten o'clock this morning, a battered package was delivered to my office. It was postmarked St. Louis and dated nearly four months earlier. I eagerly opened it and found a bundle of tightly wrapped newspapers and a letter from my former father-in-law, Nathan Carter, the first I have received since leaving Auroria.

Several of the newspapers were from St. Louis, but there were also editions from Cincinnati, Ft. Wayne and Des Moines. All were many months old but carried on their front pages news of the war and casualty rolls of appalling length.

Dear Noah,

I thank you for the letter I received about a year ago and I apologize for the delay in returning your kindness. I am sorry to report to you that my dear wife Susanna took ill not long after your letter arrived. She had a wasting disease and without laudanum she would have died in great pain. She was a wonderful woman and wife, but I don't think she ever fully recovered from Rebecca's tragic death. Of course you know I consider you my son and hold you blameless. It was the work of those bloody Mormons, who, incidentally, have yet to pay for their crime despite my continuing correspondance with the authorities.

The war rages. We now hear of unspeakable brutality being committed by irregulars in Kansas and western Missouri and there was a horrible battle at Sharpsburg in Maryland last September. I am told there were more than twenty thousand Union and Confederate casualities in a single day. Perhaps these newspapers will be of interest to you should they find their way to Virginia City.

Affectionately yours,
N. Carter

Colgan saw the pile of newspapers and began eagerly poring over them. "Good Lord!" he said. "Look at this casualty list! Where the hell is Fredericksburg? The fool correspondent doesn't say here...is that Virginia?" he snatched up another paper. "Good God Almighty!" he exclaimed, "Lincoln has emancipated the Negroes!"

I ignored him, thinking instead of Nathan Carter, alone now. I drew a sheet of paper from my desk and began writing him a return letter. As I dipped my pen in the ink, I was startled by gunfire that ended as abruptly as it had begun. Colgan had dropped the newspaper he was reading as I stood and made for the door.

"Be careful!" cried the editor as I ran into the street. I saw a cloud of dense white smoke hanging in the still air in front of the Bale of Hay Saloon at the far end of the street.

Virginia City is considerably larger and more established than Bannack. Large wooden structures and even some brick buildings rise up on both sides of Wallace Street, which extends for perhaps a hundred yards, so it took me some time to reach the foot of the street where the shooting had taken place. I carefully walked along the boardwalk, hugging the buildings, wary of any more shots.

The smoke had dissipated by the time I arrived and a group of miners had collected around a man lying on the ground. I pushed through them and saw it was J.W. Dillingham. The Texan lay in the street, bleeding profusely from his chest, his assailants gone. He was conscious and bloody foam appeared at his mouth as he tried to speak.

"Don't try to talk, Jack," I said as I knelt next to him. With some help, I managed to get him to the doctor but he lost consciousness and expired an hour later. Before he died, in a rasping voice, Dillingham told me who had shot him and why. I immediately sent word to Henry on the afternoon stage to Bannack.

Virginia City
Idaho Territory
June 6, 1863

Henry and I stood over Dillingham's body, which lay on several blocks of ice in the mortuary on Jackson Street. The deputy wore a black suit that I had purchased for his burial. I had also paid a boy to shine his boots. Henry reached out and patted the two hands crossed on the deputy's chest. "This won't go unanswered," he whispered, more to the dead man than to me.

We buried Jack Dillingham on the hill overlooking Virginia City as a cold rain fell. Just Henry and I were there along with a gravedigger and Parson Timmons, who said a few words over the dead Ranger. The chilly wind blew through my hair as Henry gazed down into the grave at the crude coffin. I felt myself shiver.

"Will you help me find Forbes, Lyons and Stinson, Noah?" Henry asked as we walked down the hill toward town.

I said I would. Then I told him of my recent interview with Professor Thomas J. Dimsdale.

"Cleveland's dead," he said with finality. "Whatever Dimsdale, Edgerton or Sanders know about my past, or think they know, cannot be proved."

I considered this for a moment. "I don't think they care about proving anything," I told him.

Virginia City
Idaho Territory
June 7, 1863

I was worried when Henry had retained Ned Ray as a deputy, but when he told me he'd deputized Buck Stinson I was truly shocked. Stinson's reputation was that of a drunk and layabout who made a meager living as a barber. If that was the best Henry could do, I had told him, then he was going to run into trouble. And now he had.

We learned that Stinson had run to Nevada City after shooting Dillingham. Henry rented a carriage from the Smith and Boyd livery stable and we set out on the two-mile ride to the neighboring town, which sat hard by the bank of Alder Creek, closer to the newest gold strike. It was a place more along the lines of Bannack, a ramshackle collection of cabins, tents and huts bisected by a muddy commercial street that offered everything from dry goods to female flesh. Like Virginia, Nevada City fell into Henry's jurisdiction.

We asked around the town and soon found Stinson sleeping off a drunk on a cot in the back of a rundown saloon. Henry dragged him out into the street by the scruff of his neck and stood him on his feet but realized by Stinson's blurred eyes and lolling head that an interrogation was out of the question.

With my help, we dragged him back to the carriage, laid him on its floor and rode back to Virginia. As we rolled up Wallace Street, Judge Edgerton and Wilbur Sanders observed us from the porch of the Fairweather Hotel. I noticed Dimsdale standing behind them. The professor made some comment as we passed by. Henry touched his hat, but Edgerton and Sanders made no response. They simply followed us with their eyes. We came to a stop in front of an empty house, and dragged Stinson from the back of the carriage and into the abandoned building. Using a logging chain, Henry shackled him to the floorboards.

Less than an hour later, Haze Lyons and Charlie Forbes appeared at the *Tribune*'s office, where Henry and I sat waiting.

"Plummer!" said Lyons angrily, "I hear you're holdin' Buck!"

"Yes, I am," replied Henry calmly, his new shotgun across his lap. "And I'm glad you boys are here. It saves me the trouble of looking for you. I am arresting you both for the murder of Jack Dillingham."

"That's hoss shit, Plummer!" cried Forbes. "We didn' have nothin' to do with that!"

Henry glared at him. "Jack told us who shot him before he died! I mean to see all of you bastards hang for it," he said coldly as he stood up, the shotgun leveled at the two miscreants.

Forbes, eyes wide with alarm, took a step back but Lyons held his ground. He was short and had a nervous tick that caused his left eye to continually blink. His narrow chin was covered by several days growth of whiskers. He wore a pistol in his waistband and I saw his fingers twitching but he wisely resisted the urge to draw his piece.

Henry stepped forward and seized Lyons's weapon. He shoved him aside with the barrel of his gun and grabbed the pistol from Forbes's holster. I suppose I should have been surprised at how meekly the two capitulated, but I had seen that murderous look in Henry's eyes for myself. He pushed his prisoners through the front door and up the street toward the house where Stinson was chained to the floor.

Virginia City
Idaho Territory
June 8, 1863

Judge Edgerton was at a window of the Fairweather Hotel, watching the proceedings on the street below. I fancied a look of disgust on his face, but it could have been just the angle of the morning sunlight.

A miners court was convened and the defendants, their counsel, the prosecutor and the judge were all seated in a flatbed wagon in the middle of Wallace Street. Miners milled around taking in the "trial" which, from where I stood, seemed to have a foreordained conclusion. Forbes was a popular figure in Virginia City with many friends. He was released after the judge refused to even indict him for murder. I could see Henry was seething with rage as Forbes stepped down from the wagon, a grin on his face, his comrades clapping him on the back.

Lyons and Stinson were indicted. Their trial was as chaotic as Henry's had been, but this time the jury consisted of only twelve miners rather than every available man in town. The friends of the accused made catcalls and yelled threats at the jurors and the judge continually had to call for silence. Henry's Virginia City deputy, Ned Ray, who was supposed to be keeping order, was leaning indifferently against a storefront watching the spectacle unfold.

I was called and testified that it was Forbes, Stinson and Lyons who murdered Jack.

"And, Mr. Coffey, how do you know that?" asked David Pemberton, who was serving as the prosecutor at Henry's request.

"Jack told me before he died. The doctor was there as well," I explained. "He said he'd gone to the Bale of Hay, found Deputy Stinson drunk when he needed him. Some heated words were exchanged and the three accused—well, the two accused men—shot Jack down without provocation."

After I testified, a young ranch hand who had witnessed the killing was called.

"At any time during this argument did Deputy Dillingham draw his weapon?" asked Pemberton.

"No, Sir, he didn't," replied the witness. "They just shot 'im like a dog."

The twelve men of the jury, several of whom were clearly troubled by the angry crowd of onlookers, stepped off the wagon bed and gathered under a nearby willow tree to deliberate.

After an hour, they all filed back up onto the wagon and delivered their verdict. Lyons and Stinson were guilty. There were howls of protest as the two men were sentenced to hang for Dillingham's murder. Suddenly, Ned Ray stepped forward and climbed onto the wagon. As Henry watched, mouth agape, the deputy held up a hand and the crowd quieted.

"Nobody wants to see these boys die!" he declared from his perch. "They are good sons of the South! I move they be granted mercy and banished from Virginia City!"

The throng seemed to be waiting for this moment because they pushed forward and loudly demanded the release of the two prisoners. The judge looked around, confused as the twelve jurors stepped off the back of the wagon, their duty completed.

"I second!" yelled another friend of the condemned men.

"Yeah, let 'em go!" someone else cried out.

"What the hell are you doing, Ray?!" Henry called to his deputy. He began to angrily push his way through the crowd, but Ray was now asking for a show of hands from those who wanted Stinson and Lyons released.

Hell broke loose as those who wanted to see the two men executed rushed headlong into a crowd of supporters of the accused. Fists flew and men dropped to the dust. Henry waded in. I saw a miner club him from behind with an axe handle and Henry drop to the ground. Another man stumbled over the sheriff and a third crashed down on top of him.

I had stepped back to the boardwalk as the fight broke out, but seeing Henry being trampled, I ran forward to rescue him. I dragged his limp body out of the melee, deflecting a blow with my forearm as I got him to safety. I looked back at the wagon where the judge was flailing his arms wildly in a vain attempt to end the violence. Men were stumbling out of the brawl hatless, faces bleeding or arms hanging limply. I watched a miner try to slash another with a knife. A man viciously kicked the face of his opponent who was on all fours in the dirt. The miner with the axe handle who'd laid Henry low was himself struck in the face with a thick chain. As brutal as the fight was, there was no gunfire.

The judge suddenly turned to Stinson and Lyons and said something. They broke into grins and Ray led them off the rear of the wagon and away from the fight, which was, by that time, winding down.

Henry had a deep cut on the back of his head, but was slowly regaining consciousness. I placed my handkerchief on the wound, lifted him to his feet and guided him slowly to the doctor's office several doors up Wallace Street. I wanted to get him there first before the line formed.

The doctor determined there was no fracture. "Looks worse than it is," he mumbled as he cleaned the wound and fixed a bandage on it.

We left the office and as I had expected, a crowd of men, who moments before had been battering one another, now sat peacefully on the boardwalk waiting for the doctor's attention.

"I need a bath," Henry croaked as I walked him toward my office. "And look at my clothes."

His usually impeccable suit was covered with dirt and dung. His shirt was filthy and torn and his hat was crushed. He was still very unsteady so, holding him by his upper arm, I steered him to a side street and into an establishment I frequented that was run by an ancient Chinese man and his wife. It was a combination barbershop, bathhouse and laundry.

"Bath," I told the tiny proprietor.

He barked something at his equally diminutive wife and she set to work fetching hot water.

"He needs his suit cleaned and his hat repaired. Also, throw away that shirt and buy him a new one."

Henry stepped behind a screen and disrobed, handing me his filthy clothing. The woman finished pouring the water into a large tin tub and Henry stepped out from behind the screen naked. The old woman ignored him and returned to her washtub where she began scrubbing his clothes. The old man busied himself repairing Henry's hat as my friend eased into the steaming water. He slowly closed his eyes as he lay back. I sat in the barber chair.

He opened one eye and peered at me. "No need to wait," he said. "I will be fine. But you can do me a favor."

"What's that, Henry?" I asked.

"See if you can learn where they went; all of them, including Ray. And, watch your back. I am afraid things have changed for the worse."

I didn't quite know what to make of his ominous remark. "I'll check on you later," I said as I left the shop.

It was mid-afternoon. I suspected Dillingham's murderers and Ned Ray had fled for good. This was confirmed at the third livery stable I visited, where I learned Stinson, Lyons and Ray had retrieved their horses and ridden west out of town just after noon. I tapped my fingers on the stable owner's desk for a moment and considered tracking them to wherever they might be holed up, but then thought better of it after I considered the three-to-one odds were I to stumble on them somewhere out on the range. When he felt better, Henry would organize a tracking party and hunt them down. I left the stable and began to walk back to the *Tribune* office.

As I passed the Fairweather Hotel, a voice called out to me. I turned and saw Wilbur Sanders standing in the doorway, fanning his pallid face with his hat.

"A word, Mr. Coffey?"

I shrugged and followed him into the lobby where I saw Sidney Edgerton seated next to Professor Dimsdale and two other men I didn't recognize. Sanders led me to a chair across from them and then took a seat to my right. The air was warm and stuffy and the two strangers were puffing cigars and peering at me through the smoke. Judge Edgerton regarded me with his dark eyes and then smiled without humor.

"That was quite a spectacle this morning, Mr. Coffey," he began. "Is that what passes for a court of law out here?"

"I'm afraid so, Judge," I replied dryly. "Miners court leastways. They seem to do better when the case is a claim dispute. As you saw, their handling of criminal proceedings leaves much to be desired."

Sanders cleared his throat. "Let me see if I understand what happened," he commented, his voice officious. "Charlie Forbes was not indicted for murder because…?"

"Because he is handsome and popular hereabouts," I interrupted.

"Yes. Even though you, yourself, testified Forbes was one of the three who killed that unfortunate deputy?"

"Correct," I said. It was at this point during the interview that I noticed Dimsdale writing in a small notebook. "What are you doing, Professor?" I asked.

The judge replied for him. "He's making notes of this discussion so I can consult them later. I asked him to be my amanuensis."

"For what purpose?" I asked.

I could see Judge Edgerton was unaccustomed to having his actions questioned. "So I can better understand the nature of the legal system here, Mr. Coffey," he replied stiffly.

"Gentlemen," I responded, "long before I arrived here I was a correspondent in the New York City judicial system and I must tell you, this seems very much to me like an official inquiry," I pinned Edgerton with my eyes. "Yet, you have no official status, Judge Edgerton, because, well, as I explained to you, there is no law in Idaho Territory. And even if we had laws, as chief justice, I believe you are acting outside your authority conducting this inquiry."

"How dare you!" Sanders shouted at me. "President Abraham Lincoln himself appointed my uncle chief justice of the territory," interjected Sanders. "Of course he has authority…"

I shook my head. "You're wrong, Mr. Sanders. Firstly, there is no law here. And there won't be until the territorial legislature writes it. And second, chief justices review appeals from lower courts. They most certainly do *not* conduct investigations."

Sanders glanced at the judge with a confused look as the older man held up his hand.

"He's quite correct, Wilbur," Edgerton conceded with a patronizing smile at me. "At present the territory has no laws on the books to enforce. Criminal or civil. It's a very odd state of affairs. The miners court is probably the closest thing you will find here to a justice system." Then he shifted his gaze to me and it slowly darkened. "As for my authority, Mr. Coffey, I wouldn't be so presumptuous, if I were you."

My eyes locked with Edgerton's for a long moment. "So, Judge, I am correct. This is an official interrogation."

"Interrogation!" he cried suddenly with a conciliatory chuckle. "My dear fellow, I am simply trying to comprehend what transpired out on the street this morning. Professor Dimsdale informs me you are a savvy observer of life on the frontier. I had hoped you would tutor me on the ways of the miners."

I smiled at him. "Very well, Judge Edgerton. If it is education you seek, then please ask the professor to put down his pen and I'll try to be helpful."

The judge motioned to Dimsdale, who closed his notebook with an annoyed glance my way.

"You may have detected an undercurrent in Bannack and over here in Virginia City," I began. "There is considerable tension between men from the north and men from the south. Most of the time their political differences are out of sight because everyone here is trying to get rich, which tends to overrule one's political persuasion, no matter how passionate that may be."

Edgerton looked around at the other men, his brow knitted, as I continued.

"Stinson and Lyons are both from the south, so they naturally back the

Confederacy. So does the judge who was presiding. But the jury, along with the men who wanted to see Stinson and Lyons hang—well, they're Union supporters. Many of them are from Pennsylvania, Illinois, and Ohio. And there are some Irishmen, Bohemians, and other immigrants who tend to have northern sentiments, if they have any leanings at all."

Edgerton's look of befuddlement was giving way slowly to one of comprehension.

"And these sympathies precipitated the free for all," he stated.

I nodded. "Ned Ray is Sheriff Plummer's deputy...or was. The sheriff thought he was a Union man but he was wrong. Ray waited until just the right moment and then called for release of the condemned men, appealing to the crowd's southern sympathies."

"That's outrageous!" cried Sanders. "They kill a good lawman and they go scot free? And another deputy sheriff orchestrates the entire fraud?!"

Edgerton again held up his hand and like an obedient dog, Sanders quickly calmed himself.

"What troubles me about the affair, Mr. Coffey, is the appearance of official...complicity. Tell me, if you can, where is Sheriff Plummer now?" he asked quietly.

"He was injured trying to stop the fight. He's resting," I replied. "As soon as he is able, he will go after the killers as well as Ned Ray..."

"Oh, I'm sure he will," Edgerton replied, his tone sarcastic. "I imagine Sheriff Plummer will be right behind them."

I shot the judge a puzzled look. "Yes, he will," I agreed as I slowly stood up. "If there is nothing more..."

"Thank you for your time, Mr. Coffey," Edgerton said. "Our talk has been illuminating."

I stopped by the office, where I was surprised to see Colgan at his desk scribbling away.

"Oh, there you are," he called as I walked in. "Did you see that insanity on the street today?"

"Indeed I did," I replied. "I was right in the middle of it; another north-south dust-up, but this time murderers were freed by a deputy sheriff, no less. I came in to write an account for the next edition."

"Excellent!" he replied, rising from his chair. "Play up the political angle...that seems to sell more newspapers. I'm dreadfully late for an appointment. I will see you on the morrow, Noah." He dashed out the door, pulling his jacket over his heavy shoulders.

I finished my account of the trial, brawl and flight of the killers. It would make for a wonderful read for anyone who wasn't there. I stuck the papers on a spike on Colgan's desk and locked the door as I left. It was growing dark, so I made my way back to the bathhouse.

The old Chinese man greeted me and then waved his hands, "Man go!" he said. "Don't know where. Leave fast. No pay. Shirt cos' fou' dorrah. Bath, clean suit, fix hat two dorrah. Shine boots flee." I dug into my pocketbook and handed him the coins, annoyed at Henry for not settling his bill. Then I searched the town for the next hour but the old man was right, I thought to myself. Man go.

28

Virginia City
Idaho Territory
July 10, 1863

The blond man is here. The day was hot and a persistent wind whipped up clouds of dust and dry dung. I was sitting in the shade of a tree speaking to some acquaintances when a large wagon rolled by, hardly a noteworthy occurrence. I glanced up at the driver thinking it might be someone I knew, but was stunned by whom I saw holding the reins.

It has been nearly six years since he leveled his carbine at me and fired, but I remember his face as though I had been shot yesterday. He glanced my way and our eyes met but his still youthful face showed no sign of recognition. Indeed, he touched the brim of his hat and smiled at me as he drove by. I felt an electric rush in my spine at the sight of the Mormon killer. I looked away quickly, making no return gesture of greeting.

"What's the matter, Noah?" asked Warren, a man I'd befriended who ran a leather repair shop off Wallace Street. Like me, he was originally from Connecticut and we occasionally exchanged stories about our home state.

I shook my head. "I'm fine...just the heat," I replied. I stared at the wagon as it continued up Wallace Street. In the rear sat two young women and two small children. The wagon the blond man drove was likely one of those that had been looted in 1857—or so I imagined. The furnishings and other goods in its bed suggested the family was emigrating somewhere.

I excused myself, walked across the street and, then on the boardwalk, followed behind the wagon. At the top of the hill where Wallace Street terminated, the man gestured to a miner loitering on the corner. The fellow stepped over to the wagon and the two exchanged some words. The man pointed to a trail that I knew led down to a small branch of Alder Creek. There was an area along the creek where wayfarers often camped. The wagon turned to the left and slowly rolled down the short hill toward the willow trees along the stream.

Shaken by the blond man's arrival in Virginia, I walked back to the *Tribune* office.

"Hotter than Hades!" Colgan declared as I came in. He was busy proofreading a copy of the newspaper. We had sold enough advertising space to publish and Colgan wanted to finish up so he could get to his afternoon "appointment." He handed me a copy.

"Here, you can proofread the back page..." He hesitated as he looked at my face over his eyeglasses. "Are you ill?"

I fell into a seat. "Yes," I replied. "The heat." He poured water from a pitcher and handed me the glass. I drained it in three gulps.

"Easy, Noah," he said, his voice kindly. "Why don't you go home and lay down?"

"I'll be fine in a few minutes," I said. "Here, give me the proof." I took it from his hand and began reading. But I only saw meaningless blacks spots on the page before me.

Two hours later, with the help of a couple of boys, we had distributed the newspapers to the establishments in Virginia where it was sold. One boy then took a bundle to Nevada City and sold them on the street there. The other lad peddled the *Tribune* to patrons at the local saloons and wikiups. Three bundles were shipped to Bannack on the afternoon stage, where Chrisman now sold them and sent the proceeds back to us.

That evening, I had my supper at Mrs. Foster's boarding house where I lived, and afterward I walked down to the campground, nervously fingering the derringer in my pocket. It was cooling off rapidly as it always does here after the sun drops behind the mountains. Darkness was closing in and I could see the cheerful glow of firelight among the willows as I descended the hill. I smelled the aroma of meat broiling and heard some quiet laughter along with the pleasant music of the shallow stream spilling over rocks. The trail crossed the creek at a point where the water was only ankle deep. It bent around the trees and I could see several distinct campfires alongside the creek.

As I walked by, alarmed faces looked my way, but I waved and smiled in a reassuring manner as I hurried by. Ahead of me I could hear the voices of small children. Then I saw the wagon. I stopped as the blond man appeared ten paces in front of me in the dusk, apparently unaware of my presence.

"Good evening, Sir," I said. Alarmed, he spun around, and then I saw him smile.

"Good evening to you, Sir," he replied. He stepped forward, holding out his hand. "My name is Micah Jordan."

I shook his hand and introduced myself. He again showed no recognition but, to be sure, my hat was pulled low so my face was in shadows.

"Where do you hail from, if I may ask Mr. Jordan?"

"Utah Territory, I'm proud to say," he replied with a grin. I arrived this afternoon. I am hoping to establish a church hereabouts."

"A church!" I laughed. "Well, that's a fine idea. You will be happy to learn there are plenty of sinners in Virginia City that need saving." I looked at him intently. My plan was to pull the derringer, put a bullet between his blue eyes and escape into the night. "Have they run out of sinners down in Utah Territory?"

He hesitated for a moment. "There are many sinners there," he stiffly replied. "But ours is a mighty church with an important message of salvation. The leadership in Salt Lake City wants to reach out to the hinterlands of the west and bring converts to our faith. Brigham Young himself has called on the faithful saints to serve as missionaries." He glanced at the two girls by the fire. "We are missionaries."

"That would be the Mormon Church of which you speak?"

"Yes," he replied, "but we prefer to call ourselves The Church of Jesus

Christ of Latter-day Saints."

"Well, Mr. Jordan, I am quite sure you will receive the welcome in Virginia City you deserve," I obversed with a genial smile. "You seem like a man who will be more than capable of leading a flock, seeing as how you live your faith."

By now Jordan didn't know what to make of me or the direction in which I had steered the conversation. Before he had a chance to respond, I asked him another question.

"Do you know a man in Utah named John Lee?"

"John D. Lee? Of course!" he replied eagerly. "Everyone in Utah knows Bishop Lee! He is one of our most esteemed elders. Bishop Lee was among those who made the hand cart trek from Missouri to Zion with Brigham Young in '47."

"Is he, now?" I asked. "Well, Sir, as it happens I made his acquaintance once some years back. I only wish I had the chance to spend more time with him then."

"That's how many people feel after they've met Bishop Lee," he proudly declared.

"Perhaps one day I will meet him again," I replied as I silently cocked the small pistol in my pocket. "In fact, I look forward to it."

In the growing gloom, I saw him nod, a slight look of confusion in the blue eyes I remembered so well. I began to pull the pistol just as a tiny boy ran forward and siezed Jordan's leg.

"Papa! Supper!" cried the tyke.

Jordan tussled the boy's hair, blond like his father's. I eased the hammer back down, abandoning my plan to kill the Mormon there and then. I smiled instead at the child and then looked at Jordan.

"It was a pleasure meeting you, Sir. I know I will be seeing you again very soon."

Jordan wasn't going anywhere and neither was I. When the time was right, I knew at least one of the Mormon butchers would finally answer for his crime.

Idaho Territory
August 1, 1863
Virginia City

I learned this morning that an unknown coward shot Henry. The scoundrel lacked the manhood to face him in a fair fight so he shot Henry from behind. The Bannack stage driver who delivered word of the assault said the injury was not life threatening but that the doctor attending him had considered removing Henry's wounded arm. I cannot say I am surprised, given the enemies Henry has made since the beginning of the year.

The last word I had from Henry before the shooting was that he'd been unable to find any trace of Forbes, Stinson or Lyons, and Ned Ray had disappeared. As for Doc Howard and his gang that Henry suspected of robbing and killing the merchant Magruder, they still remained at large.

The reader could well conclude that Henry brought the shooting upon himself and that, at best, he is an ineffective sheriff, but one must remember that this territory is inhabited by all manner of villains and the area is vast and studded with mountain peaks. It is a distance of some forty miles from Virginia to Bannack and much of the land between the towns is uninhabited except for the occasional ranch or roaming band of Indians. Fast flowing rivers and creeks crisscross the sage-spiked prairies and there are countless canyons, gulches and abandoned shacks where men may easily hide.

Without a great deal of good fortune, a hundred men—let alone just one sheriff with a deputy or two—would find it nearly impossible to locate men who didn't want to be found. These were my thoughts as I encountered Wilbur Sanders this afternoon after learning of Henry's wounding in Bannack. As usual, the day was clear and hot as I walked into the Miner's Café for my dinner. Sanders was just leaving.

"Ah, Coffey," he declared, catching my arm. He directed me by my elbow out to the boardwalk. "I was just speaking about you with some of my associates."

I pulled away from him. "Is that so?" I asked in an irritated tone.

"We are of the mind that Sheriff Plummer isn't doing near enough to bring the men who killed Dillingham to justice," he stated. "And we have wondered why the *Tribune* has not taken an editorial position on the matter."

"Sheriff Plummer was shot," I angrily declared. "Wounded in the arm. I might be taking an editorial position on the cowardice shown by his assailant. He attempted to kill the sheriff while his back was turned!"

Sanders took a step back, an astonished look on his face. I continued.

"Henry is the one person I know for certain who is trying to bring about order in Bannack and the rest of his jurisdiction; to protect the lives and property of citizens…and this is how a good man is repaid!"

"Well I know you are his friend…"

"Friendship has nothing to do with it, Sanders!" I exclaimed. "Henry is a wealthy man. He's made his money honestly as a miner and as a merchant before that. He doesn't need to serve as sheriff. Do you have any idea why he does that thankless job?"

Sanders shook his head stupidly and blinked his eyes in the face of my passion.

"Because he despises lawlessness and disorder," I said. "He won't stand by when the strong prey on the weak. You, Edgerton and your associates, whoever they may be, should thank God Almighty that the miners chose Henry to enforce the law."

Sanders tried on a conciliatory smile. "Mr. Coffey, Sir. Please. I sympathize fully with your feelings about Sheriff Plummer. But try to understand. Judge Edgerton is accustomed to citizens respecting the law and officers of the courts enforcing it to the letter. Thus far, what he has observed here has offended his sensibilities in that regard. And mine as well."

"This is mining country, for Christ's sake," I interrupted him. "What did you people suppose you would find in the mountains? Aristocrats? The men who stampeded here want to get rich. Fast."

He held up his hand. "Yes, yes, but the constant violence, the drunks, the gambling and whoring, the petty crime, the undesirables that seem to inhabit every street corner…this is what we're concerned with. And it's not just here in Virginia, but in Nevada and Bannack, too. This place will never become respectable without some semblance of order. And that can only come with a reliable sheriff supported by a strong force of dedicated deputies."

"Reliable? Explain yourself," I demanded.

He hesitated, then leaned into me and lowered his voice conspiratorially. "Think on it for a moment, Coffey. Three men who killed the deputy are free thanks to one of Plummer's deputies. A merchant and his wagon go mysteriously missing. Then the men supposedly guarding the merchant and wagon show up in Nevada City, *sans* merchant, sell the goods and disappear. No arrests made. In fact, before I arrived here two days ago, I observed Plummer in Bannack going about his business as though bloodthirsty criminals weren't running amok. What do you suppose Judge Edgerton might conclude from that?"

I glared at him. "Go on."

"Well, as I say, he might well question Plummer's…reliability."

I was shocked, scarcely believing the words I was hearing. He mistook my expression as bewilderment, nodding slowly, this thin lips pursed.

"That's right," he whispered, "Plummer would seem to be a confederate of the outlaws. Perhaps their leader."

"You son of a bitch!" I yelled in his face. "How dare you?"

It was Sanders's turn to be shocked. "Just…just a moment, Coffey," he sputtered, backing away from me. "You have no right to speak to me…"

In the street, several men stopped in their tracks to watch us.

"I am of a mind to thrash you here and now, Sanders," I cried. I glanced toward the group of men who had gathered around hoping there might be a display of fisticuffs. "In Ohio you may have challenged a man's honor without fear of standing behind your words! It is much different here, Sir! I would advise you *never* to repeat to anyone what you just said to me! That gentleman you mentioned will see to it you answer for your slander if you do! You've been warned!" And with that I pushed past him and entered the café.

As I sullenly ate my food, flies buzzing about my plate, I began to reconsider my impolitic outburst. Edgerton, after all, was the future chief justice of the territory and Sanders was obviously his second. If they really suspected Henry was part of a criminal enterprise, how might they decide to deal with him? The longer I reflected on it, the more I realized I may well have exacerbated Henry's problems.

Bannack
IdahoTerritory
August 28, 1863

Henry was far more cheerful than I had expected when I finally located him in the saloon of the Goodrich Hotel. His left arm hung by his side, almost useless, but he seemed to be in a good mood nonetheless, no doubt because he was already well into his second or third whiskey.

"That damned doctor was ready to take it off," he said. "I told him I'd shoot *him* in his arm if he tried it."

"So there is no corruption?"

"No, thank God. The damn thing was swollen up like a blood sausage at first but it's much better now," he replied. "He lifted the arm onto the table and pulled back the sleeve of his coat and shirt to reveal his wrist. "Put your fingers right here."

I did as he asked and felt a hard ball just under the skin on top of his wrist. "That's the slug that entered my shoulder and traveled down my arm. It's lodged in the wrist bones," he grinned. "I'll take it to my grave."

"Another souvenir of your career as a lawman," I remarked dryly. "No witnesses have come forward?"

He shook his head as he sipped his whiskey. "My own fault. I dropped my guard. It was dark and I heard men across the street but paid them no mind. The shot came from among them while I was walking into Chrisman's. It knocked me onto my backside. By the time help arrived, whoever pulled the trigger had run."

"Any idea who it was?" I asked.

He shrugged. "There's a long list of suspects starting with the parsimonious bastards who want me to uphold the law but don't want to ante up a couple of dollars so I can build a jail. They'd rather I hang everyone I arrest. Then there are a few miners who think I cheated them out of their claims now that the stamp mills are paying off. Or it could be Cleveland's friends, or friends of Cleveland's friends. A bunch of them would love to see me dead."

After a long pause, I smiled at Henry. "And you were once so popular!"

He laughed. "It was like this in California, Noah. The so-called respectable citizens want law but they don't want the mess that comes when you have to enforce it. I had enemies there, too, you'll remember. No surprise I have them here."

He was more right than he knew. It occurred to me I should tell him about my exchange with Sanders but I knew it would only anger him and might even move him to violence. As I was considering this, Buzz Caven came through the door. Henry saw him and waved with his good hand.

"Trouble," Caven said without preamble. "Over 't the stage office."

Henry rose and I followed him out the door. The stagecoach office was at the foot of the street near Yankee Flat. Seated on a bench before it sat a man I recognized as Tom Caldwell, one of the Oliver-Salt Lake Stage Line's drivers. He saw Henry and stood.

"Sheriff," he began, "we was robbed at Point of Rocks this mornin'. Three men, all masked. An' their horses had blankets on 'em, too, so's we wouldn't know whose they was."

Henry eyed him. "Any idea who the men were, Tom?"

Before Caldwell could answer, Judge Edgerton suddenly appeared out of the darkness with Wilbur Sanders and another man in tow.

"Sheriff, I heard the mail stage to Salt Lake was robbed," Edgerton said. "Is that true?

"Seems so, Judge," Henry replied calmly. "I'm just hearing about it for the first time from Tom Caldwell here. He was the driver."

"What happened?" Edgerton asked Caldwell.

"Pardon me, Judge," Henry interrupted in a mild voice. "I'm questioning Tom and I will determine what happened and investigate. This is no affair of yours."

Sanders tried to step forward but Edgerton's arm shot out, checking his nephew's advance on Henry. "Of course, Sheriff Plummer, of course," the judge replied coolly. "I was only trying to be of some assistance to you."

By then a crowd had collected. Some miners were calling out questions and others offering interpretations of what was going on. Henry took Caldwell by the arm and began leading him up the street toward Chrisman's.

"Let's go up to my office where we can speak in private," Henry said as the two departed. Several men began following them but Caven stepped in front of them.

"Sheriff says private, Boys," he said. "Now go about your own business an' leave 'em alone, hear?"

I glanced at Edgerton. He was watching Henry and Caldwell walk away. Sanders whispered something and the judge looked at him and gave a curt nod. Both exchanged words with the third man who seemed to agree with whatever it was they said. Moments later, the three of them were gone.

I made my way up to Chrisman's where I found Henry questioning Caldwell in his office. The driver was certain George Ives had led the gang. He was less sure about the other two robbers. They had used shotguns to hold up the stage and its passengers. All told, the robbers had gotten a little less than two thousand dollars in gold and more than five hundred dollars in coin and valuables from the three passengers.

"Ives?" Henry asked. "How would you know that if he wore a mask and draped his horse?"

"I seen the hoss had three white socks and the legs was gray dappled, Sheriff," Caldwell explained. "I know fer a fact that George bought that hoss from Mr. Oliver last fall. It were a geldin' and kinda small. Not strong enough to draw the stage."

Henry nodded. As with other stage line owners, Oliver frequently bought and sold stock out of his main stable and his way stations between Virginia City and Salt Lake.

As Henry considered what Caldwell had told him I interrupted the interview.

"Who is this Ives?" I asked.

"I haven't met him yet but it appears the deputy U.S. marshal in Lewiston has," he said as he handed me a broadside. It carried the rough sketch of a young man and said George Ives was wanted for three robberies and a killing. It called for Ives's arrest and return to Lewiston, where he was to face justice before a federal judge there. I handed the flyer back to Henry.

"I assume you've met this Ives," I asked Caldwell.

He nodded. "Last summer on the road down t' Salt Lake. We was at Diamond Ranch south o' the Snake fer the night an' he and some other fellas made camp outside. To tell the truth Sheriff, I was worried that night 'cause I didn't like the looks of Ives nor his associates. Thought they might try somethin' out on the road after we left the station, but I never did see 'em again."

"Well, they could be anywhere," Henry declared after some thought. He looked at me, then down at his wounded arm. "Care to throw in and help me hunt them down?"

I thought of Exeter Colgan. He wouldn't appreciate the extended absence as it was but I told Henry I would help since it also meant a good first hand story if we managed to capture the fugitives.

I smiled. "I'm in."

"Very well, Deputy Coffey, we shall leave at first light. We'll try to pick up the trail at Point of Rocks."

29

Idaho Territory
August 29, 1863

From a distance at first light we must have looked like three wraiths as we galloped through the thick mist that hung like a shroud in the chilled air. By late morning, the fog had burned off, revealing mountain peaks jabbing the crystalline sky. A pleasant breeze out of the north cooled us as we forded the Beaverhead, where we headed our mounts toward Point of Rocks ten miles distant.

"So Ives hasn't shown up in Bannack before?" I asked Henry.

"No," he replied, "Nor Virginia City or Nevada City either, as far as I know."

"It seems odd that he would suddenly decide to hold up a stage," I remarked. "Seems risky, I guess."

"Oh it is risky," Henry acknowledged. "With so few people in this part of the territory, it is difficult not to be known unless of course you're newly arrived. I wasn't surprised to hear that Caldwell remembered Ives by his horse."

We stopped next to a creek, and made coffee. I stood admiring the distant mountain range shimmering in the sun. We could see a herd of elk ranging across the lower slopes of the nearest peak, the great beasts intently grazing in order to put on enough fat to make it through the long, brutal winter ahead.

"Henry," I said as we resumed the ride, "you remember I told you about what happened to me. In Utah."

He looked at me earnestly. "Yes, of course."

"The man who shot me is in Virginia City. His name is Jordan."

"Are you sure?" he asked.

"Absolutely," I grimly replied. "He showed up some weeks ago. Says he's a missionary and plans to build a church."

"You spoke to him?"

"Yes, the day he arrived. He didn't remember me," I said. "As far as he knows, I'm dead. I swore I would kill any of the bastards if I ever encountered one and now I have my chance."

Henry nodded his understanding and then rode silently for many minutes. Finally, he looked over at me. "He won't fight you, you know," he replied, "being a missionary and all. He'll hide behind his Bible. I could arrest him, but it would be your word against his."

"No, you misunderstand," I declared. "I mean, I am thinking of just shooting him down, whether he is armed or not. In fact, I almost did just that."

Henry was already shaking his head. "Don't do it. That would put you on the wrong side of the law. You will have to find another way."

That was odd advice when I thought of Vedder and Cleveland and how they'd both died, so I said nothing more about Jordan.

By evening, we had reached Point of Rocks, so named because of the unusually dramatic formation of boulders. We drew up into a canyon beneath a ledge and ate a cold supper of ham and bread as Henry had decided a fire or its smoke might alert Ives and his men if they happened to still be nearby.

Henry was kneeling at the remains of a fire, his hand on the coals. "These are warm. They were here three hours ago, maybe less."

He stood up and looked around the stand of pine trees. We'd begun our third day on the trail riding south for an hour until we spotted the trees high up on the slope of a steep ridge. They provided the only cover for miles around.

On Henry's hunch, we'd ridden up to the pines and almost immediately found fresh horse droppings and the remains of a jackrabbit.

Henry pointed at some matted pine needles on the ground beneath the tall trees. "Looks like three men sleeping there," he commented. "Shot the rabbit for supper. I think they circled back to either Virginia or Nevada. There's nothing south of here but desert and Salt Lake City. They wouldn't go there with better pickings to be had up at Alder Gulch. Still, we'd better make sure." He looked over at Caven. "Buzz, ride south for another day and see if you pick up their trail. If you find it or if you run into them, don't try to take them yourself. Ride back to Virginia City and I'll meet you there. We'll get a party together to go after them."

Without a word, Caven mounted his horse and rode away at a trot. Henry looked around for a few more minutes and then we mounted our horses and rode northeast.

Dempsey's Ranch was located along a spring creek off the main trail. Shortly after noon, we rode through the ranch's gate and down a short road to a low slung log cabin. Smoke issued from its stovepipe and a big dog of uncertain breed charged us from behind the privy, its teeth barred. Henry kicked it in the side and the cur ran back to the cabin, whimpering.

A fat woman opened the door of the cabin and scowled at us. She slammed the door and moments later a fat man came through it holding a carbine in one hand and a Colt Dragoon in the other.

"What in the hell you two want?" he demanded as he approached us. He wore an undershirt that had once been white but was now stained with sweat and soot. His suspenders hung loose and he had mud-caked boots pulled over his tattered trousers. His thin hair blew in the breeze.

"We want you to put those guns up," Henry smiled. "Or I will be happy to do it for you." Henry flipped his coat aside and placed his hand on the handle of his revolver.

The man's jowls quivered and he made a face, the fat folds rolling into something approximating a smile. "No need to make no threats, Friend," he said, exposing small yellow teeth as he lowered his weapons. "We get all kinds of trash out here. Man can't be too careful."

"I understand," Henry smiled back. "I take it you are Mr. Dempsey? I'm

Sheriff Henry Plummer from Bannack. This is Deputy Coffey. We're looking for George Ives. Has he been here recently?"

Dempsey's red face went through more jiggling permutations. I believed he was trying to communicate ignorance. "Ives, ya say? No. No man name o' Ives been by here. Just some injuns t' other day come beggin'. I shot one of 'em in the foot..." As he recalled the event, he let out a string of croaks that I took for laughter. "Fuckin' redskin hot footed it out of here, I'm tellin' ya!"

Neither Henry nor I shared in the levity. "Do you mind if we have a look around?" Henry asked. Dempsey hesitated. His little blue eyes glanced back at the cabin. Then he shrugged.

"Naw, I don't mind," he said finally.

The interior of the cabin was cluttered with clothing, bedding, pans and refuse. The stench of stale sweat, bacon fat and wet dog fur hung in the air. The fat woman was seated on the edge of a bed in the one room cabin, glaring at us as we surveyed the mess. Her long black hair was uncombed and she had an enormous wart on her cheek. Her dress was as filthy as the clothing her husband wore. Henry glanced over at Dempsey, who stood by the door.

"Mr. Dempsey, would you kindly show Deputy Coffey around the barn? I'd like a few words alone with Mrs. Dempsey."

The fat man's face went rigid. He fixed his eyes on his wife with a look I could not decipher, but I reached out and tugged his arm. Henry coolly watched all of this until we were out the door.

The barn was as cluttered and unkempt as the cabin. A few sway-backed horses stood in piles of their own droppings, forlornly peering at me from their stalls. They looked malnourished and mangy. Some goats and chickens wandered in and out of the barn and tools were scattered across the floor where they had been discarded or were leaned haphazardly against the walls. I saw enormous rats in the dark corners of the barn, but I could find nothing that looked suspicious. From where I was standing, Dempsey was guilty only of being slovenly.

As we left the barn Henry approached, his steely eyes fixed on Dempsey. "You lied to me," he said to the fat man. "Ives was here with two men the other night."

Dempsey sputtered something but Henry held up his hand. "Shut up!"

he demanded. "Ives robbed a stage and he's going to jail for it. You will, too, if I decide you're his accomplice."

Despite the cool air, Dempsey was sweating profusely. His pudgy fingers rubbed the stubble on his chin and then suddenly he looked as though he remembered something important. "Did ya say *Joe* Ives, Sheriff?"

Henry glared at Dempsey.

"Cause that's what I thought ya said," Dempsey exclaimed in his croaking laugh. "*Joe* Ives! Now, there *was* a fella here two nights back name o' George...I didn't catch his last name. The woman fed 'im an' his partners and they slept out behind the barn. They's gone in the mornin'."

Henry's face was white with rage, yet he wore a smile as he reached out and genially placed his good hand on Dempsey's shoulder. "Do you know where this *George* and his companions might have gone, Mr. Dempsey?"

"Well, Sir, no...I..." But before Dempsey could complete his thought, Henry had brought his knee into the man's fat belly. A blast of air exploded from Dempsey's mouth and he collapsed to the ground holding his midsection. I heard Mrs. Dempsey's shriek of horror as she saw her husband fall. The big dog started barking but decided against attacking Henry after a bluff charge.

"You're wasting my time!" Henry growled at Dempsey, who had rolled over onto his back, his massive belly heaving as he tried to get air into his lungs. His mouth moved but there were no words.

Henry looked as though he was going to kick Dempsey as hard as he had kicked the man's dog, but I gently pushed him back.

"Let me try to help, Henry," I said.

I got the fat man slowly to his feet and led him to a discarded nail keg in the cabin's yard. I helped him sit as he continued to gasp.

"Listen, Mr. Dempsey," I whispered. "The sheriff is in a foul mood. He gets that way when he feels he can't trust somebody's word. You understand." I patted him on the back. "We need to find this fellow Ives. Now if you can just tell us where you think he's gone, we'll be on our way."

"I...I can't tell you," the fat man replied hoarsely. "They'll kill me."

"Who?" I asked. "Who will kill you?"

He stared at me, his face fearful. I glanced over my shoulder at Henry who was by the corral patting his horse's neck. "The sheriff is losing his patience," I warned him. "He will put you in jail in Bannack until he gets the truth. I wouldn't cross him if I were you, Mr. Dempsey. On the other hand, if you help us, I'm certain Sheriff Plummer will see to it you are protected and possibly rewarded for your cooperation."

Dempsey's eyes shot a look at Henry. "Howard'll kill me," he blurted. "Howard, Ives, Forbes, the whole bunch."

At the name of Forbes, I froze. "Charlie Forbes?" I asked him finally. He gave a quick nod.

I motioned to Henry and looked back at Dempsey. "Let me suggest you start from the beginning, Mr. Dempsey. Tell the sheriff what you know, who you know and, if you can, the connection between Howard, Ives and Forbes."

Idaho Territory
September 1, 1863

Henry and I had been sitting among the rocks since sun-up. We were hidden on the crest of a slope overlooking the Ruby River, peering down at what we believed to be Ramshorn Gulch, a deep ravine that ran north-south a hundred yards from the road.

"That bastard lied," I said to Henry. "There's nothing in the gulch... certainly no place for a gang of men to hide out."

Henry didn't answer. The sun appeared above the ridge behind us as he continued to eye the gulch.

Suddenly he froze. "Look!"

I followed his pointing finger and saw a thin wisp of smoke rising from what appeared to be a grassy bank along the river. "I'll be damned," I replied.

"It's a dugout!" Henry said. "They cut right into the riverbank and covered it with grass and sage...so *that's* Robber's Roost."

"I thought that story about the desperado's hideout was just talk."

Rumors about Robber's Roost had circulated for as long as Virginia City had existed, according to Colgan. Under questioning, Dempsey said he thought Ives and his men were headed to the "Roost" to meet Doc Howard, Forbes and maybe Buck Stinson and Haze Lyons. Dempsey himself had never seen the Roost but he thought the place was hidden in Ramshorn Gulch.

Henry's eyes were darting around the valley floor, assessing the best route to reach the dugout. "It's a perfect hideout for road agents what with the traffic out on the trail between Bannack and Virginia," he said.

The area was desolate and offered no escape for a miner taking his gold to Bannack or onwards to Salt Lake. The Ruby Mountains ended here and the Tobacco Root range began to the north a mile across the valley. The Ruby River flowed placidly through the gap, the road paralleling its course. As ambush locations went, Henry was right. This was perfect.

He suddenly reached over and grabbed my arm. A man had emerged from behind a screen of grass and brush. He walked across the gulch and pulled aside another screen to reveal two horses eating grain from feedbags.

Another man appeared from the dugout. He and the first man began saddling one of the horses.

"Just two men. I don't know them," Henry said. "Do you?"

"No."

One of the men mounted the saddled horse and took a rope tied to the second, said something to the other man, then rode out of the gulch toward the road. The man left behind turned and went back into the dugout.

Henry looked at me. "I can't go down there," he said. "He might recognize me. But he won't know you. Find out what you can about Ives and the others."

I stared at Henry. "This isn't exactly my line of work, Henry!" I protested.

He grinned at me. "You already look like a road agent, Noah. You've got three days of stubble, you're covered in road dust and, here," he took off his gun belt and handed it to me, "now you're armed to the teeth!"

I reluctantly strapped on the weapon. "Give me your hat," I demanded as I removed my bowler. "It has a sinister look to it." We traded hats. His was a wide brimmed affair, black and sweat stained. It was a little large, but I wore it low on my forehead. Then I cut some material from my black blanket and, using a leather thong, fashioned an eye patch.

"I like it!" Henry exclaimed. "Whenever I read your news accounts I'm always amazed at your imagination, but you're outdoing yourself today with this masquerade!"

"He may have seen me in Virginia. I don't want to take any chances." With that, I grabbed a fistful of dirt and spread it on my cheeks. I mounted and rode east for a half mile, then traversed the slope, crossed the Ruby upstream from the dugout and made my way out to the road. I came to the gulch and saw that the way down to the river had also been carefully camouflaged with brush. I pushed through and rode right up to the dugout door.

"Hello the house!" I called. There was no response at first. Then, above the babbling of the river, I heard the unmistakable cocking of a revolver. "Who's there?" came the challenge.

"Dick Jacobs!" I called. "Hold your fire!"

"State your business then!" the voice responded.

"I'm hungry. Hopin' I could get a meal an' water my hoss. Seen your smoke. I'll pay," I called out.

The dugout's door had been cleverly concealed with sagebrush, weeds and grass. Even this close it was difficult to discern that a cabin was concealed within the riverbank. The door opened and a red headed man stepped out. He was short and wore a neatly trimmed beard. He held his revolver on me.

"I kin feed ya'," he said. "Then ya' gotta be on your way. Before you dismount, drop that pistol."

I did as he said and knew Henry would be livid when I returned his LeMat covered in dust. I dismounted and held out my hand.

The man stepped forward and shook it. "I'm Red Yeager," he said. "Jacobs you say your name is?"

"That's right," I smiled, "Dick Jacobs. Just come down from Lewiston. Marshal up there took an interest in me so's I thought it were time to skedaddle."

He laughed. "All's I got right now's some cornmeal mush, bacon and coffee, but you're welcome to what you can eat."

He disappeared into the cabin and emerged a few moments later with a plate of food and tin mug of coffee. I gobbled the food greedily with my fingers. He watched with appreciation.

"I'm the cook here," he declared. "Good?"

I nodded. "Mmm...first hot grub I've had in three days" I replied, my mouth full of mush and bacon. "Who you cook for?"

He hesitated. "Some fellas. You wouldn't know 'em."

I finished the food, drained the coffee and wiped my mouth with the back of my sleeve. "Doc Howard down this way?" I asked. "If'n he is, I's lookin' to throw in with 'im."

He stared at me. "How...how ya' know Doc?"

I smiled thinly. "I tol' you, Red, I was in Lewiston. Everyone up there knows Doc...or leastways, they know about Doc. And Zachery, Page, Marshall and them."

He stood frozen, his blue eyes glancing about. Without someone to tell him what to do I could see Yeager was totally lost.

"Doc would be damned interested knowin' about me," I said reaching out and taking Henry's pistol from his hand. I slid it into the holster on my hip. "Let me ask you somethin'. A man name o' Ives come by here?"

"You seem to know a lot, Mister," Yeager said warily after some consideration. "Yeah, Ives come in last night. Had a coupl' o' men with him. His partners left early an' he left hisself just a little while ago. Said somethin' about sellin' a hoss down t' Cold Spring."

Damn I thought to myself. Henry and I had watched Ives ride off alone only thirty minutes earlier.

"That son of a bitch owes me two hundred U.S. dollars," I said angrily. "I gotta catch up with him...Cold Spring ya' say? Where's that?"

He directed me east on the road, but of course I already knew where it was. I mounted and thanked Yeager for the food. "Tell Doc I's here and lookin' t' throw in. I'll be in Nevada City. Dick Jacobs...Rattlesnake Dick some call me. Ya' remember that? Tell 'im to send word an' I'll meet 'im anyplace."

Yeager looked annoyed as he waved me away and went back into the dugout. I rode out to the trail and looked up to where I knew Henry had watched the proceedings at the dugout. I furiously waved his hat and hoped he understood he needed to hurry.

Fifteen minutes later we were galloping east toward Alder Gulch. "We'll find Ives at Cold Spring Ranch," I explained as we rode. "He wants to sell that horse he was leading."

In another hour we rode into the ranch. Dozens of ponies wandered around a big corral, picking at the thin grass or basking in the warm sun. There was a substantial cabin behind the corral and, sure enough, the horse we'd seen

Ives ride off on was tied to the hitching rail in front of it. It was a gray with dappled legs and three white socks. We dismounted and pretended to look at the horses in the corral as though we were interested in buying.

Behind us we heard the cabin door open and we turned to see two men emerge. I recognized Bill Moore as the owner of Cold Spring. His ranch served as a way station for the stages and he also bought and sold horses and cattle. Next to him stood a strapping young man of twenty-six or seven years. He glanced our way, shook hands with Moore, then mounted the gray. He spurred his horse and as he rode by us he waved genially.

"Gentlemen," he smiled, "Fine day!"

"George! George Ives," Henry called out. "How are you?!"

Ives reined in the gray and gave Henry a puzzled look. "I know you?"

"No!" Henry grinned as he pulled the LeMat. "Henry Plummer. *Sheriff* Henry Plummer. Keep your hands where I can see them and get off the horse."

I pulled the new shotgun out of Henry's scabbard and held it on Ives. He stared at us in disbelief and then did as he was told. I stepped forward and pulled a small pistol from Ives's waistband.

"What goes on here?" Moore demanded as he strode up to where we were standing. "I don't allow gunplay..."

"I'm arresting Ives for the robbery of the Oliver stage," Henry interrupted. "Step back, Bill. This is none of your concern."

Without another word, Moore returned to the cabin. Ives stood before us, his hands held at shoulder level.

"You got the wrong fella, Sheriff," he said. "I didn't hold up no stage."

"Shut up," Henry snarled. "Put your arms behind your back. Noah, tie his hands."

I did and then, directed by Henry, I helped Ives back onto the gray.

"Who were the other two and where did they go, Ives?" Henry asked.

Ives, seeing an opening, smiled. "Now that there's a good question, Sheriff. I *was* travelin' with two men until last night and they did say somethin' about a stage."

"God damn you!" Henry yelled at Ives, "I'll shoot you off that horse!"

Seeing the murder in Henry's eyes, Ives looked down at the ground. "One of 'em was called Zachery, I think," he replied after a minute of silence.

"Other was, Whiskey Bill…Bill Graves."

"Shit," Henry swore. He looked at me. "Graves must have come in with Howard. He's trouble." He looked back up at Ives. "So, where did they go?"

"Nevada. Lookin' fer women," he said with a leer. "Listen' here, Sheriff Plummer, them two ain't nothin' to me. I'll he'p you find 'em!"

Henry ignored him, gestured for me to mount as he did likewise. Leading Ives's horse, we rode west toward Alder Gulch and Nevada City.

Taking Zachery and Graves proved to be a far easier task than finding and arresting Ives. They were both snoring, dead drunk, in a rundown lean-to saloon run by a couple of Shoshone women who, along with selling a particularly vile brand of tangle leg, offered their charms for fifty cents a throw.

Henry and I dragged the two men out into the street and got them into the bed of a wagon Henry had borrowed from a livery stable. The Indian women pulled desperately on our arms, trying vainly to stop us. I handed each a coin and that seemed to cool their anger over losing the two valued customers. Ives watched the proceedings, laughing heartily over the condition of his associates.

We returned to the abandoned house atop Wallace Street in Virginia and Henry locked the three in logging chains to the floor as he'd done when he had arrested Forbes, Stinson and Lyons. Henry located Clubfoot Lane, his new Virginia City deputy, gave him some money and told him to buy food for the prisoners and to take them water, blankets, straw and chamber pots.

Exhausted and dirty from the day's work, Henry and I repaired to the Fairweather Hotel's saloon for a drink. He looked at me over his glass with a tired grin.

"Dick Jacobs, eh?" he chuckled. I pulled the eye patch out of my jacket pocket, put it on and traded hats with him again. "That's right, friend," I said with the affected drawl I'd used on Yeager. "They used t' call me Rattlesnake Dick in the Sierras. Didn't you arrest me onc't, Plummer?"

Henry laughed harder. "You missed your calling Noah! You should have been a thespian!"

"Probably better than the career I did choose," I replied as I placed his hat back on his head. "Look where *that* got me. In any event, our adventure has given me plenty to write about."

He sipped his drink thoughtfully. "Thank you for helping me," he said. "You did well. Yeager never suspected a thing and he told you all we needed to know. Very clever of you."

I gave him a pointed look. "Sometimes a little cleverness is better than brute force, Henry. I felt bad for that poor bastard Dempsey."

He shook his head. "Don't waste your pity on him. He'd shoot you in the back as soon as look at you. That's how it is here. Anyway, as soon as Buzz catches up, I'm riding back to Robber's Roost now that we know where it is. I'm going to try to take Howard and the rest there. I mean to capture them before winter. You can get a miners court convened for Ives and the other two. That should give you even more to write about."

"What about the deputy U.S. marshal in Lewiston?" I asked. "Doesn't his case on Ives and the others have priority?"

"Hell no!" Henry declared. "They answer for their crimes here first."

30

Virginia City
Idaho Territory
September 2, 1863

Now bathed, shaved and refreshed by a good night's sleep in a soft bed, I found Buzz Caven seated with Henry in the Miners Café, wolfing down his breakfast. While he ate, Henry explained what had transpired and Caven nodded his head. He even offered a rare smile when Henry told him about my outlaw impersonation.

"I want to get a couple of other guns to come with us, Buzz. It sounds like Howard is using the Roost as his headquarters. We may be able to take him."

I later returned to the office, where I found Colgan seated at his desk. He ignored me when I entered and took my seat, obviously miffed by my absence. In the silence I wrote a stirring first person account of the tracking and capture of George Ives and his accomplices by the heroic Henry Plummer and his able deputy, yours truly. I included a detailed account of my interview with Yeager in the guise of the notorious fiend, Rattlesnake Dick Jacobs. Just as I finished my story, Colgan cleared his throat, rose from his chair and made for the door.

"Exeter," I called out cheerfully, "would you mind editing this for me before you go?"

He grumbled, snatched the sheets from my hand and plopped back into his chair. I looked through some of my mail that had arrived while I was gone. There was nothing much.

"My God man! This is astonishing!" exclaimed Colgan. He read some more. "The Oliver stage held up by masked gunmen...tracked the desperado Ives for three days...Robber's Roost exists?! *You* impersonated Rattlesnake Dick?! Took Ives alive at Cold Spring Ranch without firing a shot?! Dragged his accomplices out of a wikiup in Nevada...this is an incredible account, Noah! Well done! Well done, my lad! We need to print an extra immediately!"

While Colgan engaged himself in rushing out the newspaper, I looked in on the prisoners. They sat sullenly with their backs against the walls of the building, feet linked loosely by a light logging chain locked to a heavy ring bolted into the wooden floor. They appeared to have what they needed.

Clubfoot lounged on a bench in the shade outside the door, a shotgun across his lap. A cobbler had built him a special shoe with a built-up sole, which he wore on his crippled right foot. He was another of the men from the bottom of the barrel that made up Henry's force of deputies. In Lane's case, he was a failed professional gambler. Just thirty years old, he was heavy set with a nose like a plum from too much drink. He was unshaven and clad in a once-fine suit of clothes now threadbare and dingy. Lane was sound asleep.

I walked to David Pemberton's office above a hardware store. The lawyer was hunched over paperwork when I entered, but smiled broadly when he looked up at me.

"It's Noah Coffey, the indomitable lawman!" he declared cheerfully. "I heard about your exploits from Henry! Congratulations, Sir!"

I smiled at his effusive welcome. "It wasn't quite the stuff of legend, Dave, so I wouldn't embellish the telling of it any more than Henry already has." I said. "Anyway, you'll be able to read about it in the *Tribune* and I'm sure you'll agree it was far less daunting than what you may have heard."

"Nevertheless, welcome back," he replied. "Where are the prisoners?"

"We have them chained in the empty house up at the top of the street," I explained. "We'll need to convene a miners court."

He looked at me blankly. "I suppose you haven't heard," he said.

"Heard what?"

"Sidney Edgerton has decided there are to be no more miners courts," he replied. "He was very distressed by the one he witnessed."

I thought about this for a moment. "That's all well and good, but Edgerton has no legal authority to declare anything."

"I am not so sure about that, Noah," Pemberton said thoughtfully. "He showed me the commission he was given by the attorney general in Washington. It clearly authorizes him to serve at President Lincoln's pleasure as chief justice of Idaho Territory."

"Yes, as chief justice," I replied sharply, "not as the grand potentate of Idaho Territory."

Pemberton held up his hand. "I know, I know," he said with a thin smile. "But the day will come soon when he *is* an important and influential man here and now is the time to demonstrate a willingness to cooperate with his wishes. It's not wise to stand in defiance of Edgerton."

Pemberton was right of course. The chief justice was a figure of authority whether there was established law in the territory or not.

"Very well," I replied with a sigh. "Sheriff Plummer asked me to convene a miners court to try Ives and the two others. What's to be done with them?"

He sat back, pleased with my acquiescence. "Why don't you send word to Judge Edgerton in Bannack right away. Let him decide. That's a politic and wise gesture, Noah, and I'm certain Judge Edgerton will appreciate your understanding in the matter. You've done well arresting the scoundrels. Now let the chief justice deal with them."

Virginia City
Idaho Territory
September 8, 1863

"I did not appreciate our last bit of intercourse, Mr. Coffey," Wilbur Sanders sniffed as I sat down. "Nor the public threats."

"Very rash, Mr. Coffey," scolded Professor Dimsdale. "Mr. Sanders is a man of some importance and he was merely trying to articulate his concerns about Sheriff Plummer. Concerns, I might add, that Judge Edgerton shares."

We sat inside the Masonic Hall, directly across from the dilapidated house holding the three prisoners. Edgerton had remained in Bannack upon receiving the news of the capture but had dispatched his nephew to Virginia City with his directions on how he wanted him to proceed. The trial was set for the next day. Sanders had appointed himself prosecutor and Pemberton would defend the prisoners. Doctor Clarence Bissell was to be the judge.

"Things are changing here," declared Sanders, "and you as a journalist really should be the first to see that."

I remembered David Pemberton's admonition. "First, Mr. Sanders," I said, "let me apologize. Perhaps I jumped to conclusions when we last met. It is not in my nature to be so hot headed."

Sanders leaned back in his seat with a self-satisfied look.

"But I want to tell you that I disagree with your opinion of Sheriff Plummer," I added. "He is more concerned than most hereabouts with the need for law enforcement."

"Indeed?" interjected Dimsdale with a look of doubt. "And where is Sheriff Henry Plummer, Mr. Coffey? I mean, as we speak, do you know where he is?"

I shook my head. "He and Buzz Caven left town after we returned with the prisoners. They were bound for Robber's Roost with some men to try to ambush Doc Howard and his gang..."

"And you haven't seen him since he rode out," Sanders interrupted. "In addition, there was no sign of Plummer in Bannack when I left there two days ago. Let me tell you how Judge Edgerton perceives that set of circumstances: Plummer is in business with the road agents. Indeed, we believe he is their leader."

"Leader?!" I ejaculated. "You...you can't be serious!"

Professor Dimsdale looked at me calmly. "Please, Mr. Coffey, think on it for a moment," he said. "What better position to be in if you head a criminal enterprise than to also serve as sheriff? Henry Plummer, a man who may well have a criminal past, arrives in a booming gold mining region and in less than a year, a gang of thugs follows him and almost immediately you have the disappearance of Lloyd Magruder, the killing of Jamie Wells and robbery of his father, the murder of Deputy Dillingham, the freeing of Dillingham's killers by Plummer's deputy and, most recently, the robbery of the Salt Lake stagecoach at Point of Rocks."

My head was spinning. "Jamie Wells was killed by Horan and his partners."

"How do you know?" Sanders asked. "Because Sheriff Plummer told you so?"

"Where was Plummer when the boy was killed and his father robbed?" asked Dimsdale.

I didn't know the answer.

"And then there's the question of Cleveland's murder..." began Sanders.

"Wait one moment, Sanders," I said. "Cleveland was killed in a fair fight."

"That's *not* what my investigation discovered," Dimsdale said quietly. "Not at all."

"*Your* investigation?" I asked incredulously.

Sanders jumped out of his seat. "What the hell do you think we've been doing since we arrived here, Coffey?!" he snarled at me, his brown eyes flashing. "We've been looking very carefully into what passes for law enforcement in the territory and Judge Edgerton doesn't like what he sees at all! In fact, he's appalled. So am I. So is Professor Dimsdale who, for your information, is serving as the judge's adjutant."

"But Henry Plummer..."

"You should really stop worrying about Henry Plummer and start worrying about your own appearance of...complicity." Dimsdale said after he suppressed a cough.

I then felt real fear, for me and for Henry. These men were seeing things from a vantage point that made Henry not only a suspect in their calendar of crimes, but the leader of the gang of desperados that Francis Thompson had unwittingly led into Alder Gulch.

After a silent minute Sanders took his seat. "Now, then, about the trial. Since Plummer is nowhere to be found and he supposedly deputized you, then you will serve as witness for the prosecution. I have already gotten Graves to provide evidence against Ives and Zachery. He'll be released after the trial."

"Graves?" I interrupted, "Henry told me Graves is a member of the Howard gang..."

"So says Plummer," Sanders said with a dismissive wave of his hand. "That counts for next to nothing. Graves implicated Ives as the ringleader in the stage hold-up. I want him hanged."

"I don't believe robbery is a capital crime, Sanders," I replied.

"God damn your impudence to hell, Coffey!" he was out of his seat again. "I will decide what constitutes a capital crime here. Or rather Judge Edgerton will. And he wants Ives and Zachery convicted and hanged. Immediately!"

I said nothing. Dimsdale jotted something in his omnipresent notebook as Sanders resumed his seat.

"This trial will proceed in an orderly fashion," he began reading from a sheet of paper in front of him. "A courtroom will be prepared on the ground floor of this building. There will be seats for fifty members of the public. We will select a jury from among them. The jury will be chosen in the morning. They will hear testimony in the afternoon. They will complete their deliberations by six o'clock." I thought about asking if Dr. Bissel would have a say in courtroom proceedings but thought better of it. The trial's outcome sounded very much like a foregone conclusion.

As if hearing my silent thoughts, Dimsdale looked at me pointedly. "Since you're the deputy sheriff you must provide courtroom guards and have a gallows ready should the two men be found guilty."

I couldn't help myself. "Don't you mean *when* they're found guilty?"

Sanders glared at me. "It will be your responsibility to hang them!"

I was shaking my head before Sanders had finished speaking. "That's where I draw the line. If you want them hanged, then you hang them."

Sanders looked confused. "But you said you were a sworn deputy..."

"No, I never said sworn. I was appointed," I responded with something like a smirk on my face. I couldn't help it.

Sanders looked like a fool. He glanced at Dimsdale, eyes blinking then back at me, the confusion replaced by irritation.

"Very well," he whined, "If you won't hang them, I'll find a volunteer who will."

"That shouldn't be too difficult, Sanders," I replied. "Everyone in Alder

Gulch loves a hanging."

The professor coughed. "Judge Edgerton wishes for the executions to take place immediately upon conviction."

31

Virginia City
Idaho Territory
September 9, 1863

It rained most of the day, the first precipitation in weeks. The recent daytime heat gave way to a cool breeze that swept though the courtroom on the main floor of the Masonic Hall.

I paid little attention to what was being said, instead looking around at the men that had been admitted. They were virtually all merchants and other "prominent" citizens with whom Sanders seemed allied. What miners I saw were standing at the back of the room. Other men were crowded in the street just outside the door or near the open windows. Likewise the composition of the jury seemed to lean toward "respectable" people and away from the miners who made up the vast majority of Virginia City's population. To my astonishment and anger, Micah Jordan was among them. I hadn't seen him in many weeks and had yet to decide how I would make sure he paid for his crime with his life.

Finally I was called by Sanders to give testimony:

"And the stage coach driver Tom Caldwell alerted Sheriff Plummer?"

"He did," I replied tonelessly.

"At that point Plummer deputized you?"

"Yes."

"And you tracked Ives, Zachery and Graves for two days?"

"Three days all together," I corrected him. "From Point of Rocks to Dempsey's Ranch to Robber's Roost. Sheriff Plummer captured Ives at Cold Spring Ranch. Then he captured and arrested Zachery and Graves in Nevada City."

I could see Sanders was irritated that I gave Henry full credit for seizing the criminals.

"Very well, Mr. Coffey," he continued. "Then you jailed the three suspects, is that correct?"

"There is no jail in Virginia City. The citizens here would not pay to build one. On his own initiative, Sheriff Plummer made arrangements with the owner of the abandoned house across the street to use it to incarcerate his prisoners. That's where we detained the three men."

"Thank you Mr. Coffey for the commentary. Now, Sir, will you please confine your answers to my specific questions?" Anger was edging his voice.

"Yes, Sir," I replied.

"Did any of the men make self-incriminating statements to Sheriff Plummer?"

"Objection!" called Pemberton. "That question calls for a hearsay answer, Judge."

Dr. Bissell and Sanders stared at him blankly.

"What the defendants may have said to Sheriff Plummer cannot be admitted as part of Mr. Coffey's testimony," Pemberton explained to the judge and prosecutor.

I shot a smile at Sanders.

"Well, I withdraw the question, then," he said, his face glowing red.

He curtly dismissed me and called his star witness. Bill Graves's clothing was filthy after the days he'd spent chained to the floor. He wore a dour expression on his lean, wolf-like face. His eyes were dull and he slumped in the witness chair. After a few cursory questions, Sanders stepped back.

"Is George Ives in this courtroom?" he asked dramatically.

"Uh huh," came the response.

"Where?"

Graves motioned at Ives. "Raht there." Ives stared back at him with cold eyes. Like Graves and Zachery, his clothes and body were dirty. His hair was matted on his head and he had a thin growth of whiskers on his face.

"And it was Bob Zachery who convinced you to join him and George Ives in the hold-up of the Oliver stage, correct?"

"It were."

"Graves, you bastard!" Zachery was out of his seat and moving toward the witness. Clubfoot, who I'd appointed bailiff, surprised me with an unusual display of speed and alertness by stepping between the accused and Graves, his shotgun at the ready. Zachery slowly took his seat.

It came as no surprise to me that Pemberton's defense of his clients was desultory. It took the jury twenty minutes to convict both men. As scripted, Bissel condemned them to hang in one hour's time.

"I gotta hang for robbin' a stage?!" Ives moaned looking around desperately. "That ain't right judge! Mr. Pemberton...he'p me!"

David was already out the door with Dr. Bissel right behind him. Beyond them on the street, I saw Sanders shaking Graves's hand.

It fell to me to lead the condemned men under guard back to the house. Ives was sobbing miserably.

"This ain't *right*, Mr. Coffey," he repeated pitifully over and over.

I couldn't agree with you more, I thought to myself as I padlocked him to the chain while Clubfoot covered him with his shotgun. Zachery, who was considerably older than Ives, sat down on the floor, his scarred and weathered face a mask of seeming indifference. Parson Timmons appeared with his Bible and sat with them as I walked out into the rain to the place where two ropes were slung over the stout branch of a cottonwood tree. The nooses were ready and two large boxes were set beneath them.

Standing there was a short, squat fellow I recognized as one of the men who had attended my interview with Edgerton at the Fairweather Hotel weeks earlier. He was built like a beer barrel, with a thick black beard and eyes like liquid anthracite that were presently gazing up eagerly at the ropes. Clubfoot pointed at him.

"That there is X. Beidler," he said. "He volunteered to be the hangman."

Hearing his name, Beidler turned our way. His black eyebrows met in the middle of his forehead. Without an introduction or pleasantries, he speared me with his oily eyes.

"What you waitin' fer, Coffey?" he sneered.

I ignored him and walked back through the growing crowd to the improvised jail. I suddenly wished Henry was there to restore order to the unfolding fiasco.

Night had begun to fall, so the interior of the building was dark and gloomy. Rain blew in through the broken windows while Parson Timmons, on his knees next to Ives and Zachery, was saying a final prayer. The younger man had composed himself while Zachery remained impassive.

"Mr. Coffey, the parson wrote a letter to my ma fer me," Ives said quietly. "Will ya' see she gits it?'

I took it from him and slipped it into my coat pocket before I unlocked the chain. "I will," I said, patting his shoulder. "I'm sorry George. It's time to go."

He nodded and stood. Zachery was already on his feet. I marched them out to the tree where an unruly mob waited. There were shouts and catcalls as the condemned men walked to where Beidler was standing, their heads down. Torches had been lit, casting a lurid glow over the scene.

Beidler took charge and helped the two onto the crates. He then fixed a noose around each man's neck.

Now that Ives and Zachery were standing on the two big wooden boxes, I realized Beidler had a problem. Were the condemned supposed to jump off the boxes? Was Beidler going to push them to their doom? I looked at Clubfoot and he looked back at me, equally confused.

I heard several voices from the periphery of the crowd shouting for mercy. "Let 'em go!" cried one. "You best stop this!" threatened another.

"What are you waiting for X?!" demanded Sanders. "I'll have a riot on my hands if you don't get this hanging over with."

Beidler was dumbly scratching his head studying the crates. He looked at Sanders and held his hands apart in a gesture of helplessness. Beidler may have volunteered to serve as executioner but he clearly had no experience when it came to hanging men. Long seconds began ticking away. Ives was sobbing again. Zachery was looking out hopefully in the direction of the voices that were now loudly calling for leniency.

Next to Sanders stood Dimsdale and a number of the men who had served on the jury, including Jordan, whose blue eyes were eager with anticipation. I gritted my teeth and stepped over to Sanders.

"Jesus Christ!" I swore at him under my breath. "You were supposed to build a scaffold with a trapdoor!"

Sanders looked around desperately for a solution and then strode over to some of the men who had served as jurors or been spectators. He pointed at the boxes and said something to them. They all nodded their heads and two of them grinned. They stepped forward. Three had shotguns and the other half dozen men had drawn pistols.

"Step back!" Sanders commanded. "Men, do your duty!"

The firing squad blasted away at the boxes on which the two condemned men stood, splintering them into thousands of pieces. In his terror, Ives let out a high pitched shriek while Zachery wore a look of horror as the box beneath him collapsed under the gunfire and his weight, but not as quickly as Sanders had anticipated. Rather than getting a clean drop and having their necks broken quickly, Ives and Zachery were being gradually lowered to the ground as the crates disintegrated, slowly choking as their nooses tightened.

I won't relay the details because what transpired will surely sicken the reader. I will say the two men suffered long, slow, brutally painful deaths. After three minutes of watching their desperate struggles, the crowd had stopped cheering. Only the pattering of the falling rain, the crackle of the torches, and the terrible noises made by two gagging men broke the eerie silence.

I could watch no more. I stepped over to Clubfoot and snatched the shotgun from his hands. Without thinking about what I was doing I fired a barrel into Ives' head and the other into Zachery's. Then I walked over to where Sanders stood watching with wide eyes the two nearly headless bodies bobbing on the end of their ropes. I angrily threw the smoking weapon at his feet and stalked off into the night.

Virginia City
Idaho Territory
September 28, 1863

"The war has finally taken a turn for the Union!" exclaimed Colgan as I entered the office this morning. "Look!" He handed me a newspaper from Chicago, apparently arrived in this morning's mail.

A Great Victory at Gettysburg!!!

—

Lee's Offensive Stopped by Gen. Meade

—

Great & Furious
3-Day Battle

—

Rebel Forces in Full Retreat

"It's amazing," Colgan exclaimed. "Bobby Lee was moving to take the war to Baltimore and Harrisburg. For once, the federals were ready and waiting for him!"

I had long since ceased to care what Bobby Lee did. The politicians and generals had promised a quick defeat of the Confederate rebels but the war had turned into a long, bloody massacre of young men from both sides. I pictured the rotting corpses strewn across the battlefield at Gettysburg, wherever the hell that was.

Old men who didn't do the fighting, men like Colgan, thought of the war in the abstract, a wonderful adventure they only wished they were young enough to enjoy. Looking at him, I knew Colgan wouldn't feel the least bit adventurous if a line of Confederates charged him, their bayonets gleaming. He would piss himself and run. I read a couple of more paragraphs and tossed the paper back on the desk. I could see he was disappointed that I didn't share his excitement over the "great victory."

I reached into my pocket and pulled out ten dollars in coin. "Here's the advertising payment from Carrol," I said, handing the hardware store owner's money to him.

He brightened and grabbed the silver. "About time!" He handed me five dollars. "Your salary, Sir."

I thanked him and left. My plan was to ride to Nevada City to see if Henry had appeared there, but Dimsdale stopped me on the boardwalk by grabbing hold of my sleeve.

"Mr. Coffey, I want to speak confidentially with you if I might." I looked at the hand clutching my arm and he released his grip.

"I'm sorry," he said. "Could we find somewhere quiet to talk? Please?"

Curious about what he had to say I accompanied him to the house where we had held our prisoners. I leaned on a windowsill and he stood in the middle of the room, hands behind his back as though addressing his pupils on the subject of Homer's *Odyssey*.

"Mr. Sanders told you of Judge Edgerton's concerns about Sheriff Plummer."

He glanced at me to see if he might be in physical danger, but I didn't move.

"Frankly, I believe Plummer is on his way to the States. I'm sure he saw the way the wind was blowing here; how suspicion was eventually going to fall on him." He pulled a handkerchief from his pocket and coughed into it. "Excuse me," he apologized. "In any event, there is no law enforcement…"

"Nor law," I reminded him.

"Quite so. Nor law," he agreed. "Yet, you would agree the law—that is, the commonly accepted and understood laws that govern man's intercourse—should be upheld and defended, would you not?"

Again I nodded. "Well, Mr. Coffey, that is not happening as I am sure you are well aware. Lawlessness here is—candidly—out of control. I myself have witnessed several knife and fistfights and one shooting, not to mention the killing of Deputy Dillingham in broad daylight. I understand he was a friend of yours."

"Yes, he was," I said. "He was a good man."

"Precisely!" he exclaimed, forefinger in the air like an exclamation point. "A good man gunned down in the prime of his life by fiends who walked away from their dastardly crime." He was pacing the floor. "Well, Sir, Wilbur

Sanders is organizing a Citizens Vigilance Committee in Virginia City. He is also considering one in Bannack."

"Vigilance committee?" I had heard of such a thing in California in the days before statehood. Prominent citizens in San Francisco had formed one in 1851 because they believed their police were in the pay of the criminal elements there. But I was unfamiliar with anything relating to it.

"Rather than listen to me explain, I wonder if you might attend a meeting this evening at the Masonic Hall? Mr. Sanders will chair. He's arriving on the afternoon stage," he explained. "He will outline the vigilance committee's objectives and discuss it in detail with you and the other citizens of Virginia City whom we have selected."

"It all sounds very mysterious, Professor Dimsdale," I remarked.

He smiled a thin smile. "Well, to some degree it is mysterious. Please attend and you will learn much more."

I arrived at the Masonic Hall at eight o'clock and found seated at a table with Sanders, X. Beidler and the other man from the Fairweather Hotel meeting. A third man was seated with them and I recognized him as the fellow I had seen in Bannack with Edgerton and Sanders when the Oliver stagecoach hold-up was reported.

"Ah, Mr. Coffey," Sanders said with a smile and a regal wave of his hand. "Welcome, Sir."

"Thank you," I replied as my eye roved across the faces.

"First, I would like to say, Mr. Coffey...Noah, if I may address you informally, I wish to apologize for my part in our past differences. We are both educated men and can certainly be civil to one another."

I looked at him and replied. "Yes, I agree, Wilbur. I apologize for my part, as well."

He reached across the table and I shook his hand. The other men smiled at the reconciliation.

"Introductions first," Sanders continued. "You know the professor of course. Let me also formally introduce you to Xavier Beidler. X, meet Noah Coffey. I know you two are already acquainted from that...unpleasant affair a couple of weeks ago."

Beidler stood and held out his hand, which I discovered was small but powerful as I shook it.

"Then we have Louis McKenzie," Sanders said genially.

McKenzie stood. I knew he ran a livery stable in Nevada City. He was tall, with thick mustaches and a long chin. He was completely bald and I could not judge his age. He might have been anywhere between thirty and fifty years old.

"And lastly, meet Dr. Turner Wiggins," he gestured toward the last of the men. Wiggins was also tall and I could see he was the youngest of those assembled, perhaps twenty-five years old. He was clean-shaven and neatly attired in a black suit. He had a thick head of brown hair and clear blue eyes.

"Do you practice medicine?" I asked Wiggins as I shook his hand.

"I'm a dentist, actually," he replied pleasantly. "I'm newly arrived in the city from Buffalo, New York. I am setting up shop above the Stonewall Hall. There is no other dentist hereabouts, so I hope to make a successful practice."

"Well, I have noticed many miners are missing their teeth. That could explain the absence of a dentist," I replied with a chuckle.

He didn't share in the humor and took his seat.

Sanders cleared his throat, no doubt irritated with me again. "Gentlemen, let us get down to business," he began. "We recently concluded the trial and execution of two notorious road agents, a George Ives and Bob Zachery. Thanks to Deputy Coffey's quick actions the two were dispatched to hell."

I started to say something, but Sanders held up his hand.

"Now, what did we learn from this experience? First, that the effective administration of justice here must be the prerogative of the respected citizenry, not the rabble that makes up the miners court. Second, we found that a trial can be conducted fairly but with expediency. None of us has the time or inclination for long, drawn out legal machinations. Lastly, when the criminal and undesirable elements discover we are serious about prosecuting and punishing the lawless, they will run for the hills and cease to be a problem."

There was a general nodding of heads and utterances of affirmation. I stayed silent.

Sanders stood. He rubbed his weak chin and began to pace. "However, we also learned something doesn't work. The jury. Or rather, the reliability of the jury."

"Reliability?" I asked.

"Yes, reliability," he said thoughtfully. "It occurred to me that Ives and Zachery might well have been acquitted had we happened to unknowingly select a couple of their friends to the jury. In fact, they were quite nearly rescued from the gallows." He looked at the others. "When we bring a criminal in front of a jury, we do so because he is guilty. We don't want to see that man acquitted or rescued. We want him hanged."

"If I may, Wilbur," I said. "Isn't a jury supposed to determine guilt or innocence? If you aren't going to allow a jury to deliberate, what's the point?"

He looked at me as though I were a bright pupil who had provided the class with a brilliant solution to a vexing problem. "Exactly!" he declared with a smile. "What *is* the point of a jury?"

I was confused and my face must have said so.

"A jury is completely unnecessary in the administration of frontier justice," he added as he resumed his seat.

"Unnecessary?!" I replied, my voice rising in volume. "It's a sacred tenant of the Constitution of the United States, Sanders! What the hell are you talking about?!"

Dimsdale stood. He placed his hands behind his back and looked at me sternly. Now I was the dullard who had missed the point of the lecture.

"You said it yourself, Noah," the professor declared. "Here in Idaho Territory, there is no law. No law enforcement. No administration of the law. No trial by a jury of one's peers."

"But Sheriff Plummer was elected by the miners in Bannack!" I responded. "I was there. He won by a landslide. So you're wrong, professor, there is law enforcement."

Dimsdale looked at the men to his left and to his right. "Yes, the rabble elected one of their own," he said. "And look at the outcome. Mayhem everywhere one looks."

"You know my feelings about Plummer," Sanders interjected as Dimsdale took his seat. "Hopefully we've seen the last of him this side of judgment day. But road agents and robbers still abound and we—this group you've met tonight—have decided to do something about it. There won't be anymore courts or lawyers or juries, at least not in the traditional sense."

I now understood as I looked at each man in turn. "Because you are appointing yourselves as the court, the jury and—dare I say it?—executioners?"

Sanders sat back in his chair with a smug expression.

"There is no law in Idaho Territory," Dimsdale repeated. "So we, as the prominent citizens here, have decided to take it upon ourselves to see that justice is served. And we would like you to join us."

"I didn't come two thousand miles to raise my family and build my practice in a place run by thugs and outlaws," Wiggins declared.

"That's right," agreed Beidler, his voice surprisingly high pitched for a man of such rotund bulk. "Look 'round you, Coffey. Every corner has some worthless bastard just waitin' t' roll an honest citizen."

McKenzie had been eyeing me coolly throughout the exchanges with the others and I didn't like his look.

"I lost me a coupla fine bays to theft," he remarked in his deep baritone voice. "Nobody's answered fer it. I aim to see somebody does. When these bastards watch us hang some of their own from gateposts, they'll understand we's done playin' games with 'em."

"It's really quite simple, Noah," Sanders smiled. "You commit a crime, you pay for it. With your life."

"No jail terms?" I asked "For crimes that are not capital offenses?"

"We don't make that distinction," Sanders replied, shaking his head. "Every crime is a capital crime. As the professor mentioned, we're the law now so we prescribe the penalties. The only alternative to death by hanging is banishment. Besides," he added lightly, "we don't have a jail."

"How convenient for you," I remarked dryly.

Sanders and Dimsdale both made a face at this but didn't respond.

"So what do you want from me?"

"Well, you have distinguished yourself as a lawman, Noah," Dimsdale observed. "We thought you would welcome a chance to join our committee."

McKenzie's claim about the stolen horses led me to a sudden, murderous idea.

"You know, I am not really a lawman," I finally replied mildly. "I was simply assisting Sheriff Plummer in his pursuit and capture of Ives and the others. However, I would be willing to resume my duties and join the committee if that is what you wish."

"That is exactly what I had hoped you would say!" cried Sanders with delight, ignoring my sudden change of heart. "A man of your education, integrity and determination would be a credit to the vigilance committee!"

"We have an oath of secrecy you must swear," Dimsdale said. "It is vital that no one know the identity of our members..."

"...to protect ourselves and our families from retaliation, you understand," interrupted Sanders. "We saw how friends of the accused intervened in the Dillingham case and how others wanted to free Ives and Zachery. It's the only way we can ensure our security."

In the dim, flickering light, Sanders held a Bible. I placed my hand on it and, with my right hand raised, swore the oath of fidelity to my fellow vigilantes.

I looked over at McKenzie. "You said something about stolen horses a moment ago?"

"That's right," he snarled. "Two beautiful bay geldin's. Woulda fetched me a good price. They was stole at night three-four weeks back outta my corral."

I had seen Jordan that very morning riding through town aboard a bay gelding and leading another.

"One of those bays have a big star on its muzzle?" I asked.

"Yeah!" McKenzie replied excitedly. "An' the other had a bobbed tail."

"You know Micah Jordan? The Mormon preacher?" I asked.

"No, why?"

"Because I think he stole your horses."

Since I had seen Jordan camping by the side of the creek, he had moved his wives and children to a rented house and a few acres about one mile east of town. He was holding Mormon services in his parlor but I'd heard he had a grand scheme to build his own tabernacle.

It was clear and cold when we arrived at the remote farmhouse. The windows were dark. We quietly dismounted and Beidler busied himself locating a tree with a sturdy limb. I was having misgivings, not about hanging Jordan, but about doing it in front of his family.

"Look, gentlemen," I whispered as we gathered near the front door. "Maybe we should do this tomorrow...get Jordan to town on some pretext and..."

"No!" snapped McKenzie. "He dies tonight."

With that, Sanders knocked loudly on the door. We heard some stirrings, the muffled voice of a woman and a man's response. Sanders knocked again impatiently. "Micah Jordan, open up!"

"Who's there?" came Jordan's fearful reply.

"The Citizens Vigilance Committee," Sanders said. "We need to speak to you."

The door opened a crack and I could see Jordan's bleary blue eyes peering at us from within. "What is it?"

"Please step outside," said Dimsdale.

"May I dress?"

"Yes, but be quick about it," I answered. "And tell your women to stay put and keep the children quiet." A baby had begun bawling somewhere inside the house.

After a few minutes Jordan stepped through the door, closing it behind him. We heard the locks fall into place. He was hatless and unarmed, his thick blond hair a rat's nest from sleep.

"Gentlemen," he said with a confused smile. "It's a little late for a social call, isn't it?"

"This isn't social," replied Dimsdale. "You are charged with a serious crime."

"Crime?" he looked doubly confused. "What crime?"

"Yes," I replied sharply. "You committed a crime and now it's time to answer for it."

"But..."

"Let's walk to your corral, Mr. Jordan," said Sanders in a reasonable voice. "I want to show you something."

Only starlight illuminated the penned up animals within the corral, but it was easy to see the two bays in the far corner. McKenzie pointed at them. "Where'd you git them hosses?!" he angrily asked.

Jordan blinked in confusion. "I bought them. From Dempsey."

By this time, Wiggins had retrieved the geldings. McKenzie's brand was burned onto the rumps of both animals.

"Have you a receipt?" I asked, knowing full well that Dempsey couldn't write.

"Well, no, I, I don't," Jordan began. "But I am sure Mr. Dempsey would vouch for the sale..."

McKenzie stuck his finger in Jordan's chest. "Dempsey don't sell no stolen stock, boy!"

I knew Dempsey was not that honest, but I said nothing.

"It is obvious you stole these horses, Jordan," stated Sanders flatly. "They are in your possession and you can provide no proof that you legally purchased them. Thankfully Deputy Coffey here discovered your crime." Sanders looked around at the committeemen. "Your verdict gentlemen?"

"Guilty," came the simultaneous response.

Sanders looked at Jordan's astonished and frightened face. "As executive officer of the Citizens Vigilance Committee, I sentence you to hang by the neck until you are dead."

The rush to judgement, which I had counted on, had taken place faster than I ever imagined it could.

"No!" Jordan cried. "That's wrong! I never committed a crime!"

I put my face close to his. "Never?"

He looked into my eyes and I thought I detected a flash of recognition.

"Come on!" Wiggins shoved him from behind and we herded Jordan to the tree Beidler had selected some distance from the house.

"No...no...this isn't right!" Jordan screamed as he took in the noose hanging from a limb.

"Shut up, you coward," I growled at him. "You'll frighten your family."

McKenzie tied Jordan's arms together behind his back and then with Wiggins's help the two men placed him on Sanders's horse. I had retrieved my own mount as had Beidler and we sat on either side of Jordan who was weeping.

"No...no..." he sobbed quietly as Beidler fixed the noose around his neck. "I'm innocent!"

I had heard enough from him. I grabbed the collar of his shirt and pulled

Jordan close so only he could hear me. "You're *not* innocent! You don't remember me, but I remember *you*, Jordan! You shot me in '57 at the meadow south of Cedar City. You remember? You and your people slaughtered my wife and more than a hundred of my friends. You thought we were all dead. But I lived. Now you are going to die for what you did there!"

His blue eyes opened wide with alarm. "No...I...I...was never there!" he cried in desperation.

"Stand up on that saddle you son of a bitch!" McKenzie yelled at him, "or you'll strangle to death!"

Beidler reached over and grabbed him by the arm. "Help me, Coffey!"

Together, we managed to get Jordan to his feet on the saddle with each of us steadying him from either side. He was crying again, saying a prayer between sobs.

Sanders stepped around and faced him. "Any last words?"

"I am...I am innocent...of stealing leastways!" he cried as he stared at me. "But, but I...I have...have done bad things! It is written you cannot hide from God's wrath. I confess my sins here and now. May God Almighty have mercy on me!"

Sanders stepped back and Wiggins brought a switch down on the horse's hindquarters. It bolted and Jordan dropped from the saddle. I heard a sharp crack as his neck broke. His hands and feet twitched and he voided himself. From the saddle, I looked up at his eyes, still wide with fear, even in death. He should be afraid, I thought to myself, because God would never forgive him.

32

Virginia City
Idaho Territory
October 3, 1863

Fortuitous circumstances had put Jordan at my mercy. I thought I would feel a sense of profound satisfaction this morning but whatever passion for revenge that drove me to hang the Mormon had evaporated. I was left with only a deep and hollow sense of regret.

There was no doubt that Jordan deserved to die for what he had done. But, I asked myself, *did I have the right to execute him?* There was nothing ambiguous about what I'd done to him. I had taken the law in my own hands and murdered Jordan just as surely as he had helped kill men, women and children on that long ago September morning.

"Why so gloomy?" asked Colgan from the other side of the office. He sat at his desk, a look of concern on his round face. I shrugged. "I'm not feeling well," I replied. "I believe I'll go lay down for a bit."

"Yes, good idea Noah," he smiled warmly. "You'll feel better after a rest."

Against my better judgment, I went to the stable, saddled my horse and rode out to Jordan's house again. The weather was cool and clear, the air freshly scented with the aroma of sage. My mount, a small mare I called

Miss Matilda, was happy to get out of the corral and eager for a gallop, excited by the breeze and sunshine.

We had left Jordan twisting on the end of the rope. When I arrived at the farm he was still there. His two young widows were standing beneath the body trying to decide how they were going to get it down. They were both very young and, as I discovered, sisters. The taller of the two was maybe eighteen and the other girl only fifteen or sixteen. Their eyes were red and puffy. The one I judged the older of the two had a tiny infant at her breast. Neither could have known I was among the men who had hanged their husband.

Silently I rode up to the pitiful scene and, using my knife, cut the rope. Jordan's body was stiff but I managed to catch it across my saddle and lower it to the ground as gently as I could. In the small field behind the house I found a spade Jordan had left there. He had been preparing the soil for planting some winter crop or other, maybe turnips.

I walked back to the hanging tree and looked at Jordan's wives. "I can bury him here if you like," I said. They both nodded absently. "Would you get a blanket so I can wrap him in it?"

The younger girl went to the house. I watched her and then saw Jordan's little boy seated on the back door stoop. My stomach turned over and feeling faint, I leaned on the spade.

"Are you all right, Sir?" asked the older girl. I nodded and began digging. It took me two hours chiseling away at the rocky soil to complete a grave that was deep enough. As I finished my labors, the younger girl brought me a cup of water. I sipped it and then felt myself begin to break down at her simple act of kindness. I sat down on the edge of the grave, covered my face with my hands and sobbed. One of the girls, I wasn't sure which, knelt next to me and placed her hand on my shoulder.

An hour later, I tossed the last of the dirt onto Jordan's grave and handed the spade to one of the girls. Silently, I mounted my horse and rode back to Virginia City.

I found Dimsdale eating his dinner at the Miners Cafe. "You look as though you've been mining today," he observed cheerily. "Are you hungry?"

"No," I replied wearily, "I'm not hungry." The table was empty and the proprietress of the café was in the kitchen. "Look, Professor, I cannot do this."

"Do what, my good man?" he asked, eyebrows arched.

I leaned over the table. "Be a vigilante. I cannot be a vigilante," I whispered.

He glanced furtively over his shoulder to see if anyone was listening.

"What?!" he whispered back. "You took an oath!"

"I can't kill men anymore," I replied, my eyes cast down at the table.

He sat back and observed me for a moment. "Look here," he said finally. "Jordan was guilty, was he not?"

"No...yes," I replied. "Yes...he was guilty."

"Then your conscience is clear," he smiled. "You did, we all did, what the law would have done, yes? We just took far less time to do it."

"It's not only Jordan," I said looking at him intently. "It's the killing. I can't do it."

He smiled an indulgent smile. "May I suggest you have a dram or two of whiskey? I believe you'll feel much better if you do."

I only have a foggy recollection of what happened the rest of the day. Taking Dimsdale's advice, I went to the Bale of Hay and bought a bottle of the best whiskey available. I began drinking and it wasn't long until I did feel better. Then I was asleep, my head resting on the table.

What woke me hours later was a loud commotion in the center of the room. I raised my head and searing pain shot through my skull. I had been dreaming. Rebecca was in a wagon with Micah Jordan. He had a rope around her neck and he was leering at me as they rode across the prairie. I shook the vision from my head and focused on a bizarre scene unfolding in the middle of the floor.

A short man clad in buckskins and wearing a cap made of wildcat fur stood on his toes, a savage looking hunting knife poised above his head. He was circling Exeter Colgan, whose face was pale with fear. He was wiry and agile and the two looked almost as though they were dancing.

"Goddamn nigger lovin' sum'bitch!" snarled the man with the knife.

"No...Sir...listen...please," Colgan sputtered as he held his hands out to ward off the knife, "My, my sympathies are entirely with the C.S.A! God bless Robert E. Lee and President Jeff Davis!"

Colgan was drunk, but the other man wasn't. "I seen what you writ in your damn noospaper a your'n," he drawled, his eyes sharp and focused. "You love them sum'bitchin' blue bellies and Abe fuckin' Lincoln. They killed a lotta good boys and I'm gonna kill you, Mister..."

Fully awake then, I realized this vision wasn't part of my nightmare. By his stance, I could see the man was an accomplished knife fighter. I sat frozen in my seat.

"No...wait Sir! In the name of all that is holy...you are wrong!" Colgan blubbered.

I finally began to stand up but I moved too late and too slowly. The blade flashed. Colgan was too fat to get out of its way. The long knife sliced down into his breast. It must have been razor sharp because it cut through clothing, fat, muscle and bone, from Colgan's chest all the way to his waist. The editor pulled back from the blade with a startled expression, his mouth open wide, as his insides began pouring out onto the saloon floor.

Silently, horrified miners stepped back as the grinning attacker watched his victim make a desperate attempt to hold his guts in with his hands. Blood poured freely from the gaping wound as Colgan's eyes began to glaze. He dropped heavily to his knees before falling onto his side, entrails and gore spilling unchecked around his body.

The attacker stood triumphantly over the dead editor for a moment before kneeling and wiping the knife's blade on Colgan's coat. He sheathed it, stepped back to the bar and downed what was left of his drink before calmly walking out the door.

Paralyzed, I stared stupidly at the dead newspaperman on the floor before I was jolted by a sudden explosion of spraying glass and splintered wood as the knife fighter crashed back through the shattered saloon door. He tripped over Colgan's body and fell to the floor on his back.

Henry Plummer walked into the barroom rubbing his right fist with his left hand. The man on the floor recovered, jumped to his feet, blood dripping from his mouth and nose, pulled his knife and assumed his deadly pose, blade high, feet moving.

Henry watched him, then glanced at the body, and then over at me. "Why didn't you stop this, Deputy Coffey?!" he demanded.

I stared at him, disbelieving. It was really Henry. "I…I…"

The knife fighter made a lunge, but Henry deftly sidestepped it, sticking his foot out and tripping his foe who fell to the floor. Before he could stand, Henry kicked him in the face. Stunned, the man fell back, his brutal knife clattering across the floor where it came to rest against my foot. The knife fighter rose, wobbly, and Henry delivered a furious roundhouse left to the man's jaw that sprayed blood and saliva across the bar. The blow drove the man back into the wall as Henry stood calmly, fists ready, waiting for a counter attack. The man shook his head, spit a stream of blood onto the floor and then charged Henry like a bull. Another flurry of punches and the man was face down on the floor, unconscious.

His knuckles bleeding, Henry knelt on the knife fighter's back. He produced a leather thong from his pocket and hogtied the killer's hands and feet behind his back. Then, panting, he stepped over to take a closer look at Colgan.

"He's dead," Henry remarked indifferently. He looked over at the bartender. "Close the place. I need to investigate what happened here. Go get the undertaker." He pointed at Colgan's body. "Then get this mess cleaned up."

The Bale of Hay's patrons, followed by its owner, filed out staring aghast at the slaughtered remains of poor Exeter Colgan as they exited. Henry walked over to where I dumbly sat with a glass and poured into it what remained of the bottle on my table.

"Good evening, Noah," he said, smiling warmly as he took a seat. He studied my face closely a moment. "Why, you appear to be drunk, Deputy…I believe I'll join you."

Virginia City
Idaho Territory
October 4, 1863

Colgan's body lay in a coffin behind a curtain at the mortuary. The old undertaker had somehow closed the awful wound and gotten Exeter dressed in a suit I'd brought to him. My head pounded as I counted out the nine dollars the undertaker charged me to prepare the body and provide the coffin and burial. I handed him the money. He bowed gravely and backed out of the small viewing area.

I realized as I gazed down at him that I had no real affection for Colgan. I knew next to nothing about him personally, other than that he had led a nomadic newspaperman's life and had a strong weakness for drink. I put my hat back on my head and left the mortuary, thinking as I did that, for me, communing with the dead was becoming a habit.

I found Henry where I had left him, asleep in the back of the saloon on a dirty cot. I took a closer look at him and saw that he had several days of stubble on his face. His clothing was dusty and his boots covered with mud. I tapped his arm and his gray eyes blinked open. Henry slowly sat up and pulled out his pocketwatch.

"Ten thirty," he croaked to himself. He looked around the grubby recesses of the saloon and shuddered. "We couldn't do any better than this?"

"Too drunk," I replied with a weak smile.

"Mmmm," he said by way of answering me. His eyes were shot with blood as he examined his bruised knuckles.

"I'm pleased to see you regained the use of your arm, Henry," I commented, "and not a moment too soon."

"Mmmm," he answered, his elbows resting on his knees, his head down and his eyes closed again. I let him stay like that for a bit, then reached over and gently helped him to his feet.

"At least you remembered to lock up Colgan's killer before you went around the bend," I remarked. "Thanks, by the way. Exeter shouldn't have died like that. Come on, Henry. Let's go get cleaned up, have coffee and get something to eat."

Only Henry and I were there with the undertaker and a couple of his gravediggers, who lowered the plain pine coffin into the ground not far from the headstone of J.W. Dillingham. We stood over the grave holding our hats in the bright autumn sunshine. After a silent moment we walked back to our horses. Before we mounted I reached over and took Henry's elbow.

"Things are bad, Henry," I told him.

He looked at me, his eyes then clear. "What do you mean?"

"Sanders is here," I replied. "He's formed a Citizens Vigilance Committee because he doesn't believe the law is being enforced." I looked at the ground, ashamed of what I would say next. "I joined it."

"What the hell's a vigilance committee?" he asked.

I explained what I knew, describing the trial and execution of Ives and Zachery, and the subsequent meeting at the Masonic Hall, where I'd taken the vigilante oath. His expression grew increasingly concerned as he listened.

"So, if I hear you correctly Noah, Sanders and the rest of these people have appointed themselves as the law?"

I nodded. "But it's worse than that," I continued. "Sanders wants you hanged. He believes you're the leader of Howard's road agent gang."

"How the hell did he arrive at that?!" Henry asked incredulously.

I outlined the suspicions Sanders had voiced to me. Henry's expression went from confusion to anger.

"What the hell do those bastards think I've been doing for the last month?" he asked me. "I've been looking for Howard, Stinson, Ray, Forbes and the rest, that's what! I rode all the way up to Wisdom looking for them for Christ's sake!"

"Henry, it was that gambler Butler I asked you about. And Curtis, the stage driver," I replied. "I am certain they told Edgerton and Sanders whatever they'd heard about you from Tom Cleveland. They made up their minds then and there that you were a criminal and they've now convinced themselves that, because you're sheriff, you are in a position to lead a gang of thieves without drawing suspicion to yourself."

He stared at me and I could see at first he thought I was making it all up. Then he looked away at the far mountains and considered what I'd told him. After several silent minutes, he looked back at me.

"Yes, that explains quite a lot," he said. "Edgerton doesn't speak to me; nor Sanders. I didn't understand why until now."

I nodded. "We have to convince them they're wrong about you, Henry," I suggested. "Maybe meet with Edgerton?"

He shook his head. "I don't think so," he said. "I *did* kill a man and I *did* go to prison for it. I won't deny that to Edgerton. No, the best thing I can do is to stay clear of him. Anyway, I still have the support of the miners. Remember, they elected me. If it comes to a confrontation with Edgerton, the miners will back me."

"There's something else," I said as I leaned against Miss Matilda, who was happily munching long green grass. I looked down, ashamed. "I was responsible for a hanging the other night."

"What do you mean 'responsible'?" he asked with a look of shock.

"You recall I told you about Jordan?" I said to the ground. "The Mormon preacher?"

"Yes, of course I do," he replied.

"He's dead and I killed him," I confessed as a wave of shame and remorse washed over me. "When Sanders and the vigilantes recruited me, I saw my chance for revenge without killing him outright."

"So you're having regrets now?"

"Yes. I suppose I am."

"Don't," he replied. "You found a way to do what needed to be done. Stop worrying about it."

An hour later, we sat in the *Tribune* office. I guessed I was now the editor and probably the newspaper's owner if I chose to be since Colgan seemed to have no heirs. When I had retrieved the suit of clothes for the undertaker at his rooming house, I had looked for letters or anything else that might give me an idea of any family he had left behind. All I found were stacks of old newspapers and dozens of books piled in the corners of the room.

Henry was sitting at Exeter's desk drinking whiskey he'd found in the back of one of the drawers. It was getting dark so I lit a lantern. As I blew out the match, there was a quiet knock at the door. I saw Dimsdale's face peering in at me through the glass. I gestured and he entered the office.

"Good evening, Noah," he said just before he coughed violently into his ever-present handkerchief. "I understand Plummer is in town. Do you know where…"

"Right here, Professor," came Henry's voice from the corner. In the failing light, Dimsdale hadn't seen Henry.

"Good heavens!" Dimsdale exclaimed. "You startled me!"

"Yes. I'm sure I did," replied Henry, rising to his feet and walking over to my desk. He sat on the corner and eyed Dimsdale. "I'm sorry. Anyway, here I am."

Dimsdale was nervously shifting his small frame on the balls of his feet as his eyes cut back and forth between Henry and me in time to his swaying. He brought the handkerchief to his lips and coughed again.

"So, Professor, what can I do for you?" Henry prompted.

"Well, we understand you captured Colgan's killer. This man, Mayfield." Dimsdale replied. "Where are you keeping him?"

"That's none of your concern, Dimsdale," replied Henry calmly. "And who is this 'we'?"

He stared at Henry for a long moment, eyes fluttering, then abruptly turned and made for the door. "Never mind," he said over his shoulder. "You are correct. It is none of my concern."

Henry chuckled as he watched Dimsdale scurry up the street. "Damned popinjay."

"Henry, he's got powerful friends," I replied. "Why don't you just turn Mayfield over to them? It would be a gesture of goodwill."

"Goodwill?!" He spit the word back at me and then frowned. "Mayfield is going to get a fair trial," he replied sternly. "I'm not going to let the vigilantes have him. Not today. Not ever. What kind of justice is that?"

"What the hell is the difference, Henry?" I said. "He murdered Colgan. I saw it and so did every man in the saloon. It's no different than what you said to me about Jordan."

"It *is* different," he replied. "If Jordan had gone to trial it would have been your word against his. He would have been freed. And then he would have run." He looked at me pointedly. "You knew that, of course, so you arranged to have the vigilantes do the killing for you. I applaud your initiative."

I made a face.

"As for Mayfield, he's going to stand trial," Henry declared. "And if all we have here is a miners court, then at least he gets a lawyer and a public hearing." He rose from my desk. "Is it perfect? No. But it's the *legal* thing to do. The vigilantes claim to be the law? Well, let me ask you something, Noah. Who made them the law?"

"Edgerton did," I said flatly. "*Chief Justice* Sidney Edgerton appointed by the President of the United States."

"If Edgerton is a chief justice, he ought to have more respect for the law, don't you think? Instead he's appointed himself head of some kind of damned Spanish Inquisition," Henry said, walking to the window. "When you start arresting, trying and hanging men at night and in secret, there is no justice…at least as right minded men understand the concept."

"Where *is* Mayfield?" I asked finally. "You should get him out of here. Maybe take him back to Bannack."

"That's a good suggestion."

We walked up Wallace Street to the old house. The town was quiet save for the usual bedlam emanating from the saloons and wikiups. We entered and discovered that Mayfield was gone.

"Damn it, they got him already," I said.

"No they didn't," Henry replied. In the light that spilled through a window from across the street, he was kneeling on the floor examining the padlock he'd used on the chain. "He picked the lock." He held up a nail that Mayfield had somehow removed from a floorboard.

He stood. "I was here earlier to check on him. At best, he's only got an hour head start. And I think I know where he's headed."

"The Roost?"

Henry nodded. At that moment the door to the building burst open. Sanders and Dimsdale walked in, the former wielding a shotgun. "Where's the prisoner?!" demanded Sanders.

Henry coolly looked at the pair. "Escaped," he replied. "He picked the lock and ran." He looked down at the weapon that Sanders seemed to be holding on us. "I'd lower that piece if I were you, Sanders," Henry commanded. The vigilante leader hesitated and then did as directed. "What's your business with him?" Henry finally asked.

"I'm dealing with criminals now, Plummer, not you," Sanders declared. "By order of Territorial Chief Justice Sidney Edgerton."

"Edgerton? He doesn't have any say in law enforcement matters. And neither do you, Sanders!" Henry said sharply. "Neither does anyone but me. I'm the duly elected sheriff and Virginia City is *my* jurisdiction. But you're an attorney, Sanders. Or you claim to be one. Why the hell am I explaining the law to you? You should know all this!"

Sanders looked as though he'd been slapped across the face. After a silence, Dimsdale gave a tug on Sanders's sleeve and the two departed without a word.

Henry glanced over at me with a thin smile, shaking his head. "What fools," he observed.

I watched Sanders and Dimsdale through the window as they walked toward the Masonic Hall. I wasn't so sure I agreed with Henry's assessment.

Henry asked me to accompany him in pursuit of Mayfield but I explained that, as near as I could tell, the *Tribune* now belonged to me and I had to decide what I would do with the newspaper. He said he understood and was off, headed west to the lair on the bank of the Ruby River.

33

Virginia City
Idaho Territory
October 5, 1863

It was dark by the time I completed writing my account of the murder of Colgan. I was preparing to go to press when Sanders entered the office followed by Dimsdale, Wiggins, Beidler, McKenzie and a man I did not recognize.

"Gentlemen," I greeted them.

"Noah," replied Sanders. He then turned and introduced the new face as belonging to one Silas Crown. "Mr. Crown has agreed to join the committee as a kind of sergeant at arms."

Crown was around forty years old and of medium height. I could see he was well muscled and his face was lean, tan and hard-looking beneath the wide brim of his hat. He wore short side-whiskers, but was otherwise clean-shaven.

"And what qualifies you for such a position, Mr. Crown?" I inquired.

He eyed me for a moment, evaluating the question. "I was a peace officer before I came to the territory," he replied. "In Kansas."

I glanced down and saw he was wearing two big Colts. "Peace officer?" I smiled without humor. "Well, you've made all the right acquaintances, I see. These gentlemen are very interested in maintaining the peace. As well as law and order."

He stared at me with unflinching gray eyes beneath thick black eyebrows.

"And what brought you west?" I asked.

Dimsdale cleared his throat. "That's not important. Nor is it what we are here about," he declared.

"No indeed, Professor" agreed Sanders. "We want to know why you let Plummer free Mayfield."

"Sheriff Plummer didn't free Mayfield," I replied as calmly as I could. "Mayfield picked the lock and escaped."

"So says Plummer," Wiggins interjected.

"So say I, Wiggins!" I shouted. "I was there when Henry discovered the escape!"

Dimsdale coughed. "Mr. Coffey...Noah. Did you ever actually *see* Mayfield locked up in chains yourself?" His voice was barely audible behind the handkerchief.

"Well, no," I admitted. "But..."

"There you are, then!" cried Sanders. "Yet another desperado, the very one who butchered your employer like a bullock, mind you, released to resume his criminal career in Plummer's employ!"

"God damn it, Sanders, you're jumping to conclusions!" I bolted from my chair in anger and glared at the men standing before my desk. "All of you! You're wrong! As soon as Henry discovered Mayfield's escape he lit out for Robber's Roost!"

Silence hung like a poison cloud in the office.

"Robber's Roost," Dimsdale repeated in his quiet voice. I shot a look at the professor and then eyed each of the other men in turn.

"That's...that's where Sheriff Plummer said Howard's gang has been hiding...Robber's Roost," I tried to explain. I could hear the desperation in my own voice. "Mayfield is one of Doc Howard's men! That's where Henry said Mayfield probably went!"

"It would seem Sheriff Plummer is intimately acquainted with this son of a bitch Doc Howard and his band of murderers," Wiggins suggested.

"No, you're wrong!" I cried. "Henry rode to Wisdom Ranch looking for Howard's gang! That's where Henry's been for the last month, for God's sake!"

"How ya know that?" asked McKenzie.

"Henry told me…" I stopped myself. I could see in their eyes I wasn't helping my friend. I took a deep breath and sat down. "Look, Gentlemen, let's give Sheriff Plummer a few days to find Mayfield and bring him in. That's reasonable, is it not?"

Sanders smiled thinly. "Yes. That is reasonable, Noah. Meantime, Mr. Crown here is a bona fide lawman so he has agreed to conduct his own, shall we say, discreet investigation of Sheriff Plummer's recent activities. As you suggest, it is possible our suspicions may be unfounded where the sheriff is concerned," he added, nodding in Crown's direction. "We want to give him the benefit of the doubt."

I looked over at the former "peace officer" and cringed.

Virginia City
Idaho Territory
October 10, 1863

No word from Henry for the better part of a week. I thought he might be in Bannack so I asked the stage driver to learn what he could and report back to me on his return trip. He arrived this morning with the news that Henry was not in Bannack and hadn't been there for some time, according to his mine foreman, Francis Thompson.

I concluded that he must be in pursuit of Mayfield. At least I hoped that's what he was doing.

Before me was the most recent edition of the newspaper. *My* newspaper.

Virginia City Tribune Publisher Savagely Murdered

Killer Escapes Custody
—

*Sheriff Plummer Vows
to Bring Mayfield to Justice*
—

Eyewitness Account of Slaying
—

It was true. I had been little more than an eyewitness, totally useless to Colgan. But the headline had sold all the newspapers I had printed, so at least there was a few dollars profit from my failure to save him. Exeter would have enjoyed the cruel irony.

I put on my hat, slipped on my coat, then stepped into the street. A cold wind blew down from the north but along with the bright sunshine, the autumn gold of the aspen trees glittered on the nearby hills.

I walked down Wallace Street intent on collecting some advertising bills from the grocer, haberdasher, a dry goods merchant and a blacksmith. As always, the streets were full of wagons, miners, horses and merchants. In fact, Virginia City had spawned a metropolis of sorts that stretched some fourteen miles on an east-west axis all the way to Alder, another mining camp on the far side of Nevada City. I had heard that as many as thirty thousand people now resided within its environs. What is astonishing is that, just two years ago, there were fewer than a thousand settlers hereabouts. Gold had that affect on population growth.

The grocer was not in but the haberdasher was, although he wasn't terribly excited to see me. Still, he drew some cash from behind his counter and handed me the four dollars I had come for. I was stuffing the money in my pocketbook when I encountered Sanders.

"We're meeting tonight," he said without pleasantries. "I'd like you there."

Curious, I agreed to attend and continued my collections. By the end of the afternoon I had managed to bank fourteen dollars and was back at the office preparing the next edition. Nathan Carter's package of newspapers from Madison, Detroit, Philadelphia and Boston had arrived several days earlier and the war news they contained told a woeful tale of merciless fratricide.

As I read through them I discovered that over the summer there had been a bloody siege at Vicksburg in Tennessee and draft riots in New York City. It was next to impossible to determine which side was winning the war once I read past the patriotic hyperbole the publishers of the northern papers injected into every account. The newspaper from Philadelphia dated July 25 was of particular interest because it carried a horribly long list of Union casualties at Gettysburg. And Colgan had said that battle was considered a federal victory.

I had selected those accounts for reprint then left the office and walked to the Masonic Hall. Sanders was chairing the meeting, with Dimsdale, Beidler, Wiggins, McKenzie and now Crown all in attendance. I took a seat next to Wiggins and Sanders began.

"The Peabody stage was struck by road agents last night," he announced without preamble. "Judge Edgerton spoke to the driver, who reported that the coach was attacked at Bannack Pass en route to Salt Lake City. A passenger was murdered and cash was taken from all the survivors; more than a thousand dollars. Also, a large quantity of gold dust was found in its hiding place and stolen."

Silence greeted Sanders announcement but I sensed eyes were on me. "Four road agents were involved, all masked. The driver thought they were a hunting party as he approached them but they turned and ambushed him as he crested the pass."

Dimsdale's muffled coughing broke the silence. I shifted in my seat and waited.

"The driver was unable to identify the thieves," Sanders added, "but I plan to travel to Bannack to question him myself when we return."

"Return from where?" I asked.

"Silas has located Mayfield," Sanders said, "hiding in the Gallatin Valley."

"He's at a ranch up that a'way," Crown declared. "Mayfield's got him a brother in Nevada City. He tol' me where Mayfield was. Took me all of a coupla hours t' figger it out, Coffey. 'T weren't no big mystery. Ain't seen hide nor hair o' Plummer, neither."

"We shan't worry about Plummer for now," said Sanders. "We have more pressing business. We ride out tomorrow morning to this ranch to capture and punish Mayfield. It should take us three, maybe four days."

"We?" I asked pointedly.

"The vigilance committee," replied Wiggins. "That's what we're organized to do, Coffey. Remember?"

"I'm not going," I said as I stood up.

They all stared at me. I had made up my mind with the hanging of Jordan that my vigilante service was over. "I simply don't care to be a part of anything you people are doing."

"I'm afraid you don't have that choice," replied Sanders.

"Indeed you do not," agreed Dimsdale. He raised his handkerchief to his mouth and coughed. "You swore a solemn oath of fidelity to the vigilance committee, Noah. To *us*. You cannot simply walk away from your obligations."

"Perfesser's right, Coffey," McKenzie then stood, his hand on the pistol in his holster. "You ain't goin' no place, so set down!"

I was finally beginning to understand these men and how right Henry had been about them. Sanders had cleverly assembled brawn to go along with the committee's brains. In addition to McKenzie, Beidler, Wiggins and Crown were coldly staring at me. Sanders and Dimsdale sat placidly, hands clasped before them on the table, looking my way almost sympathetically.

I reluctantly resumed my seat.

"As I was saying," Sanders said, "we'll leave at first light."

Idaho Territory
October 13, 1863

We had ridden north through the Madison River Valley, the mountains rising on both sides as we hugged the track that ran along the bank of the river. The cold wind carried sleet that stung my eyes and chilled my face. The early snows already capped the higher mountains and as night fell, the temperature dropped precipitously. We camped in the Beartrap Canyon, sheltering in a rock formation that provided a kind of roof over our heads as the river roared through a series of cataracts below. We built a fire that would have been cheerful to me were I not deployed on such a deadly mission.

The following morning was clear but very cold. Frost clung to the sagebrush and there was ice on the rocks in the river. By midafternoon we had entered the Gallatin River Valley from the west over the low bluffs that offered a striking view of the river Captains Lewis and Clark had discovered along with the Madison and Jefferson years before.

Crown led us as we crossed the river an hour later. We headed north passing several lonely ranches, the owners of which rode out to greet us, surprised to see a heavily armed platoon of white men in the remote valley.

Crown asked the location of the Bitterroot Ranch from one of the ranchers who pointed out a cabin and barn at the base of the Bridger Mountains three or four miles distant. (The reader unfamiliar with Idaho Territory's topography might well wonder how one might observe a location several miles away. It is instructive to understand that the land is what is known as high desert and the only trees that might obstruct one's view are located along the streams and creeks that infrequently cut across the landscape. Thus, one can stand on high ground and see for many miles in any direction, the sky providing a boundless canopy).

My mind was not on the scenery, however, as we approached the ranch where Mayfield was supposed to be hiding. The sun was setting so Sanders stopped us alongside a rivulet to water our horses and eat a cold supper of jerked buffalo and biscuits while we waited for darkness.

I felt a growing apprehension and wondered if it would be possible, under the cover of night, to escape. The committee's attention would be on Mayfield, not me, so I might well make it back to Virginia City unmolested. *But then what?* I asked myself for the hundredth time since we'd ridden out. After they'd dealt with Mayfield they would surely come after me, even if I tried to leave the territory. I began to realize my prospects were limited to the business at hand. As I pondered this it occurred to me that I might be able to prevent them from hanging Mayfield.

When darkness had fallen we remounted and headed toward the cabin, the lamplight flickering in its windows providing us with a beacon. The cold wind had come up and it sliced through me even though I was huddled in my heavy coat. It was decided that Crown and McKenzie would approach the front door while Beidler and Wiggins would cover the rear. Sanders, Dimsdale and I would wait, mounted near the corral and ready to pursue him should Mayfield somehow elude the men on foot.

With everyone in position, we watched from a hundred yards away as Crown and McKenzie, each carrying a deadly shotgun, rapped on the cabin's front door. We heard bits and pieces of the ensuing conversation carried to us on the wind, then nothing but the rattling of the bare branches in the willow trees above us. The ex-peace officer and the rancher looked at one another and seemed uncertain of what to do next.

There was a sharp report and I saw McKenzie driven back onto the ground as though jerked by a rope. Crown stood frozen before he finally dropped to one knee, realizing someone on the other side of the door had shot McKenzie.

The cabin went dark as Wiggins and Beidler opened up with their revolvers, even though there was no chance that the fools could see what they were shooting at. There was no return fire from the cabin. I watched Crown suddenly jump to his feet and run for the cover of a timber lean-to that served as a manger twenty paces from the cabin. On the ground in front of the door McKenzie lay motionless.

"What should we do?" whispered Dimsdale, panic in his voice.

"Wait!" replied Sanders sharply.

Wiggins and Beidler had stopped firing, probably to reload their weapons. The wind blew ferociously, kicking up clouds of dust in the corral. In the starlight I saw a flash of movement, then a horseman emerged from behind the house. He and his mount clearly knew where they were going and rode at a full gallop into the corral toward the three of us.

Sanders and Dimsdale, realizing the rider was likely Mayfield, fumbled with their carbines, but by the time they had them aimed the horseman had seen us and stopped. The gate next to us, no doubt the exit he'd intended, was closed and locked. The rider sharply veered to the right and made for the open gate on the opposite side of the corral.

I spurred Miss Matilda and she responded instantly. I galloped parallel to the rider as he approached the gate. From a dozen yards, I took aim and pulled the trigger.

The buckshot struck the horse's flank and it crumbled as it came through the gate. The rider was flung violently from the saddle, landing headfirst in the dirt. The wounded animal courageously struggled to rise to its feet, but the buckshot had done far too much damage. Seeing and hearing the pitiful suffering of the other horse, Miss Matilda became distressed and skittish. I dismounted and tied her to the fence. Walking over to the poor wounded horse, I drew my pistol and put a bullet in its brain.

By this time, Dimsdale and Sanders had recovered themselves. They were standing over the man in the dirt, who sat up but was obviously injured by the fall. As I approached, I saw that neither vigilante had thought to disarm the fallen rider so I grabbed the pistols from his belt as well as a sheathed knife he'd tucked in his boot. The man looked up at me, his face creased with pain.

"It's Mayfield," I said to the others.

Crown, Wiggins and Beidler then appeared out of the dark, panting.

"McKenzie's dead!" Crown declared. "This son of a bitch shot 'im." He kicked out viciously, his foot connecting with Mayfield's arm, which appeared to be broken. Mayfield howled in pain and fell over on his side, clutching his injured limb.

Beidler grabbed Mayfield by the collar and dragged him to his feet. "I got a rope fer' you boy…"

"No!" I shouted at Beilder and the rest. "There will be no hanging. I'm the deputy sheriff and we're taking Mayfield back to Virginia City for a trial!"

The vigilantes glared at me. My shotgun and pistol covered them as they stood in a group next to Mayfield, who'd fallen to his knees.

"Step back from my prisoner!" I commanded. My plan was to disarm them, put Mayfield on one of their horses and then scatter the rest of the mounts so I could get a head start back to Virginia. After that, I didn't know what I would do.

"Drop your weapons and get back!" I shouted as I cocked my revolver. They began to obey, but too late I saw Crown's eyes cut to my right. I felt the cold steel of a pistol muzzle on my temple.

"You drop your guns, Coffey," growled McKenzie. I did as told and turned slowly to see the rancher clutching his shoulder, blood oozing out from between his fingers.

Beidler roughly tied my hands behind my back and pulled Mayfield to his feet.

"Take them to the cabin," ordered Sanders.

Inside, Crown lit a lamp. On the floor in the corner, still sheltering from the wild gunfire, sat a spindly old man wearing a stained nightdress. "Get up!" Crown yelled when he saw him. The old man slowly obeyed. I could see he was ancient, a shock of wispy white hair topping his otherwise bald head, his mouth toothless, and his dim eyes looking about fearfully at the vigilantes crowding his little cabin.

"Who are you?" asked Dimsdale.

"Johnson," the old man croaked.

"He's my uncle," Mayfield declared. "He owns the ranch. He ain't got no part in this."

Sanders intended there to be some pretense of legality so he could later justify himself if necessary. He pointed at Mayfield. "Gentlemen," he began. "Bob Mayfield here is charged with the murder of Exeter Colgan, late of Virginia City. How do you plead?"

Mayfield responded with a look of silent disbelief.

"Very well," Sanders said quietly. "We'll enter a plea of not guilty into the record."

He looked at the professor. "Mr. Dimsdale?"

"As prosecutor," the professor replied, "I call my first and only witness, Deputy Noah Coffey."

All eyes were focused on me. "So you're the prosecutor, are you Dimsdale?" I asked contemptuously. "I would have thought a well educated man like you would be appalled at what's going on here. But, no, you're a participant."

"As are you," he replied.

"Not any more," I snapped at him. "I'll have nothing to do with the murder of this man." I sat down on a rough chair and looked at the floor.

"I'm afraid you are wrong about that," Sanders declared. "Professor, you and I both distinctly heard Noah Coffey identify the accused as Bob Mayfield, the very same man who murdered Exeter Colgan in cold blood on October the third."

I looked up at them in shock.

"I did," agreed Dimsdale.

Wind battered the old cabin as Sanders looked at each vigilante in turn. "Gentlemen of the jury, what is your verdict?"

"Jury?!" I screamed. "They're not a God damned jury, Sanders! And you're not a God damned judge! You're all killers, no better than Mayfield!"

Sanders ignored me. "Gentlemen?"

Each vigilante in turn found Mayfield guilty. The condemned man stood gripping his broken arm as Sanders addressed him.

"Bob Mayfield," he said, "the Vigilance Committee of Virginia City has found you guilty of the murder of Exeter Colgan. As the committee's presiding executive, I sentence you to hang by the neck until you are dead. You will be executed forthwith. After we hear from this man."

I watched stunned as Sanders pointed his finger at Johnson.

"You, Sir, your full name."

The old man blinked his eyes. "Johnson…Cal Johnson."

"You stand accused of aiding and abetting a murderer in his flight from justice," Sanders intoned. "How do you plead?"

I shot out of my seat, my arms still pinioned behind my back. "For the sake of all that is decent, Sanders!" Before I could finish, McKenzie stepped forward and delivered a punch to my jaw. The blow sent me crashing back into the wall. I staggered to my feet, blood pouring from my mouth. I spit several broken teeth onto the floor as Wiggins watched with a grin.

"It looks as though you'll be requiring my services, Coffey," he laughed. Crown and McKenzie chuckled while Dimsdale eyed the scene with a look of disgust before he finally turned his attention to Johnson.

"Do you know this man?" he asked, pointing at Mayfield.

Johnson nodded his head. "He's my sis's boy."

"And, did he tell you why he was here at your ranch?"

The old man had no idea what was happening. He smiled a toothless smile, saliva dripping from a corner of his mouth. "Well, now Mister, he tol' me he had 'im some trouble down there in Virginia…"

"So," Dimsdale interrupted, "he explained he was on the run, so to speak."

Johnson blinked some more and scratched his head.

"Uncle Cal!" Mayfield suddenly cried out in anguish, understanding what Dimsdale was doing, "Don't say no more!"

"Johnson, we're waiting for your answer," demanded Sanders.

"Well, yeah, I guess he said somethin' about tryin' to get to Dakota…"

"So you helped him by providing bed and board, did you not?" asked Dimsdale.

"Boy's kin," Johnson explained. "I weren't gonna turn him out."

The wind screamed through the rafters and a cold draft stabbed me in the back.

Sanders eyed the old man then looked at the vigilantes. "Gentlemen?"

I was herded outside with Mayfield, who was followed by his uncle, still clad in his filthy nightdress, now condemned to die along with his nephew. For a brief moment I thought I was going to be hanged as well, then saw that Beidler had prepared only two nooses, which waited beneath the ranch gate's crossbeam.

"You ain't gonna hang me 'er ya?" the pathetic old man asked, tears streaming down his face.

My hands were freed by Dimsdale. I held a rag to my mouth and watched as Beidler placed a noose around Mayfield's neck first and then Johnson's.

"Let the old man go," Mayfield tearfully begged. "He don't know nothin' and he ain't done nothin'!"

Before either of them could say another word, Crown kicked out the rain barrel on which Mayfield stood. A half-second later, Beidler pushed the barrel out from under old Johnson. Both men fell then writhed violently, choking at the end of their ropes, their necks unbroken.

"You fucking incompetent bastards!" I screamed through my battered mouth, blood spraying. "Don't let them die like that!"

Beidler stood off to one side with Crown and McKenzie. They were clearly enjoying the throes and convulsions of the two dying men. Wiggins had walked away. Dimsdale stood nearby, head down, but Sanders looked on, confusion on his face as he fingered his pistol, no doubt recalling how I'd dispatched Ives and Zachery. He finally followed Wiggins off into the darkness.

Mayfield's tongue protruded obscenely while old Johnson's eyes bulged nearly out of their sockets. Only their feet twitched as Crown laughed mirthlessly.

"Necktie a little too tight there, grandpaw?" he asked.

McKenzie and Beidler burst out laughing. If I'd had my pistol I would have killed all three of them then and there. But I turned, hot tears in my eyes, and walked to where Miss Matilda waited for me, still tied to the fence.

34

Virginia City
Idaho Territory
October 27, 1863

Snow was falling today, the first of the season. I lay in bed watching the wet flakes splatter against my window. I must get out of Virginia City, but winter is fast approaching and I realize now I must wait for spring before I can leave.

As I walked up Wallace Street to the *Tribune* office, the day seemed as dreary as my mood. The snow stopped, but it was raw and windless, souring my state of mind to the point where I considered detouring to a saloon to spend the day.

Just then, the morning stage from Bannack passed me and there, sitting at the coach's window, was Henry Plummer. He saw me, smiled and waved, then pointed up the street, silently suggesting we meet at my office. I arrived before he did, brewed some coffee, and turned as Henry walked through the door. With him was Francis Thompson, whom I hadn't seen in weeks.

"Where have you been, Henry?" I asked, unable to mask the worry in my voice, "All hell has broken loose here!"

"So I've heard," he replied as he shook my hand. He studied my face.

"What happened to your mouth?"

"I was kicked by a horse," I replied, not wanting to tell him what had really happened. "Lost a couple of teeth. It's nothing serious."

Henry looked at Thompson and patted his shoulder. "Francis here hit pay dirt last week! He found a vein of quartz ten feet down that was full of gold. Tell him."

"It's true!" Thompson said with an excited grin. "We were digging upstream about a mile from town, Charlie Benson and me. We hit the quartz on the surface and started digging; found the biggest vein I've seen yet! We started crushing and, my God, the dust just poured out!"

"We brought it here to see what kind of price we could get," Henry said with a smile as he produced a chamois sack from the saddlebags he was carrying. "Look!"

Astonished at the size of the bag, I picked it up. It weighed perhaps five pounds. "And there's more," Henry declared excitedly. "Much more! It might be time for you to rejoin our enterprise, Noah, because I'm about through being a lawman and about ready to start becoming truly wealthy!"

Once again, my friend proved himself to be among the luckiest men I had ever met. I poured coffee for the three of us.

"I got your note about Mayfield," Henry remarked. "Did they really hang the old man, too?"

I nodded.

Henry's face turned grim. "What about this man, Crown?"

"The Kansas 'peace officer'?" I sarcastically replied. "He's a thug they recruited to do their dirty work. Oh, by the way, he's investigating you."

"What?!"

"I told you, Henry!" I exclaimed. "Sanders suspects you're the leader of a gang of road agents! They claim you or your 'henchmen' robbed the Peabody coach and murdered the passenger."

Henry looked more annoyed than fearful. "On what evidence?"

"None!" I shouted. "They don't worry about those kinds of legal niceties, Henry! You were supposed to be tracking Mayfield. You disappeared. That puts you in league with Doc Howard, according to Sanders and Dimsdale."

Henry ran a finger over his mustaches thoughtfully, then sipped the steaming coffee.

"That's crazy!" declared Thompson, who was sitting on my desk.

"Yes, it *is* crazy," Henry agreed, regarding me with curiosity. "After Mayfield escaped, Noah, I tracked him to Dempsey's. He bought a horse there and I lost him at Beaverhead Rock. He must have headed north or doubled back to the Gallatin. I gave up and returned to Bannack."

"I heard you weren't in Bannack," I replied, perhaps too testily because my friend frowned. My voice had an undeniable ring of suspicion to it. "I had the stage driver ask Francis if he'd seen you."

Henry was silent but his cool gray eyes bored into me. "I was there for a day or so then I went up to look in on Francis at his camp."

"That's right," interjected Thompson. "I talked to the stage driver before I hit the quartz vein. Henry, Charlie and me worked almost around the clock after that."

"Satisfied?" Henry asked me, an eyebrow cocked.

I sighed. "Henry, I'm sorry…it's just that I've been around them too long." I was ashamed of myself.

"Well, you *are* one of them," he observed quietly. "Aren't you?"

"No!" I shouted again. "Not any more! I made the mistake of using them to…achieve my purposes. But after that poor old man…"

Henry completed the thought for me. "…you see them for what they really are."

We finished our coffee in silence, then Henry went off in search of Clubfoot Lane and his other Virginia deputy, Boone Helm. Francis Thompson excused himself, saying he needed to buy some excavating equipment unavailable in Bannack. Before he left, he turned over the sack of gold to me to store in the small safe I kept in a closet.

We met at my rooming house for supper after I told Henry and Francis the fare was much better there than any other they would find in Virginia City. Then we repaired to the Bale of Hay. The barroom was filled with thick smoke and the usual laughter and loud voices. Francis and I, unaccomplished as we were at cards, were happy to be spectators as Henry won hand after hand of poker. As he raked in another pile of coins, I saw Silas Crown had slipped into the saloon and was watching Henry from the far corner of the bar.

Crown had not noticed me. He stood silently, his dark eyes locked on Henry.

"Henry, Crown's right over there," I said, leaning forward so he could hear me.

"I know," Henry said, a thin cigar clamped in the corner of his mouth, his hands shuffling and dealing the cards. "I saw him come in."

The other players were oblivious to our conversation, intent only on winning back the money they'd lost to Sheriff Plummer.

"But you said you'd never seen him." I was confused.

"What do you think I was doing this afternoon?" he asked without looking at me.

While we spoke, Crown moved closer but Henry made no move. He simply read his cards and anted up.

Crown was then behind us. I rose and made as though I had just noticed him. "What the hell are you doing, Crown?" I demanded.

"Arresting Plummer," he growled.

"That's not a good idea," I replied. "He'll kill you."

He glanced at me, derision on his face. For the first time I noticed the ugly scar on his neck. His skin was pocked and he had several days of growth on his face.

I looked back at the table where Henry sat and saw he'd lost his first hand of the evening. I knew it was his habit to always quit after a winning streak. His opponents grumbled as he collected his money and thanked them politely. Then he joined Crown and me at the bar.

"Good evening," he said cheerfully. He ordered a whiskey. "Join me?" he asked the Kansan.

Crown silently eyed him. "Something on your mind, Friend?" Henry asked with a smile despite the look on Crown's face.

Sensing trouble, some men nearby looked our way but the din in the saloon continued. Someone at the far side of the barroom was playing a fiddle badly and I heard an Irish ballad raised by a clutch of grubby miners near the window.

"I know you," Crown snarled at Henry.

"Oh?" Henry replied. "Well, my friend, I know you, too. Your name isn't Crown. It's Danner. The U.S. deputy marshal in Lewiston has paper on you for the murder of a man named Jacob Schumacher. You're under arrest."

As he spoke, Henry had placed his drink on the bar and casually squared his body toward Crown/Danner, whose face had gone ashen at Henry's accusation. Just as casually and without the other man seeing him do it, Henry had his hand on the LeMat in his holster.

Crown/Danner licked his lips and seemed to be sizing up his chances.

"Stop!" boomed a voice from the door. Henry kept his eyes on his prisoner, but I looked over as Wiggins entered and pushed his way toward us.

"What's the meaning of this, Plummer?" he demanded.

Henry ignored him.

"Crown?" Wiggins asked his fellow vigilante.

Crown/Danner nodded toward Plummer. "I come in here to ask Plummer some questions, is all," he said. "He come over here like he's lookin' fer trouble."

"You're the one looking for trouble, Danner," Henry sneered. "And you just found it. In spades."

The Kansan, face white and sweating, licked his lips again. The saloon, save for the singers, was nearly silent, all eyes on the unfolding drama at the bar.

"You're mistaken Plummer!" Wiggins barked. "This man's name is Crown!"

"No it's not," Henry replied, not taking his eyes off the man before him. "And this is none of your business, whatever *your* name is. So kindly step away or you might find yourself in the same fix as Mr. Danner here."

It was Wiggins's turn to look stunned. "You...you have no authority in Virginia City to arrest anyone!" he declared finally, although he sounded doubtful of his own words.

Henry pinned the dentist with his cold eyes. "Move *back*, I said!"

Wiggins hesitated, then slowly stepped away. Henry's attention was on Danner/Crown again as he took three steps back. "How would you like to do this Danner?"

Sweat dripped off of the face of the "peace officer" as fear flashed in his eyes. He reminded me of a cornered mad dog I'd once seen just before it was shot.

Danner looked desperately at the retreating Wiggins. "Ain't you gonna do somethin'?!" he cried.

Wiggins responded by holding out his hands.

"I suppose shooting an old Quaker abolitionist in the back requires a little less courage than facing someone like me, eh Danner?" Henry taunted. It was an insult that everyone in the saloon heard and one, by the Mountain Code, that could not go unanswered.

But instead of drawing his weapon, Danner began shaking, almost uncontrollably. Suddenly he was sobbing. Seeing this, the men in the saloon shook their heads in disgust and resumed their card and dice games. Very quickly, the noise had reached its previous level. It was as though nothing had happened.

Henry stepped forward and removed Danner's Colts from his holsters as Wiggins beat a hasty retreat out the door. Gently, Henry turned the man and gave him a nudge.

"Let's go," he said. As Danner obeyed, Henry wore a slight smile that seemed to contain more cruelty than humor.

35

Virginia City
Idaho Territory
October 28, 1863

"You will release Crown this minute!" commanded Sanders. He stood in my office facing the desk where Henry sat regarding him with a look of perturbed indulgence.

"Mr. Sanders," Henry began with a patient voice. "As I told you. His name is Willard Danner. He is wanted by Missouri authorities for the murder of a Quaker in Kansas City last year. He may once have been a peace officer, as you say, but after the war began he started killing abolitionists. Jacob Schumacher is the one the Missouri federal law knows he killed for sure. It's all right here."

He held out a circular to Sanders that U.S. Deputy Marshal Hill Beechey in Lewiston had mailed to lawmen throughout the territory (I received them for Henry since he had no office of his own in Virginia City).

"This picture looks nothing like him!" declared Sanders pointing at the sketch on the notice that was supposed to represent the fugitive Danner.

Henry was beginning to look annoyed. "That's for the Missouri authorities to sort out, not you, Sanders. I dispatched a deputy to Lewiston to advise the marshal we have Danner in custody and he can come collect him."

He stared up at Sanders for a long minute. "I'm getting awfully tired of teaching you the law."

"Don't be impertinent, Plummer!" Sanders countered. "You're in enough trouble as it is."

"Am I?" Henry stood, face to face with the vigilante leader. "How so?"

Sanders realized he'd said too much. "I shall take the afternoon stage to Bannack," he said finally, "and consult with Judge Edgerton on this matter."

"You do that," Henry replied. "And when you see him, Sanders, you might ask the judge what the penalties are for obstructing a duly elected lawman acting on behalf of a United States deputy marshal. You'll find they are quite severe."

Sanders flushed, then spun on his heel and abruptly left.

"Henry," I said, exasperated. "You're pushing him too far."

"He's a shithead," Henry said dismissively as he resumed his seat to continue reading a newspaper.

Virginia City
Idaho Territory
October 30, 1863

As I sat in the café this morning, Professor Dimsdale joined me at my table.

"We had a meeting last evening and you weren't there," he said without preamble.

"That's very observant of you, Professor," I replied sarcastically.

He gave me a look, wiped his mouth with his ever-present handkerchief, and resumed. "We expect you to honor your commitments," he said.

I looked at him. "Honor?" I scoffed. "That word means nothing coming from you. You—people—*have* no honor."

"Just one moment..." he began, his tone indignant.

I cut him off. "You sit here and presume to lecture me like one of your pupils about honoring obligations and oaths? I tell you and the rest of them that you are no better than men like Mayfield. Get out of my sight before I..."

He lifted his small frame out of the chair. "I see," he sniffed through the handkerchief he held at his mouth.

I finished my dinner, but my stomach was upset. I returned to the office, ready to resume my work. Henry was seated at my desk. Mail that had arrived while I was dining was piled before him.

"Ah, Noah, my *good* friend," he smiled as he gave me an odd look. "The post arrived while you were out. There's a letter here for you."

He held up a small envelope between his fingers. "I recognized the handwriting so I took the liberty of opening and reading it."

I reached out and took the opened envelope. I removed the letter it contained and read.

Dearest Noah,

How I have longed for you since leaving Bannack...

I stopped reading. I dropped the letter on the desk and rubbed my eyes. "Henry..."

"My *faithful* and *true* friend, Noah Coffey."

"Henry. Listen. For God's sake..."

He slowly stood and I felt a pulse of fear in my chest. Unable to look him in the eye, I stood before him silently waiting for whatever punishment he had in mind. I knew I deserved it.

"You're the one man I believed would never betray me," he said sadly. "*Could* never betray me. Electa was unhappy in Bannack and I suppose she was dissatisfied with me...the kind of man I am. But *you*? My best friend?"

I looked up at him then. His gray eyes were as sad as his voice as he slowly shook his head. I saw he intended me no violence.

"Henry, listen, please. She is young," I pleaded. "Back at Sun River you gave her something she never had...you made her feel something new; something different. Then Bannack. You were gone more often than you should have been. She needed you. One day, well..."

"...you stepped into my boots and fulfilled her needs," he said bitterly. "My *honest* friend Noah Coffey. I asked you to look after her when I had to do my duty. And you certainly did."

I walked to my desk and collapsed in my chair. Seized by anguish, I slumped forward and put my face in my hands. "Henry, it wasn't like that...I, I was there. I discovered I loved her. I still love her. And she loves me."

"You could have talked to me," he replied, almost in a whisper. "A *real* friend would have talked to me about her, Noah. But you went behind my back. You deceived me."

I nodded my head. It was undeniable. "Yes," was all I could bring myself to say. "I'm sorry you found out this way."

"Is there a proper way to discover betrayal, Noah?" Without another word he placed his hat on his head, strapped on his gunbelt, shrugged on his coat and walked out of the door.

After an hour, I picked up Electa's letter and finished reading it. She had arrived in St. Louis with an Army column from New Mexico Territory she'd encountered on the road outside Salt Lake City, I was greatly relieved to learn. Electa had ridden east on the wagon of an old Swedish sutler and his wife. She had earned her keep cooking for a company of the soldiers while a kindly cavalry captain named Reno had looked out for her well-being.

I told Captain Reno about you and he recalled meeting a man named Coffey some years ago on the Oregon Trail. He said the man he remembered was a courageous Indian fighter. Now I am here waiting for a boat north to Davenport on the Iowa shore. Most all transport is headed south to Tennessee where Captain Reno says there is a Union offensive underway, so I must be patient. As I idle I cannot seem to keep my thoughts from turning to you again and again, Noah, and I am flush with desire. I long for your touch. I want only to hold your face in my hands once again. When will you come to me, my love?

After the events of the afternoon, it was a question I could not begin to answer. I gently folded the letter and placed it in my desk.

Virginia City
Idaho Territory
November 7, 1863

An ugly rumor now circulates throughout town. It was reported by an assayer that Henry Plummer weighed more than five pounds of gold dust and nuggets before leaving Virginia City a week ago, nearly the same amount stolen from the Peabody stage. I heard this from Boone Helms, a man of deplorable habits and ill looks whom Henry was forced to hire as a deputy when he could find no other man interested in the job.

I had encountered Helms before a back street wikiup this morning. He reeked of whiskey and was about to enter the ramshackle lean-to in search of some female comfort. He was about thirty and looked emaciated beneath his dirty clothing. He held a battered carbine and a pistol was jammed into the waistband of his tattered trousers. Beneath his hat, his face resembled a skull covered with skin, an oozing ulcer decorating his bony chin.

"They's sayin' Sheriff stole that gold," Helms said, completing his account.

"Who? Who is saying that?" I asked.

"Ever'one," he drawled. "It's all over town, Mr. Coffey." He glanced eagerly into the wikiup where a squaw of middle age was sprawled on a fetid buffalo robe, her deerskin shift pulled up around her waist, waiting for her next customer.

I looked away in disgust. "All right, Boone, thank you," I said. "If you hear anything more, please tell me."

There were few people I could trust in Virginia City. Whatever I asked would surely get back to the committee. But I did know of one man I believed heard all and said nothing.

The old Chinese man was just finishing a customer's shave. As I entered the small shop he glanced my way with a confused look. I had already been there earlier for my own shave. I smiled and sat on a bench, as though waiting my turn. The old woman appeared. "You wanna bat', Missa Coffey?"

"No thank you," I replied.

After a few minutes, the old man finished and accepted payment from the customer with a deep bow. He squinted at me, waiting.

"You remember Plummer?" I asked him. "The sheriff?"

He smiled widely. "Ah...yeah, yeah!" he declared. "Sheliff...goo' man. He here many time."

"That's right," I replied. "He is a good man. He paid you well?"

"Yeah, yeah," he beamed. "Vely wer!"

"Have you heard any talk about him from other men who come here? Bad talk I mean?"

His eager smile was instantly replaced by a dark frown. He shook his head.

I reached into my pocket and removed a ten-dollar gold piece. "I will pay to know what you know," I said, holding the gold up for him to see.

His tongue flicked out at the sight of the money and the old woman skittered off into the back of the shop. He glanced out the window at the empty alleyway.

"You know Engrishman?"

"Professor Dimsdale?"

"Yeah, yeah. Him," he said with a fast nod and another anxious glance out the window. "I no want no trouble...savvy?"

"Savvy," I replied.

"Engrishman Dim'dare, he say Prumma stole much gor' from stay co'. Kir mans," he said in a stage whisper. "He say to oth'a man, Prumma time is shor'."

"What other man?"

"Man come in wi' him...that den'is' man."

"Wiggins?"

"Yeah, yeah. He. Wiggin' They come for shave together."

"I see," I replied. "What did they mean, 'Plummer's time is short'?"

"Don' know," he said as he greedily eyed the gold. I handed the coin to him. He put it between his teeth to ensure it was genuine. Satisfied, he bowed deeply.

"Thank you," I said. "We will talk again and I will pay for what you know." I held my finger up to his nose. "You know I am the deputy sheriff here, yes?"

He squinted his eyes and gave me another dark look, no doubt accustomed to threats.

"Do not say anything about me asking questions," I warned him. "Savvy?"

He nodded quickly, still scowling, then scurried off behind a curtain to the back of the shop where I heard him chatter loudly at his wife in Chinese.

Virginia City
Idaho Territory
November 12, 1863

I could see by the dim light of the single lantern that McKenzie had recovered sufficiently from his gunshot wound to attend the committee meeting. Sanders was at his usual place as were all the rest, except Danner, whom Henry had transported to the new Bannack jail to await the U.S. deputy marshal.

"Well, Noah, the professor tells us you've had a change of heart," Sanders began. I took my seat and nodded.

"What brought that on?" he asked derisively. "After the trouble you made for us at the Bitterroot, we had, frankly, given up on you."

Beidler glared at me. "That's right, Coffey. You're damn lucky you didn't get hanged with them other two."

"Yes, X, thank God," I replied looking him in the eyes, "You did such a fine job as the hangman out there, I *am* lucky. I'd probably still be choking to death."

He stared back at me, his black beady eyes glinting hungrily. "Next time you point a gun at me, Coffey, you best pull the trigger."

Sanders held up his hand. "X, please," he sighed, "let us hear what Noah has to say for himself."

I looked at each of them earnestly. "You were right about Plummer," I began. "We had a falling out after I confronted him over the gold he'd brought here with him from Bannack. I believe he stole it. Well, perhaps not him personally, but some of his confederates; Doc Howard's men."

A bitter wind pounded the flimsy window frames as the vigilantes glanced at each other. I could see they were assessing my words and perhaps deciding how much they could confide in me.

"Actually," said Sanders after a long silence, "I am fairly certain that the gold you mention belongs to Plummer. He's been successful—I think too successful. He's making a fortune while the other miners in Bannack are grubbing for what's left. It's not right."

I stifled my confusion and managed to continue. "Be that as it may, Wilbur, I also agree with you that Crown was who he said he was. Now the one trained lawman who might have discovered what Plummer and his cronies were doing is gone."

I could see Wiggins nod his head slightly. "That's a good point," he interjected. Then he addressed Sanders. "Remember, after just a couple of inquiries it was Silas who learned of Mayfield's whereabouts. Plummer didn't do that; didn't even try. He just disappeared."

"Please continue, Noah," invited Dimsdale as he sat back in his chair.

I cleared my throat. "Then I considered the coincidences you pointed out. Whenever there was a robbery, Plummer was nowhere to be found. There was the business with Mayfield's escape and before that the release of Forbes, Stinson and Lyons and the complicity of Plummer's deputy, Ned Ray. I came to realize after I confronted Plummer that there were no coincidences in any of this. You were right about him all along. Plummer is directing the criminal activities of his gang. And in order to do that, as you have said repeatedly, what better position could he be in than sheriff?"

Sanders was eyeing me suspiciously. "I asked you once about his past and you refused to divulge what you knew. In fact, you lied to me. We know bits and pieces. But now I ask again. Who *is* Henry Plummer?"

I hesitated. "I met him in California. He had been elected marshal in Auroria. I was told he did a good job before I got there. Then there was a shootout and he accidentally killed a sheriff..."

"*Accidentally?*" repeated Sanders, his voice dripping with sarcasm as he glanced about at the others.

"He was absolved in that killing," I continued, "but not long afterwards, he shot another man. Henry was in love with the man's wife. He was sentenced to prison. He served just six months. He was well connected politically so he was able to win a parole from the governor on the pretext of being deathly ill."

Sanders sat back and spread his hands. "There you have it, Gentlemen!" he declared. "A convicted felon. What did I tell you?" He looked at me again. "Anything else we should know?"

"After his release, he killed another man in a brothel," I said quietly, looking down at the table. "He was arrested and jailed for that murder. But he had the sympathies of the Auroria sheriff and his deputies. They, um, forgot to lock his jail cell one night and Plummer escaped."

Sanders slapped the table with the flat of his hand. "I knew it!" he cried. "By God, I knew it!" He looked around again at the committee members. "He used his position as a lawman to try to cover his crimes! This is why we *must* get rid of him. He's a murderer, a thief and a moral reprobate! There will be no law and no order until Plummer and the rest are found, tried and hanged!"

There was a general agreement. I looked at Sanders. "If you...I mean, if we do that, what becomes of the money and property of those we try and execute?"

Sanders seemed irritated by the question. "It's forfeit to cover the cost of the proceedings, of course," he explained. "You don't believe we're doing this without the promise of some recompense, do you?"

McKenzie looked at me coldly. "I know I got me better things to do."

"As do I," agreed Wiggins.

"As do we all," declared Dimsdale. "Policing this jurisdiction is time consuming and, candidly, troublesome. Obviously Plummer has no interest in his job beyond enriching himself at the expense of the citizens' safety and well-being. Miners are being robbed and some men killed. There continues to be violence here, in Nevada and over in Bannack. And we haven't even begun to talk about the swindlers, drunks, whores, confidence men and other undesirables! High time, I say, for real law enforcement! And that comes at a price, Noah!"

This was, by far, the most impassioned I had ever heard Dimsdale on any subject.

"Let the lawbreakers and perpetrators pay for it, not only with their lives but with their purses and property!"

"Here, here," said Wiggins in a bright voice. "Very well put, Professor, very well put, indeed."

"Damn right Perfesser," McKenzie chimed in.

"So what about Plummer?" I asked.

"We need something to make the case against him airtight," Sanders replied as he peaked his fingers and cast his eyes thoughtfully on the ceiling. "The evidence is mounting but my legal training tells me it wouldn't stand up to appeal were higher authorities to, um, review it…later. In point of fact, the case against Plummer is entirely circumstantial."

"Plummer is a man of means and intelligence and, as you pointed out, Noah, he has friends in high places," noted Dimsdale, "At least in California he has. But Plummer may have friends here, too. He seems well acquainted with Deputy Marshal Beechey in Lewiston, for example."

"Yes, he is," I agreed. "In fact, Hill Beechey had recommended him for deputy U.S. marshal for this jurisdiction," I said. "But there's been a delay in his appointment. Someone evidently intervened."

Sanders nodded. "That someone would be Judge Sidney Edgerton," he said as he raised an eyebrow knowingly. "From the professor here, the judge learned of the deputy marshal's interest in appointing Plummer so he sent a letter to Beechey in order to put a stop to the appointment."

"I see."

"No, we need to proceed carefully," continued Sanders. "Hanging Mayfield was one thing. But hanging Plummer will be quite another. He has many friends, including the federal marshal. We must build our case against Plummer so it can stand up to scrutiny." He looked around the table at the faces illuminated by the flickering lamplight. The wind continued its relentless hammering against the windows. "Any ideas, Gentlemen?"

Part Four

Vigilantes

Kevin Emmet Foley

36

"I think it will work," remarked Dimsdale. Sanders frowned, less certain.

Coffey had left the meeting an hour earlier with Wiggins, McKenzie and Beidler. Sanders sat alone with Dimsdale, considering the plan.

"I really don't like the notion of engaging the boy, but I see no real alternative," Sanders replied after a long moment of thought.

"As you told them, the case against Plummer is far from convincing," Dimsdale said. "We keep talking as though there has been a wave of crime..."

"There has!" exclaimed Sanders.

"I've compiled a list, and it's rather thin, I'm afraid," Dimsdale said as he slid a sheet of paper to Sanders. "Apart from the Peabody stage affair, it pains me to say that Plummer and Coffey solved the other crimes or at least know who is responsible for committing them. The rest is mostly petty theft and non-lethal violence."

Sanders glanced at the sheet. On it was a list of reported crimes over the past two weeks:

Dutch Fred—$5 stolen
Dunbar stabbed (not killed) in fight at wikiup
Samuels, miner, robbed of gold on Bannack road.
Banfield shot in melee in Nevada City. He died from wound.
The baker LeGrau's business broken into, nothing taken

He pushed the paper away. "We need to focus on the robberies and murders," Sanders said, exasperated. "Plummer's gang was obviously behind them, so it shouldn't be difficult to link him to the Wells killing and robbery and the Oliver stage hold-up."

"How are we going to do that?" Dimsdale asked, perplexed by Sanders's accusations.

"Well, that's easy," Sanders said with a sly smile. "Horan took his orders from Plummer and Plummer executed him before he could implicate the sheriff. Ives and Zachery were Plummer's henchmen in the Oliver stage robbery."

"Yes, Wilbur, but Ives and Zachery said nothing about Plummer at their trial."

Sanders shrugged. "They were obviously protecting Plummer. So were the scum who murdered poor Deputy Dillingham."

"Dillingham?!" Dimsdale asked, surprised at hearing the name.

"Of course," Sanders replied. "Who shot Dillingham? Plummer's deputies."

"I don't see the connection..."

"J. W. Dillingham was a Texas Ranger," snapped Sanders. "An experienced lawman. How long would it be before he would detect Plummer's guilt? In fact, I believe Dillingham had found evidence to implicate Plummer. So the sheriff had him...eliminated."

Dimsdale was nodding, understanding Sanders's insinuations. "Yes, I see. That makes sense, Wilbur. It also explains why the fiends are still at large."

"Exactly!" exclaimed Sanders, pleased that Dimsdale was finally catching his drift. "Then there was the matter of Bob Mayfield and his so-called escape from custody and Plummer's sudden disappearance.

"We also have these crimes as well," Dimsdale noted, pointing at the sheet of paper. "The ones without any suspects associated with them."

Sanders slowly sat back and folded his hands behind his head. "What we *don't* have is an eye witness. Yet."

For the better part of a week Henry Plummer's health had not been good. He was so frequently gripped by ague he thought perhaps the consumption had returned. It wasn't helping that he was holed up in the clef between some rocks with Buzz Caven as a furious snowstorm ripped across the Ruby River Valley.

Plummer fought off a shiver as he pulled the wool blanket more tightly around his shoulders. Caven stoked the fire and threw another chunk of wood on the blaze. Sparks flew and the smoke hung on the ceiling above them before the relentless wind sucked it out of their refuge. Caven sat down heavily and gnawed a piece of jerked buffalo.

"When this breaks, we'll take them," Plummer said. The deputy continued chewing and said nothing. "We'll be back in Bannack by Thanksgiving. I bought a turkey, Buzz," he added with a smile. "A thieving Mormon butcher in Salt Lake charged me forty dollars for it. I'll treat you and some others to a real holiday feast when we get back. How does that sound?"

"Mmm," agreed the deputy through a mouthful of desiccated meat. "Better'n this injun shit."

Morning broke clear, but drifting snow had piled up in front of their shelter during the night. They pushed their way through with their saddles and weapons and found their horses kicking aside snow and grazing on thin blades of grass among a stand of aspens. A mile away, they saw the smoke rising from Dempsey's lonely cabin.

The night before last, Caven had been playing poker at Skinner's when he'd overheard a drunken Frosty Stump mention the names of Ray and Stinson.

"They's in Nevada," Stump had loudly bragged, "right under Plummer's nose. Hear tell they's leavin' fer Salt Lake tomorra 'r the next day...gettin' outta the territory while they still can."

Caven relayed this intelligence to Plummer who decided to try and intercept the fugitives at Dempsey's, the place they would most likely stay their first night on the trail.

After a short ride through the feathery snow, Plummer and Caven veered east, following the frozen spring creek that flowed behind Dempsey's place. Screened by brush and willows, they approached the cabin from the rear, dismounted, and secured their mounts.

They peered around the corner of the barn and could see the cabin. Despite the snow cover, the place was as unkempt as Plummer remembered from his last visit. A collection of animals wandered around in their waste, mostly ignoring the lawmen. A black colt lay on its side at the far end of the corral, frozen to death. A mare stood over the corpse, looking as if she hoped her baby would miraculously get back on its feet.

Plummer assessed the layout then looked at his deputy. "Buzz, head for those trees and work your way around to the front door. I'll make my call from the rear door. They won't expect that." He grabbed the deputy's arm. "I want you to be ready because they may try to make a break."

Caven disappeared and Plummer waited for ten minutes until he was certain the deputy had found a place to cover the front door. Then, because there were no windows facing him, he stepped out from behind the barn and strode up to the door, the English shotgun in one hand and the LeMat in his other.

Rather than knock, he simply pushed open the door and walked into the cabin. Immediately he saw Buck Stinson was asleep in the corner on a pile of blankets. At the cluttered table sat Ned Ray, eating hotcakes. The forkfull of food was poised before his open mouth and he wore a look of astonishment on his face. Dempsey, also seated at the table, had his back to Plummer. His wife was frying bacon at the stove, a sheen of sweat covering her fleshy face.

"Hello Ned," Plummer smiled. But before he could say anything more, Dempsey wheeled around with surprising speed for a fat man. His face was screwed up as he attempted to level a Colt at the sheriff's chest. Just as quickly, Plummer brought the barrel of the shotgun crashing down on Dempsey's skull. Steel met bone, sending Dempsey to the floor on his belly.

The woman screeched and threw a pan full of hot grease at Plummer. He sidestepped the scalding liquid and it splattered harmlessly against the cabin's wall. By then Stinson had begun stirring in the corner.

Plummer glared at the woman. Without a word she moved to help her husband to his feet and then sat next to him, holding a filthy towel to his bleeding skull. The LeMat was aimed at Stinson's chest.

"Don't move, Buck," Plummer ordered. "And put that fork down Ned. You look like a damn fool."

Ray obeyed.

"Spread your hands out on the table where I can see them."

Plummer called out to his deputy and Caven presently walked through the front door. Silently, he went over to Stinson, got him on his feet and tied his hands behind his back. Then he did likewise with Ray. He placed the two fugitives against the wall and awaited orders. He saw that Plummer was eyeing the stock of the shotgun with a dark look of anger.

"God damn you, Dempsey!" he exclaimed, holding the weapon in front of the man's face. "Look at that stock! It's broken because of you!"

Dempsey managed to open his pig-like eyes and closed them again with a grimace of pain. "Sorry, Sheriff," he said through clenched teeth. "I don' know these boys…"

"That's what you told me last time, you bastard," Plummer snarled. "And you remember what I did when you lied to me, don't you?"

Now the man's eyes grew wide with fear. "They…they showed up here last night lookin' for food an' a roof. I let 'em stay for a dollar a man!"

He stopped speaking as he saw the menacing look in the sheriff's bloodshot eyes and was relieved when they cut to Ray and Stinson. Plummer felt himself becoming feverish and exhaustion washed over him in dizzying waves. He wanted nothing more than to lie down in his bed and sleep. He glanced back at Dempsey then looked at Caven.

"Get them on mounts, Buzz," he said. "I need to get back to Bannack."

Noah Coffey was hanging by his neck from a cottonwood tree. There was snow on the ground and a screaming wind spun the dead man in tight circles. Somehow, his bowler hat remained on his head, yet Coffey's eyes were bulging and his tongue hung from his mouth, which seemed to be wearing a smile. Electa, who was naked, pleaded with Henry Plummer to cut the body down, tears frozen to her eyelashes. In the distance, through a white screen of blowing snow, mounted men were watching.

Plummer shook violently and opened his eyes. His sheets were soaked in sweat and through the icy window he saw it was dawn. He felt damp and chilled, but his fever had finally broken. He slowly got to his feet, stoked the fire and placed a pot of water on top of the stove so he could wash and shave.

An hour later, bleary eyed and weak, he made his way to Chrisman's, where he found Caven pouring himself a cup of fresh coffee. Without being asked, Caven produced a second mug from a cabinet and poured Plummer's coffee. The broken shotgun lay on his desk. The sheriff lifted it and again angrily examined the damage. Irritated, he jabbed the barrel into Ned Ray's ribs. The prisoner was seated in a chair before his desk.

"Look!" Plummer snapped as he threw the gun onto his desk. "That stock can't be repaired properly!"

Ray kept his eyes on the floor as Plummer sat down. He kept his coat and hat on even though the room was warm.

"All right, Ned, let me guess," the sheriff began, his tone mild. "You've been slumming with Doc Howard and his boys, haven't you?"

"No," the former deputy said to the floor.

"I've got witnesses who will testify you and Buck robbed the Peabody stage in October. And you probably had something to do with Jamie Wells's murder, too. You remember that don't you? Boy of sixteen, murdered..."

Ray looked up. "We ain't done no robbery, Plummer, nor no murder," he added disdainfully.

The sheriff quickly jabbed Ray again with the gun's barrel, harder this time. "That's *Sheriff* Plummer, Ned."

"Sheriff, I mean," Ray continued, his tone suddenly respectful. "We been lookin' fer work upcountry. Just got back here las' week."

"That is most definitely *not* what Red Yeager told me, Ned. He said you and Buck are road agents. "

Ray looked alarmed at the mention of Yeager and Plummer saw his gambit had worked. "That's right, Ned. Red says you and Buck threw in with Doc." Plummer stood up, walked to the stove, opened it and threw in several sticks of wood. He slammed the metal door noisily. "Red likes to talk, doesn't he?" Plummer asked Ray with a sly smile. "He told me quite a lot."

Ray was scowling as he considered his options. He stared up at the ceiling for several minutes then asked for coffee. Plummer obligingly poured him a cup.

"Have you had your breakfast, yet?" Plummer asked. Ray shook his head so Plummer sent Caven to the Goodrich kitchen for a plate of boiled eggs, bread and bacon.

Ray sipped his coffee. "Thanks, Sheriff Plummer," he said finally.

"You always been good to me."

Plummer reached over and patted the former deputy gently on the shoulder. "Don't get used to it, Ned," he said. "I gave you a job and the first chance you had you played me false. I'm going to make you pay for that."

Later, Plummer quizzed Stinson, who must have felt he had less to lose than Ray because he was far more talkative.

"Dillin'ham was mad when he found out Lyons and me was drinkin' instead a doin' what we's supposed to be doin'," Stinson explained, avoiding Plummer's eyes. "It were Forbes an' Lyons what shot Jack."

Plummer decided to accept this explanation of Dillingham's murder for the time being. "What about Howard and the rest?"

"We was runnin' with Doc last summer all right. Him, Steve Marshland, Romaine, Bill Bunton, um...fella name o' Carter. They's others but I cain't remember 'em all, Sheriff."

Plummer was pleased to see Caven jotting the names down. "So you were there when they stole the freighter and killed Magruder?" Plummer asked.

"No, Sir," Stinson replied, "but Carter tol' me about it. Said they killed the man what owned the wagon, sold the goods and split the money."

"And what do you know about the Peabody stage and the old man who was killed?"

Stinson bit his lower lip and thought about it for a moment. "Well, Sir, the stage, Ned an' me done that..."

"Good. That's what Ned told us," Plummer lied smoothly. "Ned also told me you pulled the trigger on the old man, Buck."

Stinson's face turned red with rage. He bunched his fists and shot a look at the jail out behind the store where he knew Ray was cooling his heels. Then he relaxed and laughed bitterly.

"He tol' you *I* shot that ol' man?" he asked. "That's a goddamn lie, Sheriff. It were Ned killed the old gent. Told 'im to hand over his money belt. Ned blew his head off on account a' he's movin' too slow."

"And Jamie Wells?" Plummer asked. "That was the young boy who was shot to pieces and his father robbed. I hanged Johnny Horan for that, but he never told me who was with him."

Stinson's lip began to tremble and tears formed in his eyes. "That boy, he went for his piece and Ned and John shot 'im out o' the buckboard. I was right mad at 'em when they did it. I says to 'em, 'Now we's all in for it!'"

"You got that part right, anyway," Plummer concluded. "You *are* all in for it. But I will try to help you, Buck. You've cooperated with me and that might have saved your neck. But Ned's going to swing and so are Doc and his people for the Magruder killing when I find them. Now where are they?"

Coffey watched the weather change. What had been an unseasonably warm afternoon was growing ominous. Clouds like sheets of steel pushed down over Virginia City from the north. A stiff, icy breeze heralded the freezing blasts that would soon follow. Outside on the muddy street, merchants scurried to conclude the day's business. Tomorrow was Thanksgiving Day, and they wanted to get home to their families and their feasts. Coffey could think of nothing for which he was grateful.

Nevertheless, Mrs. Foster had promised a chicken dinner, and he supposed that would do. ("I am so sorry, Mr. Coffey, but there are no turkeys to be had!" the spinster had apologized.)

He gazed down at the Kansas City newspaper and its screaming headlines:

Slaughter in Kansas!!!

—

Men, Women, Children Murdered

—

Lawrence Looted & Burned by Rebel Irregulars

—

Survivors Swear Revenge on
Quantrill's Raiders

The chickens had come home to roost in Kansas, he thought to himself with a humorless smile. He wondered how many of the dead in Lawrence who'd so energetically supported the Union ever expected the violence to land on their front door steps. A rag tag force of escaped prisoners of war and criminals had attacked their picturesque little town and sacked it like Carthage. He thought about Crown, now languishing in Marshal Beechey's cell in Lewiston. *He* would have enjoyed the Lawrence raid. The news account reported that few citizens had fired back at the raiders.

Through his window he could see the snow was blowing horizontally. As he watched, a wagon appeared and rolled to a stop before the *Tribune* office. A bundled figure jumped down and made for the door, shielding his face with his hat.

"Francis!" called Coffey as he watched the miner enter. "What the hell are you doing out in this weather?!"

Thompson removed his long wool coat, gauntlet gloves and a red woolen scarf. His face was raw, the boyish freckles gone. He held his fingers out over the stove, then turned around and rubbed his backside as it warmed.

"There was never such cold back in Massachusetts, Noah," he said, his teeth still chattering. "It came out of nowhere! Most of the day I was driving along in a spring sunshine and then the hammers of a frozen hell beat on me for the last couple of miles!"

"You're stuck in Virginia, now, my friend," Coffey remarked. "Do you have lodgings?"

Thompson shook his head. "No...I needed to warm up first."

"Mrs. Foster will fix you up, then. She has rooms available."

They had finished their supper of beef stew. Thompson lit a thin black cigar, which earned him a nasty look from the landlady. Coffey smiled at her and she gave him an indulgent shake of the head and disappeared into her kitchen with the empty plates. They exchanged small talk, Coffey delicately avoiding the difficult subject of their mutual friend, Henry Plummer.

"So you are off to Salt Lake?" he asked.

"Next week," Thompson replied, "Before the real weather hits. Hope to be back by Christmas." He blew out a plume of smoke.

Coffey noticed Thompson's fingers were nervously tapping the corner of the table.

"We need more equipment. Maybe a dredge. We've only gone down ten or twelve feet. No telling how much gold lies deeper."

Mrs. Foster returned, hovering around the men as she pretended to fuss with her silverware at the sideboard. The two men sat quietly waiting for her to leave. She finally took the hint and retreated to the kitchen.

"How is Henry?" Coffey finally asked.

Thompson hesitated. "Oh, he's not well. He's taken ill with some kind of consumption. He has a fever and he coughs quite a lot."

"Yes, he was quite sick in California some years back," replied Coffey with a worried nod.

"But he's having a feast tomorrow!" Thompson said cheerfully. "He had a butcher in Salt Lake ship him a live turkey, if you can believe that. It's as big as a buzzard!"

"Sounds like Henry," Coffey chuckled. "Always doing things up in grand style. He probably bought the turkey a ticket on the stagecoach to Bannack."

Thompson laughed. "Oh, yes. He's invited some…friends to the Goodrich. Mrs. Quinn is preparing everything. It should be quite a table, Noah."

"Aren't you going?"

"Well, I was. But we needed some more equipment," he said. "This was the only place I could get it. Thought I'd be back by tomorrow night, but…" he gestured out the window.

Through the kitchen door came Mrs. Foster again. She stacked some clean plates in the cupboard and loitered again at the sideboard. The little rooming house shook as the wind's velocity increased.

"Why don't we go get a drink?" Coffey suggested, giving the spinster's back a look of irritation. "I've some things I need to tell you about our friend, the sheriff."

37

If Stinson had told him the truth, then Howard and his men were going to winter at Deer Lodge. But it had been snowing almost continuously since Thanksgiving. Now mid-December, Plummer was worried that the longer he waited to go after the criminals who'd robbed and murdered Magruder, the worse the weather would get. He was also unwell, not so sick that he couldn't travel, but ill enough that a hundred mile trek through the frozen valley might prove fatal if he wasn't careful. He weighed his options as he watched the snow fall dreamily from the dull gray sky. There was no wind, just fluffy white flakes cascading relentlessly down on Bannack.

"I think I'll go after them, Buzz," he said finally. "It's now or spring but I think Doc and the rest will be gone by then if I wait."

Caven had a wad of tobacco plug in his cheek. He sat on a chair near the woodstove, whittling a stick with his pocketknife. He glanced up at Plummer and frowned.

"That smart, Hank?" he asked, brown spittle dribbling down his chin as he spoke.

"No, probably not. But I don't see much choice." He turned back to the window.

"You gonna need he'p, ain't ya?" the deputy asked.

Plummer had considered this. Taking Howard and four or five other men was a three-man job for sure. His plan was to take his captives on to the Beechey in Lewiston, convinced now that the vigilantes would summarily hang them if he brought them back to Bannack. But Lewiston was at least another hundred miles through the mountains beyond Deer Lodge. He shivered at the prospect.

"I have a couple of Deer Lodge men in mind that will help," he said. "As long as I can find them."

At the livery stable he rented a huge roan stud named Julius Caesar. He knew he needed a strong mount to get through the snow. He'd had a blacksmith repair the shotgun with some bailing wire, but the fine workmanship was ruined. He slid the weapon into a scabbard on his saddle. He had another scabbard for his carbine. Along with the LeMat, he had two borrowed Colts and he had plenty of ammunition for all the weapons.

The horse turned out to be unruly, spoiled by long summer days in the corral consorting with mares and unaccustomed to the saddle. But as he rode out of town, Plummer used a switch to let the big stallion know who was in charge. Slowly, the roan calmed down and settled into a steady, powerful gait that took Plummer northward toward Deer Lodge.

"Deer Lodge, eh?" Sidney Edgerton said thoughtfully.

Caven nodded. He was uncomfortable standing before the chief justice's desk. He felt like he was on trial.

"Been gone fer two days, Mr. Edgerton," Caven said. The judge didn't respond.

"And where is Plummer's man...Thompson, is it?" Sanders asked. The judge's nephew sat in a chair next to Edgerton's desk.

"Believe he went down t' Salt Lake City," Caven replied. "Don't know he'll be back here much afore April, seein's how we got all that snow."

Sanders met the judge's eyes, then both turned back to Caven. "Very well," said Edgerton. "Thank you for meeting with us, deputy. You're dismissed."

An annoyed look flashed across Caven's face, but he didn't reply. He put his hat on his head and left the parlor of Edgerton's home. The fire in the stove crackled loudly.

"You're sure you want young Henry to do this?" Edgerton asked his nephew.

"Yes, I'm sure," replied Sanders, an elbow resting on Edgerton's desk. "We've got to get Plummer out of the way."

"Well, I can have no part in any of your...plan," Edgerton said again as he stood. "And, frankly Wilbur, I already know too much as it is. I will send the boy in."

Henry Tilden was fourteen, the son of Edgerton's brother in Maryland. He had arrived in Bannack over the summer with a chronic cough that doctors had diagnosed as tuberculosis. They'd prescribed a dry climate, so before Edgerton had departed Ohio, he had agreed to take in the youth once he'd established his home in Bannack. The boy entered the room and nodded at his cousin. He was small for his age, his face smooth and his blue eyes bright.

"Henry, how are you feeling, my boy?" asked Sanders with a solicitous smile.

"Very well, Sir," Henry replied, surprise and uncertainty in his voice. Mostly his older cousin ignored him when they were together. "Thank you for asking."

"Henry, I have an errand for you to run for me later this afternoon," Sanders said. "I need you to ride over to the Hanson place on Horse Prairie and deliver some papers there for me. Are you up to that?"

"I can do it," the youth replied with an excited smile.

"Wonderful," Sanders said as he gestured toward a pile of papers on the desk. "It's a legal matter. I need to finish this up and I'll bring it to you when I am ready. Meantime, why don't you saddle my horse? You can ride him if you'd like."

The boy grinned widely. He loved riding and the thought of going to the Hansons' aboard Nutmeg, Sanders's gelding, cheered him immensely.

"Yes, Sir!" he agreed brightly.

Horse Prairie was a stark rangeland south of Bannack dotted with lonely cabins. It had stopped snowing but a cold wind swept the plain as darkness fell. It had been just before supper that Wilbur had presented the boy with the folio he wanted delivered to old man Hanson.

"You can dine when you return," Edgerton said dismissively when the boy brought up the subject of supper.

It was a three-mile trip. The boy found Hanson seated at his table with his wife and two adult sons. He warmed himself by their stove, ate a biscuit with honey that Mrs. Hanson had offered, then mounted Nutmeg for the return ride to Bannack.

A quarter moon hung on the horizon and stars had appeared while he'd refreshed himself in the Hanson cabin. A wolf howled somewhere beyond the crest of a nearby ridge and several dogs from distant cabins responded with furious barking. Henry shivered as he huddled himself deeper into the full-length woolen coat he wore. He tugged the scarf up around his ears and rode on.

As the trail neared Bannack, Henry saw three forms on horseback ride down off a hill in the distance, to his right. The figures stopped in the middle of the trail and waited for the boy to approach. Henry, unsure of what to do, continued to ride toward them. He stopped a dozen yards short of the men, who sat impassively in their saddles.

"Get your damn hands up!" called one of the riders.

Henry felt a stab of fear.

"You heard 'em boy," hollered one of the other men. "Put your hands up and git off that hoss!"

The boy blinked and finally did as he was told. "I...I...I have no money nor valuables," he began.

"Shut up!" commanded the third man as he dismounted.

Henry saw he was short and wore a black mask over his face. He peered at the boy through eyeholes. Completely terrified, the boy began sniffling.

The man slapped Henry hard across the face. "Shut up, I said!"

Henry broke down completely, sobbing uncontrollably as the man went through his pockets. The other two, having dismounted, were standing before the boy.

"Check his saddle," said the masked man who was roughly searching Henry. The others walked over to Nutmeg and rummaged through the saddlebags.

"Nothin' here, Hank," called one of them.

"Nor here!" replied the other bandit. "All right, boy, git on your hoss and get outta here now! Don't look back or I'll kill ya!"

Henry dropped his arms, wiped his teary face and runny nose with his gloved hand. He climbed onto Nutmeg and kicked him hard. Inexperienced riding at night, especially at a full gallop, a mile later Henry took a turn onto the main street of Bannack where Nutmeg caught his foot in a frozen hole and threw the boy into the street. As he flew through the air, Henry let out a bloodcurdling shriek that was heard throughout the town.

"He should never have been out there, Wilbur," scolded Hattie, Sanders's wife. Henry lay on his bed as she stroked his forehead. "Thank the good Lord he wasn't injured. But he is frightened out of his wits!"

Sanders ignored her and looked at the boy. Edgerton was in the room, leaning against the wall, his arms crossed over his chest, his face a mask of worry for his brother's son. As with most things Wilbur Sanders did, this had gone wrong, too, Edgerton angrily thought to himself.

"Henry, do you know who it was that tried to rob you?" Sanders asked the boy.

Henry, still in shock from his fall off the gelding, shook his head absently. Hattie held a cup of tea to his lips and the boy sipped it. He now looked at his cousin with blank eyes.

"There were three men, Sir," he said weakly.

"Three, eh?" Sanders repeated, his lips pursed. "Did they hurt you?"

"One hit me," Henry replied, eyes brimming with tears again. "But it didn't hurt."

Edgerton cleared his throat. Sanders glanced up at his uncle from the chair beside Henry's bed and then continued. "Did any of them say a name?"

The boy remained silent for almost a minute, thinking. "Hank," he said finally. "One man called another man Hank."

"Hank? Are you certain of that?" asked Sanders, his voice doubtful. "Think again, Henry."

"I am certain, Cousin Wilbur," the boy replied meekly. "Hank was the name I heard."

Now it was Edgerton's turn. "Did the man who searched you, the man named Hank, the one you said hit you, did he look like Sheriff Plummer?"

The boy stared at the judge. "I don't think so, Uncle Sidney," he mumbled.

Edgerton's dark eyes bored into Henry's. "It's just that we haven't seen Henry Plummer hereabouts for some days. It's my considered opinion that's because he's a road agent…a thief. And a killer. Now, here you are, riding by yourself at night. It's dark, so you cannot see very well. Road agents stop you and attempt a robbery. One is named Hank. That's a nickname for Henry, you know."

"Some of my friends call me that back home," the boy said with a sniffle.

"And the sheriff has the same name as you," Sanders interjected.

"So, it is quite possible you saw the sheriff tonight," concluded Edgerton. "In fact, Henry, it is quite probable it was the sheriff and a couple of his henchmen who stopped you."

The boy was blinking, confused, yet eager to please his uncle and cousin. He had seen Sheriff Plummer in Bannack. He'd even talked to him once in the fall. He remembered Plummer as a nice man who'd asked him if he ever went hunting up in the hills for jackrabbits. When Henry said no, the sheriff had offered to take him, but Cousin Wilbur had told him he couldn't go, without explaining why. The man he'd seen tonight called "Hank" was short; certainly shorter than the sheriff. He also thought he'd seen a beard beneath the mask.

"May…maybe," Henry said, his voice barely audible.

"Not maybe, Henry," Sanders said flatly. "You saw Sheriff Plummer tonight. He struck you and tried to rob you, didn't he?"

The boy was crying. "I…I…no…yes…no…I think so…"

Sanders glared down at him. "Think? Or know? This is important, boy!"

Moved by Henry's pitiful tears, Hattie stepped forward. "Please, Wilbur, you're frightening him again…"

"Come on, Henry!" Sanders shouted, seizing the boy's arm and squeezing it viciously. "Was it Plummer or wasn't it?"

The boy was crying. "It…I, I…it was the sheriff. I know it was the sheriff," Henry choked through his heavy sobs.

Sanders looked up at Edgerton, a thin smile on his lips. The judge shot him a look of contempt and left the room. Sanders swallowed, then patted the boy's arm.

"Get some sleep now, Henry. You've done well."

38

Out on the range forty miles north of Bannack, Plummer was struggling through deep snow and piercing wind. Mountains jutted up on either side, but a sky the color of lead hung so low he could only make out their lower slopes. He kept his head down so his face wouldn't be blasted raw. Caesar gamely pushed on but he could tell the big animal was suffering. His own fingertips and toes were numb, and he began to question this foolhardy adventure. Why couldn't this have waited until spring? Either he would take Howard and his men then or they'd be gone from the territory.

As he approached a line of willows and bushes, he knew he needed to be careful because there was likely a stream alongside them, although it lay invisible beneath a thick blanket of snow. He spurred his mount forward onto what he knew was ice. The stallion took several tentative steps before he heard a muffled cracking beneath and felt his stomach jump to his throat. A second later, the ice gave way and he and Caesar plunged, not into a shallow stream, but a deep river.

Probably the Big Hole you damn fool! Plummer swore at himself, realizing he'd let his attention roam. The horse was struggling with all its might in the deep, freezing water, trying to find his footing. Caeser huffed and coughed in shock and panic as Plummer desperately hung on to the saddle's horn. He calmed himself, then reached out and patted the stud's neck gently.

"Easy, boy, easy," he said quietly, pulling the reins to the left. The panicky horse seemed to relax and then followed Plummer's command. He spurred his mount and suddenly Caesar found purchase, plunging through the ice and back up onto the riverbank.

Plummer quickly dismounted and led the shivering horse to a thicket of willow trees that provided a little protection from the screeching wind. His own teeth chattering, he fell to his knees and dug into the snow all the way to the ground then brought out a handful of dry grass and twigs. In his breast pocket he found the matches he always kept wrapped in oilpaper. His clothing already beginning to freeze on his back, Plummer struck a match to the tinder but it was blown out. He lit another and, carefully shielding the flickering flame with his hands, he got the grass and twigs ignited.

He found dead trees beneath the snow, broke off their branches and built the fire up into blaze. He stripped naked and hung his clothes on bushes near the fire, hoping its radiant heat would dry everything. Meantime, Caeser had gratefully cozied up to the fire as close as he could get and was soon dozing in its warmth. Plummer placed himself between the horse and the fire and waited.

"I don't appreciate you striking the boy, X," Sanders angrily declared. "That was completely unnecessary."

Beidler smirked. "Just tryin' to make it convincin' was all."

"Be that as it may," Sanders continued, looking around at the others, the lamplight flickering on his face, "we now have our witness. Henry Tilden will swear he was assaulted by Plummer and two of his road agents on Horse Prairie on December the tenth."

Coffey frowned, but said nothing. Wiggins puffed his cigar and McKenzie sat back, satisfied. Two others had joined the vigilantes a week earlier and Coffey didn't like the looks of either of them. As Sanders went on, the newspaperman eyed Nellis Kincaid, a farrier from Nevada City. He had a hatchet face that featured an aquiline nose. It was difficult to discern where the black stubble of his whiskers ended and the smut from his forge began. He wore his battered hat and a scowl as he listened to the vigilante leader.

Matthew Horace was small, with catlike moves and eyes that seemed always to be roaming. He was clean-shaven, and wore his black hair slicked down with a foul smelling pomade Coffey suspected was bear grease. His teeth were tiny and yellow and he frequently laughed without provocation. He said he clerked at a store in Alder.

"But first things, first," Sanders was saying. "We need to find Howard and deal with him. I learned he is in Deer Lodge with his fellow road agents."

"Deer Lodge!" declared Wiggins. "You don't mean to go there in this weather, do you Wilbur?"

"In this *weather*," Sanders rejoined, "they aren't going anywhere and they won't be expecting us."

"Well, now, Wilbur, I think..." Beidler began to say.

"I don't give a damn what you think, X!" Sanders cried as he jumped to his feet. "We're going after them! Tomorrow! Are you a member of this committee or aren't you?!"

"Well, sure, but..." Beidler replied sheepishly.

"Very well, then. Be ready to ride in the morning. First light. All of you," Sanders commanded.

The weather had lifted though the sky threatened more snow. The road northward cut between the Tobacco Root Mountains on their right and the Ruby River on the left. It was well worn from previous traffic, so the going was not as slow as the vigilantes had expected. Still, the horses had to trudge through knee-deep drifts and the wind forced the vigilantes to cover their faces with woolen scarves. Sanders rode out in front of the party with Dimsdale alongside him like his shadow. Next was Beidler, then Wiggins, McKenzie, Kincaid, Horace and finally the editor of the *Virginia City Tribune*, Noah Coffey.

They crossed the Jefferson River just before nightfall at a ford where previous riders had already broken the ice. Wet and cold, they built a fire below a steep bluff on the western shore and made camp. They'd just finished eating their supper of corn mush and dried venison when an old Indian man appeared at the edge of the vigilante camp. As he wordlessly approached the warmth of the fire, Coffey could see he was ancient, probably abandoned by his people because he could no longer care for himself.

Coffey made his way to the fire and began spooning mush onto his plate. He turned and saw McKenzie, Kincaid and Beidler were standing in front of the decrepit old Indian. They were laughing and making sport of the man's miserable condition.

"God *damn* you stink, old man!" Kincaid laughed.

The Indian's dark eyes never wavered as he stared at the food Coffey held. His long, wispy white hair hung limply to his shoulders and he wore old buckskins that provided little protection from the frigid evening air.

"Oh, you hungry?" Beidler asked with a leer. "Well, Chief Stinkin' Ass, you're welcome to our food."

He walked over, took the plate from Coffey and threw the mush into the old man's face. Even though it was steaming hot, the Indian never flinched and instead used his fingers to push what food hadn't fallen onto the snow into his mouth.

"Beidler, that's enough!" called Coffey. "Kincaid, leave him alone."

"Ah, he's just a dirty ol' injun…what the hell you care?" Beidler asked without looking Coffey's way.

"Keep out of it," Kincaid sneered. "We're just funnin'."

Coffey ignored them. He walked forward, took the old Indian by the arm and led him over to where he'd laid out his blanket. He refilled the plate and handed it to the Indian who ate greedily. He was obviously starving and wouldn't live long alone in the wilderness.

"That's a mistake, Coffey!" said McKenzie with a nasty laugh. "Like takin' in a stray dog. You ain't gonna be rid o' 'im now."

"Shut up, McKenzie," Coffey snapped as he now glared at the others. "You're all churchgoers and this is your Christian way of showing charity?"

"He ain't no Christian," replied Horace.

"He ain't even human," added Kincaid. "I ain't got no more regard for 'im than a god damn cy-ote."

Coffey gave up. The Indian silently held out the plate and Coffey spooned out for him what mush remained in the pot. When he had finished eating the old man began to get to his feet as though to leave, but Coffey pointed at his blanket by the fire and the Indian gratefully lay back on it. He was asleep in seconds.

Kincaid and Horace were laughing like the fools they were at some joke one of them made as the others bedded down. Coffey leaned against his saddle next to the Indian, pulled his overcoat over himself like a blanket, and, despite the cold, drifted off into a fitful sleep.

He was jarred awake by the sharp report of a pistol. Coffey leapt to his feet, fumbling with his carbine. The morning was clear and bitterly cold but the wind had stopped blowing during the night. He looked around and saw the Indian was gone. Someone had stoked the fire, which now burned brightly. McKenzie was preparing mush and bacon.

Sanders, Dimsdale, and the others were rolling up their blankets when Kincaid and Beidler came over the rise of the bluff above the camp. Both were laughing. Beidler was carrying Coffey's woolen overcoat.

"Where's the Indian?" Coffey asked Beidler.

"Oh, he took a notion to steal this," Beidler grinned. He tossed Coffey's coat on the snow. "Me an' Kincaid stopped 'im."

"God damn you!" Coffey swore. He pulled on the coat and followed their tracks through the snow up the bluff. At the crest he saw the old Indian's sprawled form. He was bleeding profusely from a bullet hole in his head. Coffey was shocked at the contrast of the reddish blue blood against the glittering white snow.

He stormed back to the camp in a blind rage. Beidler was making a show of killing the old Indian, holding his pistol and laughing.

"Killed *that* sum'bitch dead!" he was laughing as Coffey spun him around and delivered a punch to Beidler's jaw. He felt the satisfying crunch of teeth and bone beneath his fist. He brought his right fist around and connected with the temple, sending Beidler stumbling back through the fire, his boot toppling the breakfast McKenzie had been preparing. Kincaid and Wiggins tried to hold Coffey back, but in an instant he was on top of Beidler, raining punches onto his face.

A shotgun blast split the morning stillness and Coffey froze.

"Get off him, Noah!" Sanders demanded. "Right now!"

Coffey slowly rose and looked down at Beidler's bloody face and dazed eyes.

"I'll kill you Beidler, you murdering bastard!" he panted. "I'll kill you, I swear on all that is holy!"

"Leave him be!" Wiggins said as he pushed Coffey away from Beidler.

Coffey unraveled his fists, gulped some more cold air and then turned back to his belongings.

Holding the shotgun with one of its barrels still smoking, Sanders addressed them. "We have a long way to ride today. The weather is with us. Let's get moving," he ordered.

At that same moment, Plummer was riding back into Bannack empty handed, his ammunition soaked and his resolve to capture Howard and his men gone. He had been sick for two days, nauseous and vomiting, the fever returning with a vengeance. His misfortune at the river had convinced him a winter pursuit was hopeless.

Several miners acknowledged him as rode his exhausted horse back to the livery stable. Plummer was on the verge of collapse as he returned the stallion, patting the great horse gently again on his thick neck.

"That's a good mount, Kelsey," he told the stable's owner. "I'll be back to buy him." Then, shivering, he staggered to the cabin on Yankee Flat.

39

Red Yeager yanked the biscuits from the huge iron stove, burning his fingers. They were crusted black on top but otherwise looked edible. On the stovetop bubbled a stew of buffalo and potatoes.

"Food's on," he said to George Brown.

The little man with a wide face and narrow set eyes was laying on a cot in the corner, dozing in the one room dugout's warmth. Brown rose, walked to the stove and spooned stew onto his plate. As he began to take a biscuit, the rough-hewn door burst open admitting a blast of bitter cold air into the tiny space. Eight men were suddenly crowding inside, the door slamming behind them. They all looked frozen to the bone to Red, who recognized only X. Beidler and Wilbur Sanders.

Red smiled warily at the visitors, who began peeling off coats and kicking snow onto the mud floor.

"Hello, Red," Beidler finally said through a beard thick with frost. The stocky man glanced around at the others with an expression that was both surprised and pleased. "We been lookin' fer you."

"Me?" Yeager replied, surprised. "What ya want with me?"

Sanders stepped forward and placed his hands over the hot stove. "We want you to tell us where Howard is," he said, looking down at Yeager's confused face. "We rode all the way to Deer Lodge and somebody warned him and his bunch we were coming!"

Kevin Emmet Foley

Yeager was genuinely befuddled. "Howard?" he asked. "Oh, you mean Doc Howard? Ain't seen Doc since summer, Mr. Sanders."

Now all the vigilantes were crowded around the stove. Wiggins eyed the pot of stew and biscuits hungrily. "Got enough there?" he asked Yeager.

"Sure, sure, ifn we stretch it a bit," the cook replied with an eager smile. He passed around some spoons and forks and the men took turns eating from the pot. The biscuits were broken apart and handed around.

Coffey took his biscuit half and plopped down on a stool in the corner. He ate the food without tasting it as he felt the blood return to his numb extremities. *Thank God they aren't frostbitten*, he thought to himself. *What the hell was I thinking, joining them on their absurd "scout," as Dimsdale called the misadventure.* Then he remembered. *Appearances.*

McKenzie, Horace and Kincaid mopped up the gravy from the bottom of the pot with the remainder of their biscuits and licked their fingers. It was the first hot food they'd had in the three days since leaving Deer Lodge.

"I kin make some more," Yeager said to the men cheerfully. "I got bacon, too."

"That's all right, Red," Beidler replied as he sipped from the bottle of whiskey he'd found under the table. "We ain't gonna be here long."

"That's right, Mr. Yeager," agreed Sanders. "We're almost home... Bannack is just another half day's ride. What we're here for is to question *you*."

"Me?" Yeager asked again.

Irritated at Yeager's continued questions in response to questions, McKenzie pushed him back onto the other empty cot.

"Yes, you!" he snarled. "We want to know why you warned Doc and them we's comin'."

"Warn Doc?" Yeager replied, confused again as he warily regarded the seven men crowded around him. The eigth man was still sitting on the stool, ignoring the proceedings.

Sanders held up his hand, calling for order. McKenzie took a half step back.

"Let me refresh your memory, Red," he said pleasantly. "You sent this to Deer Lodge." He held out a sheet of paper. "It's a note you wrote warning the rest of the road agents that we were coming."

Yeager took the sheet of paper from Sanders and looked at it. "No Sir, I didn' write this here letter," he said with an embarrassed smile. "Shit, I can't really write but a few words, anyhows."

"Well, then, perhaps it was this gentleman," Sanders said, stepping back and revealing George Brown, who sat on the other cot with an anxious look on his face.

"I cain't write a' tall," Brown declared.

"Shut up!" commanded Kincaid. "You writ' that damn letter. We knows it!"

Once again, Sanders had adopted a judicial air by holding up his hand. "I think the evidence speaks for itself, Mr. Yeager. You know who we are, do you not?"

Yeager looked at them blankly. "I know you, Mr. Sanders, and I know X there, but the rest o' you fellas, I ain't never seen…'cept that one there maybe…" he added as he pointed at Coffey. "He looks famil'er."

Coffey glanced over at him. "I'm Rattlesnake Dick Jacobs, Red. You remember."

The other vigilantes were looking confused. "Oh, yeah…yeah," Yeager exclaimed pointing at Coffey. "You came lookin' fer what's his name…at the Roost!"

Coffey nodded. "George Ives."

"Be that as it may!" interrupted Sanders with an angry look at Coffey. "We are the vigilance committee and we want you to tell us where Howard went, the names of those men who are part of his road agent gang, and what Plummer's role is."

"Plummer?" Yeager asked. "*Sheriff* Plummer?"

"The same," said Dimsdale.

"He ain't with Doc and them," explained Yeager, scratching his head, thoroughly perplexed. "Like I said, Doc took off last summer…"

"Where'd he go?" demanded McKenzie.

Yeager shrugged. "'Don't know, Mister."

"Who was with him?" asked Sanders.

"Last I seen, Steve—Marshland—Aleck Carter, um, Bill Bunton…"

"How 'bout you?" Horace said, nudging Brown with the muzzle of his carbine. "You're awful quiet."

"Just got here," Brown explained in a mild voice. "Yesta'day. Come up from Salt Lake on my way to Deer Lodge…"

"I don't believe you," Sanders interrupted impatiently. "Or you," he said, turning back to Yeager. "Here's what I *do* believe: Henry Plummer is the leader of a gang of road agents that have been robbing and killing innocent men in Bannack, Virginia and Nevada for the better part of a year."

"Yes," continued Dimsdale. "And this Doc Howard is his second in command. The rest of the agents—Marshland, Carter, Bunton and all the others—are part of this notorious criminal enterprise. You, Sir, are its messenger. Plummer gave you this," he tore the letter from Yeager's hand, "and told you to take it to Howard in Deer Lodge! Didn't he?"

Yeager was blinking his eyes, baffled by Dimsdale's accusation and tortured logic. "I…I ain't a messenger, Sir. I'm a cook, is all."

Wiggins stepped before the smaller man and slapped him hard across the face. "Enough of this nonsense!" he said impatiently. "We chased Howard all the way to God damned Deer Lodge through brutally cold weather, Friend, and now we want to know where he is and who is with him!"

He reached back to slap Yeager again, but Coffey rose and stayed his hand. Wiggins glared at Coffey, then pulled his arm away. Coffey again took his seat on the stool.

Sanders's hand went up. "Gentlemen," he said, his tone reasonable. "Mr. Yeager here knows how high the stakes are. So does Mister…"

"Brown," said Yeager, rubbing his cheek.

"Quite so, Mr. Brown," continued Sanders. "We need information. And for that information, we might spare your lives."

Yeager suddenly stood, his eyes bright with fear. "You gonna kill us?"

"Not if you provide the information we need," replied Dimsdale.

Yeager sat again. He looked over at Brown who was staring at the floor, his hands clutched in front of him as though in prayer.

"Well, Sir…yeah," Yeager finally began. "I guess Doc and them, well, yeah, Plummer was, uh, like tellin' 'em what to do an' all."

"Yes?" replied Sanders, his eyebrows raised.

"And, uh, well, Sir, he tol' 'em to rob them miners you was talkin' about…"

"What about the Oliver stagecoach?" Dimsdale asked quickly.

"Yeah, that, too…" Yeager said uncertainly.

"And the Peabody stage?" asked Wiggins. "Who killed the old man?"

Yeager glanced around anxiously. "Um…let's see now…uh, the Peabody stage, um, that were Jem and Steve…"

"Romaine and Marshland, you mean?" asked Sanders.

"Yeah. They done that one…"

"And Plummer ordered it, correct?" demanded Dimsdale.

Yeager nodded his head.

Coffey stood, grabbed Sanders by the shoulder and spun him around. "Even you don't believe this charade, Sanders!" he said bitterly.

Horace and Kincaid grabbed Coffey from behind. Sanders glared at him for a moment then turned back to Yeager.

"So, Red, what about the Magruder freighter?"

Yeager stared up at his inquisitor. "Freighter?"

"You remember," Sanders said helpfully. "Old man Magruder's freighter from Salt Lake that you and the rest of the gang stole."

Finally, Sanders was addressing a subject Yeager did know something about. He had been with Howard when the gang had stolen the wagonload of goods and Bunton had cut the old gentleman's throat. He'd helped hide the body in the rocks. Yeager had felt guilty about his complicity in the crime and this was his chance to come clean. He told his story to the men, who nodded their encouragement as he explained what had happened.

The room was growing cooler so McKenzie threw some wood in the stove as Yeager finished the story.

"…so Doc gave us all some money and then took off."

"Where was Sheriff Plummer while all this was going on?" asked Dimsdale.

"Plummer? Well he didn't have…" he began to reply, then saw the black looks from the men standing over him and quickly corrected himself.

"He, uh…he tol' Doc what to do."

Sanders wore a look of profound satisfaction. "Gentlemen, I believe we have broken this case!" he declared.

"Indeed!" agreed Dimsdale. "It remains for us only to round up and punish the scoundrels."

"After we take care o' these two, right?" interjected Kincaid.

Sanders looked back at Yeager grimly. "What is your Christian name?"

Yeager hesitated. "Erastus," he finally said.

"Erastus Yeager," Sanders began, turning slightly so he could also address his other prisoner, "and George Brown, you are both charged with the capital crime of aiding and abetting known felons and murderers. You have also confessed to the Magruder murder." He looked around at the other vigilantes. "Gentlemen, having heard the testimony, please raise your hand if you believe these men are guilty."

All but Coffey raised their hands.

"Innocent?" he asked.

Again, Coffey refused to raise his hand.

"Very well, we have an abstention," declared Sanders. "You men have been found guilty of the crimes for which you stand accused by a majority of the members of the vigilance committee. As its executive, I sentence you both to hang by the neck until you are dead."

"No!" cried Yeager as he shot up from the cot. "I done tol' you what happened…why should I hang? You said…"

Sanders ignored him. Brown, meantime, looked up forlornly at his captors as though he'd known from the beginning what his fate would be. Kincaid pinioned Yeager's arms while McKenzie pulled Brown from his cot and tied his hands behind his back.

"Better say your prayers, boys!" Horace leered.

Kincaid slapped him on his back as he grinned at the prisoners.

"Bout damn time we hung a coupla these bastards," said McKenzie with a satisfied smirk. "Woulda hated to ride all that way to Deer Lodge fer nothin'!"

Coffey knew he could do nothing to stop them as they shoved the bitterly weeping Yeager and the sullen, silent Brown out the cabin door. He decided to stay where he was for the night as the vigilantes went about their lethal work and departed for Bannack. Coffey knew they were all eager to get back to their homes and their families before Christmas.

He picked up the sheet of paper Sanders had left on the table and though the text was crude, he instantly recognized Dimsdale's handwriting on the warning "message."

When they'd arrived in Deer Lodge and failed to locate Howard or any of his men, the vigilantes had nearly mutinied. Sanders and Dimsdale had disappeared briefly and then emerged from a cabin with the paper, which they showed to the others. That's when it had been decided to ride back to Bannack. When they had reached Rattlesnake Creek, they'd stumbled across the unfortunate Red Yeager and George Brown. Coffey crumbled up the paper and threw it into the fire where it quickly flared and died.

In the morning, Coffey saw the two corpses hanging from the corral gate's crossbeam, twisting in the slight breeze. Both were frozen solid. He decided he didn't have enough strength to try to bury them in ground that was hard as brick. As he saddled Miss Matilda for the ride to Virginia City, Coffey noticed the dead men's horses and tack were gone.

40

Buzz Caven could see that the sheriff was seriously ill. He lay on his bed beneath a pile of blankets, shivering, sweat glistening on his face. He hadn't shaved for days, his blond hair was pasted against his head, and his usually clear blue-gray eyes were dull and bloodshot.

Caven had an elixir the doctor had prepared for Plummer. He knelt next to the sheriff, noticing the rancid smell of his body as he did.

"Here, Hank, doc said to get some o' this into ya." He gently lifted Plummer's head and put the mouth of the dark bottle to the sheriff's lips. "Sez it'll help you the fever."

Plummer managed a swallow or two, pushed Caven's hand away and fell back on the pillow. "I've never been this sick, Buzz," he managed to croak through his parched lips and throat.

Caven stood, went to the dresser and wet a cloth, then brought it back and placed it on Plummer's forehead.

"Thanks," Plummer said, his eyes closed. In a few moments he seemed to be asleep, so Caven quietly left him.

The day was unseasonably warm and sunny. Water from the melting snow dripped from the eaves but the street was still choked with ice. Wagons rumbled through town and horsemen cautiously made their way up and down the street, anxious to take advantage of the improved weather to conduct their business.

As instructed, the deputy found Edgerton and Sanders seated at the Goodrich Hotel, finishing their breakfast. He silently took a seat across from them.

"Good morning Caven," Sanders greeted him.

"Morn'."

"Coffee, Deputy?" asked Edgerton, holding the pot out.

Caven picked up his cup and the judge poured. Caven eyed the two men over the rim as he sipped the brew. Sanders was glancing around, assessing how much privacy he had.

"Caven," he began, his voice lowered, "we have a confession from one of Doc Howard's men. Red Yeager."

"Who's 'we'?" asked Caven.

"The committee," hissed Sanders, annoyed at the question. He didn't like mentioning the secret organization in public.

Caven vaguely nodded his head, so Sanders continued. "The confession was heard by all of my men."

"So?"

"*So*, Deputy, you're going to need to enforce the law. I want you to arrest Plummer. As I suspected," Sanders glanced at his uncle, "...as *we* all suspected, he is the leader of the road agent gang. He's behind the stage robberies, the Magruder affair and, most recently, the attempted robbery of my young cousin."

Caven stared at Sanders. He was not a particularly intelligent man, but something in Sanders accusation told him he needed to be careful.

"He was also responsible for the escape and flight of the men who killed your associate, Deputy Dillingham," Sanders added. "In fact, I am certain Plummer ordered the execution of Dillingham because he was about to expose the sheriff."

Caven shifted in his seat. "You're wrong there, Mr. Sanders," he said. "Stinson and Ray are in the jail for killin' Jack. Hank—er, Sheriff Plummer— tracked 'em down and brought 'em in."

Sanders blinked his eyes at this news.

"Obviously a ploy to cover his misdeeds," Edgerton interjected. "He'll no doubt release them before long."

"No, Sir, I don't think so," replied Caven. "The sheriff sent word up t' Lewiston for Marshal Beechey to come git 'em."

Judge Edgerton gave Sanders a dark look, coughed, wiped his lips with his napkin and stood. "I have business elsewhere, Gentlemen," he said rising. "Wilbur. I trust you can—*see* to this?"

Sanders nervously regarded his uncle. "Of course, Judge, of course." With that assurance, Edgerton departed the dining room.

"In any event, Caven," Sanders continued, looking back at the deputy, "we have this confession from Red Yeager and it's time to arrest and punish Plummer and his henchmen."

Caven smiled at Sanders. "You want *me* to do the arrestin' and punishin'? You got yourself the wrong man, Sanders."

"What do you mean?!"

"I ain't no lawman, Sir," he replied as though talking to a small child. "I just help Hank out, that's all."

"You're a *deputy*, man!" snapped Sanders. "This is *your* duty!"

Caven finished his coffee. "No, Sanders, I don' think it's my duty t'all. In fact, I think it's *your* duty...you and them vigilanters you're talkin' 'bout." He rose and stood before Sanders. "But let me tell you somethin', Mister. Hank Plummer has a lot of friends in Bannack. You might have one helluva time gettin' past 'em ifn you try to take Hank and hang 'im."

"Quiet!" Sanders snapped, looking around at the three or four other diners who were listening to Caven.

"Me? I'll be on my way," the deputy said as he walked out on Sanders.

Caven returned to Plummer's cabin. The sheriff was sleeping, so Caven sat down, pulled a stick of wood from his pocket and began whittling. An hour later he heard Plummer stir.

"What time is it, Buzz?" he asked.

"Little after ten."

Plummer groaned. His head was splitting and his lungs seemed to be full of mucus. He sat up on an elbow and spit into a can next to the bed. He then looked with dull eyes at his deputy.

"What's the matter, Buzz?" he asked.

Caven shifted in his chair. "Hank, I'm quittin'...bein' a dep'ty, I mean."

"Why?" asked Plummer. Caven told Plummer about his interview with Sanders. "They mean to hang you," he concluded.

Plummer gave him a weak smile. "No, they aren't going to hang me, Buzz. But I'll tell you what I'm going to do. I'm going up to Sanders's house and arrest *him*. Then I'm going to go after his vigilantes. And I'll tell you why. They don't give a hoot in hell about the law. They're a bunch of murdering thieves hiding behind Edgerton."

Caven looked at him blankly, not comprehending. "But, but Judge Edgerton, he's some kind of federal law...and Sanders, well, he's a lawyer."

"Yes," agreed Plummer as he swung his stocking feet onto the floor. "They're self-appointed law and I'm going to put a stop to them. They talk about some imaginary road agent gang? *They're* the only criminal gang I know of. Who do you think owns the Bitteroot Ranch now that old man Johnson is dead? Edgerton, that's who!"

"But..."

"But nothing," Plummer said irritably as he slowly rose from the bed, fighting off nausea. He looked at Caven and then put his hand on the deputy's shoulder. "I'm sorry. I need you, Buzz. Don't quit...not yet anyway. Now, would you please help me get cleaned up?"

Plummer felt shaky and feverish as he made his way to Sanders's house on the far side of town. Sanders lived with his wife and two children a block off the main street in little more than a large shed. Plummer broke the shotgun open to make sure it was loaded, than closed the breech. He drew the LeMat and saw it also was fully loaded. Men on the street eyed him and one or two pointed as they watched the sheriff walk to Sanders's door and knock.

The lawyer appeared and looked surprised and confused at Plummer's sudden visit.

"I want to speak with you," said Plummer firmly.

"Yes?" replied Sanders. "About what?"

"About where you've been for the last week to ten days."

"That's none of your business, Plummer!" Sanders responded indignantly.

Plummer reached out and grabbed Sanders's tie and yanked him into the street. Fear flashed in Sanders eyes as the sheriff brought the LeMat up to his head.

"Where were you?!" Plummer asked again.

"Deer Lodge," Sanders said, "On business!"

"Let's go," said Plummer. With that he turned and started walking quickly toward Chrisman's, Sanders's tie clutched in his fist. The lawyer had no choice but to follow. Sanders tried to protest, but each time he spoke, Plummer tightened his grip, choking off Sanders's words. Shocked pedestrians and shopkeepers watched the two men cross the muddy street. When he got to Chrisman's, Plummer roughly shoved Sanders through the door.

Now in his office, Plummer pushed Sanders into a chair. "What about Red Yeager's so-called confession, Sanders?!"

"I don't know…"

Plummer struck him in the mouth with the butt of the shotgun, sending Sanders sprawling onto the floor. He reached down, pulled Sanders up by the tie and placed him back in the chair.

"What about Yeager's confession?!"

Sanders's mouth was bleeding, his lip and cheek split by the blow. He looked at Plummer.

"I was on business…"

Plummer smashed him again with the butt of the gun, toppling Sanders back onto the floor, blood splattering across the desk. Plummer pulled him up by the tie again and punched him hard in the forehead.

"You son of a bitch!" Plummer growled, "what about the confession?! You will *not* leave here alive unless I hear what you have to say!"

Tears welled in Sanders eyes. Blood streamed from cuts on his head and face. "Please…I…please…"

Plummer cocked his gloved fist and Sanders brought his arms up reflexively over his face. "It wasn't just me!" Sanders whimpered, thoroughly terrified. "There were others…we went to Deer Lodge looking for Howard and his gang. They weren't there. We found Yeager and another man…"

"What did you do to them?"

"Nothing!" cried Sanders, spitting blood and mucus. "Yeager...he told us he worked for Howard!"

Plummer cuffed him across the face. "You hanged them, didn't you!" Plummer yelled into Sanders's face. "You got them to say what you wanted to hear and then *you* hanged them!"

"No!"

Teeth gritted, Plummer picked up a thick piece of firewood from next to the stove. Sanders watched him, eyes wide with horror.

"Yes!" he cried. "But it wasn't me...it was the others!"

Plummer, jaw set and ready to swing the stout pine branch, glared at Sanders. "What others?"

"Beidler, McKenzie, Wiggins, Dimsdale, some other men...and...and Coffey!"

Plummer dropped the wood on the floor with a thud. "Coffey?" he asked with a groan. "Noah Coffey?"

Seeing an opening, Sanders looked at Plummer earnestly. "Yes...Coffey. He was the one who ordered the two men hanged!"

"No," said Plummer, dropping back into his chair.

"Yes!" replied Sanders. "He put the noose around Yeager's neck!"

Plummer was staring blankly at some papers on his desk. *How could Noah be a part of any of this?* he asked himself. Then he remembered Micah Jordan, the Mormon preacher Noah had tricked the vigilantes into hanging.

"Coffey is a vigilante?" he asked.

"He's not only a vigilante," Sanders said with an urgent tone. "He's one of the committee's *leaders!*"

Was it possible? Henry felt a chill coming on. He pulled a bottle from a drawer, sipped the whiskey and shuddered involuntarily as the liquor's heat washed down his parched throat. He would not have ever believed Noah was capable of deceiving him with Electa, either.

Now he looked up at Sanders. "You're under arrest for the murder of Red Yeager," he said without emotion. "I also have reason to believe you murdered Bob Mayfield and his uncle last month."

"Arrest? You can't arrest *me!*"

Plummer stood, walked over to Sanders and placed the barrel of the

LeMat on his temple. "Or I could shoot you here and now and say you attempted to escape."

Sanders went ashen. Plummer stepped back as the lawyer rose from the chair, turned silently and walked out the door to the jailhouse behind Chrisman's.

After he'd locked Sanders up with Stinson and Ray and posted Caven as their guard, he went to the stable to ready for his trip to Virginia City.

The icy wind swirled ghostlike spindrifts down Wallace Street. Dark clouds scudded across the sky. The snow that had fallen continuously for two days immobilized Virginia City. The new year, 1864, had been rung in mostly with silence, the miners and merchants holed up and waiting for the weather to ease off. It had been a struggle for Coffey to get to his office. He was preparing another edition as Dimsdale entered clutching a leather portfolio.

The professor shook off the snow, removed his heavy wool coat and his hat and wiped his face with his handkerchief. "Bloody awful weather, this," he said.

Coffey said nothing as the little man approached his desk.

"Look here, Noah," he smiled as he reached into the folder, "I've prepared a news account of the Deer Lodge scout and our capture of the desperadoes Yeager and Brown. I think your readers will find it most interesting!"

Curious, Coffey reached out and took the sheets from Dimsdale. They were written in a precise hand with just a few words crossed out.

Every fiber of our frame vibrates with anger and disgust when we meet a ruffian, a murderer, or a marauder. Mawkish sentimentalisms we abhor. The thought of murdered victims, dishonored females, plundered wayfarers, burning houses, and the rest of the sad evidences of villainy, completely excludes mercy from our view.

Coffey looked up at Dimsdale's eager face, then continued reading.

Honor, truth, and sacrifice of self to considerations of justice and the good of mankind—these claim, we had almost said, our adoration; but for the

WHERE LAW ENDS

low, brutal, cruel, lazy, ignorant, insolent, sensual, and blasphemous miscreants that infest the frontiers we entertain but one sentiment—aversion—deep, strong, unchangeable. For such cases the rope is the only prescription that avails as a remedy.

Coffey couldn't keep from laughing out loud. "Dimsdale," he said finally, "you can't mean me to print this drivel!"

Dimsdale frowned. "Of course I do! Please, read on."

"You have treated me like a gentleman," Red said, "and I know I am going to die—I am going to be hanged. It is pretty rough, but I merited this years ago. What I want to say is I know all about the gang, and there are men who deserve this more than I do. I don't say this to get off. I don't want to get off."

Now it was Coffey's turn to frown. The professor, smile gone, shrank back as Coffey continued.

His last words were, "Good-bye boys; God bless you, you are on a good undertaking." The frail footing on which he stood gave way, and this dauntless and yet guilty criminal died without a struggle."

Coffey carefully laid the papers on his desk, sat back in his chair and folded his hands over his stomach as he looked up at Dimsdale again. Uncertain of himself, the professor smiled.

"Perhaps not Shakespeare, but certainly a colorful and informative account," he said to Coffey.

"Really more of a justification, wouldn't you say, Professor?" Coffey asked quietly.

Dimsdale brought his handkerchief to his mouth and coughed for a long time. "We would like you to publish it," he finally said. "Anonymously, of course. As a warning to other cutthroats that might consider crossing us."

"I suppose the truth about what really happened out there is immaterial?"

Dimsdale regarded Coffey almost sympathetically. "You're being naive. The truth is what *we* on the committee deem it to be, Noah," he quietly explained to the newspaperman.

Coffey thought again of Micah Jordan hanging from the tree, his little family gazing at the lifeless body swinging in the cool morning breeze.

"Where does all of this end, Dimsdale?" Coffey asked.

"When justice is served, of course!" came the professor's simple reply. "Please print that," he added pointing at the pages. "In the next edition of the *Tribune*."

41

Sidney Edgerton exploded: "You get him out of that jail now, or by God, I'll have you tried and hanged as an accomplice!"

Caven began quivering before the judge's rage. "Mr. Edgerton... Judge...I..."

"God damn you to hell, man! *Do* as I say!" Edgerton roared. "I *order* you to free my nephew! He has been illegally jailed by Plummer."

Buzz Caven had never bargained for this. Now all he wanted was to get away from Bannack as quickly as he could. He reached into his pocket and held a padlock key out to Edgerton. "I ain't gonna let 'im out, Judge," he said. "You're gonna have t'do it."

Edgerton snatched the key and, without a word, left Plummer's office with Caven following him out to the jail, where the judge opened the lock. With Stinson and Ray looking on from their seats on the floor, Sanders appeared, rubbing his eyes in the bright morning glare. Edgerton stepped back in horror at the sight of his nephew's battered, bloody face. He handed him his handkerchief and led him away by the elbow. As he did, Edgerton shot the deputy a murderous look.

By noon, Caven was on his horse riding out of Bannack at a brisk trot, determined never to return.

Because of the deep snowdrifts on the trail, it had taken Plummer almost three days to reach Virginia City. Despite the bitter cold and ferocious wind, he was surprised to find himself feeling better. He wasn't sure how he would go about finding the vigilantes, but he was determined to get them locked up and then packed off as soon as he could to the deputy marshal in Lewiston; all of them, including Noah Coffey.

Julius Caeser diligently plowed through the snow and Plummer eventually found himself in Virginia shortly after noon. The stable owner greeted him and said he had a warm stall and oats for Plummer's animal. The sheriff then went to the Fairweather Hotel and took a room.

The clerk awakened him at six o'clock as he'd requested. Plummer had sent his blue suit and boots to the old Chinese man for cleaning. He shaved himself, then dressed. Outside in the dark, beyond the windowpanes thick with ice, he heard the wind moan. He buckled his gun belt, checked the breech of the shotgun, then pulled on his coat and carefully arranged the black hat on his head. Finally, he donned his heavy gauntlet gloves and left the room.

Coffey sat at his desk, transposing an account of a battle at a place in Georgia called Chickamauga. The office door swung open and through a plume of snow stepped Henry Plummer. A small, flickering lamp illuminated his stern face and clear gray eyes. At the sight of his friend, Coffey instinctively broke into a wide grin.

"You have any whiskey?" Plummer asked. "Damned cold out there."

Still smiling, Coffey rose and produced a bottle and glasses from a cabinet and poured. "Happy New Year, Henry," he said as he handed Plummer his drink. "It's wonderful to see you again."

"Happy New Year," replied Plummer, tapping his glass against Coffey's. He shot the whiskey back and then took the seat across the desk from Coffey. "I'm here on official business, Noah."

Coffey slowly sat down, the smile vanishing from his face. He started to pour the sheriff another drink but Plummer held his hand over the glass.

"I understand you were among the vigilantes who hanged Red Yeager and another man," he began. "I'm here to arrest you for murder."

Coffey was shocked by Plummer's accusation. "Murder?"

Plummer nodded grimly. "I'm holding Sanders prisoner in Bannack on a charge of murder. He told me you and others hanged Yeager and another man. I'm going to arrest them, too."

Coffey now understood. "Well, *Sheriff* Plummer, let me see if I can clarify things for you." He recounted the story of the Deer Lodge scout, the fruitless search for Howard and his men, the forged "message," then the vigilantes' dejected ride back to Rattlesnake Creek, where they encountered the luckless Yeager and George Brown in a lonely log dugout.

"What about Yeager's confession?" Plummer asked.

"Except for being part of the Magruder killing and stealing the freighter, Yeager never confessed to anything," Coffey said. "Sanders just put the words in his mouth. They pretended they were a jury and, no surprise, found Yeager and the other poor man guilty. They strung them up to silence them and then stole their horses and traps."

"And you had nothing whatever to do with the hangings?" Plummer asked quietly.

"Of course not!" Coffey scoffed. "They were intent on hanging someone. Anyone. Yeager and Brown were in the wrong place at the wrong time."

Plummer reached out, seized the bottle and poured whiskey into both glasses. They drank silently, avoiding each other's eyes. Plummer rose and made as though to leave. He stopped, turned and eyed Coffey.

"Why were you there?" he asked.

"To learn their intentions," Coffey replied. "I am very worried about you Henry. They absolutely want you out of the way."

"I know," Plummer declared. "Sanders and that damned uncle of his tried to have poor Buzz Caven arrest and hang me, if you can believe that!" He paused and looked thoughtfully at Coffey. "You remember that day up on the hill when I told you how I felt."

Coffey nodded. "Yes."

"Sanders and his vigilance committee are the most dangerous kind of disorder there is," Plummer explained. "These are men convinced of their own righteousness because of their position and their power. I won't allow the vigilantes to continue. They have no right, no sanction and no laws to back them up. Before it's over, I will see all of *them* hanged for what they have done."

Plummer turned to leave.

"Henry!" Coffey said. "Please wait! I want to talk to you about Electa..."

"No need," Plummer replied over his shoulder. "It's over between us. Between Electa and me...between you and me, Noah. But we were friends once and I am relieved to hear you had no part in the hangings." With that, Henry Plummer was out the door.

Coffey dashed into the street, hot tears of shame and loss in his eyes. "Henry, please, be careful!" he called to Plummer's back. "They'll kill you, too!" He saw the sheriff raise a hand acknowledging the warning as he disappeared into the winter night.

In a whorehouse run by an old Dutch lady named Gilda, Plummer found McKenzie. He was lying in a bed alone, snoring. Plummer prodded him with the shotgun's barrel. The rancher's eyes popped open. In the dim light he saw the gaping twin muzzles inches from his nose.

"Get up!" Plummer ordered. McKenzie instantly obeyed. "Get dressed. I am arresting you for the murder of Red Yeager and George Brown."

Eyes locked on the shotgun, McKenzie pulled on his trousers and shirt. "Plummer, you don't know what yer doin'."

"Really?" he replied. "I think I do. You killed two men at Rattlesnake Creek. Last time I looked, that's a capital crime."

"You got that all wrong Plummer..."

"Why don't you shut your mouth, McKenzie!" Plummer interrupted, jabbing the tall rancher viciously with the barrel. "Put your boots on and let's go!"

He took his prisoner back to the hotel, bound and gagged him in his room, then continued the search. An hour later he located Horace at a gambling house. Then he found Kincaid sleeping in the back of a saloon. By midnight, three of the vigilantes were sitting on the floor of Plummer's hotel room. He removed their gags, gave them some water, secured them for the night, then went to sleep fully clothed, the LeMat in his hand.

Dimsdale arrived at the Masonic Hall early the next morning and prepared for his students. Despite the snow, the children were expected to attend. He opened his lesson plan just as Wiggins walked into the classroom.

"X told me Plummer arrested Kincaid, Horace and McKenzie last night," the dentist anxiously declared without preamble. "He charged them all with the murder of Yeager and Brown. He has Wilbur locked up in Bannack. He intends to arrest us."

Dimsdale looked at Wiggins blankly. "Well...that's not possible," he stammered. "Is it?"

"Don't be a fool," Wiggins said impatiently. "Of course it's possible. If he gets the deputy marshal here from Lewiston, we could all hang!"

The professor swallowed, then drew out his handkerchief and mopped his brow. "Well what...what about Coffey?"

"I don't know about him and I don't care about him," Wiggins replied with a shrug. "But I do know I'm getting out of Virginia. You should, too. Right now!"

Dimsdale was frightened, but he forced himself to think through the situation as though it were a rhetorical problem. "You say Plummer is holding Sanders in Bannack?"

Wiggins nodded.

"Judge Edgerton will never let that stand," Dimsdale stated. "As soon as he learns Wibur is in Plummer's jail, he'll get him out."

"Edgerton is up to his elbows in this!" Wiggins cried. "He's going to swing, too, if the marshal learns what we've been doing."

Dimsdale became impatient. "Stop and think for a moment, Wiggins! Who is Plummer? He's a sheriff appointed by a mob of filthy, ignorant miners; a miner himself with a very unsavory past! That's who the esteemed Sheriff Plummer is! Then ask yourself, who is Sidney Edgerton? He's the *Chief Justice* of Idaho Territory appointed by the President of the United States."

Wiggins's lips were pursed.

"Plummer says there are no laws in the territory for the judge to enforce so the judge has no authority until there are laws on the territory's books. Utter nonsense, I say. President Lincoln sent the judge here as the final word on legal matters, written law or no written law."

Wiggins drummed his fingers on the back of a chair. "Maybe so, but Edgerton has no authority to appoint a vigilance committee that circumvents the law."

"Merely an expediency," Dimsdale said with a dismissive gesture of his hand. "What are Judge Edgerton's options? America is at war. The United States deputy marshal is more than two hundred miles away. The vigilance committee is the *only* way we can strike fear into the hearts of the lawless. If the criminals and undesirables know we mean business, they'll run."

"We still have Plummer to worry about," said Wiggins.

"I agree with you," Dimsdale conceded. "The prudent thing to do is make ourselves scarce for a few days. That will give us time to see how all of this plays out."

As Plummer finished breakfast, the Fairweather's owner approached his table and sat down next to him.

"Sheriff Plummer," he whispered nervously, "I don't think I like the idea of you using your room as a jail cell."

Plummer glanced at the man and smiled. "Just for an hour or so, Carl. I'll be on my way with them shortly."

"That's not what I'm talking about!" the hotel owner said. "They're all vigilantes! I don't want to get mixed up in any of their business!"

Plummer frowned. "They'll be gone in an hour."

Wiggins's dentist office was closed. At the Masonic Hall, it appeared that the professor's pupils had been sent home. Beidler had disappeared. "Damn it," he swore under his breath as he walked back to the hotel.

Plummer collected his prisoners, paid his bill and took the bound McKenzie, Kincaid and Horace to the stable where he mounted them all on rented mules. His stallion was jumpy and excited, eager to get going because the weather was calm, clear and cold.

A number of men had heard of the arrests and had gathered around the stable as Plummer prepared to leave for Bannack. Among them were his deputies Clubfoot Lane and Boone Helm.

"You need he'p, Sheriff?" asked Lane.

"No," Plummer replied. "Just keep anyone back who has a mind to stop me."

"You got no cause to take them boys, Plummer!" someone called out.

"Damn you, Plummer!" cried another. "You better let 'em go!"

Plummer shot a look in the direction of the voices but nobody made a move to rescue the captives. Just in case, Plummer perched the shotgun on his thigh as he led the men and mules out of Virginia City and onto the road to Bannack.

It was after ten o'clock in the evening when the two dozen men gathered at the brewery which had opened on New Year's Day at the edge of Bannack. They sat on sacks of hops and barley or on barrels, some holding shotguns or carbines. The owner had tapped into a heavy wooden keg and offered mugs of warm beer to the assembly, but only a handful of the men accepted. The others were ardent churchmen and Masons who didn't drink.

Sanders entered and, despite his battered face, smiled when he saw the gathering. All but a few of those he'd asked to join Bannack's vigilance committee were there.

"Mr. Schultz!" Sanders called out to the brewer. "Thank you for allowing us the use of your fine new brewery as our meeting place."

The heavyset, bearded man was leaning against the keg he had tapped as he nodded in Sanders's direction.

Sanders looked around the room. "Gentlemen!" he began, "Thank you for coming to this important meeting. As explained to each of you individually, we are met with a great threat to law and order here in Bannack and, indeed, throughout the region. As you know, there is a gang of murderous cutthroats plaguing commerce and threatening the lives and well-being of honest citizens such as yourselves."

The men looked back at him intently. Sanders continued: "Chief among these villains is none other than Henry Plummer, your sheriff!"

The men glanced around at each other with surprised or puzzled looks.

"Yes, I know, an unbelievable revelation!" Sanders cried, his voice reverberating throughout the wide room. "*Sheriff* Plummer! The man you elected to protect you has been exposed as the wolf at the head of a bloodthirsty pack..."

"How in hell you know that, Sanders?" asked a miner from his perch on an upturned barrel.

Sanders pointed at the man. "An excellent question, Sir, and one I would expect from fair-minded men!" He locked his hands behind his back and began to pace in the manner of a prosecutor presenting his evidence. "Sheriff Henry Plummer," he began thoughtfully. "What do we *really* know about him?" He looked around and was met with blank stares. "Well, my friends, let me enlighten you. He has a criminal past!"

There was an audible reaction to this, a collective gasp among some of the men, followed by outcries. Sanders held up his hand for quiet.

"Yes!" he cried dramatically. "Henry Plummer was convicted in California of slaughtering the husband of his illicit lover!"

He could see the reaction from his audience was one of shock.

"This good gentleman—a man not unlike yourselves—learned of Plummer's treachery and demanded satisfaction. But Plummer was too much of a scoundrel and coward to meet him face-to-face in a duel of honor! No! Instead Plummer shot the poor fellow when his back was turned!"

The men were becoming noisy and angry. Sanders waited patiently for them to grow quiet, then continued.

"Thankfully, Gentlemen, the honest citizens and the courts of California acted swiftly. Plummer was convicted of his heinous crime and thrown into prison where he belonged!"

"How the hell did he end up here, then?" asked a fat dry goods merchant seated on a pile of burlap sacks.

Sanders nodded solemnly. "Yes...how indeed? Well, Plummer would be rotting in a California dungeon as I speak were it not for his corrupt political allies," he said, a note of sadness in his voice. "Who knows what sway he held over these so-called *friends* of his, but it was enough to win his release after just a few months."

"I never liked that bastard," called a small man standing in the corner holding a mug of Schultz's beer. "Always had that high and mighty way..."

"Right!" agreed another, a haberdasher who catered to the less reputable men and women of the town. "What about that time he came 'round demandin' we give him good money to build his damned jail?"

There was a buzz of agreement and Sanders, again, waited to be heard.

"Oh, there's more, Gentlemen, much more you should know." The room was instantly silent and Sanders raised the volume of his voice again.

"Plummer leaves this prison called San Quentin and has the gall to return to the very town where he had committed his murder! Then, one night at a bawdy house—one of his regular haunts I might add—Plummer in a state of complete drunkenness, shot a defenseless young man who simply spoke to a prostitute with whom Plummer was enamored!"

More looks of shock greeted Sanders.

"Yes...yes, I know; incredible behavior for man sworn to uphold the law! But it gets worse, I'm afraid. Plummer escaped jail before he could be tried for murdering the young man. Now a fugitive outlaw, he made his way east, assembling a gang of road agents that presently terrorize Bannack, Virginia and Nevada Cities."

"Where you hear all this?" another man asked skeptically.

"From Noah Coffey, the editor of the *Virginia City Tribune*! He's known Plummer for years and is well acquainted with his nefarious deeds! He fell out with Plummer and now Coffey is one of us; a member of the vigilance committee! Mr. Coffey could no longer stand by and watch Plummer and his thugs terrorize honest men!"

A tall man stepped forward. "Listen here, Sanders, I seen Plummer doin' his job and he's damn good at it."

"Of course he's good at it!" exclaimed Sanders in response. "He has to *appear* convincing, does he not?! But, tell me this, what better position can you think of to control a criminal gang than from the office of the sheriff?"

The tall man stepped back, vaguely nodding his head.

"Think on it a moment, Gentlemen!" Sanders continued, passion in his voice as he looked each man in the eye. "Plummer came here in complete anonymity. He took you all in with his formidable appearance, his reputation with a pistol, his fine speech and his promise to uphold the law on your behalf.

Then he proceeded to orchestrate the wave of crime that presently engulfs us!"

He could see he'd almost won them over, so he lowered his voice for dramatic effect again. "Plummer's also made himself a small fortune in Bannack, unfairly buying up mining claims and taking advantage of you and many of your friends. It's past time for him to be punished and for those who he has cheated to get back what is rightly theirs!"

"Yes!" called a miner.

"I'm in, Mr. Sanders!" said another.

"What about poor Tom Cleveland?!" called Frosty Stump from the back of the room.

Sanders eyed the men. "You've heard what kind of man Plummer really is. He stands accused of masterminding the recent stagecoach robberies and the assault on my young cousin, Henry Tilden. He must be stopped, but some of you may not have the stomach for what must be done." His hands were clenched behind his back again, and he strode with a sense of purpose before them in the flickering lamplight.

"If you do not wish to be a part of those who will set things right in Bannack, then leave now!" He stopped and swept an accusing finger over the crowd. "But I warn you, if you walk out of here, you will remain silent until such time as justice is served. If we on the vigilance committee learn you have betrayed us, there will be consequences!"

After a moment, a man stood and, without a word, walked out. A second followed him, and finally a third. After the door closed behind them, there was silence.

"Very well, then," Sanders said. "You men will now swear an oath of fidelity to the vigilance committee. You will serve the interests of law and order at my direction as its executive, without question and without hesitation."

Wiggins stepped into the light with a sheet of paper. "All of you men, please raise your right hand," he called.

The men did as directed.

"Repeat after me," Wiggins continued:

"Uniting in a party for the laudable purpose of arresting thieves and murders and recovering stolen property we do pledge

ourselves and our sacred honor each to all others and solemnly swear that we will reveal no secrets, violate no laws and never desert each other or our standards of justice so help us God.

42

The next evening, Plummer trudged into town on the back of Julius Caesar, the prisoners on their mules strung out behind him. In the dim lamplight he could see Bannack was shrouded in the snow that had fallen lightly throughout the day. He rode directly to Chrisman's and dismounted. He led the string of mules back to the jail and as he approached, he saw Buck Stinson's face at the small jail window.

"Hey Plummer!" he called, "we ain't had nothin' to eat fer two days!"

Tired and feeling unwell, Plummer found himself irritated. "Where the hell is Caven?"

"Ain't seen him since t'other day!" called Ned Ray. "And we ain't got no wood fer the stove, neither…we's freezin' our asses off!"

"Shit," Plummer swore under his breath. He looked around. A half moon peeking through broken clouds cast an eerie glow over the snow-cloaked town. He saw nobody on the street and, more strangely, heard none of the usual noise from the saloons. Plummer walked to the jail and peered in.

In the faint light he saw Stinson and Ray standing with blankets wrapped around their shoulders.

"Where's Sanders?" he demanded. The two prisoners started laughing. "You didn't think Edgerton would let you keep 'im in here, did ya?" asked Ray.

Now he understood what had happened to Caven and silently cursed himself. "When did he let Sanders out?"

"Other day," Ray replied with a smirk. "Right after you left."

Seething, Plummer returned to the mules. He yanked the prisoners off their mounts. Horace and Kincaid were not dressed for the weather and shivered uncontrollably. McKenzie malevolently glared at Plummer as he slammed the jail door angrily and replaced the padlock.

Inside the store Plummer gathered kindling and firewood from the stack next to the stove. He took three new heavy blankets from Chrisman's stock and then walked back to the jail. He laid the blankets and wood in a pile and allowed Stinson to retrieve them and then empty the chamber pots as he held the LeMat on him cocked and ready.

"I'll be back with hot food in a half hour," he told the prisoners once he'd secured them again. He walked to the Goodrich Hotel.

Quinn, the old clerk, nodded at him. "Sheriff?"

"I need food for five men," he said.

"Oh, I'm afraid the kitchen is closed, Sheriff..."

"Damn you, Quinn, don't argue," Plummer snapped. "Get me the food, right now!"

The clerk instantly scurried off to the back of the hotel. Plummer heard pots and pans rattling and the little man mumbling to himself. There was nobody at the untended bar. He found a bottle of whiskey and poured himself a drink, shot it back and then poured another, which he sipped standing next to the warm stove.

Quinn appeared twenty minutes later with a tray. "I did the best I could..."

"I'm sure it's fine," Plummer said apologetically as he paid for the food and took the tray. He looked at the clerk. "I am sorry I cursed you, Jimmy. I've been on the trail and I am not well."

"That's all right, Sheriff," Quinn replied with a look of concern. "You look tired. You should get some rest."

Plummer returned to the jail, where he delivered the food and saw that the prisoners had a fire going in the small stove in the cell. They were huddled in their blankets near it and Ray and Stinson were greedily shoving the meat and bread they'd been served into their mouths.

"I'll be back in the morning," Plummer called out as he left. He delivered the stallion and mules to the stable, then returned to his cabin.

At Edgerton's home the next morning, Plummer learned from the judge's wife that he'd left the day before, bound for Salt Lake City.

"Where is Wilbur Sanders?" he asked.

The woman frowned and shut the door in his face. He decided he wouldn't worry about Sanders for now and returned to his office. As he passed through Chrisman's store Plummer encountered a couple of miners he recognized. He greeted them, but he received only vacant looks in reply. He shrugged as he entered the office, sat down and began reading through the mail that had arrived during his absence.

Just before noon Plummer looked up to see Sanders and a half-dozen armed men standing in the door to his office. Sanders held a carbine.

"I've been looking for you, Sanders," Plummer said as he stood up. "I understand your uncle illegally released you from jail. When he returns to town, I intend to arrest him for obstructing justice."

Sanders smiled, leveled his weapon and shook his head. "No you won't, Plummer. You're through as sheriff."

"Is that so?" Plummer calmly asked. "The last time I looked, the citizens of Bannack hadn't voted to remove me from office so I believe I *am* sheriff."

"That's why we're here, Plummer," declared a ragged looking miner standing to Sanders's right. "To remove you."

The speaker was Jerome Tully, a young Irishman who'd sold his three claims to Plummer over the summer. He was a squat man with broad shoulders and huge hands. He had an old pepperbox pistol stuck in the waistband of his patched woolen trousers and appeared to be drunk. Plummer eyed Sanders's other deputies and realized all of them were miners who had sold out their claims to his company.

He turned his attention back to the vigilante leader. "I'm arresting you, Sanders," he declared. Before Sanders could blink, Plummer had drawn his pistol and had it trained on Sanders's head. "You other people, back up!"

The miners stood dumbly as Sanders, eyeing the barrel of the LeMat, slowly lowered the barrel of the carbine and raised his hands. Plummer yanked the weapon away then roughly shoved him in the chest and he reeled backward into his deputies.

"Turn around!" he ordered Sanders.

The miners were slowly backing up, all watching Plummer and his cocked weapon. Sanders finally obeyed, and faced Chrisman's front door.

"You know where to go!" Plummer said, shoving the lawyer from behind. "Move!"

The miners made way for Sanders and Plummer. None tried to stop the arrest. Outside in the bright sunshine, Plummer walked Sanders to the jail behind the store.

"Welcome back!" said Ray, who'd been standing by the window when he saw Sanders approach with his hands raised. Plummer opened the jail door and roughly pushed Sanders into the cell. He turned then and saw the six miners watching him from the street.

He strode toward them and addressed Tully. "All right, Jerry, what's all this about?"

Tully's breath smelled of stale whiskey as it plumed white in the cold air. On the far side of the street, Plummer saw other men watching the scene. The little Irishman glared at him with bloodshot eyes.

"This must have something to do with your claims, am I right?" Plummer asked. He looked at the others. "All of your claims?"

Tully started to respond but was stayed when one of the other miners grabbed his sleeve. "Let it go fer now," he hissed at Tully.

"I'm not going to allow him to let it go," Plummer declared. "Tully said you men were removing me from office. So..."

Plummer took a step back, placing his hand on his holstered pistol. Tully's eyes darted down to the weapon. He licked his cracked lips and blinked.

"I ain't gonna fight yer," he cried, his voice rising in fear. "T'wouldn't be a fair fight and well you know it, Plummer! No man in Bannack can match ya with the pistols!"

Plummer's eyes were locked on Tully. He stood before the miner and waited silently for any of the six to make a move. Despite the cold, he saw sweat beading on Tully's forehead. Plummer shifted his weight, ready.

"Fer God sakes, Plummer! I ain't gonna fight yer!" Tully's desperate voice echoed off the nearby buildings. The crowd across the way had grown, and men were pointing at the stand-off.

The six miners all began carefully stepping away from Plummer, who impassively eyed their retreat. When Sanders's deputies reached the middle of the street they scattered.

Plummer took a few steps forward and looked around at the crowd of spectators.

"I am Henry Plummer!" he called out defiantly, "the lawful sheriff of Bannack and surrounding jurisdictions, no matter what anybody else here claims to be! The citizens of Bannack legally elected me their sheriff! If the citizens wish me out of office, they can vote me out!" Plummer rested his hand on the butt of the LeMat. "But the next man who presents himself to say he intends to remove me from office will be dealt with...harshly!"

Plummer sat at his desk and considered his dilemma. He could call a miners court, but he was fearful that sympathetic jurors would acquit his prisoners. It would be worse than the Forbes affair. He'd already sent word to Lewiston but it would take weeks, maybe months before the Beechey could intervene.

Then it occurred to Plummer he could take his prisoners south to the federal authorities in Salt Lake City. He didn't know the U.S. deputy marshal there and wasn't even sure if one was posted in Salt Lake, but the weather was sure to be less severe in the valleys between Bannack and Salt Lake. He had also made up his mind to arrest Sidney Edgerton on charges of obstructing justice, conspiracy to commit murder, and fraud in the theft of the Bitterroot Ranch. He would either encounter Edgerton traveling back to Bannack or in Salt Lake City, so his decision to head south was made.

It was dark as he walked out to look in on his prisoners. He'd given them their supper, water and more wood. Sanders had protested, but Plummer ignored him. He was determined to leave with the prisoners in the next day or two but he knew he would need help if he was going to travel overland to Salt Lake City. He decided Skinner's Saloon would be the best place to recruit deputies.

He slipped a little on the packed snow as he walked gingerly along the boardwalk. The wind had come up and it blew drifts in front of the doors, forcing Plummer to step through or around the piles of powdery snow. As he made his way along, intent on not slipping, a figure lunged out from between two buildings and struck him on the back of the head with a length of pipe. Plummer, dazed, collapsed to his knees. Another blow knocked him senseless.

Plummer awoke, sprawled in the frozen street, his face wet and cold. He gently touched the back of his head then looked at his fingers and saw there was no blood. He was nauseous but otherwise he thought he was unhurt. The street was dark and empty. He had no idea how long he'd been laying there but he thought it was no more than an hour. He still had the LeMat, but his keys were missing. He picked up his hat and staggered back to Chrisman's.

Ray and Stinson were still locked up, but the others were gone. His keys were lying in the trampled snow in front of the door. Dizzy and light-headed, Plummer leaned against the door. "What happened?" he gasped.

Stinson was bundled in his blanket in the corner. "Coupla masked men came for Sanders and them others," he explained. "One of 'em said they'd be back fer us...and fer you, too, Plummer."

43

Coffey was preparing to leave his room when there came a loud knock on his door. He answered and was greeted by Charlie Benson, who was clutching his hat self-consciously in his hands and wearing a look of worry.

"Mr. Coffey, it's good to see ya, Sir," he said. "Yer landlady says I could come up."

"Charlie! How are you?" Coffey asked, confused by the man's sudden appearance in Virginia. He shook his hand. "How are the diggings in Bannack?"

"Closed down on account o' the cold," the miner replied. "Can I speak with yer in private, Sir?"

Coffey admitted him and closed the door. "What's the matter, Charlie?"

The man looked like he was about to cry. "It's Sheriff Plummer, Mr. Coffey. He's in frightful trouble!"

Coffey felt his stomach sink. "What sort of trouble?"

"Well, Sir, he put Wilbur Sanders in his jail but ol' man Edgerton done let 'im out while the sheriff were in Virginia."

Coffey nodded. "Go on."

"Sanders got a bunch o' miners and others together at the new brewery. They asked me to be there. They had this meetin'…"

"A meeting?" asked Coffey.

Benson swallowed. "Sanders said you tol' 'im Mr. Plummer killed a man back in California and went to prison fer it. Then he killed another man and ran…Sanders says Mr. Plummer were a fug'tive and that he was runnin' with a gang o' road agents!"

Coffey realized his gambit had failed. By pretending to be one of them, he'd hoped to learn if and when the vigilantes were moving against Henry so that he'd be able to warn the sheriff.

"What did Sanders ask these men to do about it?" Coffey already knew the answer.

"Don' know, exactly, Mr. Coffey. Sanders says he was goin' after Plummer is all I heard. He wanted men to he'p him. Said any man that don' want no part could leave, so me an' two, three others got ourselves outta there. Mr. Plummer paid me good money fer my claims an' give me a job, too. I got no truck with 'im. But them others sounded like they's gonna do somethin' terrible."

Coffey glanced at his watch. It was just past seven o'clock. If he rode fast he could be in Bannack by nightfall. He patted Benson on the shoulder again.

"Thanks Charlie."

Plummer's head was pounding and he still felt ill. He decided to stay by the stove throughout the day and recover. Then he'd go after Sanders and his vigilantes. When he had them this time, he'd march them straight to Salt Lake City, and he'd do it by himself.

He dozed throughout the day, took a short walk to Chrisman's to make sure the grocer was looking after Ray and Stinson, then returned to the cabin and took a long nap. He rose as the sun was setting, feeling more like himself. He ate some bacon between slices of bread, then lit a lantern and picked up the book he had been reading.

Sanders looked sternly at the others. They had all gathered, as ordered, at the brewery just after sundown.

"All right, Gentlemen. We will do this in an orderly fashion. Remember,

I am the commander of this vigilante contingent and you will do as I order. Is that clear?"

Along with McKenzie, Kincaid and Horace, there were more than twenty of the newly sworn vigilantes, most of them miners with grudges against Plummer but also a few merchants. Tully was there, holding his pepperbox revolver at the ready. The others carried a variety of weapons. Sanders could see some shotguns, a couple of carbines and a number of Colts and other handguns.

Satisfied, he continued. "We will march to Yankee Flat in good order. You men," he said pointing at the six nearest him, "will be the frontal guard. You others will cover our rear. We will arrest Plummer, then proceed to the jail and collect Ned Ray and Buck Stinson. At that point, we should be ready for a confrontation from Plummer's friends, if one is to come. They may be alerted to what is happening and try to rescue him."

The men nervously glanced at one another but said nothing.

"Who has the ropes?" he asked. A tall man pointed at a pile of coils on the ground next to him.

Plummer had dozed off. He was jolted awake by a sharp rapping at his door. Without thinking, he put aside his book, rose and opened the cabin door. A crowd of men had gathered in the alley, their breath vapor rising into the still night air. Plummer recognized several in the flickering light cast by the lanterns some of them held and instantly knew their purpose.

"State your business!" Plummer demanded, hoping to intimidate them long enough to grab the LeMat, which lay on the floor next to the chair in which he'd been sitting.

The vigilantes then seemed to hesitate in their purpose. Those at the front began nervously shuffling their feet and glancing about, uncertain of what they should say or do.

Sanders had slunk to the back of the crowd, out of the lantern light in case Plummer had armed himself, but he realized the mission was in danger of collapsing. He abruptly pushed through the vigilantes to the front and faced Plummer.

"The Citizens Vigilance Committee of Bannack places you under arrest

Plummer. For murder and robbery!"

Plummer began to slam the door, but two big miners pushed through and before the sheriff could snatch his revolver, they had seized him, tying his hands behind his back. The two men pushed Plummer out into the alley where the others crowded around him.

Plummer knew it was useless to try to dissuade Sanders so he addressed the others.

"You men know Wilbur Sanders has no legal authority in Bannack! You know that what you are attempting to do will land all of you at the end of a rope when the federal marshal in Lewiston learns about it! Stop this while you still can!"

"Shut up!" cried Sanders, his voice shrill. He knew all too well how fragile the resolve of his vigilantes really was.

"You men, listen to me!" cried Plummer. "This isn't about serving justice! It's about killing the one man who knows what Sanders and Edgerton have been up to here and in Virginia and can do something about it!"

"Gag him!" demanded Sanders.

"No!" replied a miner. "I want to hear what Plummer's got t' say!"

"Let 'im speak!" yelled someone else.

"Edgerton and Sanders came to Bannack with nothing! They aren't merchants and they aren't miners! So how can they support themselves? By claiming to be the law and hanging any man they want out of the way, then confiscating—stealing—their property! There is no road agent gang! The only murderers and thieves in Bannack are Edgerton and Sanders!"

"Silence!" screamed Sanders frantically. "Men...you will do your sworn duty! Company, forward march!"

With some pushing and shoving by McKenzie, Kincaid and Horace, the platoon, with Plummer at its center, began to slowly walk toward town. They passed single file over the footbridge that crossed Grasshopper Creek then they boxed Plummer in again as they made their way onto and up the main street of Bannack.

As they marched, Plummer saw three of the guards to his left silently drift away from their posts so he stopped walking which forced everyone to come to a halt.

"Look at those men!" he called to the remaining guards. "They know this is wrong! And they know if it continues, *they* will be hanged!"

Sanders was becoming desperate. The Bannack men were listening to Plummer, some nodding while others were looking about to see if anyone else was abandoning the mission.

Plummer lowered his voice. "Boys," he said, looking at those closest to him in the eyes, "let me go. We can all sit down at Skinner's and discuss this reasonably. I'll buy the drinks. You can hear my side of the story and when you do, you'll be as convinced as I am that Sanders and his vigilantes are the men who should be arrested and hanged."

The miners were looking at one another. Sanders was now certain his guards would free Plummer and felt a flash of fear for his own safety at the same moment. Just as he began to consider his escape, Sanders heard hoofbeats behind him. He turned and saw riders approaching the scene. As they neared he recognized Beidler, Wiggins and Dimsdale leading more than a dozen other men from Virginia City. They pulled up their horses next to the guard detail and dismounted.

"Oh, thank God!" Sanders said in a raspy voice.

In a few minutes, Ray and Stinson were bound and brought out to join Plummer. Beidler produced a sheet of paper.

"I got here a letter of execution signed by the executive of the Bannack Citizens Vigilance Committee sanctionin' the execution of…"

"Beidler, you son of a bitch," Plummer snapped. "Don't pretend this is a legal hanging. It's not. It's murder, plain and simple."

Beidler silently folded up the paper then eyed the wavering guards. "Next one o' you Bannack men who runs'll swing with 'em!" he growled.

"That's better, X," Plummer said with a contemptuous laugh. "Now you boys see for yourselves how these people regard the law."

Without warning, Beidler stepped over to Plummer and punched him in his sternum as hard as he could. With a gasp Plummer fell to his knees in the snow.

Beidler roughly pulled him to his feet. "That'll keep you quiet 'til I get that noose 'round your fuckin' neck, Plummer," he said with an evil grin.

As Sanders had predicted, friends of Plummer began to materialize out of the night. They watched the prisoners being marched up the gulch toward the gallows. Several became alarmed when they realized the sheriff was among them.

"What the hell they doin'?" asked one.

"Hangin' the sheriff," replied a miner who had been following events since they'd begun.

"They can't do that...can they?" asked a third. "What's Plummer done?"

"Don' know, but they sure as shit 'er hangin' 'im."

Word reached Skinner's and a dozen men who considered Plummer a friend ran toward the gulch. But it was all happening too fast. At the top of the gulch stood the gallows from which Plummer had hanged Horan. The guards fanned out to keep rescuers back. Torches were lit and ropes were hurled over the crossbeam.

"For Christ's sake, Sanders," Beidler exclaimed. "You only got two ropes here!"

Flustered, Sanders grabbed Henry Tilden, who had joined the crowd, and told him to run to Edgerton's home for another rope. The boy took off.

"You fuckers got no right to hang me!" cried Ned Ray. "I ain't even had a trial!"

"Yes you did!" exclaimed Wiggins. "The committee tried you in *abstentia* and we found you guilty of complicity in the death of Deputy J.W. Dillingham. Now we're executing you!"

"That's hoss shit, mister," yelled Buck Stinson. "What the hell kinda trial is that?"

"It's the kind of trial you all will be seeing a lot more of if Egderton's vigilantes have their way!" Plummer called out to the mob that had been listening to the exchange. Faced with the inevitable, Plummer felt himself grow calm, even relieved that it would all soon be over.

Henry Tilden ran up trailing a long length of rope in the snow. Beidler threw it over the crossbeam and quickly fashioned a noose. Ned Ray, struggling and crying, was placed atop a kind of crude scaffold Beidler had arranged from some scrap lumber. Without ceremony, Wiggins stepped forward and kicked the legs out from under the scaffold and Ray fell. The rope jerked violently and snapped his neck.

Plummer set his jaw and felt his stomach squirm. He closed his eyes and thought of his boyhood home in Maine, the sea and the woods, his brother and sister, his parents who had raised him so well and were so heartbroken to see him leave in search of his fortune.

He opened his eyes and saw Stinson, who'd been struggling and swearing obscenely at his executioners, suddenly fall. His neck didn't break so he kicked and struggled and choked slowly. There were cries of protest from the crowd and some walked away, sickened by the sight of a man dying so horribly. Plummer saw Beidler and Kincaid watching Stinson's death throes with fascinated looks on their faces.

"I want some time to get my business affairs in order!" demanded Plummer as he was led to the scaffold.

"You've had all the time you're going to get," replied Sanders.

Plummer fixed his cold gaze on his nemesis for the last time. Sanders seemed to shrink back from the blue-gray eyes that drilled into him.

"You're a coward and a murderer, Sanders," he said calmly as Beidler fixed the noose and stepped down off the makeshift platform.

"Stop!" a voice cried out from down in the gulch. "Stop this!"

Panting and wild eyed, Noah Coffey suddenly appeared on the execution ground that was glowing cheerily in the dark night from a score of lanterns and torches.

"Henry!" Coffey screamed as he made the circle of guards who stood before the scaffold. "Wait...Sanders!" He was pushed back as Beidler glanced his way and grinned.

"You're too late, Coffey," McKenzie said with a smirk.

Plummer's eyes were closed again and he thought of the soft autumn afternoons at Sun River holding Electa in his arms. He heard a disturbance and opened his eyes. There, thirty feet away, stood Noah Coffey, tears pouring from his desperate eyes. Despite the noose around his neck, Plummer smiled warmly at him.

"It's all right, Noah. It can't be helped," he said over the din of the excited spectators. "I forgive you, Friend. And when you see her again, please tell Electa I always loved her. You'll find my brother's address in my belongings. Please write him and tell him what happened to me. Sell off my holdings and send him the proceeds."

Coffey broke down completely, falling to his knees in the trampled snow and mud.

Plummer shifted his gaze to the mob below. "Some of you men here owe it to me to set this right after I am gone! I hope you will!"

Then he calmly looked down at his executioners. "Give me a good drop, boys," he called as he closed his eyes for the final time.

Beidler hesitated, shaken by Plummer's courage. He finally stepped forward and, with a swipe of his foot, kicked out the flimsy boards supporting the platform. Henry Plummer's neck broke cleanly.

Coffey let out a wail as nearby on-lookers backed away from the prostrate newspaperman. Some silently turned and began walking down the gulch toward town. When he finally collected himself, Coffey looked up to see the three dead men suspended from the crossbeam and the vigilantes standing around, gazing up at their victims with satisfied expressions.

By eleven o'clock the next morning, Sanders had visited Plummer's office and found his victim's ledgers and business papers. Among the latter he discovered a receipt from Taylor McKee's office. Along with appraising the value of the gold miners brought him, the assayer kept a kind of bank where customers could safely store their cash or gold dust.

"Good Lord!" exclaimed Sanders. Wiggins, McKenzie and Dimsdale moved to look over his shoulder. "He had more than fifteen thousand dollars! It's in the safe at McKee's!"

Wiggins clapped Sanders on the back as Beidler walked into the office. "X, did you sell off his horse and traps?" asked Sanders.

"Two hundred for the lot," Beidler said tossing money onto the desk. "And another hundred and fifty for the hosses and saddles o' them other two."

Sanders didn't tell them about the legal instrument he'd drawn up transferring Plummer's interest in the Plummer & Coffey Mining Company to Sanders & Edgerton, Ltd. He knew it wasn't worth the paper on which he'd written it, but when his uncle returned from Salt Lake City, he'd sign it as chief justice of the territory, making it legal. Then, Sanders knew, his financial troubles would be over.

Tully suddenly appeared outside the open office door. Sanders glanced up and frowned at the man's repulsive odor and shabby appearance.

"What is it Tully?" he demanded.

"Mr. Sanders, Sir," he said. "I come to see about me money."

Sanders waved a hand impatiently. "Good God, man! Plummer's not even cold and you're here for your money! We're working on the accounts now. We will contact you when we have your funds. Now please leave us alone!"

Tully disappeared.

"Damned mick," spat Beidler.

"Indeed," agreed Dimsdale. "An entirely worthless and beggarly race of people."

Sanders stood. "Very well, I will go take charge of Plummer's funds."

He started to leave, but Beidler grabbed him by the sleeve. "We're comin' with ya, Sanders," he said testily.

"For appearance sake, you understand," interjected Dimsdale. "We must present a united front in every aspect of the Plummer...um...matter."

Taylor McKee's assayer's office was four doors down from Chrisman's store. The vigilante leaders entered and Sanders showed the owner the receipt he'd found.

"I wish to verify that you are holding this sum," he said pointing at the total figure.

McKee nodded, then picked up a sheet of paper.

"Actually, the sheriff, that is, the late Mr. Plummer, made another deposit just three days ago...yes, here it is..." He showed them a copy of a receipt in the amount of three thousand seven hundred and sixty two dollars. The vigilantes looked at each other with broad smiles.

"I wish to have all of those funds in cash now," Sanders demanded. The assayer was a trim man of fifty years. He wore neat mustaches and his sincere brown eyes now flashed with suspicion.

"That is highly irregular," McKee replied with a frown. "I can't do that without a court order."

Sanders flushed with anger. "See here!" he said sharply, "I am an attorney acting on behalf of aggrieved miners Plummer defrauded out of their claims..."

"Hold on there, Mr. Sanders," interrupted the assayer. "I knew Sheriff Plummer and I know most every miner in Bannack. Nobody was defrauded. They sold their claims willingly to the sheriff at a fair price. Plummer knew how to extract the gold and they didn't. That's the end of it."

"The hell you say!" cried Beidler, his fists clenched. "We want that money right now or you're gonna join Plummer!"

"Shut up, X!" snapped Sanders angrily. He looked back at McKee. "Disregard this fool. Very well. I will have Judge Sidney Edgerton sign an order when he returns."

McKee was shaking his head. "I don't think so, Mr. Sanders. I know the judge is your uncle. He has a conflict of interest in this matter. No, Sir, I will not release any funds without a legitimate court order. That'll probably have to come from a federal authority in Lewiston or Salt Lake City."

Dimsdale could see Sanders and Beidler were about to explode. He stepped between them and addressed the assayer calmly.

"You are quite right, Mr. McKee," he said quietly. "This is rather a complex legal matter and it should be sorted out correctly. Let us consult with Judge Edgerton when he returns in a few days' time. Meanwhile, do we have your promise you will not release the funds until the disposition of Plummer's estate is properly ajudicated?"

McKee thought about this proposal. "Should Mr. Plummer's heirs contact me," he told them, "and present the correct legal instruments, I would be obliged to turn the money over to them. But until that happens, I will hold the funds here."

The frustrated vigilantes returned to Plummer's office where they encountered Coffey. The newspaperman's clothing was disheveled, his eyes were red-rimmed, he was unshaved and they could smell whiskey.

"What the hell do you want?" demanded Sanders.

Coffey glanced up. "You heard what Henry said. He asked me to sort out his accounts; take care of his brother and sister..."

"That won't be necessary," sniffed Sanders. "I am handling the estate."

"You?" said Coffey with a bitter laugh. "I think not. I'll retain Dave Pemberton and see that Henry's wishes for his property are respected. I'm not going to allow his killers to plunder his estate, that's for certain!"

"Watch yer tongue, Coffey," warned Beidler.

"That's what you're doing, isn't it?" asked Coffey, ignoring Beidler and addressing Sanders. "Robbing him after he is dead and out of your way?"

"No, we're most certainly not," said Dimsdale mildly. "We already told you that all of the property of the road agents—and any other criminal for that matter—is forfeit to the Citizens Vigilance Committee. The proceeds cover the cost of their pursuit, prosecution and, if necessary, their execution."

"Forfeit!" Coffey spit the word back at the professor. "It's not enough that you bastards denied him access to a court of law and due process—you remember those principles, don't you Sanders?! Now you entitle yourselves to his money and property!"

"Your thoughts on the right or wrong of what we do and how we do it are quite irrelevant, Noah," Dimsdale remarked, wiping his fleshy lips with his handkerchief. "We will do what we need to do to protect our community. I suggest you stay out of our way."

"Now, if you'll excuse us," added Sanders, "we have business to attend to."

Coffey angrily picked up his hat and left the office. When he'd gone, the vigilantes divided the proceeds from the sale of the dead man's horses and saddles.

44

Dimsdale and Sanders sat in the Goodrich Hotel. The lawyer was looking over a list of names the professor had compiled and was slowly nodding his head in agreement.

"All of these people are, shall we say, undesirables, Wilbur," said the Englishman.

Sanders continued to nod his head before finally looking up at Dimsdale. "I agree. They have to die. But we need to do it before my uncle returns."

Dimsdale sipped his tea then carefully placed the china cup on its saucer. "If Judge Edgerton should question our...actions...we have only to explain to him that these men," he pointed at the sheet of paper, "were all part of the Plummer gang."

Sanders smiled his agreement as McKenzie, who'd been stoking the fire in the stove, walked over and took the paper from Sanders. His reading skills were rudimentary, but he frowned and looked up at the two leaders.

"That damn dirty greaser with his fuckin' goats, that stupid Dutchman, Helm, Gallagher, Lane, sure, they all gotta hang. But Cap'n Slade? He's a friend o' mine."

"I'm not surprised to hear that," Dimsdale sniffed. "He's been making a damned nuisance of himself in Virginia. He fired his pistol through the ceiling of Duncan's store while he was in a state of complete drunkeness. He's going to kill someone before long. We want him out of the way."

"Yeah, but he ain't killed nobody yet," McKenzie angrily protested. "Most time's he behaves hisself. He runs a good ranch down by the Madison. Got him a perty wife. I don't see no call hangin' him. I can talk to him if…"

"Don't worry about Slade," said Sanders. "The executive committee makes these decisions and it's up to you to follow its orders."

The rancher started to say more, but Sanders held up his hand. "The first order of business is the greaser. Then Dutch Wagner."

Because of his dark complexion and his thick accent, most people in Bannack assumed Joe Pizanthia was Mexican. He was, in fact, from Sicily, a young, illiterate stonecutter by trade whose real name was Pizzana. Newly arrived in New York at the start of the war, he had almost enlisted in the Army but he had seen hundreds of coffins being unloaded at a railroad depot in Brooklyn not long after he had disembarked. He had changed his mind then and there about fighting for the Union.

Pizanthia had wandered west, working at odd jobs along the way. Everywhere he stopped he always heard about gold fields in the West from his fellow Italian immigrants. He thought his stone cutting skills would make him a good miner but he struggled with the English language and never did learn how to go about filing a claim. Finally, he'd settled in Bannack where he'd gone to work for Francis Thompson, digging out quartz that the other workers smashed into powder with machines that extracted the gold the rocks contained.

Pizanthia lived alone in a dugout shack south of Bannack with a half dozen goats he raised for their milk and meat. Boulders sheltered his hovel. He had little money and, because his English was so poor, he had no friends. He only went to town to buy staples like salt and flour from Chrisman and, along with his collection of goats, he lived on the rabbits and other small game he could kill with his old muzzle-loaded shotgun.

A steady wind out of the north raked the hillside as Pizanthia stepped outside his shack and cut some fire wood. Down below in the draw he thought he heard voices, but it was too dark to see who was speaking. He shrugged, finished his chore and returned to the dugout with the wood. He stoked the blaze in his makeshift fireplace, then lay on his cot and sang a song he had learned as a boy in Palermo.

Before long, he heard voices close by. Alarmed, he rose and grabbed the small caliber pocket revolver he always kept loaded and extinguished the candle that lit the small, dingy room. He thought Indians were prowling outside when, suddenly, the shack door was kicked open and two armed men entered.

Without thinking, the Italian shot the first man who came through the door and then the second. The first died where he fell, the bullet piercing his heart. The other man staggered back out the door clutching his groin and hysterically screaming. There were shouts and oaths. It sounded to Pizanthia like an army of men had surrounded his cabin. He stepped over to the small table and snatched his shotgun then crawled under his cot, the only cover the little cabin offered.

He heard the man he'd shot howling in pain and anger, then other voices, more urgent. After a moment of quiet there came the deafening roar of gunfire from dozens of weapons. Balls and shot pierced the flimsy wood of the shack and blew apart anything above waist level. The dugout's one small window disintegrated.

Sweating and panting in terror, Pizanthia squirmed back under his cot as far as he could until his back was against the cold earthen wall of the dugout. He heard the gunfire rise to a crescendo and then pause as the shooters reloaded their weapons.

Desperate and panicked, Pizanthia rolled out from under the cot and, steadying himself, fired his revolver blindly at his assailants through the broken window. Another fusillade forced him to dive for the cot. Before he could reach cover, a ball ricocheted and struck him in the leg. Another caught him in the shoulder. He passed out from the pain momentarily and then awoke, paralyzed with fear.

Outside in the cold, safely hidden behind a rock, Sanders looked down at Smith Ball, whom Pizanthia had shot in the hip. Blood from a severed artery poured from the wound that Dimsdale tried to patch with his handkerchief. Ball had stopped his screaming but he was in excruciating pain, gritting his teeth.

"What happened to Copley?" asked Sanders.

"Dead, I think," gasped Ball. "Hit inna ches'…oh God! Oh sweet Jesus!"

"Quiet!" demanded Sanders. "You'll draw more fire."

The vigilante leader peered over the rock at the darkened dugout. The greaser was giving as good as he was getting, that much was clear. The shack was built into the side of the hill. It had a sod roof and was timbered on its other three sides. "We need uncle's cannon!" he called back to Dimsdale. "The one we brought with us from Ohio. Send someone to fetch it!"

Men ran back to Bannack and returned in twenty minutes carrying the short barrel of a mountain gun that fired a small caliber shell.

"Place it there," ordered Sanders, pointing at a spot thirty feet from the windowless west wall of the shack. The men obeyed, loaded the weapon and fired. They forgot to cut the fuse of the shell because it went straight through the hovel and exploded against rocks on the east side. Fragments sent men there diving for cover as the gunners reloaded and fired at the chimney, believing Pizanthia might be hiding in it. The shell blew the stone apart but had little effect otherwise. Sanders held up his hand and shouted, "Cease fire!" He then waved several men forward from his position behind the rock.

Kincaid and Horace reached the door of the shack first. It was blown off its leather hinges. Dust and smoke filled the interior as they peered into the darkness. A torch was brought forward and they spotted a pair of boots beneath the cot. Kincaid stepped over the dead body of Copley, grabbed the boots and dragged out the still form of Pizanthia.

"Goodamn greasy son of a bitch!" roared McKenzie as he drew his Colt and fired all the chambers into the wounded man on the dirt floor. Another vigilante appeared with a length of rope. They dragged the body out and hung it from a makeshift gallows someone had fashioned with a long pole leaning over a boulder. Sanders appeared holding two pistols and began firing them at the body. Others joined in, blasting the corpse with all manner of firearms.

"Fry him in his own grease!" screamed a man who had set the dugout on fire. Smoke billowed from the shack's interior and, in minutes, the timbers and roof were ablaze. The body, riddled with bullets, its extremities hanging off the torso by tendons and gristle, was cut down and dragged by the mob to the burning shack. Smiling, Sanders and Dimsdale watched several men pick up what was left of Joe Pizanthia and throw his remains into the inferno.

Dutch John Wagner sat in Skinner's saloon nursing his frost bitten fingers. The young German miner had come from Bavaria to Bannack by way of California. Mildly retarded, he had experienced nothing but bad luck panning his claims and made barely enough money to feed himself. He didn't even have a place to live, so poor had the results of his mining efforts been. Still, Wagner was popular among the other German miners, several of whom had taken pity on their "poor little brother" as they took to playfully calling him. They bought him an occasional meal or let him sleep in their cabins when it was cold. John—his real name was Johann—was grateful for their help.

One of his friends had told him the night before of rumors that some men from Virginia City suspected Johann had something to do with "Plummer's gang." Wagner had no idea what the man was talking about, only that he'd seen the sheriff hung by a mob two nights earlier. That was enough to make him afraid for his own safety, so he had attempted to run away that morning.

He rubbed his fingers together again, blew on them, and saw that the tips of several were beginning to turn dark blue. He knew that was bad but what was he to do? He didn't own a horse so he had been forced to walk. He'd gotten as far as the Beaverhead River, but the wind came up, brutally cutting through his thin clothing. With his hands wrapped in rags for want of real gloves, he'd turned back for Bannack deciding to take his chances there rather than freeze to death out in the endless, snowy valleys. Perhaps his friend was mistaken. He'd done nothing wrong. Why would anyone wish to harm him?

The saloon was as noisy and smoky as usual, but Wagner could also sense a tension. Men glanced out the window. Others smoked their pipes or cigars while they spoke to one another in hushed tones. One man kept his pistol on the table in front of him as he played poker. Skinner himself was drinking, and while that wasn't unusual, he didn't seem to pause in his libations. He just poured and downed glass after glass of whiskey as his eyes cut to the saloon's door for no apparent reason.

The room went suddenly silent. Wagner looked up curiously. In the distance, to the south of town, he heard gunfire. It sounded like a battle had begun. Then there was a pause and the alarmed men in Skinner's began looking at one another. Soon there was more gunfire and then another pause. The card games slowly resumed and the barroom din returned. Then, again, silence as a loud report shook the building in which they sat. Wagner now wondered if the federals and the rebels had somehow brought their war to the mountains. A second blast was followed by more shooting that seemed to continue for many, many minutes. Finally, the gunfire ceased.

"What the fuck's goin' on out there?!" called Skinner from behind the bar.

"Vigilanters," replied an old miner, a pipe wedged into his mouth. "Seen Sanders with men headin' south after sundown."

An hour passed. Wagner, with little money to spend, had nursed a beer and a whiskey. His fingertips were throbbing as the wind beat against the saloon, the glass shivering in its frame. Men were drifting out into the night, a blast of freezing air sweeping through the room each time the door was opened. Skinner was preparing to close so Wagner asked if he could sleep on a cot in the back.

The landlord nodded, holding his hand out. "Ten cents."

Wagner paid with the last money he had. He found a vacant cot and lay down on it fully clothed, pulling the thin, dirty blanket up over his head. He had just drifted off to sleep when he felt something poke him in the head. He pulled the cover back and found himself looking down the wide barrel of a Sharp's rifle. The saloon was empty, lit only by a dim lantern. Skinner was standing behind the bar looking at the ten or twelve men crowded around Wagner.

"Get up," ordered the man with the rifle.

The young German obeyed and flashed a wary smile. "*Was ist los*?" he asked, forgetting he should speak English. "V'at...v'at you vant off me?"

A man Wagner knew as Sanders stepped forward. "Are you John Wagner?" he asked. "Dutch John Wagner?"

"*Ja*...but I am no' Dutch," he said with a confused grin. "I am *Deutscher*."

The questioner smiled thinly. Another man was tying Wagner's hands behind his back, but the young German offered no resistance. Sanders eyed him.

"You might as well confess," he said. "We know you were part of Plummer's gang of road agents. Red Yeager told us."

The English was coming too fast for Wagner. He thought he understood what Sanders was saying, but wasn't sure. "*Ja*...Plummer...that sheriff. You mans hang him," he said with a helpful look and a hopeful smile.

Sanders looked around at the other vigilantes. "So you admit your guilt?"

"*Ja*, sure!" Wagner said blinking.

"Then, John Wagner," Sanders intoned. "You are sentenced to die."

"Die!? *Nein!*" cried the German, suddenly understanding what was happening. "I do notting! Please, Mister, I no vant to die!"

Ignoring the pleas, his captors dragged Wagner from the saloon as he cried out in German and broken English. In a stable a few doors down from Skinner's, a rope was slung over a beam. Wagner, by then begging pitifully for his life, was helped up onto a buckboard where Beidler fixed the noose. Without ceremony, Beidler shoved the young miner from behind. The vigilantes cheered lustily as they watched Wagner's death dance. When the body grew still, Sanders turned to address them.

"Gentlemen, we have more work ahead of us!" he announced. "I'll need volunteers to join me in Virginia!"

45

Coffey was defeated, wracked by grief and guilt. He had failed Henry and his friend had died as a result of his stupidity. Certainly he'd warned him about the vigilantes. Repeatedly. But he now knew he had not done enough to save him.

He and Chrisman, along with Charlie Benson and a couple of other miners Henry had befriended, had returned to the gallows the morning after the hangings. They had cut down the bodies and Coffey had stood over Henry's frozen corpse, looking for a long time down at his friend's peaceful gray face.

The men wrapped the corpses in sheets then carried them up a nearby hill to the town's cemetery. The weather was again taking a turn for the worse. The wind whipped up the snow on the ground, blasting and stinging their eyes. The ground was frozen solid so digging decent graves was out of the question. To accommodate this inconvenience, the miners had built a stone shed where Bannack's dead could be stored until spring when proper graves could be dug. The crude mausoleum would keep the corpses preserved while preventing birds and animals from desecrating them.

They lay Henry inside beside the other bodies, then closed the door and sealed it with rocks. Coffey looked around at the other men as though seeing them for the first time.

"Thank you, Gentlemen," he said as he shook each man's hand. "We must make sure that Henry is buried properly, come spring. He was a good and decent man. He made mistakes, but he didn't deserve to die like he did."

"Mr. Coffey, what are ya gonner do about them vigilanters?" asked Benson, his eyes rimmed with red. The miner had wept like a child as they'd wrapped Henry in the sheet.

"Do?" Coffey replied with a shake of his head.

"You ain't gonna let 'em off, are ya'?" asked Willis Chrisman, the storekeeper. He was a young, rotund man of about thirty. "You're a deputy, ain't ya?"

Coffey now understood. "No, not anymore, Willis," he quietly replied, casting his eyes onto the snowy ground. "I'm getting out of the territory." Coffey knew the others were disappointed but they said nothing as they walked back to town together.

Now, three days later, sitting in the *Tribune* office, Coffey was slowly becoming drunk. He watched the snow fly horizontally outside his window in the dull afternoon light and shivered a little as a draft of cold air cut through the office. He stood and walked to the stove, stoking the fire and adding a log. When he turned, he saw Dimsdale standing at his desk. He didn't bother greeting his guest. Coffey ambled back to his seat and dropped down into it, silently observing the professor, who thrust a sheaf of papers at him.

"An account of the capture and execution of the road agent leader Henry Plummer and his accomplices, Ned Ray and Buck Stinson."

Coffey made no move to take the papers. Instead he stared up at Dimsdale with dull eyes. The professor dropped the papers on his desk.

"When you are sober, Coffey, see to it that is published, *verbatim*," he commanded. Without another word, Dimsdale turned and left.

Coffey poured himself a big drink and took a long, slow sip. Then he picked up the papers and began reading.

Sanders had arrived in Virginia City just after noon and walked with Wiggins, Dimsdale and Beidler to the building that was under construction on Wallace Street. It had no roof as yet, but heavy pine beams had been put in place for the purpose of supporting one. Snow covered the bare earthen floor. Tools and lumber lay scattered by the carpenters Beidler had told to leave. The vigilante leaders agreed the location was ideal as they trooped back to the Masonic Hall and prepared to make the arrests.

Emboldened by the killing of Henry Plummer, more men had joined the vigilantes in the days since the sheriff had been hanged. There were at least thirty armed men waiting as Sanders strode into the meeting hall. He found a chair, stood on it, and called for order.

"We have formed you into six platoons!" Sanders announced. "Captain Wiggins will lead the first unit and arrest Clubfoot Lane. The professor will lead his men and take Haze Lyons. He's in Nevada City. The fool thinks we forgot about him. Captain McKenzie, you and your men find Boone Helm. Kincaid, you'll take your men after Jack Gallagher. Captain Horace there will bring in Bill Hunter! Finally, my men will arrest Frank Parish!"

Now the newest vigilantes were looking at each other in confusion. While the other men named might well be road agents, as Sanders alleged, most knew Frank Parish as a harmless, sickly drunk who only made a nuisance of himself, begging for food and money on Wallace Street.

"Parish?!" called out one of the new men. "What's he done, Mr. Sanders?"

Sanders peered at his inquisitor. "I have it in confidence he was among Plummer's road agents," he barked, irritated at the question. "He's also an undesirable this town doesn't need!"

There was some grumbling but no further questions.

"Very well, let us move out. We will gather after dark at the unfinished building with the prisoners!"

The crisis had come. Seeing the circumstances, we admitted neither vacillation nor delay and the citizen leader, summoning his friends, went up to the party and gave the military command, "Company, forward march!"

Coffey felt a wave of disgust so he sipped his drink. *Citizen leader,* he thought to himself. That was how Sanders now regarded himself. Of course Dimsdale couldn't name any vigilantes in print, ostensibly because if any were identified, the friends of the executed men might seek revenge. Coffey knew the real purpose. Secrecy was required because if the names of the vigilantes were ever documented, they one day might have to answer for their crimes.

On the road Plummer heard the voice and recognized the person as the leader. He came to him and begged for his life...

Despite the effects of the whiskey, Coffey felt anger welling up in his chest. It wasn't enough the vigilantes had taken his life; now that little son of a bitch Dimsdale intended to dishonor Henry Plummer's memory, as well.

Soon after the party formed and returned to town, leaving the corpses stiffening in the icy blast. The bodies were eventually cut down by the friends of the road agents and buried. The "Reign of Terror" in Bannack was over.

Coffey slammed his fist down on the papers. Gripped by anguish and impotent rage, he covered his face with his hands and wept bitterly for his dead friend.

Word had spread throughout Virginia City and then on to Nevada that the vigilantes were in search of new victims. The news excited many and soon men on foot and horseback were streaming up Wallace Street. The fierce wind had subsided and snow fell gently in the still, cold night.

The half erected building, cast in lantern and torchlight, appeared almost festive as the first of the prisoners arrived. Clubfoot Lane and Boone Helm, dressed as slovenly as usual, were brought in, followed by Jack Gallagher. Then Haze Lyons was dragged in, struggling and cursing his guards. Finally, Sanders appeared, leading the small form of Frank Parish. The little man was bent double, limping on a crippled leg and sobbing. Still his captors nudged him along with their weapons, but the spectators could see Parish was a sick man, his face ashen and withered.

Hands on his hips and wearing an expression he thought conveyed confident authority, Sanders watched as the five condemned men were lined up under the nooses that had earlier been slung by X. Beidler from one of the stout cross beams. A place beneath the sixth noose remained vacant until the men sent to find Bill Hunter finally showed up empty handed.

"Somebody blew," explained Horace. "Hunter ran!" Annoyed, Sanders had the sixth rope removed from the beam. He then directed the vigilantes posted outside the structure to guard the proceedings. A phalanx of gunmen arranged themselves on the street so they could keep one eye on the growing mob and the other on the hangings.

Sanders affected his prosecuting attorney personae. He pointed at the condemned men, a look of determination on his face.

"You have each been found guilty by the Citizens Vigilance Committee of being accomplices of Henry Plummer! We know all of you have committed crimes as part of Plummer's notorious road agent gang! You have been sentenced to death by hanging, execution of same to take place forthwith!"

Lane was furious. His arms were tied loosely before him, so he took off his hat and slammed it on the floor, glaring at Sanders all the while.

"Yeah! You hanged Plummer!" he bellowed. "You killed him so's he couldn't tell Marshal Beechey about what you and these other bastards been doin' here!"

Jack Gallagher, taking a different tact, stepped forward. "I ain't never been no road agent, Mr. Sanders," he pleaded. "I'm a gamblin' and drinkin' man... but I sure ain't never killed nobody, nor robbed a man...can't I be spared, Sir?"

"No, Jack, I'm afraid not," Sanders replied matter of factly. "The evidence against you is overwhelming." Gallagher might have asked to see or hear that evidence, but he simply hung his head and resigned himself to his fate.

Meanwhile, Boone Helm stood speechless. He'd wet himself and his eyes were wide with terror. Lyons struggled furiously with the three vigilantes who were trying to hold him steady. Parish continued his pitiful sobbing.

Clasping his hands behind his back, Sanders stepped back. "Gentlemen," he ordered the execution detail, "do your duty!"

Vigilantes stepped forward and lifted the prisoners onto barrels. Using a ladder that he leaned against the crossbeam, Beidler climbed alongside each man and positioned the nooses. When he completed his task he stepped down, rubbing his hands together, his thick beard hiding a smile.

Clubfoot Lane looked down darkly at his executioners. "Y'all are gonna' roast in hell!" And with that, he leapt off the barrel to his death. Helm and Parish cried out in fear at the sight of Lane's body swinging under the beam, its legs violently lashing out.

McKenzie, standing behind Gallagher, pushed the condemned man. Gallagher dropped from the barrel and his neck snapped audibly. Out on the street, a lusty cheer went up.

Now it was Helm's turn. Horace stood behind the deputy whose eyes were clenched shut. Using a stout board, Horace pushed Helm awkwardly off the barrel, but unlike Lane and Gallagher, his neck did not break. As the noose gripped flesh, Helm's tongue shot from his mouth, his eyes bulged, and blood exploded from his nostrils. The spectators grew quiet as they took in his death throes which were underscored by Helm's choking and gagging. Slowly, he ceased to struggle and, finally, many long minutes later, he died.

Haze Lyons had watched with a look of horror. He'd stopped resisting because Beidler had taken all the slack out of his rope. The noose was taut and Lyons understood what that would mean.

"I don' wanna die like that!" he cried out desperately, "Give me some rope so's I'll drop!" Beidler obliged, bringing his ladder forward and leaning it on the beam behind Lyons. He climbed, let out the required slack then, without warning, shoved the man from behind.

Lyons fell a few feet, the rope jerked and he was quickly dead.

The still air held the stench of voided bowels, emptied bladders and blood. Only little Frank Parish was left. He had closed his eyes and was praying as fast as the words would come.

"May I?" Dimsdale asked Sanders, his eyes flashing with excitement. Sanders held out his arm by way of invitation. The professor stepped behind Parish and, using a wooden pole, tried to push Parish from the barrel. But the sick man had decided to he didn't want to die. He teetered on the barrelhead, crying out in terror as Dimsdale futilely prodded him again and again.

The vigilantes watching the scene began to laugh at the sight of the little Englishman, now sweating profusely from his exertions, unable to dislodge the doomed man. Even Sanders was smiling before McKenzie finally pushed Dimsdale aside and practically threw Frank Parish from the barrel.

Out on the street, some of the guards fired their weapons in celebration. Others cheered. Sanders shook hands with the members of the Citizens Vigilance Committee, then good-naturedly patted the embarrassed Dimsdale on the shoulder as the professor mopped his face with his handkerchief. As he shook Beidler's hand, Sanders winked because the two men had already calculated the value of the forfeited property.

As the corpses slowly swung beneath the thick beam, indeed the mood became celebratory. Whiskey was passed around and there were more shots fired, cheering and some jeering, too, as miners came up to the skeletal building for a closer look at the dead men.

Snapped out of his sleep by one of the gunshots and the sounds of revelry, Noah Coffey rose and went to the window. He had no idea what was happening so he donned his overcoat and ventured over to the execution site just in time to see Lane's body being lowered. Without thinking, Coffey strode up to Sanders.

"Henry's lynching wasn't enough for you?!" he asked Sanders, his voice bitter with recrimination.

"Careful," Sanders warned him with a menacing look. He pointed up at the four remaining bodies. "*You* could be next."

Coffey made a lunge at Sanders's throat but Beidler and McKenzie grabbed him before he could reach their leader. They pushed him to the muddy floor and then stood over him, pistols in their hands. Coffey got to his feet and staggered back out into the street, gulping the cold air. He saw spectators drifting away from the carnage, some shaking their heads, but most heartily laughing at the massacre they'd just witnessed.

"What in God's name is the matter with you people?!" Coffey screamed at them as he stood in the middle of the snow-shrouded street. "How could you let this happen?!"

A few of the retreating faces glanced back at him then just as quickly looked away. In a moment most of the on-lookers had evaporated into the darkness. As he watched the last of them disappear, Coffey suddenly felt himself spun around.

A gloved fist hit him squarely on the chin and he stumbled back in pain and shock. Other hands caught him as he was punched in the belly. Another fist landed on his temple and he fell to the frozen street. A boot kicked him painfully in the ribs and then he felt himself lifted to his feet again.

Two men firmly held his arms behind his back. He saw McKenzie and

Kincaid standing before him. They took turns punching him in the face. Hot blood sprayed from Coffey's mouth and broken nose. A brutal kick connected with his testicles and his knees buckled. He suddenly vomited, but the arms held him fast. Through swollen eyes he saw Kincaid and McKenzie step back with looks of disgust. Behind them, Dimsdale and Sanders stood by, impassively watching the beating. Kincaid stepped forward and delivered a combination of vicious blows to Coffey's face, his gloved hands dripping blood.

The arms released Coffey and he fell to his knees, then over onto his side. Another brutal kick broke a rib, but he felt nothing because he'd already lost consciousness.

"That's enough!" called Sanders. "I think we made our point with this distinguished journalist. Perhaps now he'll understand there's small profit in asking so many questions, eh Professor Dimsdale?"

"Indubitably," Dimsdale remarked dryly.

46

The old Chinese woman tisked as she applied dressings to Coffey's shattered face. She saw his cheekbone was broken and his eyes were swollen closed. She had pulled out his broken teeth as best she could and wrapped a bandage tightly around the man's bruised ribs. He lay naked on the rope bed, oblivious to her ministrations and it occurred to her he might never wake up.

Her husband appeared, looked at the man he knew as Coffey and joined his wife in tisking. He had made a thin brew of some medicinal herbs he kept in jars displayed on a shelf. He attempted to get Coffey to drink but he couldn't rouse him. He picked up the heavy poultice he'd made and applied it to the angry black and blue knot on the man's forehead.

Coffey had appeared at his shop door in the middle of the night. He could barely stand and his face looked like chopped beef. The old man had helped him to the bed and Coffey had immediately passed out. It was almost twenty-four hours later, and the couple wondered aloud if they should summon a doctor. They didn't trust white men and especially disliked the doctors, whom they considered ill-educated quacks. As they debated, they heard Coffey stir.

The old woman tottered over to him and placed her cool hand on his temple. She saw him try to open his eyes before he grimaced painfully. She tisked some more as she gently dabbed his face with a wet cloth. He tried to croak out some words but she placed her fingers on his lips and shook her head. The old man made another attempt at helping him with the broth he'd made and this time Coffey managed to get some down. The old man smiled with satisfaction before he and his wife let their battered patient drift off to sleep.

Sanders had finished giving his orders to the main body of vigilantes. He mounted his horse and led them northward. The man he'd dispatched ahead to locate Howard's men had returned to say that he'd found Steve Marshland laid up in a shed at the Clarke ranch twenty miles to the west, recovering from a fever. Mindful of the last failed search for Doc Howard, Sanders had taken the precaution of scouting ahead. The vigilante he'd sent had spent the night at the ranch with the sick man before returning to Sanders.

Two dozen vigilantes in double file were heavily armed and well clothed for the weather as they crossed the Jefferson River. By sundown they had the shed surrounded.

Horace and Wiggins entered. It was pitch black inside. Horace struck a match and saw a form lying on a pallet in the corner. He lit a lantern and several candles. Wiggins saw a shotgun and revolver on a table near the bed, so he took them out of the reach of the sleeping form.

"Steve...wake up," Horace said, nudging the man. Slowly, Marshland sat up, blinking bleary, bloodshot eyes. He slowly swung his feet out of the bed and rubbed his face. He was clad in long johns and wore a stocking cap on his head. He coughed, hacking up phlegm that he spit onto the floor.

"God, I'm sick," he announced to his visitors. "I think it's pneumonia."

"Sorry to hear that," replied Wiggins with a sly smile and a wink at Horace. "But I believe we have just the remedy for you."

Horace laughed at the joke as Marshland looked more closely at the two men. "Who are you?" he asked as he suppressed another cough.

"Members of the vigilance committee," Wiggins answered as he stepped to the door and opened it. "We're here to arrest and punish you, Steve."

He waved his hand and a few moments later ten more men were standing around taking turns warming themselves by the fireplace that Horace had stoked into a crackling blaze.

Marshland rose silently and pulled on his trousers and a shirt. He then sat back down on the bed where he rubbed his face with both hands.

"Fellows," he said in a refined Eastern accent. "I am not a well man and I have no idea why you would want to arrest or punish me."

"You are one of Doc Howard's road agents, is why," said Sanders.

"Doc?" asked Marshland, genuinely puzzled. "I haven't seen him for nearly a year."

"That's a lie," declared Dimsdale, removing his coat and hat. "You were with him last May when Lloyd Magruder was robbed and murdered."

"But I wasn't," Marshland said calmly. "Last spring I was looking for work around Bannack. I couldn't find any so I did some panning on the Rattlesnake."

"I'm afraid we don't have the time or inclination to discuss what you were or were not doing last May, Marshland," said Sanders as he stood over his prisoner. "What we really need to know from you is where the rest of your friends are."

Marshland coughed violently and spit again. "Friends?"

"You remember them," Sanders said agreeably. "Aleck Carter, Bill Bunton, Lowery, Romaine, and the rest. Come now, we need your help, Steve."

Marshland rubbed his eyes. His brown hair was matted and his long face was drawn and pale, days of stubble covered his cleft chin.

"Well, let me see. Bunton was in Deer Lodge, the last I heard. At Smith's ranch near the Cottonwood, I believe."

"What about them others?" interjected McKenzie.

"I really have no idea where those men are," he said, looking about earnestly at the vigilantes. "I do know Carter and Romaine. I played cards with them back in Nevada City. But Gentlemen, other than Bunton, I have no idea of the whereabouts of the men you seek."

Sanders consulted with Dimsdale, then looked at the other vigilantes.

"Gentlemen, those of you who find Steve Marshland guilty, please say 'aye'."

The poll was unanimous. Marshland looked around him in fear and confusion. "Guilty?" he asked, blinking. "Guilty of what?"

"Of being a party to the robbery and killing of Lloyd Magruder," replied Sanders sharply. "You are hereby sentenced to hang by the neck until you are dead."

The hour was late and the vigilantes were cold and hungry. Marshland tried to plead with Beidler who, along with five others, marched him barefoot through the deep snow to a tall cottonwood tree behind the ranch house. Without ceremony they quickly carried out the execution. The vigilantes stayed the night in the shed and departed with the morning's first light for Deer Lodge, leaving Marshland's barefoot corpse twisting forlornly in the violent, arctic wind as a warning to others.

Coffey was able to take a few steps, although he gasped with each one as searing pain shot through his ribcage. His head pounded and he could see only through the narrow slits of his swollen eyes. One ear was ringing and he was afraid he might lose his hearing in it. The old Chinese couple helped feed and bathe him. But as battered as he was, Coffey knew then that he wasn't going to die.

In an odd way, the beating had also awakened him. He was determined to get to the *Tribune* office as soon as he could. Thankfully, they had not injured his hands, so he could still write, still set type.

The old man appeared with a bowl of the foul tasting herb concoction he kept pouring into Coffey's mouth. He tried to wave the man away but ended up choking the brew down. As he nodded his thanks, the old man responded with a wide grin at Coffey's twisted face. Then the old woman rewrapped the bandage around his ribs and changed the dressings, tisking all the while.

Sanders's vigilantes easily hunted down Bill Bunton at Smith's ranch north of Deer Lodge, but he proved to be tougher and far more reticent than Marshland. He was a large, remarkably ugly man with a wide, pockmarked face. His head was covered with black stubble and he refused even to look at Sanders as he was interrogated while he sat at the plank table.

"You stranglin' sons o' bitches is gonna string me up anyhow," he said angrily, ignoring Sanders's demands for names and places. "So's it don't matter if I say I ain't part of no road agents or if I say I am..."

"True enough," interrupted Dimsdale, the handkerchief over his mouth as he felt another cough coming on. "But we do need your help nonetheless and I'm afraid we haven't much time to...um...persuade you to assist us."

The professor stepped back as Kincaid came forward holding a thick, short branding iron he had found in a shed behind the ranch house. Bunton glanced up at Kincaid and fear flashed in his eyes as Wiggins and McKenzie grabbed him from behind and two more men extended his hands onto the table.

Without a word Kincaid brought the iron down onto Bunton's right hand, smashing bones and tendons. The prisoner screamed, but his cries were drowned out by the wind that roared relentlessly through the eaves. Blood splattered across the table and onto the coats of the nearest vigilantes who watched the next blow land on Bunton's left hand. Somebody passed a tobacco plug around as the bar continued to pulverize helpless man's fingers and hands.

Blubbering and frantic, Bunton tried desperately to pull away from the table while the vigilantes struggled to pinion him. Others stepped in, helping to hold Bunton in place as chunks of flesh and bone flew about the room. As he wielded the iron bar, Kincaid's face and chest looked as though he'd just butchered a cow.

"For...God's...sake...stop!" Bunton finally howled. "I ...I... know...I can tell you where...where Carter is! Stop! Please stop!"

Kincaid was poised to deliver another blow but Sanders reached out and stayed the gore-drenched bar with his gloved hand.

"Very well," he said quietly as the big man was released. "You know where Aleck Carter is? So?"

Bunton was holding his crushed hands in his armpits. His face was twisted in pain as he rocked himself forward and backward. He managed to open an eye and look at Sanders. "The...the last I seen Aleck—oh, God! Oh, God in heaven! It hurts!"

"Yes?"

Bunton was gasping, spittle dripping from the corner of his mouth. "Gimme a drink o' whiskey...please! Oh, Lord...oh God in heaven!"

Dimsdale held his silver flask to the man's lips and Bunton drank deeply. "Aleck...Aleck...last I seen him a month or so back, he said he was gonna go to Hell Gate...oh...he's got a squaw up that way...Oh, God...gimme another drink!"

Dimsdale let him have a sip then capped the flask and placed it in his coat pocket. "All right, then, Mr. Bunton," said the professor. "What about the others?"

Bunton's eyes popped open. He looked fearfully at Kincaid, who was holding the brutal iron bar at the ready. "No! Please...no! I only knows 'bout Carter...I swear to God! I cain't tell you where them others is!" he cried in desperation.

"You've been a great help," Sanders said with a kind smile and a pat on Bunton's shoulder. He then pointed at the dripping iron bar that Kincaid held. "I'm very sorry it had to come to—that—to encourage your cooperation."

Believing the worst was over, a look of relief passed over Bunton's pug face. "Oh, thank God! Thank God!"

Sanders nodded amicably. "Yes, a prayer is in order, Bill. You see, we've decided you're to hang for killing Magruder. Red Yeager told me it was you who cut the old man's throat."

"Hang? Me?!"

Some of the vigilantes laughed at the question. "Yes, I'm afraid so," Sanders said sadly. "X?"

Many of the men he passed on the street averted their eyes at the sight of his mangled face. When others realized the man they were looking at was Noah Coffey, they held their hands over their mouths in horror. Coffey ignored them as he limped toward the *Tribune*. He had a stop to make first, so he turned into the narrow alleyway and found the old Chinese man at work over a tub of laundry.

"Missa Coffey!" he cried, eyes wide with astonishment. "You shou' no' be up!"

Coffey pressed a twenty dollar gold coin into the man's withered hand. "For your kindness, Uncle."

Embarrassed by the tears in Coffey's eyes, the old man flushed and bowed deeply.

The old woman thrust aside the curtain that screened the couple's living quarters, took one look at Coffey and began weeping silently. He walked over to her and, without a word, patted her wrinkled cheek.

"I will be all right, Auntie," he said before he kissed her forehead.

Unused to such displays of affection, the old woman stepped back with a cackle. She chattered something at him in Chinese and wagged her finger in his face. He guessed she was demanding he get back into his bed. But he'd slept enough and he had done far too little. It was time to act. He thanked both of them again then he left for his office.

On the bank of the frozen Hell's Gate River was a collection of tents, wikiups and some crude dugouts. A band of Indians had erected a half dozen tipis a hundred yards away on the opposite shore. As the vigilantes rode up just before noon, they could see smoke curling from the cluster of buffalo skin lodges.

Hearing the arrival of men on horseback, an old man emerged from one of the dugouts. He was surprised at the sight of more than twenty heavily armed white men staring back at him. Their eyes looked hollow and cruel. One of them dismounted and approached.

"We're looking for Aleck Carter," Sanders declared without any greeting. "Where is he?"

The man pointed out at the tipis. "Over yonder…with his squaw."

"Who are you?" demanded Sanders.

"Perkins," he replied. "I trap 'round here."

Sanders detailed several vigilantes to retrieve Carter and bring him to Perkins's dugout. He watched them ride over to the tipis and then went inside the cabin with his fellow vigilante leaders, telling the others to make do with whatever shelter they could find.

Perkins had a pot of soup on his stove. He offered it to Sanders, Dimsdale, Beidler, Wiggins and McKenzie, who ate greedily and didn't thank him. They heard several gunshots ring out from the direction of the tipis but ignored them as they wolfed down the food.

Presently the dugout door swung open and a man wearing only trousers was shoved into the cluttered room. He was in his mid-twenties with long black hair cinched off in a ponytail. He wore a thick black beard and resembled a wild animal to the four men who were just finishing their soup.

"You are Aleck Carter?" asked Dimsdale as he dabbed his mouth with his handkerchief.

"Who wants t' know?" demanded the enraged prisoner.

"That's not the correct attitude, I can assure you," replied Dimsdale mildly as he placed his handkerchief in his pocket. "Not the correct attitude at all. So I ask again. Are you Aleck Carter?"

"Yeah," snapped Carter. "Who're all o' you?"

"The Citizens Vigilance Committee of Virginia City," replied Sanders, his booted feet stretched out to the stove, which contained a pleasantly warm fire. "We've been looking for you and your cronies."

"Huh?"

"Your compatriots. Your fellow assassins," Sanders replied, his tone annoyed. "Doc Howard, Lowery, Romaine and all the rest who robbed and killed poor old Lloyd Magruder at the direction of Henry Plummer."

"Plummer?" Carter asked scratching his head. "He's the sheriff in Bannack, ain't he?"

"Was," Wiggins smiled. "We're the law now. We've already taken care of most of your friends, but we need to know where the last few are hiding."

Carter slowly realized his predicament and understood there was no point in reasoning with the vigilantes, only telling them what they wanted to know. He began nodding his head.

"Well Sir, Lowery, I think he's up t' Fort Owen. I seen him there a week ago or thereabouts. And Bill Bunton, he's..."

"We know about Bunton," interrupted Sanders. "What about Doc Howard?"

Carter looked puzzled. "Doc's been gone a long time...close to a year, I reckon."

"You want to tell us about Magruder?"

Carter sat back in an empty chair. "Sounds like you know's most o' what happened."

"Red Yeager was helpful," Sanders replied, "but we're always interested in learning more."

"Red!" replied Cater angrily. "That bastard can never keep his trap shut!"

"Oh, he's pretty quiet now," laughed McKenzie from his seat by the stove as Beidler and Wiggins chuckled at the rancher's witty rejoinder.

"Well," continued Carter, "old man Magruder, he was a real nice gent. Doc and me and Bob, Page, Romaine and a couple others, we met him on the trail from Salt Lake. He was on his way to Virginia City with this freighter full o' all kin' o' goods: tools, guns, women's pretties, food stuffs, whiskey, amanition..."

"Yes, yes..." interrupted Sanders impatiently, "And what happened?"

"We kinda guarded the old fellow until we got close t' Bannack. Then Doc says we'll kill him when we take the cutoff trail over to Alder Gulch. We was camped for the night, maybe ten, twelve miles outta Virginia when Bunton cuts Magruder's throat. He didn't suffer any. Died quick in fact. We took the wagon on t' Nevada City an' sold most of the stuff there, split the money...then we all scattered."

"And Plummer?"

Carter frowned. "What about him?"

"He directed you in this heinous crime, did he not?" asked Dimsdale urgently.

"No, Sir. Why would he do somthin' like that? He's the law...or was. What happened to Plummer, anyhow?"

Sanders rose from his seat, ignoring the question. "Well what about Plummer's deputies...Lane, Helm, Gallagher...the others? Surely they were involved!"

Carter shook his head. "Don't know any o' them boys. Sorry."

"And the stage coaches? Did you rob those?" demanded Dimsdale.

"No, Sir," Carter said flatly. "When was that?"

"In October and November...you and your gang of road agents weren't part of either of those?"

"Like I said, we broke up after Nevada City," replied Carter. "I wouldn't really call us no gang, neither, Mister," he added with a helpful smile. "Doc, he ain't none too smart and the rest, well, they's just looking fer an easy stake was all. I felt bad about old Magruder though. He should'n'a been killed like that. He shared his food and whiskey with us..."

"Shut up!" cried Sanders, who gestured at Beidler. "X, get him out of here!"

Beidler pulled Carter to his feet as McKenzie began to tie his hands behind his back. The young man looked at Sanders and Dimsdale.

"Wait a second now!" he said, panicking, "I done told you what y'all wanted to know...what's this?"

"You didn't think you's gonna walk outta here alive, did ya' boy?" growled McKenzie as he cinched the knot tightly around Carter's wrists.

With that they marshaled the half-naked man out into the snow and shut the door. Sanders and Dimsdale sat silently, avoiding eye contact. They listened to Carter's cries of protest and pleas of innocence and soon after his choking as he slowly died. They rose, still silent, and walked out to where the dead man was swinging, his feet twitching.

He looked at the weary vigilantes shuffling indifferently in the deep drifts beneath the trees. More snow had begun falling, collecting on their shoulders and the crowns and brims of their hats. Sanders could see their bloodlust had spent itself. They wanted to go home.

"Carter confessed everything!" Sanders announced. "As we knew, Plummer ordered the murder of Magruder and theft of the freighter as well as the stage robberies! We have one or two more scores to settle!" he added brightly. "Are you with me, Men?!"

Several new vigilantes shook their heads and mounted their horses.

"Mr. Sanders, we done our part," one of them said as he wheeled his mount to face the leaders. "Most of us, we got livin's to tend to. We're headin' back."

"Very well!" Sanders said angrily. "Those of you who want to leave, do what you wish. But speak not a word of what you saw or heard on this scout!"

Two more men mounted their horses and joined the others for the long ride back. Sanders looked around at the remaining fourteen or fifteen men.

"Gentlemen, we have shelter and hot food, so let's enjoy it!" he called out, trying to sound as cheerful as he could. "We ride out for Fort Owen in the morning!"

Coffey had finished his account and read it again carefully. He scribbled out a line here and changed a word there, but was mostly satisfied with it. He managed to stand shakily at the composing table and began setting the type.

The ride to Fort Owen had been brutal. Snow fell continuously on the horses and men as they trudged through drifted banks three and four feet deep. They could see only a few feet ahead through the gray, silent gloom and, once, McKenzie feared he had lost the trail entirely.

Several of the vigilantes had pleaded with Sanders to turn back, but he insisted they ride on. It took them another day to reach Fort Owen. They located Lowery in a lean-to. He tried to run but Horace shot him in the leg. With no "trial" at all and with the mechanical movements that signaled their physical and emotional exhaustion, the vigilantes hanged Lowery from a tree limb. Beidler placed the noose around his neck and the others hoisted him up. Nobody had the strength to give him a drop. None of them cared how Lowery died. They left him choking beneath the limb as another bitter night closed in.

47

J.D. Slade had fought in the Mexican War as an infantry officer so he was known around Alder Gulch as "Captain" Slade. He had been among those who'd drunkenly applauded the work of the vigilantes the night they'd executed Clubfoot Lane and the others.

"There's trash that needed dyin', if anyone did!" he'd told his wife afterwards.

On the day of his own execution, Joseph Slade rode out to Virginia from the Madison Valley, where he owned five hundred acres of prime rangeland. At forty, he had money and wonderful prospects. He waved to Maria as he rode past the cabin he'd built for her with his own two hands. She was a beautiful woman of Spanish heritage with raven hair and fair skin. He had met her in New Orleans several years earlier and she'd married him early in 1861. She waved back with a smile, but inwardly she was glad to see him go to town. He could have his drunken binge and sleep it off there.

Steep, barren foothills of the Gravelly Range separated the Slade place from Virginia City, but the snow had mostly stopped and the afternoon was clear. It took him an hour to cover the distance and he arrived in front of Star Billiard Hall shortly before sundown. There were a dozen horses tied up in front of the establishment, which along with billiard tables, featured liquor and cards.

Several men greeted him with handshakes as he entered and one bought him his first drink. He had another whiskey, then a third. In very short order, he had become belligerent. He shoved a miner who had inadvertently bumped him. He'd argued with a neighbor about the price of beef, calling the rancher a "bastard." He then accused the bartender of shorting him on his change, loudly calling him a cheater and coward.

One of Slade's friends heard this and walked over. "Joe, that's enough. Durant's a good fellow. You shouldn't talk to him like that."

Slade, staggering, pushed the man away, turned around and leaned heavily on the bar with a sullen expression. He stayed quiet for a time, then began muttering to himself about the sons of bitches that ran the town.

"Who the fuck they think they are, anyways!" he called out, pushing himself back and turning to regard the room.

Some men at the card tables glanced his way.

"What are you bastards lookin' at?" he yelled. "You lookin' fer a fight?"

The card player he was addressing ignored him. "I'm talking to you!" Slade cried out, walking over and jabbing the man in the arm with his finger. Accustomed to Slade's behavior, the player glanced up and then looked down at his cards again. Slade reached down, grabbed the cards out of the man's hand and threw them on the floor. By this time, Durant had seen and heard enough of Captain Slade. A big man, he swung himself over the bar and grabbed the drunk by the arm, walked him to the door and shoved him out into the night.

At that moment, a column of horsemen led by Wilbur Sanders was passing by in the street. Behind them trailed a dozen more horses carrying packs. Slade silently watched them ride by, swaying on the boardwalk before stumbling down Wallace Street toward the Bale of Hay. The bartender there didn't care much about behavior, only money, and he still had plenty of that.

At the Smith & Boyd livery stable, Sanders slowly dismounted. "Men, you have performed heroically," he said to the others, who remained mounted. They stared back at him with glassy eyes, his words barely registering. "I will make an accounting of the property we've confiscated from the criminals," he gestured at the string of horses, "and contact each of you shortly about your share." With that, Sanders, followed by Dimsdale, led his horse into the stable as the others rode off to their respective homes.

Sanders could see that the journey to Fort Owen had taken its toll on the diminutive and diseased professor. Dimsdale coughed continually and looked sallow, but he had stayed the course without complaint.

"What ya' want to do with them horses and packs, Mr. Sanders?" asked Boyd, the stable owner.

"Just corral them until I find buyers," replied Sanders wearily. "And hold the packs, saddles and traps here until I have a chance make an inventory of their contents."

In an hour, Sanders and Dimsdale were dining on roasted pork in the warmth of the Fairweather Hotel. Sanders finished his meal and pushed back from the table.

"Did you see Slade on the way in?" he asked.

"Dispicable," replied Dimsdale. "Truly an obnoxious reprobate."

"A landed one, too," replied Sanders thoughtfully. "He owns that rangeland along the Madison with hundreds of head of fine looking cattle grazing on it."

Dimsdale stifled a yawn. The comfort of the hotel made the exhaustion he was feeling all the more acute. "Wilbur, surely you are not suggesting we…"

"Yes, I am," Sanders interrupted. "I'm tired too, but Slade is here in Virginia and there is no time like the present."

The professor nodded as he yawned. "Let's go get some stalwarts and arrest Slade," he finally agreed.

The rancher was sleeping on the floor of a dive. The owner of the Bale of Hay had run him off an hour earlier so he had staggered to the ramshackle saloon perched on the edge of a ravine. It was filthy and drafty, full of failed miners on their way to oblivion. Along with liquor, the dive's owner sold opium to his patrons and several were in the back, laying on wooden pallets, smoking oriental pipes. The sickly sweet smoke combined with the rancid odor of unwashed bodies and stale beer to produce a nauseating stench.

It was just before midnight when Sanders walked in followed by Dimsdale, Horace, Wiggins and McKenzie.

"Where's Slade?" he demanded.

The barman pointed toward the corner at a body curled up on the grubby earthen floor. Wiggins and Horace pulled the captain to his feet, disarmed him, and frog-marched the dazed rancher out the door and up Wallace Street to the Masonic Hall.

"You're a disgrace, Slade," declared Sanders with a look of disgust. "And we're all sick to death of you."

Slade slowly looked up. Beginning to comprehend his predicament, Slade was weeping pitifully and shaking his head in agreement. "I know, I know, I know," he lamented as mucus dripped from his nose over his thick mustaches. "I…I can't control myself Mr. Sanders…"

"Look at you," snarled Wiggins. "You smell like a goddamn goat."

"I know…I know…it's just that, I wish…I, I, I'm sorry!" Slade blubbered.

The vigilantes had placed Slade in a chair before Sanders and Dimsdale. McKenzie and Horace stood behind the prisoner, glancing at each other and exchanging sly smiles over the man's misery and fear.

"You're sorry," Dimsdale repeated, his voice dripping with disdain. "Well, my friend, the committee is tired of your sorrow. We're tired of *you*. You're a drunk and a danger to the community; a danger to the little children I teach. You have no right to live."

Slade continued sobbing. "I know…I know…I know…"

"You see, Slade," Sanders explained in an expansive voice as he leaned back in his chair, "our aim is to make Virginia City, indeed the entire region of Alder Gulch and Bannack, a safe place, where a man can prosper and raise his family. Dr. Wiggins here has three children. Two of them attend the professor's academy. How would you feel if, during one of your benders, you happened to fire a weapon that killed one of the doctor's little ones on his way home from school?"

The rancher shook his head and said nothing as he mopped his nose with his sleeve.

"Well, Captain, we're not going to wait to find out!" Sanders continued, his tone dark. "We are exterminating the vermin who endanger those children and the honest citizens of Virginia. I speak not only of the criminals but also of the undesirable social elements as well. You, I am afraid, fall into the latter category."

Through the alcoholic haze, Slade now knew why he was sitting in the Masonic Hall.

"Slade, I've seen you drunk. You are lucky indeed that one of these miners hasn't taken a notion to slit your throat," said Wiggins.

Slade was gazing about at his inquisitors as he forced himself to think clearly. "Mr. Sanders...all of you...you are right," he moaned, his voice growing weaker with each word. "I shall reform myself. I...I shall stop drinking strong spirits; live a different kind of life...if...only you'll...let me?"

Sanders pushed himself out of his seat. "We're past that point, Slade. You should have thought about this a long time ago."

Slade buried his face in his hands. His pathetic sobbing filled the room. "Oh my God...must I hang?! Oh...my poor, dear wife..."

It was all Horace could do to keep from laughing out loud at the condemned man's woe. He grinned at McKenzie, who covered his mouth with his hand. Sanders shot them both a stern look, and Dimsdale was shaking his head at their antics.

Sanders stepped around the table and gently patted Slade on the shoulder. "Come along, Joe. It's time."

Maria Slade had become worried when her husband had not returned by midnight. That wasn't like him, no matter how drunk he was. Shortly after three o'clock in the morning she had managed to get a mule in the traces of a buckboard and drive it as fast as she dared along the desolate snow covered trail that led over the hills to Virginia City. The night was bitter as she crested the rise above the silent town. The snow reflected the half moon so it seemed almost as bright as day to her as she made her way onto Wallace Street.

Bundled against the cold, her eyes darted around as she drove the wagon along the deserted street. She passed the Masonic Hall and the Fairweather Hotel. She saw that her husband's two favorite haunts, the Star and the Bale of Hay, were dark and shuttered. There were other saloons and any number of foul wikiups that seemed lively, but she was loathe to search those.

She decided to ride back up Wallace Street, returning when it was light if she failed to find her husband.

As she neared the top of the street, she passed a corral and thought she saw a figure standing near its gate. She reined in the mule and climbed down to investigate. As Maria approached, she could see more clearly that a man was hanging by his neck from the crossbeam of the corral's gate. She put her knuckles to her mouth, slowing her walk. The corpse's back was to her. She hesitated, then reached out and took hold of the cuff of the trousers and slowly turned the body.

Captain Joseph D. Slade's tongue and eyes were protruding from his head, which was hanging at a crazy angle, the noose biting into the flesh of his neck. Maria blinked. At first, her mind was unable to register the sight of her dead husband. Then she let out a series of shrill screams that split the peaceful winter night.

48

Sanders had slept soundly for more than twelve hours. He awoke in his bed in the Fairweather Hotel, shaved and then carefully dressed. It was almost three o'clock when he began his walk to the livery stable, eager to make an accounting of the property the vigilantes had appropriated from the men they had hanged. In his head he already counted himself a wealthy man.

Now he could move his family out of that dreadful shack in Bannack and over to Virginia City where the business opportunities were far better. He also had his eye on the Slade place. With that and ownership of Plummer's holdings along with his share of the dead sheriff's cash, he could stop worrying about putting food on the table and start concerning himself with attaining a high public office in the Territory of Montana that President Lincoln had promised Judge Edgerton he would soon establish. Sanders thought attorney general was an appropriate station for a man of his caliber. Given his passionate prosecution of the Plummer gang, his uncle would no doubt agree.

Sanders smiled and nodded at the town's respectable men that he passed along the way. At first, he didn't notice their angry looks, but when he had cheerily greeted Bernard Starling, a wealthy newcomer who was constructing a large commercial building on Wallace Street, the man had frowned and strode away without a word.

Sanders paused, confused by Starling's odd rebuff. He looked back up the street. The sun was beginning to drop behind the distant mountains but it was clear and commerce was bustling along as usual. Everything appeared normal, so he shrugged and entered the livery stable.

Dimsdale was waiting for him. He looked distressed and without a word he shoved a newspaper at Sanders. It was the *Virginia City Tribune.*

"Excellent!" declared Sanders. "He published your account..." Sanders interrupted himself. His jaw dropped as he read the banner headline beneath the newspaper's masthead:

Vigilantes Murder Sheriff Henry Plummer!!!

—

An Eyewitness Account Herein of a Most Cowardly Act

—

*W. Sanders & Other "Vigilance Committee" Members
Hang Shf. Plummer Without Charges or Trial*

—

Many Citizens Outraged

Sheriff Henry Plummer of Bannack was hanged January 10 past by members of an organization calling itself the Citizens Vigilance Committee. The secret "Committee" is led by Wilbur Sanders, late of Ohio, who arrived in this city last spring. He is the nephew of Mr. Sidney Edgerton, Chief Justice of Idaho Territory.

Sanders felt the sweat break out on his wide forehead. He tore his eyes away and looked at Dimsdale. "How...what...?"

"Read on," replied the professor, tapping the page furiously with his forefinger.

Sheriff Plummer, who had served this jurisdiction with distinction since his election last year, was dragged from his home by armed men led by W. Sanders and hanged without benefit of a trial nor were any official charges preferred against Sheriff Plummer. This gross miscarriage of justice, which took place while Judge Edgerton was absent from the city, was witnessed by scores of

Bannack citizens as well as your correspondent. A number of men considered rescuing Sheriff Plummer but were held at bay by armed associates of W. Sanders. In addition to the noble Sheriff Plummer, two other men, Buck Stinson and Ned Ray, were executed without due process of the law.

Sanders was trembling. "Has this been...?"

"Yes, of course!" snapped Dimsdale as though speaking to an imbecile. "Everyone from here to Bannack has seen it."

Sheriff Plummer was a successful gold miner and owner of the Plummer & Coffey Gold Mining Company. Inquiries conducted the morning after Sheriff Plummer's murder revealed that W. Sanders, Professor T. Dimsdale, Dr. T. Wiggins, L. McKenzie and X. Beidler demanded that Plummer's holdings be turned over to the Vigilance Committee by T. McKee, the Bannack assayer. Mr. McKee correctly told the men he would not until they provided him with lawful documents.

Panic passed through Sanders like a bolt of lightning. Sweat dripped onto the newspaper page. His throat was dry and his stomach churned.

Your correspondent, a deputy sheriff lawfully appointed by H. Plummer, sent word of the murders to the United States Deputy Marshal in Lewiston soon after the killings. Readers will be interested to know that a letter reached Sheriff Plummer's Virginia City office following his death appointing the late sheriff deputy U.S. marshal for this district of Idaho Territory.

Weak in the knees, Sanders sat back on a hay bale. "What...what do we do, Thomas?" he asked, his voice barely audible.

"It's obvious, is it not?" replied Dimsdale through a violent cough. "Coffey must die. Immediately."

"But Hill Beechey..."

"Forget about him," Dimsdale snapped. "If and when Beechey comes here to investigate, we'll have established Coffey as one of Plummer's road agents cleverly installed as the editor and publisher of the *Tribune* after Plummer had its rightful owner murdered."

Accustomed to reconstructing events to fit inconvenient facts himself, Sanders nodded his head in sudden agreement.

"Yes! Yes!" he replied enthusiastically. "Coffey is no doubt one of the desperadoes who held up the Oliver coach."

Dimsdale had his hands clutched behind his back, his forehead knitted in thought. He looked like what he was, a teacher. After a long moment he held up his forefinger.

"Coffey was also with Plummer when he assaulted Henry Tilden on Horse Prairie," replied Dimsdale. "I heard young Henry say so myself."

"Exactly!" exclaimed Sanders as a flood of relief swept over him. He stood and placed his finger on his chin. "Professor, the people deserve the truth. Not *this* clabber." He rattled the newspaper in his hand. "Murder! How dare he? Once we eliminate Coffey, you'll publish an edition of the *Tribune* that corrects all of this!" He gave the professor a meaningful look. "After all, you'll be its new owner and publisher."

Dimsdale bowed slightly and smiled. "It will be an honor and a privilege to set the record straight."

Coffey approached the Masonic Hall on unsteady legs. It was dark and a wispy snow fell. He saw a lantern glowing inside. He'd considered running, but it was no use. He had heard they'd ridden all the way to Fort Owen to hang a man. How far would he get?

His only shield now was that he had publicly exposed the vigilantes for what they were. His only weapon was the truth. He decided he would try to persuade them to disband and lie low. If they attempted to hang him, surely the outraged citizens he had been speaking to all day would stop them.

"Ah, good evening Noah," called Sanders cheerfully as he entered the room. "Thank you for joining us."

Despite the warm greeting, Coffey could see McKenzie, Wiggins, Beidler, Kincaid and Horace glaring at him from their seats around the table. They all had copies of the *Tribune* before them.

"Thank you for asking me, Wilbur," Coffey replied with a genial smile that revealed several missing teeth. His lean face was still covered with hideous bruises and he was forced to hold himself up by leaning on the back of a chair because of the broken rib. "I see the *Tribune*'s circulation is up among members of the committee."

"I don't think sarcasm is going to serve you particularly well today," said Dimsdale from behind his handkerchief.

"You have violated our trust and your sacred oath to the Citizens Vigilance Committee, Noah," declared Sanders. "You've revealed the names of some of our members. We also couldn't help but notice you accused us all of murdering Plummer."

"You did murder him," replied Coffey.

McKenzie started to rise, but Sanders seized him by the sleeve. He slowly resumed his seat.

"No, no, you see, there you are wrong," Dimsdale scolded. "We just returned from a scout during which we eliminated nearly all of the road agent gang Plummer controlled..."

"Professor, who are you trying to convince?" Coffey asked angrily. "I hope it's not me."

"No indeed," replied Sanders. "No indeed. But as the professor was saying, during our interrogations of some of the gang members, most notably Aleck Carter, we had it confirmed beyond a reasonable doubt that your friend was a notorious cutthroat and robber."

"*Reasonable doubt?*" spit Coffey. "Stop pretending you're someone who respects the law, Sanders! You're a disgrace to your profession. You have no more regard for the law..."

Sanders angrily slammed his fist down on the table. "I *am* the law!"

The room grew still and Coffey could see a couple of the men looking out of the corner of their eyes at their leader. Sanders cleared his throat and regained his composure.

"There is no question whatever as to Plummer's guilt. And as for the property he forfeits, we intend to distribute it to his many victims. So your charge that we were going to take it for ourselves is a complete fabrication."

Coffey reached into his jacket pocket and withdrew the copy of the Constitution. He slowly opened it.

"This is the Constitution of the United States of America, Gentlemen," Coffey declared. "We may be living on the very edge of civilization, out of sight and mostly out of mind of the rest of the country, but *this*,"—he held up the crumbling document—"is the law. Not Sanders. Not Edgerton. Not any of you ."

He began to read:

"In all criminal prosecutions, the accused shall enjoy the right to a speedy and public trial, by an impartial jury of the state and district wherein the crime shall have been committed, which district shall have been previously ascertained by law, and to be informed of the nature and cause of the accusation; to be confronted with the witnesses against him; to have compulsory process for obtaining witnesses in his favor, and to have the Assistance of Counsel for his defense.'"

Coffey looked at each man carefully. He settled on Wiggins, whom he decided was probably the one man present who might listen to reason.

"You men are in trouble," he said to the dentist. "Marshal Beechey will be here in a week, two weeks at the most. When he arrives, he will conduct a court of inquiry because I sent him a letter that explained what you have been doing. There are many here in Virginia and many more in Nevada and Bannack that believe you all to be murderers. You no longer have the support of the citizenry. In fact, I'm not sure you ever did. Regardless, you've wantonly killed men. You've acted unlawfully, no matter what Sanders or his uncle might say. Hill Beechey will discover the truth whether I am alive to tell him or not. So, Gentlemen, I suggest you disband this committee tonight and disappear. Otherwise," Coffey pointed directly at Wiggins, "it will be *you* at the end of a rope."

Sanders jumped to his feet, strode around the table and slapped the Constitution from Coffey's hand. The two men stood toe to toe.

"Perhaps he's right," Wiggins suddenly declared. Sanders spun and faced him.

To Coffey's surprise, Kincaid agreed with Wiggins. "I know Beechey," he said. "And he ain't gonna be satisfied 'less he gets t' the bottom of things."

"That right!" agreed Coffey. "Beechey is a tough and determined lawman. So was Henry Plummer. That's why you killed him; because Henry stood between you and your...your plunder! But unlike Sheriff Plummer, Hill Beechey has federal law enforcement authority in this jurisdiction," he said as he passed his extended forefinger slowly over all of them. "None of *you* will be able to hide behind Judge Sidney Edgerton when Marshal Beechey gets here."

"This is utter nonsense!" exclaimed Sanders. "My uncle is the last word when it comes to legal matters in the territory, not Beechey! Why, my uncle authorized us..."

"Quiet you fool!" interrupted Dimsdale harshly, but Coffey smiled knowingly.

"I thought so," he said. "Edgerton's been with you from the beginning. Well, that means he'll hang, too!"

Sanders was glowing red with embarrassment. He had somehow dragged his uncle into this and now he feared facing the old man when he returned to Bannack. When Edgerton read the *Tribune* and saw his name had been linked to the committee, he would skin Sanders alive. He steadied himself against the table as he shivered at the thought of his Uncle Sidney's rage.

"Why don't you gentlemen think about what I have said tonight," Coffey suggested as he painfully bent to pick up the Constitution. He neatly folded it and placed it back in his jacket pocket. "Deliberate. When you do, I think you will all agree with and act on my advice. Good evening."

Coffey turned, placed his bowler hat on his head and was almost to the door when he heard the click of a Colt hammer. He stopped and turned. McKenzie's revolver was leveled at Coffey's chest.

"Git your ass back here, Coffey!" the rancher commanded. He gestured with the barrel of the pistol and Coffey obeyed, moving back to the spot where he'd been standing.

"You're a slow learner, boy!" McKenzie continued as he eyed Coffey's battered face. "You got the shit kicked outta you. That shoulda told *you* to run. But you're still here."

"That's right, McKenzie!" Coffey replied in a firm and defiant voice that belied his fear. "I *am* still here!"

Horace leaned over and picked something up off the floor. He rose and Coffey could see a long length of rope.

"You ain't gonna be here much longer," Horace snarled.

The hall had exposed beams, so Horace selected one and tossed the rope over it. Beidler stepped around from his seat and casually began tying the noose. Dimsdale slid a chair near Beidler as Kincaid walked behind Coffey and tied his hands behind his back.

Everything seemed to be happening in slow motion to Coffey, who realized he'd overplayed his hand and was about to die. *Well, they overplayed their hand, too,* he thought to himself. *This is what will happen to every one of them when the real law discovers what they've done.*

He remembered Henry's brave death and was determined to follow his friend's example. He closed his eyes and his thoughts turned to his lovely Rebecca, her pale face looking up at him from a bed of purple and gold flowers. Then he thought of Electa, her laughter and her small, lithe body eagerly taking him during those long winter nights.

Sanders was impatiently pacing the room, his face etched in worry as he thought again of Sidney Edgerton.

"Let's get this over with!" he called in an annoyed voice to Beidler. "I need to get back to Bannack."

The brutish hangman ignored Sanders as he focused on making the noose as tight as possible. "Need to make sure a fellow vigilante dies quick," he said finally, proudly holding up his handiwork.

"Get up on that chair," ordered McKenzie. Coffey obeyed. He watched Beilder stand on a stool to secure the end of the rope to the beam.

The hangman jumped down and looked up at Coffey. "Hope I left ya 'nough slack there, Coffey," he said with a cruel grin.

Kincaid and Horace joined him in the joke, but Coffey could see that Sanders, Dimsdale and Wiggins were agitated.

The vigilantes stood back. "Now you know how that Momon preacher felt," declared Beidler.

"For God's sake, X, get on with it!" demanded Sanders.

Beidler stepped forward and studied the chair. He decided to kick out one of the back legs in the hopes of breaking it and collapsing it under Coffey's weight. That might or might not break the man's neck but he supposed it didn't really matter either way, as long as Coffey was dead. He drew his foot back, but before he could deliver the kick, the door of the hall flew open.

"Halt or you die where you stand, Sir!" bellowed Nolan Harris Tofton the Fourth. He was holding his pistol on Beidler, who's foot was frozen mid-kick. Tofton strode into the room followed by a dozen tough looking men, all dressed in gray uniforms. They held pistols and carbines on the vigilantes, who were staring at the invaders in stunned silence.

"You, with the beard!" Tofton barked as he gestured at Beidler with the pistol. "Step back!"

Beidler, mouth agape, obeyed. As he did, McKenzie raised his pistol. One of Tofton's men saw the movement and fired. The bullet struck the rancher in the chest and drove him back to the wall. He collapsed to the floor, blood pulsing in scarlet gouts from a hole where the bullet had split his heart in two.

Kincaid tried to draw his revolver, but Tofton fired first, hitting him in the head, the bullet splattering gore on the other vigilantes.

"Anyone else care for a dance?" asked Tofton calmly as the thick smoke from his weapon drifted to the ceiling.

The sudden violence had shocked the surviving vigilantes. They stood dumbly staring at their dead comrades.

"Corporal Nickerson, release that poor Yankee on the chair, if you please," Tofton smiled. "I am quite sure he deserves to be hanged, but I don't believe we'll let his execution occur tonight."

The soldier who'd shot McKenzie holstered his revolver and quickly released Coffey, who scarcely could believe he was looking at the Virginian. He walked over and embraced Tofton, who gently patted him on the back.

"How...how...who..." Coffey began, blinking back tears.

"Later," Tofton smiled down at him. The smile disappeared as he looked closely at Coffey's battered face. "We need to get out of here, Noah. Quickly." He turned to his soldiers. "Men, disarm these bastards, then secure and silence them."

The troops instantly obeyed. They soon had Sanders, Dimsdale and the rest tied to chairs and gagged. Coffey watched them go about their work, too stunned to speak.

There had only been time for Coffey to retrieve and saddle Miss Matilda. An hour later, he found himself riding fast through Nevada City and out into the Ruby River Valley in the company of Tofton and his platoon of Confederate cavalry. They headed south and rode furiously through the night. At first light, they came upon an abandoned cabin along a frozen creek. Clouds were moving in and the wind had picked up. The men dismounted, unsaddled their horses and hobbled them so they could roam and graze on exposed grass.

Now in the cabin, a fire warming them, Tofton offered Coffey a drink from his silver flask, which he gratefully took. The gray clad troops ate a breakfast of jerked beef and were soon asleep on their bedrolls.

As they sat together among the snoring soldiers, Coffey looked at Tofton and shook his head. "How the hell?"

Tofton laughed. "Our young friend, the abolitionist, Mr. Thompson found me in Salt Lake City. I was there recruiting these men and more like them for service. Indeed, when Francis located us at our bivouac, we were about to ride for Texas and then onwards to Virginia."

"I thought you'd be back east fighting by now, Colonel," replied Coffey.

"Actually, I'm a brigadier," corrected Tofton as he pointed at the epaulet on his shoulder with a tired grin. "I felt I deserved another promotion. In any event, my men and I were just days away from riding out when Francis came to me to say that Henry was in danger. He said you told him shortly before Thanksgiving you believed these, um, what did he call them? Vigilantes? That the vigilantes were going to hang Henry. I asked for some volunteers to help me, but," he looked sadly at Coffey, "we arrived in Bannack too late to save Henry, as you well know."

"Henry should have gotten away while he could," Coffey muttered. "He knew how dangerous they were."

"Not his style, Noah," replied the officer. "Henry would *never* run from danger. You know that."

Coffey looked over at Tofton. "But how did you learn about me?"

"I can read a newspaper, Sir!" he said, bushy eyebrows raised. "You have a gift for inflammatory copy, I must say! When I read your account in Bannack of what happened to Henry, I was certain there was a rope waiting for you, too. It seems I was right."

"You were," conceded Coffey with a sad nod of his head. "I thought I could reason with them. You saw for yourself how persuasive I was." He looked over at the tall officer, his Van Dyke whiskers neatly trimmed, his long hair elegantly pomaded. "Thank you, by the way, Nolan. I owe you my life."

"Not at all, not at all," smiled Tofton as he stood and stepped over a sleeping soldier. He laid his tall frame down on a rude wooden platform that was supposed to serve as a bed. He looked over at Coffey. "But, my friend," he continued, "I am truly exhausted. We can talk more later. Meanwhile, let's get some sleep. I want to be out of this God forsaken territory as fast as my horse will carry me."

"Amen," agreed Coffey.

Part Five

From the Journals of Noah Coffey

49

New York City
July 14, 1876

    A letter arrived this morning that set me to thinking again about my days in the West. It was written by Sumner Howard, the United States attorney in Utah, who is prosecuting John D. Lee for the Mountain Meadows Massacre, as the crime has come to be known. He wishes me to appear as his key witness when Lee's trial commences this September at Beaver, Utah.

    I have mixed emotions about going west again. The trip will be far easier than the one I made with Rebecca nearly twenty years ago, now that the transcontinental railroad is complete. But my life is different now. In those bygone years, I had nothing to hold me here. Today, I have my responsibilities as the editor-in-chief of the *New York World* and, of course, I have my little family.

    Nevertheless, I feel a sense of duty to Rebecca and to Henry, two young people cut down in the prime of their lives by forces they didn't fully comprehend. I still feel a profound sense of guilt over the death of my first wife. She was young and beautiful and she died believing in me.

    And I also feel regret over how I deceived Henry and destroyed our deep friendship; how I failed to act more forcefully when I knew his life was in danger. The best I could do was expose his killers for what they were and even that effort mostly failed.

Montana became a United States territory in May of 1864, not long after I escaped death at the hands of the vigilantes. I learned later that Sidney Edgerton became its first territorial governor and established Bannack as the capital. Wilbur Sanders, always in his uncle's shadow, was appointed Montana Territory's first attorney general. X. Beidler, the amateur hangman, was elected to the new territorial legislature where, ironically, he voted to pass laws. I don't know what happened to the other leaders, but I do know that none of them were ever brought to justice. Either Hill Beechey never received my letter exposing the vigilante lynchings or, more likely, the powerful Judge Edgerton intervened.

My rescuer, Brigadier General Nolan Harris Tofton the Fourth, got his wish. He returned to his beloved Virginia and fought valiantly alongside General Robert E. Lee in the closing days of the war. On April 1, 1865, Lee ordered Tofton to lead a desperate attack to try to break through the Union lines dug in around Richmond. It was a forlorn hope, as I am sure my friend knew. But I can see him gallantly saluting General Lee before mounting his steed, drawing his sword like the cavaliers of old, and courageously leading his cavalry to glory.

A federal sharpshooter's bullet felled Nolan. He was the first among his men to die in what became the final Confederate attack at Richmond before Lee ordered the city evacuated. Just two weeks later, the war ended.

The cunning Professor Thomas J. Dimsdale met his fate in 1866 when he died of tuberculosis. I had hoped it would be at the end of a rope, which he richly deserved. In 1868, a collection of stories came my way entitled *The Vigilantes of Montana, Being a Correct and Impartial Narrative of the Chase, Trial, Capture and Execution of Henry Plummer's Notorious Road Agent Band.* I realized as I read it, my hands shaking with rage, that Dimsdale had compiled these lies in defense of and justification for what the vigilantes had done. No doubt Edgerton and Sanders had been his copy editors because it presented both men as sterling examples of morality.

I was able to deny the vigilante leaders my friend's considerable riches. Upon returning to New York in the summer of 1864, I contacted Arthur Plummer, Henry's brother, at his law office in Boston. I informed him of Henry's death and how his killers were attempting to steal his brother's estate. Many months later I received a letter from Arthur that read in part:

Again, I wish to humbly thank you for all you did for Henry and our family. My aged parents were of course heartbroken to learn of Henry's untimely death, as was our sister. After I arrived in Bannack and visited Henry's grave, I contacted Mr. Taylor McKee as you advised me to do. You were right about him because he proved to be an honest man. He told me Wilbur Sanders had repeatedly attempted to appropriate Henry's fortune through a number of legal maneuvers, but Mr. McKee stood up to him and accepted my claim as Henry's legal heir. Mr. McKee and a David Pemberton also intervened when Sanders tried to steal Henry's mining company and claims, and turned those over to me as well.

The letter from the U.S. attorney is compelling. It explains that it has taken all these years to bring John Lee to justice because the Mormon Church had shielded him from prosecution, apparently concerned that his testimony might implicate important church leaders in the crime. Other than the little children who were kidnapped by Lee and thus were too young to remember what happened, my testimony is needed to ensure his conviction:

Your late father-in-law, Mr. Nathan Carter of St. Louis, was extremely persistant in his pursuit of justice for the death of his daughter and the other members of the Fancher-Baker party. Over the years, we received more than fifty letters from him demanding the prosecution of those responsible.

How ironic. The man who orchestrated the brutal murder of more than one hundred men, women and children is afforded every opportunity to defend himself while a score of innocent men were hanged on the whim of self-appointed executioners in Montana. And I had been witness to both crimes.

I arrived at my small house overlooking the East River at suppertime. It was a pleasant summer's evening and out on the back lawn a table had been set by the water. I heard laughing, so I walked to the corner of the house and saw my son playing with a ball and stick.

"Ah, Henry!" I called to him with a smile. "You are playing at baseball, I see!"

"Trying father!" the boy replied as he tossed the ball in the air and attempted to swing the stick in order to hit it. He missed, so I spent a few minutes "pitching" the ball to him and he finally struck it, then, giggling, ran imaginary bases as he has seen the men do at the professional baseball matches we have watched together.

"Dinner is served, Sir!" called Nellie, our Irish servant, as she carried a platter of chicken out to the table on the lawn.

"Run along and wash your hands, Henry," I tell my son and he reluctantly obeys after I promise to play more baseball with him after we dine. He almost knocked his mother down as he burst through the back door she was trying to exit.

"Careful Henry!" Electa scolded him. Then she looked at me with a smile, still as beautiful as the day I first saw her at Sun River. She handed the bowl she was carrying to Nellie before kissing me demurely on the cheek. I took in her lavender scent; noticed the threads of silver in her hair glittering in the setting sun. I kissed her gently, then took her hand and led her to the water's edge.

"I must go west again," I said quietly. "To Utah."

"Utah? But why, Noah?"

I looked out over the rippling water, felt the cool breeze on my face and remembered the wrinkled copy of the Constitution hanging on my office wall. Then my eyes met hers. "To see that justice is finally served."

Author's Notes

You can visit Bannack, Montana and see the ghost town where much of this story took place. Now a state park, it lies west of Dillon, off Interstate 15. When you arrive, you'll wonder why in the world anyone would wish to live in a place as barren and foreboding as the desolate hills around Grasshopper Creek. But gold was a magnet and men didn't care where it was found. They only cared about getting their share of it. In some cases, more than their share.

About forty miles east of Bannack along Highway 287 lay the towns of Virginia City and Nevada City, preserved much as they were when this story took place. Both are well worth visiting because you will discover that most of what you've read here is true, as are all of the salient events I have described.

Indeed, much of the "documented history" you will see in Bannack and Virginia City was authored by none other than Professor Thomas J. Dimsdale in a book you can purchase from the University of Oklahoma Press called *The Vigilantes of Montana*. But thanks to the diligence of two historians, R.E. Mather and F.E. Boswell, much of Dimsdale's story has been challenged. In their book, *Hanging the Sheriff* (Historic Montana Publishing) the real Henry Plummer emerges from the shadows.

This novel is my attempt to shed more light on the terrible injustice perpetrated by the Montana Vigilantes against Henry Plummer and the many other men known to have been their victims during the murderous winter of 1863-1864.

I would like to thank my friend Johnny France, the legendary former sheriff of Madison County, Montana, for showing me the Slade Trail and introducing me to the Montana Vigilantes during a horseback ride through the Gravelly Range in 2003. My father-in-law Lee Howard, my son Patrick, and my daughter Katie all offered many excellent suggestions and lots of encouragement along the way. My novel would not have been possible without the support and love of my wife, Susie. And, finally, I cannot thank Annette Chaudet enough for believing in Henry Plummer and in me.

If you are as fascinated as I am by the events of that long ago Montana winter, please visit my web site at www.wherelawends.com for links to more information about the Montana Vigilantes. You can also read an excerpt from my new historical novel, *Fort Enterprize*, the remarkable true story of William Eaton and Presley O'Bannon, heroes of America's first war on terror.

Kevin Emmet Foley
Bozeman, Montana
2008

Photo: David Bassin

About the Author

Kevin Emmet Foley has been a public relations executive for most of his career. He owns a successful broadcast publicity firm in Atlanta and has been married for thirty-three years to Susie Foley. The couple has two grown children, Patrick and Katie, and they live in the Atlanta area. Kevin spends a good deal of time in Bozeman, Montana, where he enjoys fly fishing, golf, hiking and horseback riding. Where Law Ends is Kevin's debut novel, which he began writing in 2004. He is currently at work on a new historical novel, *Fort Enterprize*, the remarkable true story about America's first war on terror.

Printed in the United States
142159LV00002B/1/P